THE LEGEND OF THE FIREWALKER

BY

STEVE BEVIL

THE LEGEND OF THE FIREWALKER
Copyright: Steve Bevil

ISBN-13: 978-1492285182
ISBN-10: 1492285188
Second edition. Updated 2014.

Book Cover Design:
Baub Alred and Steve Bevil

Interior Design: Steve Bevil

Find out more about the author and upcoming books:

Blog: http://stevebevil.blogspot.com/

Twitter: http://twitter.com/steve_bevil

Facebook fan page:
http://www.facebook.com/stevebevilwriting

To my best friend John, who believed that I could tell a story,

to my sister Shahara, who encouraged me to write it,

and to all who went along for the journey.

CONTENTS

CHAPTER ONE

AWAKE

It was the end of the spring semester. Leah had never been a fan of staying at Lawrence Hall, the all-girls dormitory on campus, but she had promised her mom she would the year before. It was evening and the Illinois University at Cahokia Falls (IUCF) campus was buzzing with students celebrating the end of the school year and the end of finals.

Leah, on the other hand, didn't have celebration on her mind. This semester had been a difficult one and she was looking forward to going home. "Oh my God, Amanda!" she shouted. "You didn't!"

"What?" asked Amanda sheepishly.

Leah rolled her eyes and shook her head. "I can't believe you kept your date with Hector last night after you made up with Steve," she said.

Amanda had a glowing smile across her face. "Of course," she shrugged. "Steve and I—well, you know."

Leah shook her head in disbelief again. "Know what?" she asked, through squinted eyes. "The other day you were just complaining how you and Steve belonged together." She paused to adjust her leg more comfortably on the bed. "How there was no one in the world you would rather be with and how you two were destined to get married."

"We are, we are," repeated Amanda, while flipping her long, straight, blond hair as she teased it in the mirror. "Hector is too much of a townie, anyway."

Leah drew a deep breath and sighed heavily as Amanda spun around the tiny-sized dorm room in her new sundress. The red and gold dress fit snugly against her small frame and complemented her slightly tanned skin. Amanda reached down to slide on a pair of shoes she had purchased earlier in the day with Steve at a summer shoe sale at the mall near campus. After staring intently in the mirror again, she repeated teasing her hair.

Impatiently, Leah glanced at the clock. "You know you're going to be late," she said.

"I won't be late," said Amanda, confidently turning to face her. Amanda's green eyes sparkled and she had a huge grin on her face. "So, how do I look?"

"Late," uttered Leah, while glancing at the clock again. "Steve said he would meet you downstairs like seven minutes ago."

Amanda frowned and then picked up her cell phone. "See," she said, holding it up. "No calls, no text — so he must not be here yet."

"That was his point in asking you to meet him downstairs." Leah glowered.

Amanda smiled and then enthusiastically sat down next to her on the bed. "Okay — what's wrong?" she asked.

"Nothing, really." Leah shrugged. Amanda raised her eyebrows and continued to stare at her. Leah sighed. "It's just — it's just that last night, I asked Lafonda to come hang out with me when you didn't answer your cell phone."

There was a brief silence and then Amanda pursed her lips. "I'm sorry," she said, offering her a quick hug. "I was ... busy."

"Oh, okay," nodded Leah. "I wonder if Steve knows what you mean when you say you're busy."

"Oh, he does," winked Amanda. "Trust me, but he probably thinks it only applies when we're together." She paused and then shrugged happily. "Oh, well."

Leah rolled her eyes and sighed again. "Okay, Amanda," she said softly.

Amanda dropped her eyes and then abruptly looked more concerned. "But seriously," she said. "Are you okay? Are you still having bad dreams?"

"Night terrors are more like it," Leah blurted, in a half-joking way. "That's why I asked Lafonda to come over." She paused. "I thought it would help me sleep better if I had someone else in the room. But all she did was talk me to death about getting an A in her fencing class."

"Is she still going on about that?" Amanda asked. "I wish she would just get a boyfriend." She grinned. "I wish you both would just get a boyfriend."

"Amanda, I think you've got that covered for all of us," chuckled Leah, while eyeing Amanda's cell phone. "And speaking of boyfriends, Lafonda has Jim, remember? And are you sure Steve's not waiting for you downstairs?"

"Ugh!" she moaned. "Stop trying to get rid of me. And besides, Steve is fine."

Leah shook her head and Amanda reached out to give her a quick hug.

"Look," Amanda said, "I'll be back tonight in time to tuck you in."

Slowly, Leah nodded and then forced a smile. "Well,

when you come back, please leave Steve at home." She pointed to the half-packed boxes stacked in front of her closet door. "I still have to finish packing up the rest of my things tonight, and you know my parents, they'll be here right on time tomorrow to pick me up."

"Okay," said Amanda halfheartedly.

"Amanda!" Leah ranted. "I barely got any sleep last night and I've hardly slept at all over the past two weeks, studying for finals. The last thing I need is to be up late again while you and Steve play house."

"Okay, okay, I got it!" retorted Amanda. "Don't go having an emotional dump on me." She paused for a moment and then grinned. "Look, you and me, we survived freshman year. You know, all the midterms and finals, the late-night cram sessions. And let's not forget the parties!"

"Yeah," said Leah impatiently. "And let's not forget about all the late-night phone calls from all of your ex-boyfriends, begging you to come back."

Amanda grinned. "You know that I appreciate . . ."

Amanda was interrupted by a quick knock to their dorm room door. The knocking was to the tune of "Shave and a Haircut."

"That could only be Steve," said Leah, as she and Amanda stood up.

Leah headed over to her small wooden desk, which was adjacent to the foot of her bed. It was identical to its twin across the way, which was Amanda's desk. Leah's side of the room was reminiscent of her first week at school. The wall to the side of her bed, which once displayed pictures of friends taken throughout the year and an academic calendar, was now bare.

Amanda's side of the room, however, still displayed various posters and pictures of celebrities and perfect male models. Leah was glad she soon wouldn't have to wake up to teen heartthrob Justin Bloomer's face every day. She thought it was bad enough to have to see his posters, but Amanda also loved to blare his music.

"I'm coming!" said Amanda enthusiastically, as she headed towards the door.

She looked in the mirror one last time, stopping to fix her dress. Amanda opened the door and Steve immediately scooped her up, giving her a huge hug. His broad shoulders and muscular arms looked enormous compared to her small frame.

"Hello, gorgeous!" he said enthusiastically, putting an extra emphasis on the word *hello*. "I know that I just saw you this afternoon, but I've missed you already."

"Steve!" she blurted, sounding annoyed. "You'll wrinkle my dress."

"Aw! You look great, honey!"

Amanda frowned, but after she noticed Leah was staring at her, she gave Steve a quick kiss and then maneuvered out of his grip. "How did you get up here?" she asked.

Steve stepped into the room, leaving the door open behind him. He reached out to embrace her in another hug, but this time she was quick enough to get away. "The lobby doors to Lawrence Hall aren't locked until after nine," he sighed. "And it's only a little after seven. Besides, you're late missy. I've called you like several times!"

"Oops!" said Amanda, pausing to look at her cell phone and then placing it back on her desk. "But wait a minute. Don't change the subject; I asked how you got up here. Guys aren't allowed on the floor or in the elevator without a female escort."

"He probably used his baby blues and flirted with

some girl to get up here," sighed Leah, chiming in.

Steve took his attention off of Amanda and looked at Leah for the first time since he entered the room. "And you know it!" he said with confidence. "And I asked her out on a date for later tonight. So, let's wrap this up early."

"Ha!" said Amanda, stepping away to smooth out her dress in the mirror. "You had better not."

"Let's just stay here!" he chuckled, while stumbling over towards the bed. "We can have a party here with Leah."

Leah quickly snatched a blue IUCF T-shirt off the edge of the bed before Steve sat down. "Must you sit on my bed?" she moaned. "Don't you guys have some packing to do?"

"Yes, but I doubt we would spend our time packing," he grinned, reaching for Amanda as she walked past the bed. "Besides, we have all day tomorrow." Amanda smiled and then happily sat on his lap. "Let's have some fun Leah. It's our last night before summer!"

Reluctantly, Leah looked up at Steve as she folded the blue IUCF T-shirt and placed it into the now open box on top of her desk. The last thing she wanted to do was waste time hanging out with Steve and Amanda. She was exhausted because of finals and lack of sleep. She wanted nothing more than to move back home to St. Louis for the summer with her parents, no matter how eerie that sounded to her. The room itself just seemed to drain her and no matter how tired she was, the fear of the nightmares kept her awake. She was already embarrassed by the middle-of-the-night screams that she was sure awoke her neighbors on the floor. It was about the only time Leah was glad that Amanda was away at night as much as she was.

"You guys!" Leah whined, in a half-annoyed way. "I really need to get to stuff." Suddenly, the sound of a door opening and closing filled the room from the hallway. "Great. Here comes Lafonda."

"Hey, guys!" said Lafonda, in a cheery voice. She took one look at Steve and then suddenly looked confused. "Uh — hey, Steve?"

He smiled. "Don't look so surprised, Lafonda," he chuckled. "We officially got back together this morning."

Lafonda took a seat on Amanda's bed and allowed her long, shiny black hair to drift off to one side. "I don't know why I am surprised," she said with a smile.

"Me neither!" said Amanda enthusiastically, while clasping her hands into her lap.

Lafonda slightly chuckled and then rolled her eyes quickly, in an attempt to go unnoticed. "Are you guys done packing?" she asked. "I'm almost done. I promised my grandmother that I would be all packed and ready to go early tomorrow morning."

"Great," said Steve. "Then let's all do something!"

"Ugh!" exhaled Leah, sounding clearly annoyed. "I thought you guys had plans. And look around you; does she look packed?"

Lafonda looked puzzled as she scanned Amanda's side of the room. "Why haven't you started packing?" she asked. "What time are your parents coming tomorrow?"

"They're not," Amanda answered with a smile. Lafonda looked confused. "I convinced my parents to let Steve drive me home — all the way from Illinois to Louisiana."

"Oh," said Lafonda, while nodding. "But wait — when do you plan to pack?" Her eyes were wide as she looked around Amanda's side of the room again. "Everyone must turn in their dorm key and be out by

4:30."

Amanda laughed. "Oh, Lafonda," she said, rolling her eyes. "We will have plenty of time tomorrow." Steve smiled big while Amanda stroked his cheek. "Isn't that right?"

"Yes, ma'am!" he said enthusiastically.

"Well, on that note," said Leah abruptly, "it's time for everyone to go because I have tons to do."

Amanda and Steve were still into each other and hadn't acknowledged Leah. She glared at them and frowned.

"Okay, you two," said Lafonda, standing up. "Let's go."

Steve and Amanda still didn't move.

"Now!" she demanded more forcibly.

"Ugh — come on, Steve!" said Amanda with a grin, as she stood up from his lap. She stroked his cheek again. "It's time."

Slowly, Lafonda headed over to Leah as Amanda led Steve out of the room.

"How are you doing, kiddo?" she asked.

"Good, I suppose," said Leah, shrugging her shoulders. She took a deep breath. "The nightmares aren't so bad."

Lafonda suddenly looked concerned. "Is it because you're not sleeping?"

"Hmm — that's a possibility," said Leah, as she released a slight chuckle.

Lafonda pursed her lips. "Leah," she said, "I hope you don't mind, but — what have you been dreaming about?"

Leah's eyes blinked a few times and she began to fidget as she continued to fold more shirts. "I ... I," she stumbled. "I feel so tired and down all the time." She paused as she reluctantly looked around the room. "I feel

fine when I'm in class or at the gym. I feel like it's this
…"

"No offense to you, Lafonda!" yelled Steve from the
hallway. "But why do women have to be so bossy?"

Lafonda shook her head and then smirked. "I know he
didn't say what I think I just heard," she said with a laugh.

Leah took a deep breath and then continued speaking.
"I just think it's the stress of school and, and …"

"And Jamie?" Lafonda asked, sounding more
concerned.

Leah took another deep breath and then proceeded to
fold a pair of sweatpants. "I really need to get packing,"
she said offhandedly. She forced a smile. "But I do
appreciate you asking how I'm doing."

"It's okay," said Lafonda, reaching out to give her a
hug. "If you need anything, just know I'm next door."

Carefully, Leah placed the sweatpants in the box and
turned around to say goodbye to Lafonda as she began to
close the door. "Will you … stop by tomorrow?" Leah
asked.

"Of course," Lafonda smiled, poking her head around
the door. "I still need your address. I plan to visit you in
St. Louis this summer."

Leah smiled as Lafonda closed the door. A little time
passed and she no longer heard Lafonda scolding Steve
for the comment he'd made earlier; just faint laughter and
the chatter of voices from other girls on the floor could
be heard. Leah wiped the sweat that was beading on her
forehead as she continued to pack. She reached up to the
built-in shelf above her desk and grabbed a rubber band
to pull back her hair.

It sure is warm in here, she thought to herself. She leaned
over to stretch out her hand over the air conditioning and
heating unit that was underneath the double-paned

windows to check to see if it was on. *Well, that would explain it — the air conditioning isn't on.*

She opened the panel to the controls and messed with the knobs, but nothing worked. Frustrated, she slammed the panel shut and opened the window.

Leah continued packing and started humming to herself to pass the time. She thought of turning on the radio but remembered that she had already packed it. She entertained the thought of turning on the TV, but unplugged it instead. *No distractions!*

As she worked, Leah used the bottom of her white shirt and the corner of her sleeve to stop the sweat from running down her face. Now and then, a drop or two would fall on a box. After drawing up her shirt again to pat her forehead, she noticed that it was completely soaked. "Ugh!" she uttered. "This is so disgusting!"

Irritated, she headed towards the door and caught a glimpse of herself in the large door mirror that had been a must-have for Amanda. She frowned as she reluctantly examined herself in the mirror. Her pulled-back, shoulder-length brown hair was fuzzy, and loose strands of it stuck out arbitrarily. Her fair skin, now covered with sweat lines, was also red from all the wiping.

Leah shook her head and glanced down in defeat but immediately noticed that her once white shirt was covered in dust and the bottom half was wet and misshapen. "Ugh!" she groaned. "I look like crap!" Quickly, she turned her gaze from the mirror. "I must look like a homeless person standing next to Amanda. No wonder I can't find a date!"

She made a quick assessment of her side of the room and pretty much decided that everything was packed. *I guess it's time for a shower,* she thought sarcastically.

Leah opened her closet door and pulled out the clean

clothing and hand and body towels she had put aside for herself while packing. Stepping out into the hallway, she immediately noticed the lights at her end of the floor were off. It was incredibly quiet, being that it was the end of the semester and the last day before move-out. "Someone on the floor must be playing a joke," she murmured.

She headed over to try the hallway light switch located on the opposite wall, but nothing happened. *Gosh,* she thought. *The circuit breaker must be tripped or something — and on our last day here.*

Paying careful attention not to bump into the round tables in the common room, she slowly headed towards the bathroom. "Well, at least the bathroom lights are still working," she said aloud.

She froze as soon as she entered the bathroom because it was equally quiet. "This is definitely weird," she mumbled, while shaking her head.

Leah placed the items she was holding on one of the sinks lined against an enormous wall mirror. She looked down to wet her toothbrush under the cool water as the shadow of what looked like a person entered the shower area. She jerked up. "Hello?" she called out.

Her stomach twisted in knots as she waited, and her hand trembled slightly as she shut off the water. The silence was deafening, and she cringed at a muffled creaking noise. "Relax, Leah," she sighed, composing herself. "It's probably just the water pipes in the shower."

Leah bent over again to rinse her mouth out with water, when a soft, high-pitched wail reverberated from the shower area. "Hello?" she cried out.

Instinctively, she looked into the large mirror and immediately turned around to scan the room. The sound continued to screech like grinding metal. "What is that?"

she mumbled.

Leah looked intently around the room for anything that could have made the noise. *Surely, the person in the shower must have heard that,* she thought. Taking a deep breath, she shook her head.

"These nightmares have me so paranoid. I need to get a grip on myself!"

She turned back around to begin brushing her teeth, but another high-pitched sound pierced the air. "Leeah!" a voice shrieked out.

Leah froze instantly. Goose bumps shot down her back. "I know that voice," she stuttered, her hands trembling in fear. "It's that woman's from my dreams!"

Panic rippled throughout Leah's body and her heart throbbed forcibly against her chest. She struggled to move. "Leeeahh!" the metallic voice rang out again — this time louder, echoing and bouncing off the walls.

Frantically, Leah's eyes raced around the room for the source of the sound. "This can't be real," she said, her voice trembling. "It's — it's just a dream." As Leah spun around, her mind flooded with images of the shadowy figure that hunted her in her nightmares. "This just can't be!"

Suddenly, a loud bang came from one of the shower stalls, followed by the sound of quick footsteps. "Move Leah, move," Leah whispered.

Quickly, she scanned the room and against one of the walls, shoved in a corner, was an old broom. With broom in hand, Leah crept over to where she heard the noise to defend herself from what she thought was her mysterious attacker. After all the terror-filled nights, she didn't want to run anymore. She didn't want to live in fear. She wanted to face her pursuer.

"Aaaah!"

The sound of two different screams echoed throughout the hallway and the bathroom. "Oh, my God, Leah!" said Lafonda, stepping out of the shower stall. "You scared me."

Still a little shaken, Leah stood there with broom in hand. She took a couple of deep breaths to try to relieve the tightness she still felt in her chest. *What will people think about this one?* she thought, as her cheeks and ears reddened. She could only imagine what people were saying about her and her middle-of-the-night screaming. "Lafonda, I — I ..."

"I forgot my body wash," Lafonda grinned, but it quickly faded into a look of concern. "Wait — Leah, are you okay?"

Leah tried to force a smile. "I'm fine," she said, trying to sound convincing.

Lafonda secured the towel wrapped around her and frowned as she scrutinized Leah's face. "But you don't look okay," she said.

"I'm fine," Leah said again, now more convincingly than before. "Really, I was just frightened by the noises."

Two girls from the floor entered the bathroom. It looked as if they were unaware of what had just transpired, but they looked on suspiciously.

"Frightened?" asked Lafonda, in a low whisper. She quickly took the broom out of Leah's hand and placed it back in the corner. "And what noises?"

"You didn't hear the noises?" asked Leah. A worried and tired look washed over her face. "But you were ... in the shower, right?"

"Yes," said Lafonda, still puzzled. "But I didn't hear any noises." She paused. "Wait, I did bump the shower wall with my elbow; and I did yell out from the pain."

"No, that wasn't it!" interrupted Leah. "And you

didn't call my name?"

"No," Lafonda said, while shaking her head. "I didn't call your name."

"I must be just rattled because the stupid hallway lights aren't working, and the heat," Leah stammered.

"What do you mean?" asked Lafonda, as she peeked out into the hallway. "The hallway lights are working." She paused. "I know that there is a storm —"

The sound of someone fast approaching could be heard from the hallway and they both turned their attention towards the bathroom entrance. A tall and slender girl who lived on the floor stood in front of them. She was trying to catch her breath. "Lafonda!" she let out. "I thought I heard your voice. I just walked past your room and I think your phone was ringing."

"Oh, shoot!" said Lafonda, pausing to secure her towel again. "That must be my grandmother calling about tomorrow." She started to take off running, but noticed that Leah was following behind her. "Wait — aren't you going to get your shower?"

"Oh," said Leah, while staring at the towels in her hands. "I guess I forgot my body wash too."

Lafonda smiled and Leah trailed behind her as Lafonda darted off towards her room. The hallway lights were on just like Lafonda had said and the air was cooler. Several girls from the floor were laughing as Leah walked past them. *I wouldn't be surprised if they were laughing at me with all the craziness going on in my life. And Jamie's death hasn't made things any easier,* she thought.

She was pretty sure everyone knew about her nightmares due to her frequent middle-of-the-night screaming, but she had started to feel proud of herself. It was the end of the school year, and even with everything, she had managed to finish the semester without withdrawing from school like her mom and Amanda had wanted her to.

Leah took a deep breath and relaxed her shoulders. She was determined not to let anything get to her. The following day she would be home in St. Louis, and she could put the whole nightmare behind her.

The narrow hallway from the bathroom to her dorm room opened up to the common area that was frequently used by the girls on the floor to hang out. On most nights, you could find people playing cards or studying at the round tables. "Hey, Leah!" one of the girls from the card game called out. "You think we'll have a chance to get a good night's sleep with this storm?"

Another girl at the table let out a stifled chuckle. "I mean, it would be nice to sleep through the night for once without your screaming." Sounds of laughter suddenly filled the room. "Maybe you should sleep with the lights on!" the girl laughed.

Leah could feel her cheeks turn red as the blood rushed to her head. "Sure!" she let out, her voice shaking with anger.

She walked quickly to her room; trying to beat the laughter before it ended. Forcibly, she closed the door behind her and sighed heavily as she pressed her back against it. "Can this be over any faster?" she yelled. In frustration, she tossed her toothbrush and her towels on the floor. "Ugh!"

At that moment, a gust of wind rushed violently through the open window, knocking the lamp on her desk onto the floor. The room was suddenly in complete darkness. "Grrreat!" she said, in a drawn-out huff.

She bent over to pick up the lamp but felt a little uneasy as lightning from the approaching storm created strange shadows around the room. As the sound of thunder filled the room, she stumbled to find the socket to plug in the power cord. *Duh*, she thought. *I should just turn on Amanda's lamp.* As she reached out to turn on the lamp, she paused. She had an eerie feeling that someone was standing behind her. *No one is behind me*, she thought, as she extended her arm to turn on the lamp.

"Aaah!"

There was a burst of light in the room followed by a loud crack as the lightbulb from Amanda's lamp shattered into many pieces, landing across the table and the floor. Startled, Leah jumped back, withdrawing her hand. At the same time, the door to her closet slammed shut, causing her to let out a stifled scream. Quickly, she spun around, her heart pounding against her chest.

Leah stood in the dark frozen with fear. Through the darkness, she could see that a strange mist had begun to fill the room, and when lightning struck, there was no thunder to follow.

Leah dared to take a step forward. She felt the glass from the lightbulb crunch beneath her tennis shoes, but there was no sound from the crunching glass. Leah waved her hand through the air, and the air seemed to ripple like water. Nervously, she looked around the room. She noticed the light underneath the door from the hallway was gone, and she could no longer hear laughter. The posters of male models on Amanda's side of the room, which once were vibrant with color, now appeared to be in black and white. "It's like my dreams!" she stuttered, in a panic. "Everything is washed in gray!"

Suddenly, there were shuffling noises all around her, and goose bumps formed on her arms and legs. She took a deep breath in, and when she let it out, she saw it take form in the air. Her heart was racing fast now. Leah bolted towards the door. "Help!" she yelled.

Spontaneously, the closet doors from both sides of the room flung open, stopping her in her tracks. Several small shadows darted in and out of the closets. Leah screamed in horror because she had seen them before, surrounding her, chasing her, in her dreams.

She took several steps back. Now, her back was against Amanda's desk. Frantically, her hand searched the table. She was desperate to find something to protect herself with, but little stabs of sharp pain suddenly shot up her arm. Leah looked down and shards of glass from the lightbulb had sliced into her palms and fingers. Among the tossed paper and glass, she could make out a small shape in the darkness. Instantly, Leah recognized Amanda's cell phone. She plunged for it, causing a wave of ripples in the air.

The phone, closer now, was no longer washed in gray, and the light from the LED display illuminated the apple-red color in the darkness. Without hesitating, she dialed 911, but there was no dial tone, just silence.

Abruptly, a high-pitched wail filled the air, and goose bumps rushed down her back.

"Leeah!"

CHAPTER TWO

NIGHTMARES

Nathan let out a huge gasp as he suddenly awoke from sleep. He instantaneously sat up in bed. His face and chest were drenched with sweat and his palms tingled. His heart pounded ferociously against his chest and his breathing was labored.

Frantically, he looked around the room only to be caught off guard by the piercingly bright sunlight that crept through the curtains to his bedroom window. Groggy, he shielded his eyes, as faint memories of the dream that had just terrified him began to replay in his mind. *Who is she?* he wondered. *And why am I having the same dream about her over and over?*

Every night since returning home from school for summer, he has dreamed about her. The dreams have become so frequent that Nathan stopped counting the number of times in which he awoke in the dead of night drenched with sweat. For hours, he would stay awake, trying to recall some small detail about her, to identify her, retracing her steps.

Nathan shivered. He always remembered her tousled brown hair and the blood that glowed brightly against her fair skin. "It all seems so real," he murmured. He also remembered her flailing arms as she fought desperately against an unseen attacker. "This just can't be real," he reasoned.

Like he did on most nights after awakening in the darkness, he sat in bed recalling the scratches and blood on her, and trying hard to remember from whom she'd been defending herself.

Suddenly, Nathan shivered again. He didn't want to admit what his mind had been circling for weeks. "The scratches," he muttered. "There were so many of them, and they appeared all at once. She just couldn't keep up her defense." He slowly shook his head. "It was like she was overwhelmed, as if she was fighting against more than one person."

He looked down and was drawn to the tingling sensation in his hands. The sensation in his palms was just as frequent as his dreams, and he found it equally annoying. The first couple of nights home, he thought maybe his hand had fallen asleep, that he was just sleeping wrong. It wasn't until both hands started having a prickly feeling that he actually considered something was amiss.

On most days he just ignored it, and it usually went away before he finished brushing his teeth. His only working theory was that the tingling was from all the heavy weightlifting he'd been doing and that he might want to consider investing in some workout gloves. Now that he was back home, he was taking full advantage of the weight room at the Devaro Mansion. He detested using the gym at school because the weight room was always crowded. But despite that, he'd still managed to keep a somewhat consistent workout schedule.

Since returning home, he had also made a concentrated effort to sleep in and to avoid Lafonda Devaro as much as possible. He had managed to avoid her at school practically all year, only having to see her during the holidays, when they returned home for breaks. It was easy for him to avoid her most of the time because they lived in different houses. Nathan lived with his grandfather Rodion, in the medium-sized, two-bedroom cottage behind the main house and near the garden. His grandfather, the caretaker for the Devaro estate, maintained the grounds on the property.

It wasn't that he didn't like Lafonda — they had actually been close while growing up. But once they entered high school, her new friends and their big houses, fast cars and money kind of complicated things. Although in his mind the money issue created distance between Lafonda and him, he knew he could always count on her if he ever needed her.

The Devaro Mansion was the only home he had ever known, and the Devaros were the closest thing he had to an extended family. Without them, it would be just him and his grandfather. As far as he knew, his grandfather had always worked for them.

It was still midmorning when he finally decided to get out of bed. Nathan's hand prickled as he pulled back the curtains and opened the window. He took in a deep breath as the warm air rushed across his bare chest. *I'm up a little earlier than usual,* he thought with a sense of accomplishment. He rarely got out of bed before noon.

Nathan showered, put on a pair of shorts, and wore his favorite IUCF T-shirt. He bought it when he first arrived on campus the previous fall, and it was his favorite because it had no sleeves. He hated wearing anything that was too constricting, especially on his arms.

He stared in the mirror at the now over-washed T-shirt and thought it was interesting that before, he had never desired to wear an IUCF one, even though campus was a short commute away. Nathan felt that he ended up at IUCF by default and had never really put thought into attending anywhere else. Lafonda, on the other hand, had been set on going there since high school. He thought this was mainly because her father, Avery, and her grandmother LaDonda were both alums of the school.

Nathan's stomach grumbled as he entered the hallway. As he got closer to the kitchen, he heard his grandfather mumbling something in Russian over the sound of rattling pots and pans. "What the heck is he looking for?" Nathan muttered. "We never use the kitchen."

Apart from drinks and snacks, they normally cooked or ate at the main house. This was mainly because neither of them could cook very well and both loathed washing dishes. Nathan was convinced that if it weren't for Lafonda's grandmother, everyone would starve. Lafonda wasn't a wiz in the kitchen either, and after her dad accepted a position in England, her parents were hardly ever home.

Nathan entered the kitchen to find his grandfather on his knees with his head buried in one of the bottom kitchen cabinets.

"So, what's for breakfast, Grandpa?" he asked teasingly and with a half grin.

"I'll grandpa you!" Rodion answered from inside the cabinet.

"I don't smell anything burning, so you're obviously not cooking," laughed Nathan.

The rattling and clinking sounds of metal abruptly came to a stop. Nathan's grandfather stood up, revealing a slender man with an olive skin tone. His hair was white but full, and his face was sprinkled with signs of age. Although Nathan's skin was pecan in color, his grandfather in his youth probably looked much like Nathan.

"Well," Rodion said, after taking a deep breath. "Look who decided to join the living and actually start their day before everyone else goes to sleep."

Nathan smiled and casually leaned against the small wooden island in the middle of the kitchen. "It's summer, Grandpa," he whined. "Plus, I had all morning classes last semester, and based on that alone, I think I am in need of some much deserved shut-eye."

"Oh, I'm sure you were stuck with all morning classes through no fault of your own," Rodion chuckled. "And I'm sure it has nothing to do with procrastinating, or playing video games, or perhaps registering late, or all of the above."

Nathan sighed heavily. "Can't I do anything without Lafonda keeping tabs on me?" he groaned. "What else did your annoying little spy report?"

Rodion frowned. "First, as if I need to have a spy to know what my only grandson does; and second, I thought we had agreed that I was too young looking and too handsome to be called grandpa." he retorted. "You know that I'd rather you call me Roy."

Rodion had taken to the nickname Roy after Lafonda had started calling him that several years before.

"Grandpa!" Nathan whined, through glaring eyes. "Did she happen to mention that I almost made the Dean's List last semester? If it weren't for my Spanish class, I would have gotten all As."

"No, she didn't," grinned Roy, returning back to his search. "But I do recall her mentioning something about *her* making the Dean's List and earning all As both semesters."

"Ugh!" groaned Nathan. "Whatever." His stomach continued to growl as he perused the refrigerator. "Is there anything to eat?"

"I don't know. You will have to look for yourself," said Roy, shuffling through the pots and pans. "And how do you expect her to know all this information about you when you barely speak to her?"

"Whatever," mumbled Nathan, continuing his search.

The metal clinking sounds from the cabinet ceased again. "Ah-ha!" shouted Roy. "I found it!"

Grudgingly, Nathan closed the refrigerator door and eyed the small orange juice bottle in his hand before opening it. "Do we have anything else?" he complained. "Like, perhaps, food?"

Triumphantly, Roy stood in front of him with a medium-sized silver-colored pan in his hands.

"You spent all that time looking for a pan?"

"Yes. I like to spend my time aimlessly looking for pans I don't need," Roy said, sarcastically. He grinned. "LaDonda is baking a multilayered cake for Lafonda's birthday party tomorrow, and she didn't have all the pans needed at the house."

"That's tomorrow!" exclaimed Nathan, almost spilling orange juice from his mouth.

"Yes, tomorrow night, actually," said Roy. "And I guess it's safe to assume you don't have a birthday present."

"Uh, yeah," stuttered Nathan, his face turning red now. "I guess you can say that."

Roy smiled, pulled out a brown box from underneath the kitchen island, and began to pack it with various cake pans. "I've already taken the liberty of getting a gift for you to give Lafonda," he said, gesturing towards the hallway. "It's in the hallway closet."

Nathan's face continued to redden as he looked apologetically at his grandfather. "Thanks, Grandpa," he said. "For helping me not to look so bad."

"No, problem," answered Roy with a grin. "Now, do me a favor and help me carry this stuff over to the main house. Do you think you can grab the presents from the closet?"

"Sure thing!" said Nathan, heading over to the closet. "So, what did I get her?"

Inside the hallway closet, next to the front door, were several presents on the top shelf. One in particular, with a large red ribbon wrapped around it, stood out. The shiny red box was really small compared to the others, and the big red ribbon around it dwarfed it in comparison. Based on the size, Nathan guessed it probably was a ring, or a necklace, or some piece of small jewelry.

He headed back into the kitchen, presents in hand, and laid them across the table. "So, which one of these is mine to give?" he asked.

Roy glanced up and followed Nathan's gaze to the small red box. "You pick," he said. He paused and then casually pointed. "Why don't you give her that one?"

Reluctantly, Nathan reached out, but then hesitated. "Are you sure?" he asked. "It looks expensive. What's in it?"

"It's a surprise," said Roy enthusiastically. "For both of you."

"For both of us?" Nathan asked incredulously. "I doubt that I will be too excited about Lafonda receiving another piece of jewelry." He grinned. "I think her boyfriend has that covered."

"Well, I think this one will be special," said Roy confidently. "Now, let's take this stuff over to LaDonda before she starts calling me."

With presents in tow, Nathan followed his grandfather across the sprawling green lawn and towards the white colonial mansion adorned with large white pillars. The warmth of the sun felt nice against Nathan's skin, and he suddenly had an urge to hit the pool. *I wonder why he's being so cryptic about what's in the red box,* he pondered.

His grandfather suddenly stumbled in front of him, and Nathan soon began to question who should be carrying the brown box. "Maybe I should be carrying the pans?" he called out.

"I'm fine," uttered Roy, while attempting to secure the box in his hands. "I know you think I'm an old grandpa, but I can handle it." He attempted to glance back at Nathan. "However," he added, gesturing over to the garden with his head, "the weeds have really sprouted up in the garden this year. You think you can help me by cleaning up the garden before you leave for camp? You do remember that you leave for camp on Friday?"

Nathan sighed. *Is it that soon?* He'd thought he would have more time to relax before being thrust into camp to watch over some whiny teenagers.

Although he had turned nineteen about a month earlier, Nathan would hardly consider himself in the same category as the younger teens that normally attended camp. "Of course!" he responded quickly. He said it with such enthusiasm that he almost convinced himself. "I'm almost ready to go."

"Nice try," chuckled Roy heartily. He gestured again. "Let's go through the back. I propped the kitchen door open earlier."

As they neared the back of the house, Nathan could hear voices and sounds of laughter out by the pool area. At first glance, it appeared to be Lafonda and her boyfriend, Jim. He noticed the palms of his hands started to tingle again as he placed the gifts out on the kitchen table. "Where should I put these?" he asked. "Are you hiding them until the party?"

"Um — no," said Roy, while unloading the box. "Avery and Amelia want to talk to Lafonda after she opens their gift." He paused to examine one of the larger cake pans before placing it on the counter. "And because of the time difference in London, LaDonda is having a pre-birthday lunch celebration today."

"Uh, that's cool," muttered Nathan, while occasionally glancing outside the window at the pool area. "But I'm starving now." Unconsciously, he massaged the palms of his hands. The tingling sensation was starting to make his hands feel numb. "What time does this birthday lunch thing start?"

"Soon," said Roy, eyeing Nathan suspiciously as he rubbed his hands. "LaDonda went to pick up lunch from the Dardings' Italian restaurant in town."

Nathan pursed his lips. "Well, I'm sure that was Lafonda's boyfriend's idea," he muttered.

"Actually, it was his parents'," Roy responded with a grin. "You know they've always been fond of Lafonda."

"Yeah, yeah," Nathan spouted, slightly irritated. "And I'm sure they can't wait for Jim to marry her." He continued to massage his hands. "And I don't know why Jim's parents would name the restaurant after the family name when they're not even Italian!"

"Okay, what is wrong with your hands?" demanded Roy. "Do you need some ointment or something?"

Nathan suddenly looked embarrassed and dropped his hands to his sides. Roy stared at him as if he had just caught Nathan's hands in the cookie jar. "I think we'd better get some ointment," he added sternly.

The outside door to the kitchen opened and Nathan and his grandfather both turned to the sound. Slowly, LaDonda entered the house with a tray of sandwiches in her hands, followed by Jim and Lafonda. Jim was also carrying a tray of food. Lafonda was still wearing her bathing suit and occasionally used the towel around Jim's neck to pat the water that fell from his hair onto his body.

"You can place that one over here," said LaDonda, directing Jim to place his tray next to hers. She smiled. "Make sure you thank your parents again for me for lunch."

"No problem, Mrs. Devaro," Jim responded eagerly. "Do you think it will be enough?"

"Way too much," commented Nathan. "I'm sure we could feed a small village with the leftovers."

LaDonda frowned, and Roy quickly gave him a disapproving glare. "Um — Nathan," Roy stammered, "you were starving just a second ago."

"Well, I appreciate the generosity," said Lafonda, wrapping her arms around Jim's waist. She gave him a hug followed by a quick peck on the cheek. "I'm glad that your parents are so giving and that they taught their son well."

Jim smiled a huge grin of approval, and Lafonda turned around just in time to receive a disapproving glare from Nathan. She responded with a sarcastic smile.

"Oh!" exclaimed LaDonda. "It's almost time for your parents to call. Let's move to the front living room and open presents."

"Okay," said Lafonda cheerfully. "Let me run upstairs and quickly change clothes."

"Do you think you might want to put on a shirt?" sneered Nathan, while glaring at Jim.

Jim eyed him and then forced a smile. "Nope," he said, running a hand across his bare abs and chest. "I'm good."

Roy loudly cleared his throat and then shook his head. "Here, Nathan," he said, handing his grandson a plate with two sandwiches. "I know you wouldn't want to waste any food."

The spacious front living room of the Devaro Mansion was fully arranged with white and beige furniture. LaDonda had decorated the room with a New Orleans French Quarter style. Each window in the room was adorned with intricately patterned plush draperies, and in every corner was a large potted plant. The contrasting walnut floor made all the white and beige furniture pieces inviting. Sunlight easily filled the room through the enormous picture windows, and the silver picture frames and various antiques on the mantel shone brilliantly in the natural light.

LaDonda stood in the center of the room with cell phone in hand while occasionally peeking outside the window. "You guys go ahead and open the presents," she said.

"Happy birthday, Lafonda!" said Jim enthusiastically, before anyone else could. He handed her a slim rectangular box. "Here. Open mine first."

"I don't have to be psychic to know what that is," mumbled Nathan.

Both Roy and Lafonda turned to face him and frowned. She then rolled her eyes and focused her attention back on Jim. "It's beautiful," she said, opening the gold box.

"What a surprise," muttered Nathan. "Another gold necklace; how original."

"Do you like the charms?" asked Jim, referring to the gold letters J and D that dangled from the necklace.

Nathan chuckled and then quickly tried to stifle his laughter. "Wasn't that so thoughtful of Jim to give you such a fine piece of jewelry to wear around your neck?" he asked Lafonda sarcastically. "Jim, my man, you really outdid yourself this time." He grinned again. "I'm sure Lafonda will wear it every day!"

Lafonda glowered and pursed her lips while Jim attempted to reach around her. "Here, babe," he said cheerfully, ignoring Nathan. "Try it on."

Lafonda's shoulders seemed to cringe slightly at the sound of the word *babe*. "Thank you, again," she said, while gently touching the gold letters that now lay flat against her chest. "It's lovely."

Next, she opened several gifts from Roy. "I hope the IUCF T-shirts will fit okay," he grinned.

She smiled reassuringly. "I'm sure they will," she said, taking a pause. "But why the sunglasses?"

Roy grinned again. "I'm sure they'll come in handy eventually," he said. "Maybe out by the pool. You'll figure it out."

She eyed him suspiciously and then shrugged. "Okay, then," she said with a smile, giving him a big hug. "Then they're all perfect."

Reluctantly, Nathan headed over towards the table. "I guess I'm up next," he mumbled. The only gift left on the table was the small red box with the huge red ribbon. He could feel Jim's glare bearing down on him as he reached for the box. Nathan loudly cleared his throat and stared back at him, and Jim slowly stepped back. "Happy birthday!" said Nathan, gracefully handing her the box.

Lafonda beamed. "Thank you, Nathan," she grinned.

"But wait," said Nathan, appearing confused. "You don't even know what's in it yet."

"Whatever it is, I'm sure it's brilliant!" she said, glancing over at Roy.

Carefully, she unraveled the red ribbon and placed it and the tiny red lid on the table. Lafonda's mouth slowly fell open and her eyes began to tear as she spoke in a whisper. "I thought I'd lost it for good."

Jim leaned over her shoulder and Nathan carefully inched closer to see what was in the box. Lafonda smiled as she tried to choke back her tears. "And it's just as beautiful as the day I lost it," she said. "All those years ago." She turned to look at Nathan and then at Roy. "Where did you find it?"

"I found it about a month ago while tending to the rose bushes behind the main house," said Roy, quickly placing an arm around Nathan before he could speak. "You know, where you kids would play when you were little." He gave Nathan a slight nudge. "Nathan thought it would be nice to clean it up and give it to you as a surprise for your birthday."

"Um — yeah — right!" stumbled Nathan, quickly chiming in.

"Okay, so what is it?" interrupted Jim, sounding annoyed.

Lafonda turned to glower at him before carefully removing the small gold object from the box. "It's the locket my grandfather gave to me before he died," she said in a low voice. "I was only seven when he gave it to me." She paused and her eyes swelled with tears again. "I lost it shortly after and I guess I never really stopped looking for it."

LaDonda smiled. "Yes, I remember the day he gave it to you," she said, stepping away from the window. "Jackson really wanted you to have that locket." She paused to peer out of the window again. "You know, it originally belonged to Nathan's mother."

"My mother?" asked Nathan, in a high-pitched voice.

"Yes, Nathan," LaDonda said, while glancing at Roy. She cleared her throat. "Grace gave it to Lafonda's grandfather shortly after she had you." She paused again and then enthusiastically looked back from the window. "Okay, everyone, let's continue this party outside!"

"Huh?" muttered Lafonda. She looked confused. "How come?"

"Come on," said LaDonda, while ushering everyone out the front door. "But wait for me, hun." She took Lafonda by the hand and then held up her cell phone. "I want you to walk out with me, but let's get your parents on the line first."

The noon sun was set high in the summer sky and reflected a red glare into Nathan's eyes. It took him only a moment to realize that it wasn't the sun causing the red glare, but the shiny new red Ferrari sitting in the driveway.

"Oh, my God!" Lafonda screamed.

"Happy birthday!" smiled LaDonda, taking the phone from Lafonda as she bolted towards the car.

"It's my car!" Lafonda yelled. "It even has the color seats I wanted!" She turned to look at her grandmother. "I can't believe it!"

"It's from me and your parents," explained LaDonda, before speaking on the phone.

Jim suddenly looked animated, and he had a huge smile on his face. "It's the new Ferrari Spider," he said, with excitement in his voice. "It has over 500 horsepower."

"Thank you, thank you, Grandma!" repeated Lafonda, giving her a long hug and then taking the phone to talk to her parents.

"Um," stuttered Nathan. He leaned into his grandfather and then gestured towards Jim. "Was he in on this?"

Roy paused to take a deep breath and then sighed happily. "Well, that's what happens when you sleep and everyone's awake, son," he chuckled. "You miss things."

"Okay, Dad," said Lafonda reassuringly over the phone. "I will drive safe and wear my seat belt." She smiled. "I love you too. And tell Mom that I really love the gift and that I really miss you guys so much! Yes, I will call again after my test drive."

Lafonda handed the phone back to her grandmother and squealed. "I am so excited!" she yelled, opening the door to the convertible and sliding in.

Without hesitation, Jim eagerly jumped into the passenger seat. "You ready to take this baby for a spin?" he asked.

Lafonda smiled as she turned the key in the ignition. She then turned to look at Nathan. "Hey!" she said. "You want to take it for a spin when we get back?"

Jim frowned. He appeared taken aback by her offer. A brief moment passed, and then Nathan shook his head. "Nah, that's okay," he said. "We can go for a spin tomorrow."

"Oh — okay," she responded slowly.

"Let's go, babe!" shouted Jim over the roar of the engine.

She smiled again and then put the car into gear. Jim impatiently started to tap his fingers on the dashboard. "Are you sure you know how to drive this thing?" he asked.

"Yep, and I just need one thing," she said, as she put on her new sunglasses that hung from the crest of her shirt. She waved one hand in Roy's direction as the red car sped down the U-shaped driveway. "Thanks, Roy!"

Nathan spent the rest of the afternoon helping his grandfather prepare the den for Lafonda's birthday party. He thought the den was quite nice, actually, and the Devaros often used it as a family room that also housed a small library in its mezzanine. He would often stare out the mezzanine window, especially after the first snow, while enjoying the sounds of the crackling fireplace from down below.

LaDonda was busy in the kitchen making the birthday cake but made several appearances to make certain that the room was decorated just right: not too many balloons, but festive with color.

In the evening, Lafonda went over to Jim's house to show her new car to Jim's parents and some of their friends. Nathan hid away in the cottage, hoping not to be forced by his grandfather to accompany her. He wasn't comfortable at all around the Dardings and didn't want to try to fit in with them especially since most of their conversations, one way or another, were about cars, boats, vacations and money.

Quietly, he lay in bed while allowing his gaze to aimlessly float around the room. He immediately noticed a bottle of Wool's Ointment for the treatment of fungus and other ailments caused by eukaryotes on one of his pillows. Roy had obviously put it there for him to use to solve his hand-scratching problem.

Nathan sighed. He thought about taking out his suitcase to start packing for his time at camp, but his mind kept wandering elsewhere. He glanced over at the two picture frames of his parents that were nestled in the corner of his desk. One of the frames, the one that appeared aged and carved out of wood, was of their wedding photo. The picture and the frame were his mom's, so he would often take it to school with him and on extended trips.

Why did she give her locket to Jackson? he thought, letting out a stifled yawn.

He then looked at the other photograph, of a beautiful

pregnant woman. He had studied her picture many times before, paying attention to every line and detail. Her smile in the photograph was bright and hopeful, but there was a sadness to her eyes. Her dark hair was long and full, and when he was little, he would often tell people he was the son of Pocahontas.

Was she sad because she had lost the love of her life to a car accident several months earlier? he pondered. He often studied his father's face in the wedding photo and wondered what he was like. *Did she somehow know that she wouldn't survive the pregnancy?*

When he was younger, he would often ask Roy many questions about his father and mother. But he'd stopped asking questions years earlier because he could tell it was painful for Roy to relive the memories about his only son and his son's beautiful wife. Nathan let out a huge yawn as he turned off the light. His eyes grew heavy and his mind ceased to ponder. Soon, his eyes gave in to the darkness, and he was asleep.

CHAPTER THREE

PARTY

Nathan sat quietly on the edge of his bed, staring at the black blazer hanging in his closet. Roy had taken the liberty of having it dry-cleaned so that he could wear it to Lafonda's birthday party. He had dreaded this moment all day and regretted falling asleep so early the night before. He had awoken much earlier than usual, and instead of hanging out at the Devaro Mansion and risking the chance of being volunteered to continue party preparations, he opted to weed the garden instead.

Nathan was positive that if Roy hadn't been so pleased to have this labor of love marked off his to-do list, he would have been enlisted for Operation Party Hearty straightaway. But Nathan wanted to avoid at all costs the why-aren't-you-excited-we-are-having-a-party glares from Roy and LaDonda.

Based on past experience, Nathan knew that the entire day would be a mad rush with cooking, baking, decorations and discussions of expectations for the night. All of which would annoy him just as much as the constant delivery of flowers Lafonda would receive from admirers and her boyfriend Jim.

Now, if I could just get out of attending tonight's party, he thought. He noticed the dark tan forming on his arms from being out in the sun. "Maybe I could suddenly have a stomachache or have a heatstroke from working in the sun all day." He huffed. "Or maybe I can just say I'm sleep deprived."

Nathan suddenly recalled he wasn't able to sleep the night before. Twice he had awaken in the middle of the night, just like all the other nights, with his heart racing and his body covered in sweat. His bed sheets were always wet, and he changed them so frequently he was sure Roy probably thought he was wetting his bed.

"That would be an interesting conversation," he chuckled to himself.

From his window, Nathan heard the sound of cars driving up the main driveway and the closing of car doors. *I guess I'd better get ready,* he thought, *before —*

There was a knock on his bedroom door. "Nathan," called out Roy. "Are you ready in there?"

"Too late," said Nathan quietly.

There was a knock on the door again. "The guests have started to arrive," said Roy. "And I'm sure Lafonda is expecting you at the party."

Quickly, Nathan sprang to his feet and slid into his white dress shirt and black pants. "Nathan!" Roy called out again, this time twisting the knob to the door impatiently. "What are you doing in there?"

"Okay, okay!" Nathan groaned, barely opening the door. "I was getting ready."

Roy stood in the doorway with a perplexed look on his face. "I've never known you to take this long to get ready," he said. "You said you would shower and be over to the main house hours ago."

"Uh-oh," stuttered Nathan, while looking around the room. "I thought I had time to pack a little for camp."

"Nathan," said Roy reassuringly, while staring at the almost empty suitcase, "I know it can be hard sometimes, trying to fit in."

"Ugh," Nathan sighed. "Here we go."

"And I know some of Lafonda's friends can seem a bit snobbish at times," Roy continued, "but you shouldn't let that stop you from going to Lafonda's birthday party."

Nathan stood in front of his grandfather with a bored look on his face, so Roy decided to just save the lecture. He took a long look at his grandson and then smiled. "You look handsome," he said, fixing Nathan's blazer collar. "But not as handsome as your grandfather."

Nathan's face frowned. "Whatever, Grandpa!" he teased.

Roy grinned and then placed his hands on Nathan's shoulders. "I just want you to have a good time and have some fun for a change. Okay?"

Nathan smiled. "Okay."

The U-shaped driveway to the Devaro Mansion was packed with cars; and if it hadn't been for Lafonda's red Ferrari, the driveway could easily have been mistaken for a BMW car sales lot. Jim Darding had bought a new silver BMW the previous year, which in Nathan's mind would explain the popularity of the car and the color in the driveway.

Jim was popular in town mostly because of his parent's money; his good looks were just a bonus. Jim Sr. and his wife, Frannie Marie, owned several restaurants in town and around campus. They were also into real estate and sold most of the homes to the parents of the people at the party and rented most of the apartment units on campus to their children.

"Now that Lafonda is dating Jim, next year the driveway will be full of red Ferraris," Nathan chuckled to himself.

The den that was often used by the Devaros as a

family room was more decorated than when Nathan last saw it. There were flowers in every corner, on every table, and on any flat surface that could hold a vase. In years past, Lafonda would often receive flowers for her birthday, but this was a lot more than usual. Right away Nathan attributed the room's resemblance to a flower shop to Jim. Also, there were balloons of various sizes in a variety of colors sprinkled throughout the room. The banister to the staircase that led up to the library in the mezzanine was wrapped in purple ribbon. Next to the staircase was a long table covered with a red tablecloth. On one end of the table were presents in different-sized boxes, and on the other was an enormous multilayered cake with purple, red and white icing.

LaDonda really does like a lot of color, Nathan thought.

He straightened his jacket and nervously ran his fingers through his hair as he passed by a group of young women who were laughing and having a conversation. One of them, a young woman with blond hair and emerald-green eyes, smiled at him as he walked by.

I need to find a mirror, he thought. He had gotten dressed so quickly earlier, trying to convince Roy that he was ready for the party, that he hadn't remembered to comb his hair. *I hope I look okay. Roy did say I looked handsome tonight. Um … on second thought, I think I'd better get to a mirror.*

Nathan turned around and headed towards the bathroom, but bumped into a tall guy who was carrying two drinks. "Sorry," said Nathan apologetically. He looked down to see if anything had gotten on his white shirt. "Who are all these people?" he mumbled underneath his breath. "Are they all here for Lafonda?"

Nathan looked across the room. It was full of faces that he hadn't seen before and none of the recognizable faces of friends from the past.

These are probably friends of Jim's, he thought. *Who would now be Lafonda's new friends.* He continued to look around the crowded room. *But then again, they could all be friends Lafonda made this past freshman year — none of whom I would know because I avoided Lafonda practically all last year.*

Suddenly, Nathan felt out of place because he didn't have anyone to talk to. He decided to skip the mirror after seeing the long line forming outside the bathroom, and instead of walking over to the other side of the house, decided to get a drink. The young woman with the blond hair and green eyes was standing with a drink in her hand next to the drink table. Her eyes were fixed on him and if it weren't for the three guys trying to engage her in a conversation, he could've sworn she was waiting on him.

He was caught a little off guard by the drink options on the table. After a year of being exposed to frat parties on campus, Nathan expected to find cups of beer or some kind of alcoholic beverage on the table. "I don't know why I'm surprised to find fruit punch," he chuckled. "LaDonda will probably still consider us kids even when we're thirty."

Nathan stood by the table holding his cup of punch. Eagerly, he scanned the room looking for a familiar face but would occasionally find the young woman staring at him. *What's her deal?* he thought. *She is obviously beautiful, and based on all the attention she's getting, I doubt if she needs another guy to add to the adulation.*

"Nathan! Over here!" called someone over the music and the chatter. Across the room he caught a glimpse of a short, older woman with big hair waving her arm in the air. She was standing next to a younger-looking man.

Reluctantly, he headed towards her. "Okay, LaDonda,

you can stop waving now," he mumbled. "I can see you."

"Nathan!" she called again.

"Ugh. Why is she still calling my name and flagging me down?" he protested. "Doesn't she see me walking over to her?" Painstakingly, he raised his hand to wave back. "This is so embarrassing," he muttered. He automatically scanned the room to see if anyone else was witnessing the uncomfortable display. "Maybe if I wave back she'll stop."

"Come, come, Nathan," she said eagerly, motioning her hand at him. "I want you to meet someone. I want you to meet Jonathan Gregory Black."

She beamed. "You remember the Black family, don't you Nathan?" she asked. "Dr. Gregory Black, Jonathan's father, and his wife, Patricia, attended our church for years before moving abroad to pioneer a church in India." Enthusiastically, she turned to look at Jonathan. "How old were you when your family moved there?"

Jonathan was tall and slender and wore a pair of dark, square-rimmed glasses that occasionally slid down to the tip of his sharp-angled nose. His dark hair was in contrast to his fair skin. Nathan took note of Jonathan's sharp cheek bones and his piercing blue eyes that set noticeably behind his glasses. "I believe I was seven," he said, with a slight British accent. "I also believe Nathan, Lafonda and I used to attend Sunday school together."

LaDonda turned her gaze to Nathan and stared at him intently as if she was awaiting a response.

"I don't remember," Nathan shrugged.

Her smile suddenly turned sour after hearing his answer.

"I'm sorry. I just don't remember." Nathan sighed. He hardly remembered anything from when he was seven.

"Well," continued LaDonda, "I am so excited to have

you back in town with us." She had a disconcerted look on her face, but eventually sounded elated again. "And I was so excited when your parents called me to confirm that you would be helping out with camp this year!" She smiled. "I know it may not be as interesting or prestigious as being a summer fellow with your father and my son, Avery, at the British Museum in London, but I am so grateful you decided to join us."

"Oh no, I am excited too!" shouted Jonathan, pausing to reposition his glasses on his nose. "I haven't been to the States in years and I am most interested in learning more about the historical sites."

"The historical sites?" moaned Nathan. He had a bewildered look on his face. "Here?" He huffed. *I wouldn't consider anywhere in this town of historical significance,* he thought. *And why on Earth would someone pass up a summer fellowship in London to be here to look after some whiny teenagers?*

"Yes," responded Jonathan enthusiastically, "I can't wait to see the cliffs overlooking Lake Charleston again. They were once used by the Northern Cahokia tribe for rituals and ceremonies." He smiled. "When I was little, I used to go up there with my father during his excavations of the area. Tomorrow I plan to meet with the director of Archeological Studies at the university, Dr. Janet Helmsley. She's coordinating a new dig site and the excavation of one of the Cahokia caves behind the cliffs."

"Jonathan is following in his father's footsteps by studying archeology and theology at Oxford University," said LaDonda proudly.

Nathan quickly rolled his eyes. "Well, good luck with that," he said.

LaDonda frowned at Nathan and then smiled at Jonathan. "Will you need a car to help you get around while you are here?"

"Oh," responded Jonathan, "My dad arranged for me to stay with the Dardings while I am here, until camp starts on Friday." He paused to reposition his square-rimmed glasses on his nose again. "They were kind enough to allow me to use one of their vehicles," he beamed. "It's a nice car too. I believe it's a gray or silver BMW. I really like it!"

"You and everyone else," muttered Nathan underneath his breath.

LaDonda sighed while keeping a watchful eye on the party. "I told Gregory that you could stay here with us," she said. "But your father insisted that Jim Darding wouldn't hear of it."

Jonathan smiled and then laughed. "Yes, Mr. Darding was adamant about my staying with them," he said. "My dad and Mr. Darding are good friends. Mr. Darding came to visit us in London when dad was appointed a trustee of the British Museum."

"Okay," said LaDonda, with a grin. "Well next time, you will have to stay with us."

"Well, I'm all out of punch," announced Nathan impatiently. "And I promised the birthday girl that I would find her as soon as I got here." He smiled weakly and began to inch away. "It was nice meeting you, or seeing you again, John, and I guess I'll see you at camp on Friday."

"You too," said Jonathan, repositioning his glasses again. "Oh, and it's Jonathan."

"Right — Jonathan," replied Nathan, attempting to walk away before LaDonda could demand his attendance. He took a deep breath and sighed heavily. "Gee," he groaned, when he was out of earshot. "That took forever!"

Nathan headed over towards the table with the fruit

punch and carefully maneuvered through the groups of people. The beautiful girl with the sparkling green eyes and her entourage were no longer there. *I wonder where Lafonda is anyway?* he pondered to himself. *I'd better find her quick and say hello, or I will never hear the end of it.*

He scanned the room. *I hope she doesn't expect me to dance with her like last year,* he thought, recalling the torture of having to dance in front of people, and with Lafonda. *I would rather give blood than do that again.*

Ultimately, Nathan decided to stick to the security of the table instead of aimlessly searching through the crowd to look for her. He didn't want to risk looking silly. He noticed that the majority of the people at the party appeared to be college students and that most of the older people were gathered together in little pockets near the entrance to the den or fringes of the party. He caught a glimpse of Roy and LaDonda near the table stacked with gifts and cake. It looked like she was still having a conversation with Jonathan.

Carefully, he continued to look around the room, stopping here and there to see if he recognized anyone at the party. He stopped again when he saw the blonde with the green eyes. She was standing in the center of the crowded room, but without her entourage of admirers. The sequins on her strapless black dress glimmered in the light as she occasionally shifted from side to side. She was engaged in a conversation with a young woman dressed in a white, fitted minidress that flared out slightly from her waist. The light fabric lay gently on her luminous dark skin, and her long dark hair lay in silky curls on her shoulders. Nathan thought she was just as beautiful as the blonde.

He gasped. "Lafonda!" he blurted out. He was so loud that a few people turned around. "That's Lafonda?"

Nathan blinked his eyes and looked intently again at the woman in the white dress, this time expecting to see something different. After blinking and adjusting his eyes several times, he finally shook his head in disbelief.

I guess everyone deserves to look good on their birthday, he thought, internalizing for what seemed to him an overnight transformation.

For a second, Lafonda turned in Nathan's direction. When their eyes met, she smiled a huge grin. "The jig is up: I've been spotted," he said. "I guess I'd better head over there."

Reluctantly, Nathan navigated through the crowd and towards the center of the room. He had approached Lafonda and the blonde from the side, and for the moment, had gone unnoticed as he stood behind them.

"So, Amanda," said Lafonda sympathetically, while tossing her long black hair off to one side. "Have you heard from Leah — you know, since the accident?"

"Is that what people are calling it these days?" scoffed Amanda, while running her fingers through her straight blond hair. "All I know is that Steve and I had returned to the dorm room to get my cell phone, and there was Leah in the middle of the room, covered in blood, and threatening to hit people with my lamp!"

"So you haven't gone to visit her at the hospital or tried to call her?" Lafonda asked, sounding disappointed. "Amanda, she was your roommate."

Amanda huffed. "After what I saw that day," she said, "I'm terrified of her." Her sparkling green eyes appeared to flicker with fire in them. "I mean, even Steve was scared to enter the room, and he's built like a football player! I'm telling you, Lafonda, she was like a wild woman — Tarzan's mother gone crazy!" She shrugged. "I guess a couple of girls were playing cards outside the room and heard her screaming. I think they tried to help her."

"Yes," said Lafonda, "I was in my room when I heard the screaming and all the commotion out in the hallway."

Amanda rolled her eyes. "She was going on and on about monsters and about something attacking her."

"Yes!" agreed Lafonda. "And we were trying to help her, but she was so frantic, so terrified. She wouldn't let anyone get near her."

"I guess it was just a matter of time before Leah lost it," shrugged Amanda.

"What do you mean?" asked Lafonda, appearing confused.

Amanda frowned and her green eyes gawked at her incredulously. "Everyone noticed how strange she was acting after her roommate Jamie died in the first semester, Lafonda," sneered Amanda. "And it doesn't take a genius to know she was having nightmares with all that late-night screaming." She leaned in. "But honestly, could you blame her mother for having her committed?"

"Amanda, I don't think Leah's crazy!" Lafonda snapped in disbelief. "I just wish we could have helped her."

"Well, the only people that could help her were campus security guards," Amanda concluded coldly. "It eventually took five security guards to subdue her; thank goodness somebody called the police."

Lafonda shook her head. "By the way, did you ever find your cell phone?" she asked.

"What happened?" interrupted Nathan, sounding confused and finally making his presence known. "Did this happen on campus?"

"Um, how long have you been standing there?" asked Lafonda, sounding annoyed. "You could have said something — but then again, it's you."

"Sorry," said Nathan, appearing frustrated. "But really, I didn't mean too. It's just — it's just that ..." His mind started to spin now. He wanted to tell Lafonda everything; that there were so many similarities in the story he just heard and the estranged girl he had been dreaming about. *How could this be?* he asked himself.

He had convinced himself so many times before that it was just a dream, but suddenly there was proof she could be real. Nathan's palms began to sweat and he felt his face becoming flushed. *And if she's real, then the unseen assailant would be real too!*

"Um, Nathan," said Lafonda. "It's just that what?" Suddenly, she paused and stared intently into his face. "Um, Nathan, you don't look so good."

"He's fine," interrupted Amanda, her green eyes sparkling brighter. "Isn't that right, handsome?"

"Uh-huh," stuttered Nathan.

"Well, that doesn't happen often," responded Lafonda with a smirk on her face. "Nathan Urye lost for words."

"I'm fine," he answered wearily. His mind continued to spin. *Yeah, I'm fine,* he thought sarcastically. *No big deal. Just that my reality isn't real and bloody girls and monsters are my new reality.*

Lafonda sighed and then stared at him suspiciously. "Amanda, this is Nathan," she said. "And Nathan, this is Amanda."

"Well, Lafonda!" said Amanda in a Southern drawl. "Where have you been hiding this handsome man?"

Lafonda took a long look at her and then rolled her eyes. "Nathan also goes to IUCF and just finished his freshmen year," she sighed. Reluctantly, she turned to look at him. "Nathan's grandfather is our caretaker, and they both live here on the property."

"Well," said Amanda flirtatiously, "I've never seen you on campus. How about you treat a lady to a dance?"

"I think ... I need a drink," stuttered Nathan, sounding a bit bewildered. "Or most likely to sit down." He tried to force a smile. "And I would love to, but my feet are barely good enough for walking, let alone dancing."

Amanda's eyes appeared to flicker with fire in them again. "Oh — well, we will see," she said, taking him by the hand. "I love a man with strong hands."

"Oh, brother," said Lafonda, underneath her breath.

Amanda turned around and displayed a wide grin. She then happily focused her attention back on Nathan. "Ready?" she asked, gently squeezing his hand.

Nathan suddenly had a blank look on his face. "Uh ... yes," he stuttered, still sounding confused. "On second thought, I'm ready. Let's dance."

"What?" blurted Lafonda.

"Hey guys, what's going on?" asked Jim, suddenly joining them. He stood next to Lafonda while snapping his fingers and dancing slightly offbeat to the music. "Let's dance, babe!"

"You have strong arms," grinned Amanda, squeezing Nathan's bicep.

Abruptly, Lafonda grabbed Jim's hand to stop him from snapping his fingers. "Not right now, babe," she said, forcing a smile. "How about you go get us some punch?"

"But I'm not thirsty," whined Jim, sounding disappointed.

Lafonda crossed her arms, frowning at Jim, and Jim lowered his head. "Okay," he said, reluctantly walking away.

"And you," Lafonda said, grabbing Nathan's arm, so

that Amanda would drop his hand, "if anyone is going to be dancing, it's the birthday girl." She leaned in and then took him by the hand. "You owe me the first dance, remember?"

"Uh — Lafonda!" Amanda moaned.

"Uh — Amanda?" protested Lafonda. "Go find Steve!"

Triumphantly, Lafonda led Nathan out to the dance floor, and he nonchalantly followed. "Lafonda," he said slowly. "Um — what just happened?"

Lafonda looked up towards the ceiling and then quickly rolled her eyes. "I don't know," she said. "You tell me." She relaxed her arm a little, so that he could lead. "One second you wanted to sit down, and then suddenly you wanted to cut a rug with Amanda."

"I, I don't remember," Nathan said, sounding flustered.

Lafonda glared at Nathan. "You don't have to play dumb," she said. She gestured in Amanda's direction; she was standing with her entourage of admirers again. "Amanda has that effect on men."

Nathan slightly shrugged and then shook his head. "Who is Steve?" he asked.

"Steve is Amanda's boyfriend," she grinned. She tilted her head to look around the room. "And I don't even think he's here."

"Lafonda," he said, taking a pause, "I apologize if things got weird back there." He recalled what he had overheard from them earlier. "Things have been a little … strange lately."

"Yeah, for both of us," she said, after catching a glimpse of Jim watching them on the dance floor with two drinks in his hand. "You know, Nathan," she continued, "you're not that bad of a dancer — when you're not thinking about it."

"Oh," he responded, sounding surprised. "I didn't realize moving to this slow of a song is considered dancing."

She smiled. "Nathan," she uttered softly, "what happened to us? I mean, to our friendship?" She looked longingly into his eyes. "I almost never saw you at school, and you barely even speak to me now that we're home."

Nathan twisted his lip. *Well*, he thought, *you and your friends are rich and I'm not and I feel like an outsider because of it.* He opened his mouth to speak, but closed it again. *And to top things off, I keep dreaming about a girl that I believe is being attacked by monsters.* He sighed. "It's complicated," he finally responded.

"What's so complicated about it?" she asked. "Why don't you just tell me?" Lafonda suddenly appeared a bit flustered. "Is there something that I did wrong?"

He paused for a moment. He could feel the tingling sensation starting to build in his hands. "You wouldn't understand," he said.

Lafonda frowned and stopped dancing. "How can I understand if you won't tell me?" she protested, crossing her arms.

Nathan quickly looked down. His hands started to tremble now. "Lafonda," he sighed impatiently. He then softly placed his hands on her shoulders. "Just trust me. This has nothing to do with you." He paused. "You did nothing wrong."

"Hey, guys!" interrupted Jim, while holding out the two drinks in his hands.

"Nathan!" said Lafonda suddenly. She had a look of concern on her face. "Your hands — are they shaking?"

Nathan could feel his face turning red and he quickly withdrew his hands from her shoulders. "I think I'd better go," he stuttered nervously.

"Nonsense," spouted Jim. He had an ornery look on his face. "You can hold the drinks while I dance with my girlfriend."

"Jim — don't start," warned Lafonda.

"No!" he said, with a shrug. "You're obviously now in the mood to dance, so let's dance." Lafonda frowned, and in protest Jim shoved the two cups of punch into Nathan's hands. "Here!"

"Jim," said Nathan sternly. "Please take these drinks back. I am not in the mood for this."

"Ha!" blurted Jim, while nodding his head. "No, I think you are more than capable of holding the drinks while we dance."

"Oh," sneered Nathan. "And I think you are absolutely incapable of not being a complete jerk!"

"Stop it guys!" exclaimed Lafonda. "I'll take the drinks." She reached for the two drinks in Nathan's hands and glared at Jim. "And Jim, you can dance by yourself."

"Forget it!" Jim huffed, attempting to bypass her. "I'll take the drinks."

Suddenly, Nathan's hands shook uncontrollably and fruit punch began to spew erratically from the cups. Desperately, he tried to control his hands, but couldn't. Just as quickly as it had all started, it was over; and both cups were now empty.

Nathan's eyes met Lafonda's as he slowly realized where all the juice had gone.

"Who's the jerk now?" said Jim coldly, as he tried to wipe the red juice from his white shirt and black jacket.

Nathan allowed his eyes to follow Lafonda's gaze as she began wiping her dress. "I'm sorry," he stuttered. He looked on in horror at the once flowing white dress that was now stained in red and stuck to her body. "I am so sorry." Several people that were on the dance floor had horrified looks on their faces and some tried not to let on how bad her dress looked by turning away. "I'm just gonna go," he muttered, turning to cut through the crowd.

CHAPTER FOUR

PARTY'S OVER

Nathan passed by LaDonda and Roy on his way out of the room. He could tell by the perplexed looks on their faces that they were curious as to why he was in such a hurry. He was pleased that neither stopped him because he was way too embarrassed to stick around, and he didn't want to relive what had just happened by having to explain it to them.

He kept his head down low, and his hands continued to tremble uncontrollably as he bolted towards the front door of the Devaro Mansion. He was outside now and the summer night air was cool. *What is wrong with me?* he worried, taking a moment to look down at his hands.

His hands looked normal besides the shaking and they felt warm even against the cool air. After careful inspection, he also noticed that they were a bright red. *That must be from the fruit punch. The juice must've stained my hands.*

"Hi, Nathan," said a voice that was unfamiliar to him.

Immediately, he shoved his hands into his front pockets and turned around to find Jonathan Black staring at him from the front door. Nathan gave a quick smile and tried to turn away, but Jonathan proceeded towards him anyway. "Uh — hi, Jon," he said, after clearing his throat.

"It's such a beautiful night," said Jonathan, while looking up towards the sky. "Oh, and look, there's also a new moon." He smiled and then returned his gaze back to Nathan. "And I prefer Jonathan, by the way."

"Oh, yeah, sorry about that," said Nathan, appearing slightly anxious. He took a few steps backwards towards the cottage. "I'll remember that, *Jonathan*."

"I thought I would turn in early to get a good start out at the Cahokia Caves tomorrow, before meeting with Dr. Helmsley," Jonathan announced quickly before Nathan could inch away. "Tomorrow is supposed to be a beautiful day as well." He paused, briefly repositioning his glasses. "Would you care to join me?"

"What?" asked Nathan surprised. He was hoping the conversation wasn't going to last long. "Join you?"

Jonathan grinned. "Well, I was talking with your grandfather and —"

"Uh-huh," uttered Nathan while nodding. He expected anything starting with "I was talking to your grandfather" to be followed by a request of some kind. "You were talking with my grandfather."

Jonathan paused again and took a dry gulp. "I was talking with your grandfather and LaDonda —"

"LaDonda!" interrupted Nathan again.

"Can I please finish?" asked Jonathan. He paused for a second, as if he was awaiting a response. "I'll take your silence as a yes."

Nathan raised his eyebrows and Jonathan smiled.

"After learning from Roy and LaDonda about your Cahokia ancestry through your mother," Jonathan continued enthusiastically, "I thought you might want to join me tomorrow at the dig site."

Nathan's eyebrows were still raised and were now accompanied by a frown. "Dig site?" he muttered,

"Tomorrow? At the caves?"

"Yes!" exclaimed Jonathan. "It's so exciting that after all these years they are still finding stuff!" His eyes were as wide as saucers now. "Considering that whatever we discover is a part of your history, you could learn firsthand more about yourself and your people."

I think I've learned enough about myself for one day, Nathan thought, recalling what he had just learned from Lafonda and Amanda about the reality of his nightmares. He got a warm feeling in his chest and began to think about his mother. Besides the fact that she had married his dad, Michael Urye, he didn't know a lot about Grace Sequoya. Everything he knew about the Cahokia tribe, he'd learned on school field trips to the Northern Cahokia Tribal Museum.

He soon realized that Jonathan was still there and decided to fake a yawn. He thought about stretching to add to the effect, but remembered how red his hands were and opted to leave them in his pockets instead. He also noticed that his hands continued to tremble slightly, but figured it was a good idea to just leave them there. "Thanks for the invite," he said. "But I think I'll pass. I still have to pack for camp on Friday."

Jonathan's bright blue eyes were still filled with excitement. "Did you know that the Cahokia tribe once occupied most of what is now Southern Illinois before they became known as two separate tribes?" he asked. "And that most scholars attribute the separation to a massive drought that caused famine in the area?"

"Yes!" howled Nathan, yawning with both arms stretched out in the air. He now thought exposing his hands was worth the risk.

But Jonathan's eyes continued to gleam. "Archeologists have found artifacts that suggest there was a migration of clans from the tribe's southern borders to this area right around Lake Charleston!" He grinned. "Can you guess why they migrated to this area?"

Nathan huffed and began to stare at the cars lined up around the driveway. "Uh ... the water?" he mumbled.

"Yes, exactly!" cried Jonathan, while quickly fixing his glasses. "Isn't that amazing?"

"Yes. Amazing," sighed Nathan.

Jonathan smiled and enthusiastically nodded his head. "And did you know —"

"Jonathan!" blurted Nathan, and Jonathan looked so startled that Nathan lowered his voice. "Not that I wouldn't mind continuing this most stimulating conversation, but I did promise my grandfather that I would ... that I would ... let the dog out."

"Oh, you have a dog!" said Jonathan, enthusiastically. "Isn't that wonderful?"

Nathan frowned. He didn't quite understand why he would use the word *wonderful*. Jonathan continued to smile and repositioned his glasses again.

"What kind of dog is it?" he asked.

"Uh ... uh," he stuttered, trying to think of something.

"Yoo-hoo, Jonathan!" called an all-familiar voice. They both turned around to see LaDonda standing at the front door to the Devaro Mansion. She was waving her hand, trying to get Jonathan's attention. "Good, you're still here!" she shouted. "I would like for you to meet someone before you leave."

Jonathan smiled. "Well, I guess I'd better see what she wants — or rather, see who this person is," he said. "Then, I guess I'll grab the car and head out."

Nathan opened his mouth to say something, but then paused after looking at the sea of identical silver BMWs parked around the long U-shaped driveway. "Good luck with that," he chuckled.

Jonathan caught his gaze and then chuckled too. "Thanks," he said halfheartedly as he headed towards the house. "I guess we'll have most of summer to talk."

"Where is he going?" asked LaDonda, when Jonathan got to her.

"Oh," said Jonathan, walking back inside the house. "He said he had to let the dog out."

"The dog?" she asked, sounding confused. "What dog? Nathan doesn't have a dog."

The walk back to the cottage was agonizing. Nathan's mind was going a mile a minute. He was worried about his constantly trembling hands and his dreams about Leah. The thought of all this being real and not just a dream was frustrating. His mind just kept circling, coming to the same questions over and over, for which he had no answers.

How could this be possible? he asked himself sitting on his bed. *How am I dreaming about her?* He sighed heavily while kicking off his shoes. *Am I psychic, or something?*

Nathan felt like he had just entered into a freak show starring himself as the main attraction. The voice of the show announcer played in his head, *Step right up to see the boy who can see you in his dreams and make an awesome milkshake with his trembling hands.*

"I need to get off this weirdness train!" Nathan shouted, throwing himself down on his bed. "Why do I have to be so weird?" He stared hopelessly at the ceiling. "I'm already the poor brown kid who lives behind the Devaro Mansion."

He shook his head and groaned. "After tonight, with the whole fruit punch incident, I'm sure everyone has added strange or weird or worse — loser — to my trophy case of adjectives." He sighed again. "And to make matters worse, I can't get the shocked look on Lafonda's face out of my head."

He paused, remembering how beautiful she had looked in her white dress and with her silky, curly black hair. "I'm such a loser!" he said aloud. "I ruined her dress and I definitely ruined her birthday." He raised his hands up to the ceiling and examined them. "This uncontrollable shaking has to stop, and so do the nightmares," he moaned. "But what am I supposed to do?"

With his eyes, he traced over his red hands, which seemed to tremble intermittently now. Frustrated, he sprung out of bed and headed into the small bathroom connected to his room. He began to scrub his hands with soap and water in an attempt to get some of the red out.

Nathan looked up at himself in the mirror and noticed the pattern of red dots splattered across his white shirt. "Great!" he said. "My only good white shirt!"

Slowly, he dried his hands, which he noticed were now bright red from all the scrubbing, and then took off his jacket and white shirt. Nathan eyed his favorite IUCF T-shirt, which was resting on the back of his desk chair, but decided not to put it on because he normally slept without one, anyway.

"Ugh!" he moaned, suddenly scratching the palms of his hands. "I thought I was done with all the scratching!" Abruptly, he tried to scratch the palm of his hand with his teeth. "Okay, I give up!" he yelled. "This must be a rash, or something!"

He rolled his eyes. "I hate to admit it," he sighed, "but I'm all out of ideas. Where's the ointment Roy gave me?" There was a sudden knock on his bedroom door, and Nathan launched himself to lay flat on his bed. "You can come in Roy!"

"It's me — Lafonda."

Nathan quickly sat straight up in his bed. *Lafonda?* he thought. *She never comes over.* He began to fidget with his hands. "This must be serious," he muttered. "She must be really upset about my ruining her dress, not to mention her birthday party."

"Can I come in?" she asked. "I understand if you're busy. I can come back later."

Nathan opened the door to his bedroom to see Lafonda standing there with a slight smile. She looked different than the last time he'd seen her: traumatized and soaked with red fruit juice. She had changed clothes and had a calm, almost relieved, look on her face. Without the makeup and fancy clothing, she looked more like the Lafonda that he was used to. Her hair was still curly, but it was Lafonda all the same.

"You can come in," he stuttered.

She smiled and stepped into the room. Nathan noticed her deep brown eyes pause for a second as she did a quick scan of his chest. "Sorry," he said, quickly throwing on his favorite IUCF T-shirt.

She took a seat on the edge of his bed. Nathan decided it was best to keep his distance, so he moved back the two photos of his mom and dad and hopped on his desk.

Lafonda took a dry gulp and then gently tossed her hair over her shoulders. "I thought I would stop in to apologize," she said. She paused and then suddenly laughed. "I also wanted to see if you needed any help walking your dog."

"Oh, about that ..." stuttered Nathan, becoming flush in the face. "I didn't mean to lie to Jonathan. I just needed to get away."

"No need to explain to me," she grinned. She paused. "But you might want to explain it to Jonathan. I think the cat's out of the bag on that one."

Nathan diverted his eyes and then cleared his throat. "Uh, so why are you apologizing?" he asked. "If anything, I'm the one who should be apologizing. I ruined your dress and your birthday party."

"Oh, Nathan, you can be so dramatic sometimes," she replied with a grin. "You ruined my expensive dress, yes, but you didn't ruin my birthday party. And just to ease your brain, I won't be scarred for life."

He laughed. "Now, I didn't go so far as to think I scarred you for life!" he said with a sly grin. "I do give you some credit, though. You are more resilient than most girls."

She smiled in response, but the smile quickly faded. "I shouldn't have put you in that position tonight," she said with a more serious tone to her voice.

"What position?" he asked.

"I shouldn't have put you in between Jim and me," she said. She paused again, taking a moment to catch her breath. "And for that, I am truly sorry."

"Oh, that!" he grinned heartily. "I hadn't noticed."

"Well, all the same, I am sorry," said Lafonda.

Nathan smiled reassuringly. "It's no big deal," he said. "Considering that I ruined your dress, I think we're even."

Lafonda chuckled and so did he, but suddenly his eyes became wide. "Wait. I hope Jim isn't upset with me?" he said. "I hope he doesn't think I was trying to steal his girlfriend?"

She grinned while shaking her head. "No, Nathan," she mocked, "he doesn't think that."

"Is he upset that I spilled juice all over him?" he asked eagerly. "I'll make sure to apologize next time I see him."

Lafonda quickly rolled her eyes. "You've already

apologized, Nathan," she sighed. She took a deep breath and then released it slowly. "Really, it isn't necessary."

"Then I don't get it," he groaned. "What's the problem?"

"The problem isn't you or anything that you did," she explained. She ran her fingers through her hair, placed her folded hands on her lap, and chuckled. "Jim and I were having problems long before the fruit punch incident."

"Oh," said Nathan, "I see." He sounded at ease again. "Well, I figured it would happen sooner or later."

Suddenly, a few frown lines appeared on Lafonda's forehead. "What would happen?" she said.

"Well," he said, pausing to reposition himself on his desk, "it's just the way he would say and do things."

Her eyebrows were raised. "Okay," she nodded, "carry on."

Nathan smiled. "Well, like the way he would make assumptions about the way you felt about things," he stammered. "And the way he would make decisions for both of you without asking your opinion." He paused and then smirked. "Oh, and let's not forget about his most recent attempt to mark his property."

Lafonda let out a huge laugh and placed her hand on the charm around her neck, which Jim had given her earlier. "I know, I know," she chuckled, while running her fingers across the gold letters J and D. "I really shouldn't be wearing this necklace and I don't want to encourage him."

"Well," Nathan shrugged, "then, take it off."

She smiled and then fumbled to undo the clasp to her necklace. "Can you?" she asked, positioning her back towards him.

"Sure," he said, springing enthusiastically from his desk. "I'll be more than happy to get this off your neck."

She moved her long black hair off to the side and Nathan carefully removed her necklace. She turned around to look at him, and he had a huge smile across his face. "Do you want me to throw it away?" he asked.

"Ugh, Nathan. No!" she spouted, quickly taking back the necklace. She stared at him with contempt and then shook her head. "And why are your hands so red? Is that from the fruit punch?"

Suddenly, they both turned around. The sound of car doors opening and then closing could be heard from Nathan's bedroom window. "It's nothing," he stuttered, clutching his hands. "Like you said, it's from the fruit punch."

She sat in silence, staring at him. Nathan knew she was scrutinizing his answer.

"Well," he said, while clearing his throat, "it sounds like your guests are starting to leave, so I guess you'll want to get back to your party."

"Most of them were here for Jim anyway," Lafonda responded slowly. "And since he isn't here …"

"What? He left?" exclaimed Nathan. He had a surprised look on his face, but it quickly dissipated following a knock on his bedroom door. "Now, that has to be Roy."

Nathan slid off his desk and trotted over to open the door.

"Nathan," said Roy, "have you seen Lafonda?" He had a perplexed look on his face. "I can't find her anywhere, and Jim's car isn't in the driveway."

"How did you notice?" Nathan snickered.

Roy paused and then gave him a disapproving look.

Nathan huffed and then quickly rolled his eyes. "She's here," he moaned, stepping aside so that Roy could see in.

"Oh," he responded, appearing shocked. "You're here." His face softened and then he directed his attention to Lafonda. "We couldn't find you," he said. "Did you know that Jim left the party? When we couldn't find you, your grandmother and I thought that maybe you had gone with him."

"Well, here she is, safe and sound," joked Nathan.

Lafonda cast her head down and then diverted her eyes for a second before speaking. "Yeah," she uttered, softly, "I spoke to Jim before he left." She hesitated. "We both decided that it was a good time to call it an evening."

"Oh," responded Roy. His eyebrows were raised and Nathan could tell that he was trying to be reassuring. "It was that bad, huh?"

"No, everything is fine," she said. "Like I was just explaining to your grandson a few seconds ago, everything is fine, and I plan to talk to Jim in the morning."

"Sounds good," said Roy. "But not too long after you and Jim disappeared, so did everyone else at the party." He laughed. "It was as if someone sent out an emergency news bulletin. This just in: Jim and Lafonda have left the building."

"Probably more like a text message," commented Nathan.

The sound of car doors opening and closing and engines roaring before speeding down the driveway could still be heard from Nathan's window. Lafonda sighed. "I don't want to be rude," she said. "I'd better get back to my guests."

A buzzing sound emanated from Roy's pants pocket. "No, don't get up," he said eagerly to Lafonda. He reached into his pocket for his cell phone. "It's LaDonda.

And she's probably wondering where I went too." He paused while looking at the two of them and then smiled. "LaDonda and I will take care of the guests. You kids keep talking."

Roy shoved his cell phone back into his pocket and turned to leave the doorway. Nathan started to close the door behind him, but the door was quickly reopened, startling Nathan.

"Why are your hands so red?" Roy asked, with a perplexed look on his face. "Have you been using the ointment I gave you?"

"Yep," said Nathan, holding up the ointment from his desk. "I have it right here."

Roy frowned and then stared at him incredulously. "That doesn't answer my question," he said. "I have long caught on to your plays on words since trying to treat you for the chicken pox, when you were seven."

Lafonda let out a stifled chuckle.

"Okay, Grandpa," said Nathan, sounding annoyed. "I thought you were leaving." The frown lines on Roy's forehead deepened and he continued to stare at Nathan.

Nathan sighed heavily. "It's the fruit punch!" he groaned. "My hands are stained from the fruit punch."

"Next time I come to this room," said Roy, "that ointment bottle had better have been opened."

Reluctantly, Nathan nodded while attempting to close the door again.

"And used!" Roy said.

Lafonda laughed uncontrollably. "What was that all about?" she asked.

"I don't know," Nathan said, shaking his head. "I swear it has to be from the fruit punch."

"No, not that!" she laughed. "Roy and his you-kids-just-keep-talking bit."

Nathan shrugged. "I don't know," he sighed, sounding tired. "Move over." Sluggishly, he walked towards the bed and gave a forced smile. He placed his hand behind his head as he rested on a pillow. "He probably was just shocked that we were talking without being made to."

"Nathan," Lafonda said in a soft voice, taking the spot next to him.

Nathan noticed that she smelled good; almost like caramel candy. Instantly, he became embarrassed when Lafonda noticed him taking a whiff of her hair.

She smiled. "Do you remember getting the chicken pox?"

"How could I forget!" he exclaimed. "For almost a year you constantly reminded me that I gave it to you and that I caused you so much pain and misery."

Lafonda laughed heartily. "Well, you did!" she said. "And mine was the worst. I just couldn't stop scratching!"

"Yeah, I remember," said Nathan, laughing now. "And LaDonda and your mom kept chasing you around the house. They couldn't get you to put ointment on or to stop scratching!"

"I still have some of the scars," she laughed, tears forming in her eyes.

She sat up in bed, and there was silence in the room now. "You know, Nathan," she said softly, "we may be older and in college now and have new friends and different interests, but you and Roy will always be a part of my family, and we will always have our memories about the chicken pox."

CHAPTER FIVE

STEPHEN MALICK

It was Friday and camp day had finally arrived. Nathan had spent most of the morning and the day before packing for his time away at camp. LaDonda had been looking forward to this day since Nathan and Lafonda returned home for summer.

"So," said Roy, arriving at the doorway to Nathan's bedroom, "all packed for your four weeks at leadership camp?"

Nathan sat with two suitcases flung open on the floor. They were a part of a set of four suitcases he had used to pack for his first year away at IUCF. Around him, clothes hung from half-open and closed dresser drawers or were tossed on and around his bed. He figured he could probably fit all that he needed for four weeks into one suitcase, but to avoid any opposition from Lafonda and LaDonda, he'd opted to pack a second one as well.

"Well," said Nathan, with a smile on his face, "I probably would be done if I didn't have to spend time guessing what Lafonda and her grandmother would want me to wear this summer." He paused for a moment while glaring at the second suitcase. "I mean, besides a few shorts and a couple of T-shirts, what else do I need?"

Roy cleared his throat. "Well, that's probably why they want me to give you this," he said, handing Nathan a gold sheet of paper.

Nathan's face frowned. "What is this?" he asked.

"Just keep reading," smiled Roy.

"Guys are to wear a suit and tie for the closing ceremony!" Nathan blurted out. "A suit and tie in the summer?" He continued to stare at the gold paper and in frustration plopped down on the edge of his bed. "Why on earth would someone want to wear a suit jacket and tie in the middle of the summer?" He shook the paper in Roy's direction. "Did you look at this?" he cried. "She also wants us to bring Dockers or slacks to wear!"

He glared at Roy as Roy tried to hold back his laughter.

"I swear," he ranted. "Every year that woman comes up with more and more ridiculous stuff!"

"Now, Nathan," said Roy, while trying to control his laughter, "you know how much the Leadership Camp means to LaDonda."

"Grandpa," he moaned, standing up from his bed in frustration, "there is nothing on this list that says pack shorts, T-shirts, or even gym shoes!"

"Okay, okay, let me see," said Roy with a chuckle. He quickly scanned the list of items on the paper. "It's there. It falls under bring comfortable and loose clothing."

"Ha!" shouted Nathan. "And right under that we have Dockers, khakis and loafers listed as examples."

"Just pack a pair or two," sighed Roy, placing the gold paper on the desk.

"I am not wearing slacks during the summer when it's like 85 degrees outside," he protested. He drew a big breath and sighed. "And I don't even own loafers!"

"Then what are those?" asked Roy, pointing to a pair of brown leather shoes covered in dust in Nathan's closet.

Nathan's eyes suddenly grew wide. "Come on!" he

cried. "Those things are so old and I haven't worn them since like tenth grade!"

"Good," responded Roy with a smile. "That means they should still fit."

Nathan gritted his teeth and glowered at him.

"I'll take that as my cue to exit," said Roy. "You have your list now."

"Yeah," Nathan mumbled, underneath his breath. "Whatever."

"Happy packing!" concluded Roy, still trying to control his laughter.

Contemptuously, Nathan eyed the gold paper sitting on his desk and then tossed it on his bed amidst the other jumbled items. He sighed. While he enjoyed helping out with the leadership camp and serving as a camp counselor, Nathan detested the whole ritual for the first day at camp. He loathed the packing, first day check-in and sitting for at least an hour in the cafeteria listening to LaDonda's welcome-to-camp speech. Besides the enjoyment Nathan got from hearing the high school kids complain about how boring the first day of camp was, the first night would be quite uneventful.

This sucks! he thought, and then reluctantly looked at the chaos of clothing in his room. *And I'm sure Roy is expecting me to clean up this mess before I leave.*

An hour or so passed, and he finally finished packing what he thought was a good balance between appropriate attire for summer and LaDonda's clothing request. Grudgingly, he also tossed his old pair of brown leather loafers in the suitcase. Next, he cleaned his room, and he almost didn't mind it. It gave him a welcome break from the constant thoughts about the absence of his nightmares and how boring camp would be.

Since Lafonda's birthday party, the past two days had

been quite normal. For two nights in a row, there wasn't a single tingling sensation in his hands, nor did he wake up in a cold sweat from the same dream that had plagued him for weeks. Although he was relieved not to have the tingling or the uncontrollable shaking in his hands, he couldn't stop thinking about the mousy-brown-haired woman who was the star of his dreams.

He remembered what Lafonda had said about the girl at her birthday party. There were so many similarities between her and the girl in his dreams. *Could it be the same person?*

Now that the dreams had stopped, Nathan found himself even more consumed with finding out if they were actually real and helping the girl. He sighed as images of the fair-skinned girl replayed through his mind. *At least I have a name,* he thought. *Leah.*

There was a quick knock on his bedroom door, and Nathan jumped and turned around to find Roy smiling in his doorway. "Looks like you're almost done in here," Roy said.

"Yeah," muttered Nathan, sounding a bit surprised. He'd been so distracted by his thoughts about Leah, he hadn't noticed that he had folded the last item to be put away.

"You'll have fun," said Roy, reassuringly, and with a grin. "Don't look so … spaced out."

Nathan paused, giving himself a moment to return back to reality and then he nodded. Roy cleared his throat. "Um, Lafonda has already started packing her car," he said. "I assume you guys will actually ride together this year?"

"Uh, yeah," stuttered Nathan, pausing to grab a suitcase. "No problem."

"Good," said Roy. "Because LaDonda has already left

for campus, and I don't want to have to drive you over there."

"Okay, Grandpa," said Nathan, while shaking his head.

Outside the cottage, Nathan saw Lafonda struggling to load what looked like several overloaded suitcases into the trunk of her new Ferrari. Casually, he approached her from behind. "So," he said in a playful tone, "need any help?"

She put down what looked like a humungous suitcase in comparison to her size and faced Nathan. Her long black hair, still slightly curled from the party, danced softly across her windswept face. The small gold locket around her neck occasionally caught the sun's rays and reflected brilliantly in the light.

"Good afternoon to you too, Mr. Urye," she responded with a confident grin. She paused, tucking a lock of hair behind her ear. "It's so nice of you to volunteer to place all my bags in the trunk for me. You're such a gentleman."

"Sure, sure," he mocked her, with a huge grin. "So, what time do we have to be there?" he asked. "Shouldn't we have been there hours ago to help with check-in?"

She leaned against the car and grinned. "Not this year. My grandmother said this year she had enough counselors volunteer to work check-in, so we're off the hook."

"Oh, really?" mumbled Nathan, while loading the trunk. "Well, that's no fun."

Lafonda had a surprised look on her face. "Really?" she responded, folding her arms. "I thought you would enjoy not having to wake up early in the morning to work check-in, especially being that it's summer."

"True, true," he said, pausing to catch his breath in between loading Lafonda's bags. "But I was looking forward to seeing all the excited faces turn sour after the first night."

She shook her head. "Nathan," she said in a weary voice, "you never cease to amaze me."

"Yeah. And ditto here," he responded. He stood up straight and leaned back to stretch his back. "So, how much crap are you taking to camp anyway?"

Lafonda glowered at him, and he protested by shaking his head.

"Leadership camp is only for four weeks, Lafonda," he continued. "And it's not like you're going to Rome, the Devaro Mansion is only 22 minutes away."

"I hope that explains why you only packed two suitcases," she retorted in a disapproving tone.

"Hey, you kids ready to hit the road?" asked Roy, arriving from the main house. He grinned. "LaDonda's already called twice to see if you two have left the house. I told her you two were happily riding over together."

Nathan turned to examine the almost full trunk and scowled. "I guess we'll be leaving as soon as I finish stuffing the trunk with the rest of Lafonda's entire wardrobe," he said.

She rolled her eyes and pursed her lips into a sarcastic smile.

Roy cleared his throat and grinned. He gave Nathan a hand with the last of the suitcases while Lafonda climbed inside of the car.

"Thanks, Grandpa!" smiled Nathan. "You've still got some life in those arms of yours."

Roy slightly chuckled and then huffed through his nose. "Go get in the car," he responded halfheartedly, "before I show you just how much life I have left in these arms."

Nathan smiled at his grandfather and then proceeded

to open the door to Lafonda's Ferrari. He paused and then a puzzling smirk appeared on his face. "Uh, Lafonda?" he asked, sounding bewildered. "Why are the seats and interior of your car a light blue?"

Immediately, she sat up straight while quickly examining the vehicle. "What?" she responded innocently.

With wide eyes, Nathan gawked at her and took a few steps back from the open car door to look at the vehicle. "You are aware that your car is red and the trim is a light blue," he said. He paused again and then slowly shook his head. "And you don't see a problem here?"

"No," responded Lafonda slowly. "Blue is my favorite color."

He stood there looking at her with wide eyes. "And it never occurred to you to maybe just ask for a blue car?" He suddenly released a quick snicker. "I don't know why I didn't notice it before," he continued with a perplexed look on his face. "Surely, I would have said something earlier."

"Just get in the car, Nathan!" she spouted, sounding annoyed. She had a smug look on her face. "And it's not light blue. It's carta da zucchero."

"And what is that?" he grinned, "Italian for light blue?"

"Can we go now?" demanded Lafonda, clearly irritated.

He slid into the passenger seat. "Okay!" he said in a high-pitched voice. Nathan inspected the blue trim in her car again and mumbled. "Good luck when it's time for resale."

Roy approached the driver's side of the car and sighed while slowly shaking his head. "Can you two please play nice while driving into town?" he asked.

Lafonda looked up at Roy and smiled reassuringly. "Don't worry, Roy," she grinned, "we'll be fine."

Roy took a deep breath and then released it quickly. "Okay," he said. "Now please, don't go over the speed limit, and let me know when you get into town." He glanced over to the passenger seat at Nathan, and his chest heaved again. "And Nathan," he said, "do you have your cell phone?"

"Yes," said Nathan, sounding annoyed as he patted his pockets.

Roy looked away and then back at Nathan again. "Good," he said. "Then use it."

Nathan smiled.

During the summer, the back road into town from the Devaro Mansion was always lush with greenery. There were so many trees alongside the road that they often blocked out the sun. Occasionally, there would be pockets of sunlight, and you could spot deer grazing amidst the trees or along the road. But on cloudy days and just before nightfall, the dense cluster of trees made the road seem mysterious. It was still inviting, yet quite menacing.

"What time is it?" asked Nathan, while looking at the clock on the leather dashboard to Lafonda's Ferrari. "It's suddenly so dark."

"Yeah, it is darker," Lafonda agreed, removing her sunglasses. She chuckled. "I noticed things were a little darker through my sunglasses, but then again, they always are."

He glanced over at her and laughed too. Nathan squinted as a prism of gold light reflected from her locket. "I see that you're wearing the locket your grandfather gave to you."

She quickly glanced down before returning her focus

back on the road. "Yeah," she smiled, placing a hand on the locket.

Nathan settled back into his seat and turned to look at the locket again. He smiled. "You look good," he said. Abruptly, his eyes fluttered and he began to stumble. He could feel his cheeks turning red. "I mean … it looks good on you."

She turned to face him and smiled. A few moments passed, and Nathan abruptly cleared his throat. "So," he said, while awkwardly clasping his hands, "how does Jim Darding feel about you not wearing his necklace?"

She turned to look at him again, and her happy face quickly turned sour. "Um, Nathan, is that really any of your business?"

"Okay then, don't tell me," protested Nathan. "It's just that I noticed yesterday you were gone most of the day." He cracked a smile and then snickered. "And it didn't help my curiosity any that every time someone called looking for you, LaDonda kept saying you were at Jim's place."

There was a brief silence, and then slowly Lafonda opened her mouth. "Jim and I," she said abruptly, "decided to take a break. At least for the summer, anyway."

Nathan thought he saw what looked like a half smile creep onto her face.

"I hope this didn't have anything to do with me or the fruit punch," he said.

"No, Nathan," she said, sounding annoyed again.

He smiled. "All right," he said with a grin, "I won't ask again."

They sat in silence for a while, and as the car continued down the road, Nathan thought about the events of that night. In his mind, he recalled his shaky hands and the stained white dress. He also remembered overhearing the conversation Lafonda was having with her friend Amanda and how suddenly he'd wanted to dance with her. *Now, that was definitely weird,* he thought. *But I wonder what Leah looks like. I bet if I saw a picture of her, I would know for sure if she was the same person.*

"So," he said, taking a long pause before continuing, "any news about your friend?"

"What friend?" she asked suspiciously. "Are you talking about Amanda?" Her face distorted into a slight frown as she tried to glare at him while keeping her eyes on the road. "She has a boyfriend, you know."

"No," he sighed. "Your friend Leah." He took a deep breath. "I overheard you and Amanda talking about her. Is she okay? Is she still in the hospital?"

Lafonda sat in silence for a while before slowly answering. "The last time I heard anything about her was two days ago," she said. "She's still in the hospital as far as I know. It's been a few days since I've spoken to her mother." She paused. "I haven't spoken to Leah since the day she was committed to St. Lucas Memorial Hospital in St. Louis."

"Okay," muttered Nathan, sounding slightly sad.

"Why?" she asked. "I mean, why are you asking?" Lafonda's face softened. "Did you know Leah?"

Quickly, Nathan sat up straight again. "I don't know," he said. "She does sound familiar. Do you have a picture of her?"

Lafonda paused, and her eyes fluttered for a second before she said, "No, not with me. But I'm sure there's a freshman class photo of her in the school's yearbook." She smiled. "We all took pictures right before the end of the semester. We should be able to find a yearbook once we get to campus."

She stopped mid-sentence and squinted as they drove around a corner. Nathan looked on, but looked slightly confused. "What's wrong?" he asked.

Lafonda blinked her eyes a few times and then quickly shook her head. "Uh, nothing," she said. "It's just so dark all of a sudden." She exhaled. "And I swear a dog or something darted across the road."

"Well, then turn your lights on, Lafonda!" Nathan said. "You're going to hit something if you can't see."

"Yeah, but it's not even five o'clock yet," explained Lafonda. "I don't want to look silly driving with my lights on when the sun is still out!"

"Ugh, just turn your lights on, Lafonda," he said in a weary voice. "It won't matter what people think if we hit something or have a car accident.

Suddenly, Lafonda gasped and the red Ferrari swerved.

"What — what happened?" asked Nathan, sounding panicked.

"Did you see that?" she shouted. "Something just darted across the road!"

"What?" he asked. "Another dog?"

She looked into her rearview mirror. "I don't know," she said. "It was dark. I couldn't make out the shape from the shadows."

Nathan followed suit by scanning the road behind them and then the trees. "It probably was a deer or a fox crossing the road," he said. "Now you know why I asked you to turn on your lights."

"Oh, my God!" complained Lafonda, cringing slightly and then squinting.

"What now?" he groaned, while quickly scanning the road and the trees again. "I don't see anything."

"Not on the road!" cried Lafonda, still squinting. "The car behind us is driving way too close and they have their high beams on."

He spun around to see what she was talking about, only to be repelled by the car's bright headlights. "Who is that?" he spouted.

"I don't know," she muttered through clenched teeth, "but it's quite annoying." She paused and then abruptly turned to look at Nathan. "Wait, did he just speed up?"

The roar of the engine from the vehicle following close behind them could be heard as it accelerated, and its lights grew closer and closer. Both Nathan and Lafonda turned to look at each other as the vehicle weaved dangerously close to Lafonda's car.

"Um, Lafonda," said Nathan, with a hint of fear in his voice, "I think he wants you to move."

"Um, Nathan," she responded angrily, "you think?"

Lafonda continued to drive along the road with both hands clenched tightly around the steering wheel. She suddenly became focused and only moved when her eyes occasionally made contact with the rearview mirror.

Nathan noticed that her hands appeared to clench tighter and tighter as the new red car gradually accelerated. "Uh, Lafonda," he said, while keeping a watchful eye on the still approaching vehicle, "you're not pulling over."

Her dark brown eyes made contact with the rearview mirror again and her lips pursed with concentration as she accelerated.

Nathan's eyes grew wide as he watched the dial gradually move up on the speedometer. "Look, don't piss them off!" he shouted. "Just move or pull over!"

"I know, I know!" she yelled.

Nathan's face suddenly looked beleaguered. "If you know," he snapped, "then why the heck are you accelerating!"

"Look, Nathan," she explained with a confident grin, "I'm driving a Ferrari, and if this guy thinks he can keep up with me, well, let's find out!"

Nathan sighed heavily and shook his head. "Whatever," he said. "I guess this is the part of the movie where I buckle my seat belt and say a prayer before we have a car accident!"

"You are so dramatic, Nathan!" she shouted.

"Dramatic!" he cried, while gawking at the speedometer. "Look who's talking!" Nathan noticed the trees alongside the road were now whizzing by in a blur. "One hundred miles per hour!" he yelled. "Lafonda, this guy is not going to give up!"

The headlights from the tailgating car continued to dance side to side as it attempted once to pass Lafonda's vehicle.

"I don't think so!" Lafonda groaned, shifting gears and slamming down the accelerator.

In response, the engine of the unknown car behind them roared and proceeded to drive on the approaching-traffic side of the roadway. Nathan could now make out the metallic silver car as it drove beside them, matching Lafonda's speed. "Lafonda!" he yelled. "Let the guy pass us already, before another car comes!"

"Okay, okay," she spouted. "But can you see who it is?"

"What? No!" he yelled, only pausing briefly to look at the silver vehicle. "The windows are tinted, and besides, what difference will it make if we're dead!"

"Ugh!" she huffed, and the red Ferrari began to decelerate. "What a freaking jerk!"

Nathan sighed, and his chest heaved in relief. "Yeah, he's a jerk," he said with a nod. "And you're freaking crazy!"

Suddenly, Nathan's mouth fell open as they both realized what was approaching from the top of the hill in front of them. "Lafonda!" he screamed. "A truck is coming!"

"I know, I know! I see it," she stuttered, a hint of desperation settling in her voice. "But he's not passing me! He keeps matching my speed!"

The approaching truck drew closer as the silver car next to them continued to match Lafonda's speed. They could hear the horn of the approaching truck.

"Are you crazy!" Lafonda yelled, while gawking at the person behind the tinted windows.

"He's not going to stop!" Nathan cried, his palms sweating and his heart racing now. "Just brake, Lafonda! Brake!"

"I am braking!" she yelled.

"Then just pull over, Lafonda!" he moaned. "Just pull over before you get us killed!"

"I'm trying to," she stuttered, "but there's nowhere to pull over to!"

Nathan frantically looked to the right side of the road, but she was right, there was no room for the red Ferrari. The entire right side of the road was lined by a deep ditch. The blaring horn from the approaching truck grew louder, and so did the sound of Nathan's pounding heart against his chest.

"Why don't you just come to a complete stop?" he yelled. But before he could continue, he noticed something moving fast among the trees. It looked as if something shadowy was moving alongside them. He squinted, and as the shadowy shape continued to move quickly through the forest, he was sure it was some sort of animal. It wasn't until the creature appeared out of the forest, with what looked like supernatural speed, that he was able to see what seemed to be a black and lean disheveled-looking dog. The creature's bright blue eyes immediately connected with Nathan's as it paced the small side road coming up ahead of them.

"Wait!" he yelled.

"What!" responded Lafonda in sheer panic, her hands still gripped tight around the steering wheel.

"Don't stop, pull over there!" Nathan said. "There's a side road up ahead."

Lafonda looked frantically over the dashboard. "Where?"

Nathan's eyes connected with the creature's piercing blue eyes again. "Over there!" he shouted, pointing towards the side road.

The adjacent road was close now, and Lafonda had only seconds to react. She immediately slammed on the brakes to make the turn as the tires of her red Ferrari screeched to a stop. The silver car that had tormented them quickly switched lanes right before the big, long semitruck passed them by in a whirl.

"Let's not ever, ever, ever do that again!" cried Nathan, taking in a deep breath, which made his chest expand.

Lafonda sat motionless as the car idled on the single-lane dirt road. "I hope you're not planning on mentioning this to Roy or my grandmother," she said.

"Oh, and ruin your reputation as Ms. Perfect Attendance and Ms. Honor Roll?" mocked Nathan in a high-pitched voice.

"You wouldn't!" she gasped.

He smiled at her and gloated. He was happy that he finally had something on her. Lafonda stared at him and glowered. "Whatever!" she responded, rolling her eyes in protest. "Where did that dog go, anyway?"

Nathan scanned the road. "I don't know. You probably killed it, and it's lodged underneath the car, somewhere."

"Don't be ridiculous, Nathan," demanded Lafonda. "You can be so immature sometimes."

She shook her head and began to back the car out onto the main road. Nathan continued to scan the road. "Well, so far it looks like you're clear," he chuckled, "Unless it's still stuck underneath your car."

Lafonda sat in silence and occasionally scowled at him on their way to campus. Nathan thought it was weird how his mind kept tossing over thoughts about the blue-eyed dog and not about his recent game of Russian roulette with Lafonda. He was definitely more focused on what he had seen amongst the trees: a black dog that appeared out of nowhere and seemed to move as fast as a cheetah.

Things just keep getting weirder and weirder, he thought. *This sounds strange, but it was like the dog magically appeared.* His mind continued to ponder as he focused his attention outside the car. *He appeared right on time. And stopped right on the road that we needed to see.*

Nathan turned to look at Lafonda and took her silence to mean that she was still upset about his new trump card over her oh-so-perfect existence. He tried to stifle his chuckle, but Lafonda noticed, anyway. "I'd really like to know who that jerk was," she said. "I would love to give them a piece of my mind." She smacked the steering wheel. "Ugh! Why didn't I think of getting their license plate number?

Probably because you were too busy trying to kill us! Nathan thought, as Lafonda rambled on.

As they pulled into the street that led to IUCF, Nathan could see the buildings and monuments that were easy markers for the campus. Although he had only been away from school for less than two months, he was still surprised that nothing had changed. The only thing that was odd or different was the absence of students, and that was due to summer.

As the red Ferrari pulled into the parking lot of Lawrence Hall, the dorm in which they would be staying, Nathan instantly recognized the sleek silver car with tinted windows sitting in the parking lot. "Well, it looks like we've found our jerk," he said, pointing to the tall, slender guy who had just appeared by the trunk of the silver car.

Lafonda gripped the steering wheel tightly as she screeched into the adjacent open parking spot. Surprisingly, the guy didn't even flinch or respond to the loud sound. "That's what that car is!" said Nathan aloud. "He's driving a Chevy Camaro."

"I don't care what he is driving," moaned Lafonda, quickly springing out of the car. "Excuse me," she demanded, walking right up to the guy. "Do you realize that you almost killed us back there?" The guy didn't respond, so Lafonda became more infuriated. "Hey!" she demanded, her hands on her hips now. "I'm talking to you!"

Nathan had seen that stance from Lafonda before and knew all too well that the guy didn't know what he was in for. Slowly, the dark-haired guy placed one of his suitcases on the ground and glanced once at her from above the rim of his dark sunglasses. His solemn and chiseled face gave way to a smirk before it became a full-blown smile. He casually closed the trunk to his car and adjusted his black leather jacket. "Sweetheart," he said, removing his sunglasses, "if you're going to insist on getting behind such a powerful machine, maybe your boyfriend here should teach you how to drive it first."

"What?" she exclaimed, completely taken aback by his comment.

"Don't get your pretty face in a knot," he continued. "I know cars can be confusing for the ladies, but I think I can find some time out of my busy schedule this summer to teach you." He grinned. "I mean, all you have to do is ask, and I'll see what I can do."

"What?" she cried again.

"Here, I tell you what," he continued, pulling back his leather jacket and revealing the orange leadership camp shirt Nathan detested. "I'll be working here this summer as a camp counselor, and you can ask for me at the front desk. The name is Malick."

"Ugh!" she groaned. "Look, I won't be asking for you!"

"But your shirt says Stephen Malick," interrupted Nathan.

"Just Malick," the tall, slender guy responded sharply. He paused and whispered to Nathan, "By the way, you have my condolences."

"What — why?" asked Nathan, obviously confused.

Malick gave one last look at Lafonda. "I'm sure you've got your hands full with this one," he said to Nathan, walking away.

"Ugh!" she screamed.

"What?" asked Nathan, startled.

"He's a counselor at camp with us?" she yelled. Nathan stepped back as Lafonda's hands curled into fists at her sides. He thought her eyes were going to bulge out of their eye sockets. "Ugh! I need to speak with my grandmother!"

CHAPTER SIX

LEADERSHIP CAMP

Nathan awoke to the sunlight that pierced through the tiny crack in the curtains to his dorm room window. Each night before going to bed, he did his best to come up with a new way to try to keep the sunlight from waking him up in the morning. He tossed and turned several times in bed trying to block out the sun and fall back to sleep before his alarm went off. After several attempts, he gave up and just stared at the ceiling of the all-white room. He was still reluctant, however, to turn off his alarm clock and dreaded every second and every minute that went by because he knew he would soon have to get out of bed.

I don't know how Lafonda lived in this dorm all last year, he thought. *Staying here is definitely starting to feel like punishment.*

It was the end of the first week at camp, and Nathan already desired his cozy bed at home. He glared at the white walls and ceiling. "And I thought where I stayed last year was bad. Compared to this place, Douglas Hall is way better." He let out a stifled yawn as he sat up in bed. "I'm actually impressed that Lafonda would even stay here."

Things were pretty quiet as far as his nightmares were

concerned, and he hadn't had any problems with his hands either. In fact, he hadn't had a bad dream or a problem with his hands since he left home for camp, but that didn't stop him from frequently thinking about Leah. Besides the strangeness of it all, he often wondered if she was okay or if she felt alone in all this.

More and more he found himself wanting to reach out to her, to comfort her, or at least to let her know she wasn't alone, that he too had strange things happening to him. Most importantly, he wanted to tell her that he had dreamed about her and possibly witnessed everything that happened to her that night. He wanted her to know that she wasn't crazy.

"I can't let her stay in that hospital. There is nothing wrong with her." He shook his head. "I know I'm not crazy," he murmured. "It's just too much of a coincidence between my dream and what happened to her. Now, before I go running off to go rescue her and to avoid looking like an idiot, I need to confirm what Leah looks like. I need to see a photo of her." He paused. "Lafonda did say there was a photo of her in the freshman yearbook."

Nathan's thoughts were interrupted by the sound of a bouncing ball outside of his dorm room. The sound stopped and was followed by a quick knocking session on the door.

"Jonas …" he said underneath his breath. "Why is he up already and still bouncing that stupid basketball?" He released a long drawn-out sigh. "If I have to tell him one more time to stop bouncing that ball inside, I'm going to take it away from him."

Nathan hopped out of bed and opened the door to a tall, shaggy-haired teenager.

The boy's slender frame towered over Nathan as he

anxiously looked down at his camp counselor. "Is it time to eat yet?" asked Jonas. He continued to dribble his basketball. "I'm starving."

"Jonas," said Nathan, trying not to sound annoyed, "why are you up?"

"What do you mean?" he replied, his inquisitive eyes peeking beneath his curly dark hair. "We have to get up for breakfast."

"Yeah, but it's only 6:30," explained Nathan. "They don't even start serving breakfast till 7:30."

"Oh," responded Jonas nonchalantly. He paused for a moment but quickly began to dribble the basketball more fervently.

"Would you cut that out?" Nathan demanded. "You're going to wake everyone else up."

They both paused and turned their heads to the sound of doors opening and closing. Two other campers, Andy Jolie and Hugo Mattingly, wandered sleepily towards them.

"Is it time to head downstairs?" asked Andy.

"Nope," responded Jonas, while pretending to make basketball shots in the air. "Not quite time yet."

"Oh, okay," nodded Hugo, his big arms barely squeezing past Nathan and into his room.

"What are you doing?" asked Nathan, clearly annoyed. "Get out of my room and off my bed."

Another door in the hallway opened as Jonas continued to bounce his basketball.

"If you keep that up, I'm going to take that ball away from you," warned Nathan.

"Oh, okay," answered Jonas, instantly stopping and beelining straight into Nathan's room.

"Uh, where are you two going?" protested Nathan, as Andy followed suit.

"Is it time for breakfast?" asked a new weary-eyed addition to the conversation.

"No!" sighed Nathan, stepping away from his door. "Go back to bed!"

"Back to bed?" the newcomer responded. "But it's almost seven!"

Nathan sighed again and turned around to face the three overgrown teenagers now engrossed in a conversation about IUCF basketball in his dorm room. "Don't mind me," he grumbled, while grabbing a towel from the closet, "I guess I'll get me a shower."

"Okay," nodded Jonas, pausing briefly to acknowledge him. "We'll wait for you. We can all go down to breakfast together."

"Great!" responded Nathan sarcastically. He huffed. "And this is only week one."

Later, after his shower, Nathan spotted Lafonda downstairs, sitting at one of the elongated tables alongside the large cafeteria windows. She was seated with some of the other counselors she had become acquainted with since arriving at camp. Oddly enough, besides Jonathan Black, they were all students at IUCF. Also odd was the fact that Jonathan wasn't at the table this morning.

Jonas and the other campers assigned to Nathan's floor had already gotten in line for breakfast and now were dispersing amongst the tables of other campers staying on other floors.

"Nathan!" groaned Lafonda, as he approached the table.

He wasn't the slightest bit surprised by her expression. It was quite obvious to him what was next, as he stared at the sea of orange shirts at the table.

"Where is your camp shirt?" she asked, trying to stifle

the demanding tone in her voice. "You know that my grandmother will be upset with you if you're not wearing your shirt again."

"I know, I know," he answered, rolling his eyes. "I plan to put it on after breakfast."

She glowered at him. "Whatever, Nathan," she said. "Seems like a waste of time to me to have to go upstairs after breakfast to change shirts.

Nathan shook his head and moved towards the breakfast line. He loathed wearing the bright orange camp leadership shirt and detested even more that his name was written on it. "Why can't I just wear my IUCF shirt?" he said to himself. "They were already on the Illinois University campus and almost everyone there was from the school or from the area."

He walked back with his tray of food and sat down on the opposite end of the cafeteria table on purpose. He glanced over at Lafonda and was surprised that they hadn't killed each other yet. Nathan returned his gaze to his food and shook his head. He couldn't understand what Lafonda's grandmother was thinking when she assigned them to the same group of campers.

"Good morning, Nathan," said a chipper voice. "How are you this morning?"

He looked up from his plate of pancakes to find a blue-eyed girl with carefully groomed locks of long blond hair staring at him. Everything about her seemed perfect. Not a single wrinkle in her clothing; not a single strand of hair out of place. Nathan was shocked to see how well the bright orange leadership shirt looked on her. With her long, beautiful eyelashes and rosy complexion, he concluded that she probably made just about anything she wore look good.

"Are you enjoying your pancakes?" she asked.

"They're pancakes," he responded, while taking a couple gulps of orange juice.

"I doubt it if he even remembers your name," commented the blond-haired guy with the same color eyes standing next to her.

"I'm Angela," she announced cheerfully. "Angela Greystone."

Nathan took a bite of his pancakes. "No, I remember," he stuttered, while covering his mouth.

"Yeah, right," contributed Lafonda from across the table.

Angela smiled. "We met earlier this week," she continued. "And this here is Alan Donovan."

"Right," Nathan responded with a nod. He paused and stared at the two of them before continuing. He couldn't get over how they looked like the female and male versions of each other. "Are you guys twins, or something?"

"No, we're not related, but we get that all the time," said Alan. "It's because of our innate fashion sense."

Nathan let out a stifled chuckle, barely avoiding spitting out his orange juice. "Your what?" he asked with a grin.

"Our innate fashion sense," repeated Alan. He had a sincere look on his face. "We were just born knowing what looks good together. It's a gift."

Nathan sat in silence while staring at Alan and then suddenly started laughing hysterically. "You're not serious, right?" he asked.

"Never mind Nathan," said Lafonda. "He can't even remember to wear his leadership shirt in the morning, let alone know anything about style or fashion." She paused to glance down the table and glared at him. "Isn't that right, Nathan?"

"Yup," he responded sarcastically, "you've got me all figured out."

Normally, he wouldn't readily agree with her, but he was too distracted by the sudden appearance of Jonathan Black. Since the beginning of camp, Jonathan had appeared more and more tired and wasn't the carefully dressed and punctual person that Nathan assumed he would be after meeting him the night of Lafonda's birthday party at the Devaro Mansion. Nathan was so curious as to why Jonathan was late picking up his group from leadership classes and why he looked so disheveled, that he was willing to wave the white flag to Lafonda.

"Well, there goes my counterpart," remarked Erin Rosales.

Nathan knew Erin because her father was the chief of police for Cahokia Falls, and although they had attended the same high school, they really hadn't spoken to each other until Spanish class the previous semester. He was surprised to learn from Lafonda that Erin had decided to be a counselor at Leadership Camp this year. They'd been friends in high school, and Lafonda had encouraged her to sign up to be a counselor at the end of previous semester.

"Your partner may not like to wear his leadership shirt, Lafonda," Erin smirked, "but at least he doesn't stand you up or have you and your group waiting. Yesterday, I had to escort our group of campers back to the dormitory from classes by myself."

"Good morning, Erin," said Jonathan, taking a seat next to her.

"Nice of you to join us," she responded, pushing back her tray of food and crossing her arms.

"I am so sorry," said Jonathan immediately in response, "I promise to do better next time."

"Next time!" she huffed, while tossing back her shoulder-length brown hair. "You try escorting fourteen teenagers by yourself and see how you like it."

"Uh, actually," interrupted Jonathan, while repositioning his square-rimmed glasses on his nose, "you mean sixteen."

Erin stared at Jonathan blankly with a red face while everyone else at the table waited to see if she would explode. Jonathan paused for a moment and then took a dry gulp. "See, actually, there are ninety-six kids at camp this year," he continued slowly. "A group of eight boys and eight girls for each set of counselors."

"Okay," responded Erin. "And what does that have to do with you being late all the time?"

Nathan listened intently for the answer to that question, and so did everyone else at the table. Jonathan opened his mouth to start saying something, but instead turned to look at Nathan.

Nathan was startled. *What? Why is he looking at me?*

"Nothing," Jonathan answered softly. "I just lost track of time, reading."

"Reading?" said Erin. "You're just tired and late all the time from reading?"

"Well, that might be close to the truth," Nathan chuckled to himself. He really couldn't imagine Jonathan Black up to anything else but reading.

Everyone else at the table looked like they had drawn the same conclusion and had begun to lose interest in the conversation.

"Well, and where exactly are you reading?" asked Erin more forcibly. "The guys on your floor say they can't find you after lockdown in the evening. They say they knock on your door and you never answer."

"They must be mistaken," stuttered Jonathan.

"Ah, give it a rest!" rang a new voice to the conversation.

Everyone at the table turned their heads to find a smirking Stephen Malick walking past them to sit at one of the smaller tables alongside the window.

"He's cute," perked up Angela.

"How can you tell?" asked Lafonda, sounding slightly annoyed. "He always has his sunglasses on."

Angela grinned. "I like the sunglasses. It makes you daydream more about his cute brown eyes. Plus it adds to his bad-boy image."

"Bad-boy image? Cute brown eyes? Please don't add to his psychosis!"

Angela smiled and corrected her posture. "Someone should invite him to sit with us," she continued, her cheerful voice sounding more upbeat and almost melodic.

"For what?" steamed Lafonda. "Leave Mr. Wonderful over there by himself!"

"Why not?" asked Alan, mockingly. "Do I detect a little apprehension, Lafonda? Are you afraid he won't like you?"

"Uh, you don't want to go there," cautioned Nathan. "The first day of camp Mr. Wonderful over there almost drove us off the road."

"What?" interrupted Erin. "That arrogant ass drove you off the road?"

"I still think he's cute," interjected Angela.

Suddenly, everyone was interrupted by the sound of someone clearing their throat. They looked up to find LaDonda Devaro standing there with a big smile on her face.

Instead of the bright orange leadership shirt, LaDonda wore a gold one. "Good morning, everyone," she said.

"Uh, how come she gets a gold shirt?" whispered

Alan. "My tan would look a lot better in gold."

"Shhh!" whispered Angela.

"It's the end of the week," announced LaDonda, "and as planned, if the weather permits, we will be having a bonfire on the beach of Lake Charleston. So, I'm looking for volunteers to help Argus, the tourist and recreation manager for the lake, to set the fires. Any volunteers?"

There was silence at the table, and Erin, Angela and Alan looked away from LaDonda. Quickly, Nathan also looked away. He was hoping not to be called on.

"I've already asked the group of counselors at the other table to volunteer to carry over the coolers, lawn chairs, snacks and marshmallows," LaDonda continued optimistically before pausing again. "Okay, so no volunteers? I guess I'll have to volunteer somebody."

Nathan thought he could feel LaDonda's eyes scanning over him. It was like heat from an infrared laser.

"Nathan," she called out.

"Why me?" he mumbled.

"Nathan, since you have shown such fine leadership at camp already by wearing your leadership shirt and following the rules," said LaDonda, "I am appointing you responsible for setting the bonfires for the rest of camp."

He could feel another infrared laser on him, but this one came from Lafonda. Slowly, he turned around and discovered she had an overzealous smirk across her face.

"What?" exclaimed Nathan. "The rest of camp? You have to be joking!"

"It's only on Fridays, Nathan," said LaDonda with an encouraging smile.

"But that's enough work for three people!" he moaned. "Besides, how is Lafonda supposed to escort sixteen hormonal, hyper teenagers back to the dorms by herself on Friday evenings?"

"While I am more than happy to see Nathan finally have to do some work," interjected Lafonda, "he does have a point."

"The bonfires aren't until later in the evening," explained LaDonda. "So, he should have plenty of time after his counselor duties to set up the area."

Feeling defeated, he slouched back into his chair. "And ... what about help?" he cried.

LaDonda smiled. "As far as additional help ..." she said, searching the room.

Everyone's eyes at the table diverted once more.

"Ah, yes! Stephen!" she called out. "Can you please come over here for a moment?"

Instantly, Angela's eyes lit up, and she gave Stephen careful attention.

"Yes, Mrs. Devaro," he answered promptly while taking a position next to her.

"Oh, I'm running late!" said LaDonda. "I told Argus I would meet him five minutes ago." She appeared slightly flustered. "Okay, Stephen, I need you to help Nathan prepare for tonight's bonfire," she explained before walking away. "And Nathan, Argus will meet you guys around 6:00, which gives you plenty of time to have dinner before you leave to set up the bonfire."

She took a few steps forward before pausing again to say firmly, "And Stephen, take off those sunglasses. I don't believe your grandmother would approve of you wearing them inside."

"Yes, ma'am," he responded, promptly removing his sunglasses. He took a few steps towards Nathan. "So, I guess you're Nathan?"

"Um, yes," Nathan groaned. "We met the other day, remember? You drove us off the road nearly killing us?"

"Oh," Malick responded. He had a blank look on his

face, but it soon faded into a sly grin. "Where is that girlfriend of yours?" His sly grin quickly turned into a full-blown smile after his eyes connected to a fuming Lafonda. "The offer is still on the table to give her one-on-one driving lessons."

"She's not my girl!" Nathan responded quickly. "She's just a friend." He glanced over at Lafonda and could have sworn he saw smoke coming out of her ears. "Can you meet me at the north entrance to Lake Charleston?"

"Sure," said Malick, while smiling at Lafonda. "What time?"

"Well, LaDonda said Argus will be expecting us around 6:00," Nathan said, "so, I guess that means he will be waiting for us at the bonfire pits around Lake Charleston. How about we meet at 5:45, which will give us plenty of time to make it down the trail to the lake?"

"Not a problem," Malick said, while shooting Lafonda one last smile before walking away.

"Ooh, Lafonda, he is so cute!" squealed Angela. "And I think he has a crush on you."

"Give me a break, Angela," responded Lafonda, obviously annoyed. "The guy's a narcissistic jerk and doesn't care about anyone but himself."

"Well, everyone makes mistakes," shrugged Angela. "And I think this narcissistic jerk may deserve a second chance."

"I don't have time for this," grumbled Lafonda, rising from the table. She sighed. "Come on, Nathan, let's go. It's almost time to escort our group to their morning leadership class."

"I don't know, Lafonda," continued Angela, also rising. "I have a special feeling about this one."

"Yeah," commented Alan, following behind her. "I'm sure it's just your hormones."

The rest of the morning seemed to drag for Nathan and possibly for some of the campers by the solemn looks on their faces. The first class they attended talked about persuasive communication and how to inspire people to work together and to share goals. Nathan found that class somewhat interesting and was surprised he didn't have a hard time keeping his eyes open. He found the next class on exploring leadership styles a real snoozer, and by the third class, Lafonda had to keep nudging him to prevent him from falling asleep.

As the day progressed, the summer sun combined with the notorious Illinois humidity had everyone screaming for cold pop or ice-cold water. To make matters worse, the air conditioning unit stopped working during the last class of the day. Nathan was positive that no one was paying attention, and even after several attempts by campers and Nathan himself, the instructor refused to cancel the class. It wasn't until Lafonda pointed out that it was cooler outside and that they could finish the lecture outdoors that the instructor was willing to relocate.

Nathan thought it was definitely cooler under the shade of the trees than in the classroom. He welcomed any breeze at this point, and with evening approaching, the sun was much more bearable. As the instructor went on about the importance of having integrity and what it means to be an integral person, he gladly allowed his mind to wonder elsewhere.

The birds, the trees and the few students walking on campus were an easy distraction. It wasn't until everyone started to stand up that Nathan realized the lecture was over. As the campers started to assemble in line over by Lafonda to be escorted back to Lawrence Hall, a familiar shape caught his eye. He thought that maybe one of the campers had walked away but quickly realized that the familiar shape darting across the quad was Jonathan Black.

Where is he heading off to so quickly? Shouldn't he be helping Erin escort their group back to Lawrence Hall? He kept a watchful eye on Jonathan as his group headed back to the dormitory.

Jonathan darted up the steps and into the Katherine Schmidt building. Nathan assumed Jonathan was most likely going to see Dr. Helmsley, since the Department of Archeological Studies was housed there. Nathan knew this because he'd had a class in the lecture hall of that building during his first semester.

"So, are you ready to spend time with Mr. Wonderful this evening?" asked Lafonda, interrupting his concentration.

"Do you mean Malick?"

"The one and only," she sighed, as they walked back to Lawrence Hall. "I hope he won't be more of a nuisance out there than a help."

Nathan's mind began to wander back to Jonathan as Lafonda continued to complain about Malick. "Did Jonathan say anything about leaving camp early at breakfast this morning?" Nathan asked.

"Nope," Lafonda responded confidently. She paused for a moment and then shrugged. "Well, at least not that I remember. Why are you asking?"

"I was just curious," he said.

Nathan was more than just curious but definitely didn't want to involve Lafonda at this point. She would more than likely make a big deal about it, but he wanted to know what Jonathan was up to first.

At dinner that evening, Nathan felt more than a little restless. He was so deep in thought about everything that had happened over the past two weeks that he might as well have been sitting in the cafeteria alone.

Lafonda, Angela, Alan and Erin were so involved in trashing Jonathan for leaving Erin alone again that they didn't notice how quiet Nathan was. And if it weren't for Alan's request for him to pass the ketchup bottle, he would have thought they didn't realize he was there at all.

Erin continued to complain about how Jonathan, for the third time that week, had said he needed to leave the afternoon class early, and that this time, he claimed he needed to go back to Lawrence Hall to talk to LaDonda.

Nathan was puzzled to hear this. Even if Jonathan made a mistake and meant that he was meeting LaDonda at Schmidt Hall, he knew that he wasn't telling the truth because LaDonda was waiting for Nathan in the lobby after they had returned to Lawrence Hall.

Malick was waiting with her. She wanted to remind them both about meeting with Argus after dinner to prepare for the evening's bonfire. *Unless LaDonda is skilled at being at two places at once, Jonathan was definitely hiding something.*

Nathan noticed Jonathan never showed up for dinner either, which made Erin angrier because she couldn't yell at him. Malick didn't show up for dinner either, not that he ever sat with the group or anyone else, anyway.

Shortly after dinner, Nathan reluctantly headed out to meet up with Malick. The walk over to the north entrance to Lake Charleston wouldn't take long, so he waited until the last possible minute.

The north entrance was actually located on Lawrence Road, which ran directly behind Lawrence Hall. In the beginning of the first semester and towards the end of the second, when the weather was nice, Nathan would often go out to the lake to get away from campus, even though the time probably would have been better spent studying.

As he crossed over Lawrence Road, his thoughts were still occupied with the events of the past two weeks: his nightmares; the possible reality of Leah; his periodic burning, red and itchy hands; the mysterious blue-eyed dog; and now the strange behavior of Jonathan Black. He wondered what other bizarre and crazy things he would encounter this summer. Aliens, maybe?

The north entrance to the lake was really a trail through the forest preserve that surrounded the lake. The trail was about a 15-minute hike to the lake, which also connected to another trail that led to the Cahokia Museum and the Cahokia Caves, located behind the cliffs overlooking Lake Charleston. As he approached the entrance, Nathan was surprised to see Stephen Malick waiting for him. He had just assumed that Malick would be late or wouldn't show up altogether.

"This should be interesting," he mumbled to himself.

Malick continued to lean against the forest preserve sign. "Hey man, about time you showed up!" he said with a grin.

Instantly, Nathan pulled out his cell phone. "It's barely 5:45," he snapped.

"Ha, my watch said 5:45 two minutes ago," Malick boasted.

"Whatever," mumbled Nathan. "Let's just get this over with."

Quickly, Nathan trotted past Malick and entered down the trail first. Nathan had used this trail many times before, so he had no doubt about what direction he was going as the trees began to darken out the evening sun. He found himself picking up his pace as they walked deeper and deeper into the forest. He didn't want to pretend that he liked Malick and hoped that if he walked fast enough, he wouldn't have to put up with any pretense or have some fake conversation with the guy. Irritatingly, because Malick was taller than Nathan, his longer legs actually allowed for him to keep up.

"So," said Malick with excitement in his voice, breaking the silence. "You ready to get that bonfire going and perhaps burn down the forest?"

Nathan froze. He stopped his crusade to somehow turn his fast pace into an unnoticeable sprint out of the forest to glare at Malick. He wanted to give him the most pissed-off look possible. He wanted to paint him a clear picture without saying a single word.

After a moment, he finally responded to a smirking Malick. "Look, let's not pretend that you actually give a crap about anyone, let alone this forest," Nathan scowled. "You might as well drop the act. If given a chance, you probably would love to start a forest fire, destroying the trees and everything in it!"

"Ouch!" said Malick, as Nathan continued on his warpath down to the lake.

"What's got your underwear in a knot?" shouted Malick as he trotted after him. "You and your girlfriend are so uptight!"

Nathan froze again, but this time he stopped to size Malick up. Malick stopped too, but he was more concerned with fixing his hair, as it blew effortlessly in the wind.

You've got to be kidding me, Nathan thought, as he stared at the James Dean replica standing in front of him. *Is this guy just a bad-boy wannabe, or does he just naturally look and act this way?* He shook his head. *The guy might be taller and a little older than me, but I can definitely take him.*

With confidence, he moved closer towards Malick. "Look, I know you are from like Planet Stephen Malick, or something," he spouted, "but here on Earth people usually don't appreciate their lives played with!"

"Oh, that," Malick responded, as if he had been caught off guard. "I thought you were over that; you didn't seem too bothered by it the other day."

"If the *it* you are referring to is you forcing us off the road with your car," Nathan yelled, "then yes, I am definitely, absolutely bothered!"

"It was just a joke!" stammered Malick. "I swear — you and your girlfriend act like you have never played chicken before."

"Great!" scowled Nathan. "I'm glad that you had a good laugh at the expense of others. And for the last time, Lafonda is not my girlfriend!" He shook his head and immediately continued on his blaze down the path.

Frustrated, Malick trailed behind him. "Fine!" he yelled. "If that is what you guys tell people — I mean, it looks like something more is going on there than just friends."

CHAPTER SEVEN

A LITTLE COMPETITION

As the summer sun descended in the sky, the cliffs overlooking Lake Charleston created a foreboding shadow of the night to come. A welcoming cool breeze embraced Nathan, causing tiny ripples in the water and golden shimmers to dance carelessly across the water's face.

Nathan stood there as he normally did upon first sight of the water, but this time it wasn't just the beauty of the lake that captured his attention. It was something that Malick said in the forest that bothered him. There was no doubt in his mind that Malick was a jerk and he shouldn't put much thought into the ramblings that spilled from his mouth. He contemplated what Malick had said about him and Lafonda and just shrugged his shoulders. But what was it that he said that bothered him so much?

Another breeze passed over him, embracing every inch of him, but he was unable to relax and receive it. "But why?" he asked himself. He paused and then examined the palms of his hands. They were tense but normal. But why were they so normal when he was so tense? And why was he so upset?

He drew a big breath, sighed, and thought that Malick was right. He wasn't that upset about the car thing.

Granted, he wasn't particularly thrilled that he'd been forced to depend on Lafonda's driving skills for his life, but he wasn't angry about it.

He paused for a moment, and then suddenly, he realized why he was so irritated. With everything going on that summer; with his hands, the strange occurrences, and Leah, he felt like everything was coming at him all at once, and now that he was a counselor at leadership camp, he had no time to deal with anything.

Nathan sighed again and relaxed his shoulders. The last thing he wanted to do now was build bonfires with Stephen Malick. He glanced down at his hands, but disappointment washed over him. The last time he remembered being this frustrated, his hands had shaken so uncontrollably that he'd spilled fruit punch all over Lafonda's dress at her birthday party.

He had hoped that he had figured out the whole hand thing: that his hand problem was synonymous with him getting upset or stressed. But they were not even red; no tingling, no shaking, nothing.

"What are you waiting for?" interrupted Malick with a slight grin.

"Nothing," he responded grudgingly. Nathan looked up at Malick and dreaded having to work with him. He secretly wished that his hands would shake uncontrollably around Malick's neck.

Malick froze for a second and glared intently at him as if he knew what he was thinking. But suddenly he looked away. "Is that the guy?" he asked, pointing to a tall, slender man approaching them.

Nathan rolled his eyes. He found it hard to even think about anything else other than his current frustration with not being able to solve his hand problem or the mystery behind his dreams. "Oh, and let's not forget the mysterious dog," he mumbled aloud.

"What?" asked Malick, appearing puzzled. "What dog?"

"Nothing," Nathan responded quickly, while shaking his head to focus. "That must be him. Who else would be out here stocking the bonfire pits?"

Malick chuckled as he walked past Nathan and headed towards the silver-haired man.

Nathan kicked a few of the small round pebbles that filled the shoreline before following Malick.

As they approached the middle-aged man, he looked up at them, and his eyes squinted as if they were focusing to see something. Once his eyes connected with Nathan's, he smiled. "You must be Nathan," he said with a grin, while reaching out to take Nathan's hand.

The man's striking blue eyes were warm and youthful, and his weathered tan skin suggested he'd frequently worked outside in the sun. He was a silver-haired man with a long ponytail, and his hands were slightly bigger than normal and strong looking. Nathan also caught a glimpse of what looked like a red-colored tattoo on the man's right forearm.

"Yes, yes," the man continued, while shaking his head at Nathan. "Let me show you and your buddy here what to do."

"Buddy?" Nathan chuckled to himself. He wouldn't consider Malick a friend, let alone a buddy. He glanced over to find a grin on Malick's face. He too found the comment a far stretch.

"So, I guess you're Argus?" Nathan asked.

"Ha-ha," laughed Argus, "the one and only!" He gestured with his head. "Come now; follow me while we still have sunlight." He continued to laugh to himself. "I'm sure LaDonda is keeping you boys hopping."

Both Nathan and Malick glanced at each other. Nathan found Argus both fun and a little strange, but decided to just keep quiet.

"He probably doesn't get a lot of visitors," whispered Malick with a grin. Nathan tried not to laugh at his comment.

"Okay, boys," said Argus while keeping a watchful eye on Malick. They stood by a large old wood bin. "I did you guys a favor by stocking the bonfire pits already, but the ones at the end there may need a little more wood." He placed his hands on his hips and suddenly had a grin on his face. "Unfortunately for you, I completely emptied out the wood bin doing so."

"So, you need us to stock all the wood bins for you?" interjected Malick.

"Close, but not exactly," said Argus. "There are smaller ones around the beach, but I need one of you to stock this one while the other sets the fires. It would be best to do all this while the sun is still out. If you do this separately, you should be finished before it gets dark."

"Well, I volunteer to set the fires," said Malick quickly.

"What?" complained Nathan. "Why do you get to do the easy job?"

"What?" responded Malick with a sly grin. "Your job is not hard."

Argus left briefly and returned with a wheelbarrow. In the barrow lay a small white bottle. "And look, there's even a wheelbarrow!"

Nathan reluctantly took the wheelbarrow from Argus. *Why do I get the feeling Argus only stocked the pits so that he didn't have to do the work of stocking the wood bin himself?*

"Okay," said Argus. "Now, the wood is stored in the large bin next to the Hiking and Camping Center, over the top of that hill." He pointed the way. "And I'll be there finishing up some invoices if you have any questions or problems." He reached down to pick up the small white bottle. "Oh, and you will need this."

"What's this for?" asked Malick, staring curiously at the bottle.

"Exactly what it says on the bottle," responded Argus. "Lighter fluid." He glared and appeared to be scrutinizing Malick. "How else do you expect to set the fires?"

Malick paused with the small bottle in hand and looked out at the fire pits. "You've got to be kidding me!" he exclaimed. "There's got to be at least fifteen pits out there."

"Well, you're really only set up for twelve," retorted Argus.

"This little bottle for twelve fires?" mocked Malick.

Argus shook his head while raising one eyebrow. "Oh, and you will need these," he continued, reaching into his pocket and handing over a single book of matches.

Malick stood there with a look of disbelief across his face as he stared at the small bottle of lighter fluid and the book of matches in his hands.

"What?" chuckled Argus as he headed to the path that led up the hill to the Hiking and Camping Center. "You didn't expect me to leave a blowtorch with some teenagers."

"Teenager?" yelled a frustrated Malick, so that Argus could hear him. "I'm twenty-one!"

"I thought he was older," Nathan said to himself. He turned to gawk at the wheelbarrow. "Look, Earth to Planet Malick," he said in a demanding tone. "Wheelbarrow or no wheelbarrow, you're crazy if you think I'm going to stock this wood bin from way up there all by myself."

Nathan waited impatiently as Malick continued to stare

at the book of matches and bottle of lighter fluid in his hands. Malick had a weird, frustrated look on his face.

"What's the problem?" Malick finally responded, as if springing back to life. His eyes now had a gleam to them that made Nathan nervous. "A strong guy like you should have no problem bringing the wood from up there."

"Yeah, probably so," responded Nathan cautiously. "But the question is, do I want to?"

"Well, before you put on your grumpy pants," continued Malick with a grin, "I'll make you a deal."

Nathan cocked his head and stared at Malick suspiciously. "Okay, go on; let's hear it. What's cooking in that head of yours?"

"Now, that's not fair," said Malick in a halfhearted way as if offended. "You haven't even heard what I have to say."

"Believe me, I wish I didn't have to."

"Anyway," continued Malick with a grin. He was holding up the items in his hands now for Nathan to see. "How long do you think it will take me to start all twelve fires?"

"Well," said Nathan, taking a pause, "I would say at least fifteen minutes."

"Fifteen minutes!" blurted Malick, almost dropping the items in his hands. "It will take that long just to soak the wood with lighter fluid!"

"Okay, okay," responded Nathan with a shrug. "Twenty minutes."

"You got to be kidding me, right?" asked Malick, while waving the small white bottle in his hand. "I probably will use this entire bottle on the first pit alone, and then I'll have to try and ignite the other pits from it — without lighter fluid!"

"What's your point already?" groaned Nathan.

Malick paused shortly before speaking, and his eyes had that same flicker in them as before.

Nathan's stomach began to twist in knots as Malick opened his mouth to speak.

"Would you agree that the Hiking and Camping Center with wheelbarrow in tow is about a five-minute walk from here?" Malick asked with a grin.

Nathan glanced up the hill and then nodded. "I would say less than that," he responded confidently.

"Good," Malick responded equally confidently. "I'll make you a deal. If I fail to have all twelve of these bonfires burning bright before you return with your first load of wood, I'll help you stock the wood bin."

Nathan glanced up the hill again. He had been up there plenty of times before over the years and he was pretty sure that he was familiar with the area. *It should take me about five minutes total to run up there, fill the wheelbarrow, and race back*, he thought. *And even if it takes a little longer, there is no way he will have all twelve fires set by then.*

Nathan extended his hand. "You're on!"

"Nothing like a little competition," responded Malick, shaking Nathan's hand.

They grinned at each other before quickly parting ways. Nathan grabbed the wheelbarrow and pushed it as fast as he could up the path leading to the Hiking and Camping Center. Sweat beaded on his brow as he reached the top of the hill. Lungs laboring, he figured it must have taken only about two minutes.

From the top of the hill he could easily see the Hiking and Camping Center only a few yards away. And behind him, he couldn't see the fire pits down below, but a trickle of smoke began to appear in the blue sky. *Wow, that was quick*, he thought. Malick must have gotten the first fire started.

Nathan approached the Hiking and Camping Center and the large storage bin was right where Argus said it was, which was exactly where Nathan remembered it to be. With a full wheelbarrow in front of him, he quickly descended back down the path. It wasn't quite evening yet, so the sun's rays continued to beat across his sweat-drenched brow. Nathan's heart pounded against his chest as he ran. He was sure that he'd gotten a splinter or two in his hands from grabbing the wood so fast. Coming up the hill and filling up the wheelbarrow took a little longer than he had expected, but he guessed he was only approaching five minutes. He wasn't exactly sure, but he didn't want to risk losing time by stopping to pull out his cell phone to check.

"Why am I so worried?" he mumbled through laboring breaths. "There is no way Malick can light twelve fires in under fifteen minutes, let alone ten."

Halfway down the trail, a gust of cool air with the scent of burning wood passed over him, providing a welcome relief. As he hurried down the path, something about the sky caught his eye. To Nathan's surprise, the evening's blue sky wasn't so blue anymore. Darkening the sky was what looked like one mass of black smoke. As he got closer, twelve continuous pillars of smoke began to emerge out of the once huge mass.

He can't be done. Nathan pushed himself down the hill harder and faster now. He couldn't believe his eyes and had to see for himself. "He can't be," he murmured.

As he got closer, he could definitely tell the smoke was rising from the shoreline, right about where the fire pits would be. When he reached the bottom of the hill, he abandoned his wheelbarrow in astonishment. All twelve fire pits had been set ablaze with a continuously burning fire in each pit. Only the first pit had begun to cinder as its flame flickered in and out.

"Looks like that first one might need some lighter fluid," joked Malick as he approached him from the side.

"Um," stammered Nathan, his words escaping him. "How did you —? And you still have lighter fluid?"

"Yup," Malick boasted, "and with plenty to spare." He had a smug look on his face and shook what sounded like a half-empty bottle. "And how did you make out?"

"What do you mean?" asked Nathan, with an obvious look of frustration. "I don't know how you did it, but I obviously lost."

Malick smiled wide and his eyes continued to gleam.

"So?" asked Nathan, as he wiped the sweat from his brow and on to his dirty shirt. He couldn't help but notice how relaxed and clean Malick was; not one speck of dirt or one drop of sweat.

"So ... what?" Malick asked.

"So, how did you do it?" demanded Nathan. "How did you finish so fast? I mean, it should have taken you at least fifteen to twenty minutes."

"Nah, it didn't take that long," he smiled. "Five minutes tops."

"Whatever," responded Nathan. "You must have gotten help, or something."

"Are you implying that I would cheat?" Malick replied sarcastically.

"Give me a break and drop the act. You aren't necessarily playing for the good guys."

"Well, I guess I should leave you to your work then."

"I don't understand why you're upset," said Nathan, while reluctantly walking back to the wheelbarrow. "I mean, I'm the one who lost." He raised his eyebrows and impatiently waited for a response from a quiet Stephen Malick.

"Okay ... well ... um," stuttered Malick, "I guess since you will be here for a while filling the wood bin, you wouldn't mind keeping an eye on the bonfire until everyone else arrives."

"Sure, of course," responded Nathan sarcastically. "Anything else?"

"Nope," said Malick with a shrug, "I figured there is no reason for me to wait out here with nothing to do."

"Really?" snapped Nathan. "Well, you can just sit back down over there and watch your bonfires!"

"Fine!" replied Malick, and he stormed away.

Nathan sighed. He decided to just ignore Malick and to get to work. As far as he saw it, he had lost the bet and wasn't going to a sore loser even if he thought Malick cheated.

On his third trip down the hill, he noticed that the wood bin was filling up faster now than when he first got started. He looked up after emptying another load of wood to find Stephen Malick standing next to him with his own cart.

Confused, Nathan asked, "What are you doing?"

Malick unloaded his cart of wood and had a wide grin across his face. Nathan was surprised to see he had a smudge of dirt across his forehead. "Helping you, of course."

"Why?" Nathan asked, sounding shocked and confused.

"Well, I couldn't just sit there and watch you do all the work, so that when Lafonda arrives, she can rave on about how hard of a worker you are," Malick chuckled. "And besides, I don't think sitting on the sidelines would win me many brownie points. I know she is already planning my downfall. I don't have to add fuel to the fire."

Nathan shook his head and laughed. "All right," he said, "I owe you one."

"Nah, let's just call this one even," Malick said with a smile.

Nathan and Malick continued to stock the large wood bin as the evening sun gradually fell from the sky, setting behind the cliffs. The reddish-orange flames from the fire pits provided enough light along the beach as they finished filling the wood bin.

"I can barely smell any trace of lighter fluid," said Malick.

"Good," said Nathan with a smile. He paused to brush off the dust and chips of wood from his clothing. "I noticed the smell earlier and had hoped that it would burn off."

"You think we have time to head back to the dorm for a shower?" asked Malick.

Nathan kneeled down by the water's edge and splashed water on his face and arms before responding. "Nope," he said, "I expect everyone to arrive any minute now."

Malick grinned and kneeled down next to him. "I guess this will have to do," he chuckled, after cupping his hands and placing them into the water.

"Well, good luck with that," grinned Nathan, while taking a look at the silver necklace now visible around Malick's neck.

"What?" asked Malick, with a confused look on his wet face.

Nathan laughed. "I don't think the water can help you," he responded.

"Why?" Malick asked, innocently.

"Because you smell," he laughed.

"Ha-ha," chuckled Malick, while taking a whiff under

his arm. "You don't smell too hot there yourself, buddy."

Nathan stared at him and then grinned. "So, are you going to tell me how you finished so fast?" he asked.

Malick let out a big laugh. "I told you," he said. "It really didn't take that long."

"Okay," responded Nathan sarcastically. He paused for a second before asking his next question.

Malick had responded defensively the first time he questioned him about wanting to be called by his last name, but Nathan was still curious and decided it was worth a try to ask again.

"So," he continued carefully, "why Malick instead of Stephen?"

Malick's eyes connected with Nathan's as if he was about to say something, but he stood up and walked over to one of the bonfires, instead. Nathan followed suit as Malick sat down and stared blankly into the fire.

"Because my father is a self-centered, manipulative jerk!" Malick blurted. "And I don't want anything to do with him, let alone be named after him."

There was silence, and they both stared into the fire. Nathan was surprised by Malick's response and didn't want to irritate him more by asking questions.

"I only signed up to be a counselor this summer to get away from him," Malick continued. "Being at home always makes things worse. And if it weren't for my grandmother, I wouldn't be here either."

"What do you mean?" asked Nathan, unable to fight his urge to pry.

"My grandmother and LaDonda know each other," Malick said. "LaDonda told my grandmother that she was looking for more counselors, and I decided it was a good way to get away from my father — as well as piss him off."

Nathan had a confused look on his face. "Why would he be mad at you for being a camp counselor?" he asked.

Malick huffed. "He wanted me to take an active interest in one of his organizations this summer," he said hesitantly. "He said it would be good for me ... and the family tradition. Yeah, like I would be interested."

The tranquility of the lake was interrupted by the sounds of approaching chatter and laughter from the forest. Nathan and Malick both turned their heads towards the entrance to the lake. Through the dark, Nathan caught glimpses of campers on the trail as beams from their flashlights bounced off of them, creating shadows amongst the trees.

"I believe it's showtime," said Malick. "And I think I see LaDonda."

"Yeah," added Nathan, "and I *know* I hear Lafonda."

They both laughed.

CHAPTER EIGHT

THE FALLEN ONES

"So, how did it go, Mr. Nathan?" asked a cheery Lafonda.

Malick grinned and ran his hand through his hair. "I'll leave you guys to your conversation," he said.

Lafonda pursed her lips and glared at Malick before returning her attention back to Nathan. "So," she said, sighing lightly, "how did it go?"

"Not too bad," he grinned.

"What's so funny?" she asked.

Nathan glanced over at Malick as he walked aimlessly around the other fire pits. He looked back at her and smiled again. "Nothing," he said.

Lafonda rolled her eyes. "I found a copy of last year's yearbook," she said with a sigh. "I checked and Leah's photo is definitely in there."

"How did you find it?"

"Being back on campus, I have been thinking more about Leah lately," she continued. "I remembered that you wanted to know what she looks like."

"Cool. Do you have it with you?"

"No," she said. "I actually ran into Jonathan Black in

the lobby after dinner and he had it with him."

"So, Jonathan finally showed up, huh?" Nathan asked with a smile.

She laughed. "Yes, Erin really let him have it."

He grinned for a moment and then paused. "Why on earth would Jonathan Black be carrying around an IUCF yearbook with him?"

Lafonda stood silent and then took a quick glance out to the lake. "That's a good question," she said. "I didn't think to ask."

Nathan scanned the beach and the fire pits. Malick was having a conversation with LaDonda, and some kid was playing dangerously close to one of the fires. *Jonas,* he thought. "I don't see Jonathan," he said. "I wonder if he has it with him."

"Oh, I have it," said Lafonda reassuringly. "I borrowed it from him. It's upstairs in my room. I can show you her picture tonight when we get back."

"Sounds like a plan," smiled Nathan. He looked around the beach again. "I still don't see Jonathan anywhere."

She looked around too. "I don't see him either. But I know I saw him with his group before we got on the trail." She sighed. "Anyway," she said with a shrug, "I better get back to the girls. And please do something with Jonas before he burns himself."

Nathan nodded. "Believe me," he chuckled. "I know."

She grinned and then headed towards a group of girls who were talking and laughing around one of the bonfires.

Jonas spotted Nathan and waved excitedly at him.

Nathan shook his head. "Jonas," he groaned.

"Hey!" called out Lafonda. "By the way, good job with everything tonight."

Nathan smiled.

"I agree," added LaDonda walking over to Nathan.

Malick was following behind her.

"I was just talking to Stephen about this and would love it if you two would get the fires going again for me next week." LaDonda paused and then placed a hand on Malick's back. "I spoke to Argus over the phone and he said that you two were easy to work with. And Stephen here has already agreed to do it."

"Argus," Nathan grumbled. He stared blankly at her, thinking that of course Argus was pleased because he and Malick did all the work.

"So, what do you think?" she asked.

He crossed his arms and shifted his glare into the trees. "About what?" he pouted. "I thought you already assigned me for the rest of camp."

LaDonda placed her hands on his shoulders and smiled.

"Oh, all right," he agreed reluctantly. "Sure."

"Thank you, Nathan," she responded cheerfully. "I'm sure Roy will be proud of you for all the work you've done." She cleared her throat. "Have you called him since you left for camp?"

"Um, no, not yet," he stammered.

"Well, I guess you can tell him all about it when you call him tonight," she said.

"Jonas!" she called out and walked quickly in his direction. "Get out from over there. You are too close to the fire!"

Nathan and Malick glanced at each other and both laughed heartily.

"So, who is Roy?" Malick asked.

"Oh," smiled Nathan. "Roy is my grandfather. He works for LaDonda and maintains the grounds of the

Devaro estate."

"Okay," Malick nodded. "So your grandfather is the caretaker."

"Yup," Nathan said. "We stay in the cottage behind the main house."

"Cool," said Malick, with a nudge. "Now I know where to find you when camp is all over."

"Ha, okay," chuckled Nathan sarcastically.

LaDonda gave a good scolding to Jonas about tossing rocks, cans, and whatever else he could find around the beach into the fire. She then recruited him and some of his friends to help set up the refreshments, tables and chairs carried down the trail by some of the other counselors.

Lafonda sat around one of the pits with some of the girls from her floor; Erin, Angela and Alan were seated with them. Nathan thought about joining them but changed his mind because he doubted that Malick would want to hang out with Lafonda and the others. He had almost walked past the group when he noticed Jonathan Black. Three girls were sitting around him, and he looked like he was the center of attention.

"What's going on over there?" Nathan asked.

Lafonda stopped her conversation with Erin and looked up to acknowledge him. "Oh," she said with a pause. "Jonathan is sharing some of the Cahokia legends with some of the campers."

"Oh, hi Malick," said an upbeat Angela. She quickly made space between her and Alan. "Are you going to sit down with us?"

Malick stared blankly at her for a moment before finally glancing at Nathan. He almost looked embarrassed.

Nathan cleared his throat while giving him a slight

nudge. He then took the seat that was closest to Jonathan.

Malick ran his hand through his hair before taking the seat next to Angela. "Umm — sure," Malick uttered through pursed lips.

"So," said Nathan so loudly that Jonathan spun around.

"Oh, Nathan," he responded, surprised. "How long have you been sitting there?"

"Not long," he said, with scrutinizing eyes.

Jonathan rubbed his red eyes from underneath his square-rimmed glasses. They appeared irritated and puffy. "Well, nice to see you," he said wearily.

A couple of the girls seated around him giggled while he continued to speak.

"I was just sharing some of the Cahokia legends with Samantha, Christina and Eva Marie here."

"Hi, I'm Eva Marie Evans," said the girl with the short wavy hair. "And this is Samantha Darding and Christina Williams."

Samantha ran her fingers through her long, brown, curly hair, placing a lock of it behind her ear. She smiled. "My friend's call me Sam," she said.

"And let me guess," said Nathan with a grin. "Chris?"

"Nope, just Christina," she giggled.

Jonathan opened up a black and green spiral notebook that was sitting in his lap. "I was just explaining how the Cahokia Indians —"

"Wait," interrupted Nathan. "Did you say Samantha Darding? As in Patricia and Jim Darding?"

She placed a loose lock of her hair behind her ear again and smiled. "Yes," she nodded readily. "Patricia and Jim are my parents."

"I knew that Jim had a little sister," Nathan said, sounding surprised. "But I thought when he said little, he

118

meant little."

"No, not that little," she laughed. "I'm sixteen."

Jonathan cleared his throat. "Well, Nathan probably already knows this, but the Cahokia Indians have several stories that are part of their folklore, or religion," he said with a smile. "We know a lot of these stories because they have appeared quite frequently in their paintings and in their writings." He paused to reposition his glasses. "I would say the most commonly known story is the legend about the Fallen Ones. Wouldn't you agree, Nathan?"

Nathan raised his eyebrows and shrugged. He wasn't even sure if he knew the story, let alone anyone else. "Probably," he replied slowly.

Suddenly, Jonathan perked up, his tired blue eyes getting some life in them. "Nathan here has Cahokia ancestry," he smiled and nodded. "His mother's tribe was a descendant of the Cahokia American Indians."

Jonathan paused as if he was waiting for Nathan to say something.

Nathan looked embarrassed as Samantha, Christina and Eva Marie stared at him. Over the flames of the fire, Nathan could see that Malick was looking at him too, but Nathan wasn't sure if he had heard what Jonathan said. Most of the people around the fire, including Lafonda, were still having their own separate conversations.

Christina threw back her long brown hair and leaned in towards Nathan. "Is it true?" she asked.

Nathan answered slowly. He wasn't too thrilled about the sudden attention. "Yes," he said.

Both Christina and Eva Marie grinned at each other and then beamed at him. "That's awesome," they giggled in unison.

"Indeed, it is awesome," added Jonathan excitedly. "See, years ago, when they started excavating the caves and mounds in this area, they found that almost every wall had the same symbols written on them. When the symbols were finally deciphered, they all included some aspect of the story about the Fallen Ones."

He paused to reposition his glasses again. "Most scholars agree that the Legend of the Fallen Ones is a part of Cahokia mythology on how the world began — you know, their creation story."

"This is exciting!" shrieked Eva Marie. "Tell us the story — or legend."

"Does it involve any cute guys?" asked Christina enthusiastically.

Samantha, Christina and Eva Marie looked at each other and laughed.

"Cute guys?" shouted Angela over the fire. "I have to hear this story. I'm in."

Jonathan smiled as everyone around the fire, including Lafonda, Erin, Alan and Malick, listened closely.

"There really isn't a Cahokia symbol for cute," said Jonathan. "But the symbols tell a story about five angels that were created out of the heavens in the beginning and shared in the power with the creator of the heavens as givers of light."

"Cute male angels," said Angela. "I love it!"

Jonathan laughed. "Well, I don't know how cute you will find them by the end of the story," he grinned. "See, according to the legend and the hieroglyphs found in the mounds and on cave walls, one of the five Angels of Light, as they are sometimes referred to, had a thirst for power and wanted dominance over all of the heavens." He held up a page in his black and green spiral notebook. "The Cahokia Indians used this symbol quite frequently when talking about this angel."

Nathan squinted and cocked his head a little. He was

trying to make out the sketch in Jonathan's notebook. After a few moments, he could see that he was staring at a drawing of a broken wing that was engulfed in flames and constricted by a serpent.

"Some other cultures tell a similar story," said Jonathan, placing the notebook back in his lap.

Silence fell around the fire, and Nathan was surprised to see that Jonathan still had everyone's attention.

"So, the legend is the same story as the origins of the devil in the Bible?" asked Nathan.

"Not quite," smiled Jonathan. "The popularly held belief that Satan, also known by his angelic name Lucifer, was once a prideful angel that rebelled against God is mostly based on inference. This isn't written explicitly in the Bible. It is quite clear, however, that Lucifer was not the mirror image of his angelic brethren Michael, Raphael, Uriel and Gabriel." He paused. "But he did find refuge in and allegiance from his other brethren Lucas, Lucius, Laban and Luke."

"Who are they?" asked Nathan. "I've never heard of them."

Malick chuckled and Jonathan frowned. He gave Malick a stern look over his glasses before continuing.

"See, the Bible gives a fair account about the fall of one angel," Jonathan said, "but according to the Cahokia legend, the story doesn't stop there."

Nathan's face frowned. "But the Bible —"

"Yes," continued Jonathan, "the Bible does make references to other fallen angels, like in the book of Jude, for instance, but who they were and what their names are, the Bible does not say."

"So, according to the legend," said Nathan, "these other guys Lucas, Lucius, Laban and ..."

"And Luke," said Jonathan.

Nathan smiled. "And Luke, are the other fallen angels?"

"Or other Angels of Light," Jonathan said.

Lafonda bounced her leg impatiently as her long, silky black hair drifted off to one side. "Okay, I think Nathan finally gets it now," she said. "Can we move on with the rest of the story?"

Nathan rolled his eyes and pursed his lips in protest, and Lafonda smiled back at him.

Jonathan gave a quick smirk and turned to another page in his notebook. "See, the other four fallen angels each had a similar symbol like Lucifer's," he said. "Just absent the serpent — but each still engulfed in fire."

"That's intense," said Alan.

"The legend goes on to say that after Lucifer and the Angels of Light failed to take over the heavens, they were forgotten and cast into the void," said Jonathan.

"What's the void?" asked Alan with a frown.

Jonathan paused and smiled again.

Nathan could tell that he was enjoying all the attention.

"Most scholars agree that the void was on the surface of the Earth, or the physical plane," explained Jonathan, "before the creation of man, before the creation of the sun, water and land."

Jonathan took another pause and noticed that Lafonda looked annoyed again. "And so, continuing on with the story," he said, "for thousands of years, the Fallen Ones were banished to the void and toiled in darkness. The story goes on to say that it was there they realized their weakness, because not even with their collected powers could they pierce light into the darkness."

Samantha gasped and covered her mouth. "They were sentenced to darkness forever?" she asked. "That's really sad."

Christina and Eva Marie both let out a huge laugh. "Leave it to Samantha to feel sympathy even for the devil," grinned Eva Marie.

"It just seems so sad to be in the dark, forever," Samantha said, her cheeks turning a bright red. "But I hope they stay there because I'm not like Angela, and I never want to meet them — let alone date them."

Quickly, Angela sat up straight, and her blond hair bounced readily on her shoulders. "Hey!" she spouted.

Jonathan closed his notepad with a thud. He had a grim look on his face. "We aren't that lucky," he said. "See, to their surprise, light eventually did pierce the darkness, and as it says in the legend and in the Bible, they rejoiced and cried out to the heavens."

Behind his dark-rimmed glasses, Jonathan's blue eyes grew wide, and his voice became softer. "But they had been replaced," he said. "To their dismay other heavenly bodies had replaced them, and just as many stars had populated the sky. There was a new creature on the face of the Earth: man. That is, us. See, they are still bound to the void, the same plane we live on," he explained. "And they are angry because all of this — the stars, the water, the land — was created for us. According to the legend, man was given dominance over the face of the Earth and, even in our weakness, made lord over all the angels."

"Ha! I'm sure they were happy about that," said Alan sarcastically.

"According to the legend," said Jonathan, his voice returning back to normal, "they vowed to destroy us, to condemn us to the same fate that waited for them."

"And by the same fate you mean ..." said Nathan.

"Damnation," said Jonathan.

"This is one cheery story," said Alan.

"But if we are on the same plane with the fallen angels," said Lafonda with a curious look on her face, "how come no one ever sees them?"

"According to my research," Jonathan said, "the Cahokia Indians believed that Lucifer was given dominion over the underworld, and his brethren, the other fallen angels, were given dominance over the spiritual plane, which is a parallel dimension that coexists with our world." He paused to reposition his glasses on his sharply angled nose again. "In their mythology, Lucifer is often referred to as the root or source of all evil, and evil is represented by the serpent in the symbol."

"It's just a myth," blurted Malick. He had a blank, cold look on his face.

Lafonda glowered and placed her arms across her chest. "Jonathan," she said, while keeping a watchful eye on Malick. "You don't actually … believe this stuff, right?"

Malick looked sternly at Lafonda. "Myth," he groaned.

She turned her head away from him and stared into the fire.

Nathan looked uncomfortable as he looked at Lafonda and then at Malick. Alan sighed while adjusting the gold leadership shirt he'd commandeered from LaDonda, and Erin tossed dirt from her shoes. A shiny purple hairbrush suddenly materialized in Angela's hand, and Jonathan stumbled through pages in his black and green notebook.

"And most excitingly," said Jonathan, breaking the awkward silence, "we have found a new symbol!"

Nathan turned his attention away from Malick and Lafonda and focused on Jonathan again. "A new symbol?" he uttered.

"Yes!" Jonathan said, while holding up another page from his notebook. "It's another symbol depicting fire, but do you see the difference?"

Nathan leaned forward. His face frowned while staring at Jonathan's sketch of the symbol. He thought it was peculiar that somehow it looked familiar. "Is that what I think it is?" he asked.

Malick shook his head and placed his hand slightly over his mouth.

"Yes," replied Jonathan, his blue eyes glowing bright. "It's a man!"

Lafonda crossed her legs again and leaned forward toward the sketch. "What does that mean?" she asked.

Jonathan closed the notebook and smiled. "We aren't exactly sure yet," he said. "Dr. Helmsley and I just uncovered it yesterday." He paused to clear his throat. "Since then, I have been poring over all the books and archival documents at the Cahokia Museum and haven't been able to find that symbol or a reference to it anywhere. Dr. Helmsley believes we'll be able to determine what it is after we uncover what's behind the cavern wall."

Malick had a perplexed look on his face. "Cavern wall?" he asked. "And who is Dr. Helmsley?"

Jonathan's eyes sparkled. "Oh, I'm sorry," he said excitedly. "I am leaving out the best part!" He leaned over and placed his notebook into his backpack. "I've been assisting Dr. Janet Helmsley, a professor of archeology at the university, with the excavation of one of the Cahokia caves," he said, pointing towards the cliffs overlooking the lake. "I've been helping since I first arrived in town."

He paused, positioning his backpack close to his side. "Dr. Helmsley is also the director of Archeological Studies at the university," he continued. "I first learned about the new excavation site after reading an article she had published in my dad's journal." He smiled, lightly chuckling to himself. "Well, technically it's not his journal. My dad is the editor of the *Oxford Journal of World Archaeology*."

With his index finger, he slid his glasses back to the bridge of his nose again. "Dr. Helmsley believes that behind the wall is a hidden chamber that might provide more insight into the tribe's culture," he said. "It is truly exciting. We really don't know what we will find. Dr. Helmsley said that I will definitely share the credit in the discovery and that in itself is amazing — I might even have a byline in the article!"

"That really is great!" Nathan said to Jonathan with a smile. "Umm, congratulations — with your discovery." He glanced at Malick and couldn't help noticing he looked distracted or in deep thought.

"Yeah, congratulations," added Malick, finally coming back to life. "So, when do you expect to get a peek at what's behind the wall?"

Jonathan paused for a second and gazed into the fire before speaking. "Well, it probably will be at least a couple weeks," he said. "I was thinking that Nathan might want to join us when we first enter the hidden chamber."

Angela stopped grooming her curly blond hair and passed her hairbrush to Alan. "Now, that is even more exciting," she said. "Let's all go!"

Alan glared at the shiny purple hairbrush in his hand and placed it in Angela's lap. "I am not holding your hairbrush for you," he said, rolling his eyes. "And why on earth would I want to go inside some grubby cave?"

"Come on, Alan!" she whined, tossing her hair. "It could be fun. Where is your smell of adventure? Your taste for history?"

"Yeah," commented Erin. "Lord knows nothing

exciting ever happens around here."

Lafonda laughed. "Your *smell* of adventure?" she asked teasingly. "Your taste for history? Where did you get those from, Angela?"

Alan looked anxious and crossed his arms. "Whatever," he said flippantly. "I'm not going."

Angela gave Alan a devious grin and then smiled happily.

"Whatever, Angela," he protested. "You are not going to convince me."

Abruptly, Erin sat up straight and glared at Jonathan. "So, a few weeks?" she said. "Does this mean we can expect more unexplained disappearances and more tardiness from a distracted Jonathan Black?"

Everyone laughed.

Jonathan's cheeks became flushed and almost matched the redness in his eyes. "Sorry," he said, sounding embarrassed. "I promise to work on my communication. It's just that I get so excited. But this is not an excuse."

Erin grinned. "It's cool, Mr. Indiana Jones," she said. "Just don't forget us little guys when you become famous for all your discoveries."

He smiled. "Thanks," he said.

"But hold on," cautioned Erin. "We still are going to talk later about some things."

"Understood," nodded Jonathan with a smile.

Angela cleared her throat. Her eyes were brighter, and her voice was bubbly. "Hey," she said. "Have you tried researching on the Internet, you know, for that symbol?"

Jonathan stared blankly at her, and Alan tried to hold back his laughter.

"What?" she asked with a shrug. "It's worth a try."

CHAPTER NINE

PREMONITION

Nathan opened up his eyes slowly as they adjusted to the darkness. He had a view of what appeared to be the night sky. His head was cloudy and he was a little confused. He continued to blink while his mind tried to focus. He could clearly see what looked like the stars and the moon, but they were a lot more vivid than usual. They appeared almost animated. The stars and the moon appeared to flicker playfully with one another.

"Am I dreaming?" he asked himself.

His thoughts were coming together now, and he was becoming aware of his body. He could tell that he was lying on his back but on an unfamiliar surface. There were little prickles of something underneath him. He stretched out both his hands to sit up and immediately noticed something bendable and soft pass through his fingers. It almost felt like plastic.

Nathan looked down to examine what was between his fingers and paused before looking all around him. "Where the heck am I?" he wondered. "This can't be grass." He was sitting in an open field that was surrounded by small and large trees. There was a stone road to the left of him that ran alongside a series of small hills.

Nathan blinked his eyes several times and held his hand to his head. "I might need to be on medication, or something. Or maybe I already am on drugs. Because everything is gray. There is no color."

He looked down at his hands again and then at his clothes. *Whew*, he thought. *I can see the color in my skin and in my clothes. For a second I thought I was going colorblind.*

He hoped one of the campers hadn't put something in his drink. "This is not funny. It'd better not be Jonas," he said to himself.

Nathan turned his attention again to the gray-looking grass that was all around him. *It's like — frozen*, he thought. *And it feels weird — like plastic.*

He stood up and continued to look around him. The trees were motionless, and the air was humid and stagnant — no breeze, no sign of animals or people, and no sound.

He quickly clapped his hands together to test his theory and was relieved to hear the sound they made as it echoed back at him. He was caught off guard when a small branch beneath his foot snapped with no sound.

Cautiously, he picked up the branch and examined it. Next, he picked up a rock from the stone road and tossed it, but again there was no sound. "This is definitely strange," he murmured. He was relieved that he could hear himself. "Everything but me seems frozen, lifeless, muted."

Nathan glanced up at what he thought was the night sky and was amazed at how brilliantly the stars and the moon shone, considering that his entire view, apart from himself, seemed shrouded in gray.

He crossed over the stone pathway and climbed up

one of the larger-sized hills. Almost at the top, he froze. A cold shiver ran down his back. The silence that gripped the entire area was abruptly broken. The sound was all too familiar to him — everything was, the sky and the lifeless trees.

He heard the sound again; this time it lingered amongst the trees. "Somehow I know I've been here before," he mumbled to himself. "And that was definitely a scream, and I am pretty sure it was Leah's."

Everything flooded Nathan's mind at once: his dreams about Leah, her face as she fought in desperation against an unknown attacker, the speckles of blood on her pale skin, and the scratches on her arms and legs.

Nathan's heart pounded against his chest. He was definitely frightened for Leah as he had always been, but this time it was different. This time, he actually felt like he was there. He wasn't a spectator watching everything unfold; and this time, dream or not, he planned to do something about it.

In a matter of seconds, Nathan was down the hill. Frantically, he headed in the direction of Leah's screams. If it weren't for the sudden tingling in his hands, he probably would have kept running recklessly towards the screams.

"Okay Nathan, calm down and think. If this is like all the other dreams, then Leah is in trouble and she is being attacked."

His hands felt warm, like they had at Lafonda's birthday party. He looked down and saw that they were red. He clenched them into fists. "I don't have time to think about my hands right now!"

Cautiously, he continued down the stone pathway. *I need a plan*, he thought. *I need to find something to fight with.* He thought about stopping to look for something, but every time he did so, his stomach twisted in knots. He couldn't bear the thought of wasting time to look for something when Leah's life was in danger.

He considered going back and picking up a tree branch he saw along the way, but he came across a large oak tree at the end of the pathway. "I've seen this tree before," he said to himself.

His eyes quickly caught the first line of the all-too-familiar words carved at the base of the tree. "De mortuis nil nisi bonum," said Nathan. "Speak no ill of the dead."

Just about everyone in town knew the saying because it was carved in the large tree that stood right outside Grimm Cemetery. "I must've awoken in Lynn Field. But how in the world did I get there?"

He rubbed his head and stared again at the familiar words, trying to make out the second line, but he couldn't because someone had scratched through them. No one in town could make out the second line either, and no one knew who had scratched it.

Nathan looked up and then back at the big oak tree. He caught a glimpse of the glaring moon before it disappeared behind a wisp of gray clouds. "How could this be? Besides my funky gray vision and the psychedelic sky, everything seems so real." He glanced up at the gray branches and leaves of the big oak tree and shook his head. "This has to be a dream."

He froze. A cold shiver ran down his back again and another scream filled the air. *Yeah*, he thought, *and Leah is supposed to be in a mental hospital right now. And yet, here I am, running towards her outside of Grimm Cemetery.*

He made his hands into fists again, but they trembled uncontrollably and felt like they were on fire. "Dream or not, I have to save Leah," he said.

Grimm Cemetery looked the same as it always had.

The only noticeable difference was that everything had a grayish hue to it. It was almost like looking at a black and white photo. Nathan approached the stone-and-iron fence to the cemetery and paused. He was surprised that even the plants that wrapped themselves around the black iron gate were gray.

The gate was supported by two stone columns, one on either side. Carved in the stone of one column were the words Grimm, and on the other Cemetery. Nathan was familiar with the urban legend surrounding Grimm Cemetery, but he regarded it as such and didn't want to waste time even thinking about it. He wanted his thoughts focused on finding Leah. He took a deep breath and let it out slowly. "I have no idea what's waiting for me in there," he said to himself.

A leaf from one of the plants wrapped around the gate grazed him across the neck, causing him to spin around quickly. Startled, he tripped over a loose stone and flew headfirst into the gate. The gate swung violently open and slammed into one of the stone pillars.

Nathan wiped his brow. "Whew," he said. He was relieved that the absence of sound also applied to the iron gate. "This lack of sound may actually work to my advantage."

The plot of land that was Grimm Cemetery gradually elevated up three levels. As soon as Nathan entered the gates, he saw the top of the large obelisk towering on the third level. He quickly darted past the rows and rows of battered, old headstone crosses and hid behind some of the taller gravestones and monuments scattered here and there. Carefully, he made his way to the stone steps that were at the end of the pathway. His heart pounded so loudly against his chest that he swore it was probably the only sound that could be heard for miles.

The stone steps, like the stones that made up the iron black gate, were badly weathered. Pieces of stone crumbled beneath his feet with each step he took. Before he reached the top, he paused. He could hear the sound of voices a little ways off in the distance. It almost sounded like someone was conducting a ritual or chanting. Nathan continued carefully up the stone steps to the second level. He could now see the array of mausoleums that decorated the landscape. He had never ventured this far into the cemetery before and in the past had only visited the cemetery to play games of chicken with friends.

As he had on the first level, he cautiously made his way to the stone steps at the end of the pathway. Nathan compared the many mausoleums to the cemeteries of New Orleans. He had visited New Orleans once with LaDonda and Lafonda during one of LaDonda's trips to visit family. Just like in New Orleans, it truly had looked like a city of the dead.

Slowly, Nathan approached the stone steps that led up to the third level. The voices grew louder and he could definitely tell there were multiple voices. It sounded like chanting, but Nathan couldn't decipher what it was. He strained his ears to hear more, wondering what language it was. It sounded like Latin.

At the foot of the stone steps to the third level, he was close enough to see much of the tall white obelisk that stood at the center of what looked like a memorial plaza. He crept up the steps, trying to catch a glimpse of who was doing the chanting.

There was the faint sound of crying beneath the chanting voices and someone whispered softly, almost peacefully. He dared to inch a little closer to the top, and that's when he saw them: three hooded figures dressed in long red cloaks.

Quickly, he took a step back and crouched down again, his heart beating frantically against his chest. "What the frig is going on?" he murmured.

He inched up again to take another look. *They're not shrouded in gray,* he thought. *They're in color!* He paused to wipe the sweat from his brow. "It looks like they're performing a ritual. But for what?"

The red-hooded figures stood with their backs towards him, their hands stretched out in the air. It looked like they were praying or worshipping something. Around each figure's waist was a decorative gold, tasseled rope that hung from their hips and stretched out to the ground.

Nathan followed the trail of gold with his eyes. The gold tasseled rope shone against the deep-red cloaks. "What's that on the ground?" he wondered, while straining his eyes to see.

He gasped. At the foot of each hooded figure lay several bodies strewn across the brick-and-mortar floor.

A sick feeling gripped his stomach. So far he had gone unnoticed and didn't want to chance being seen, but he had to see their faces. Nathan swallowed hard and then dared an inch closer. "Leah!" he gasped.

He clenched his fists again. "What are they doing to her?" he muttered. "And the others — who are the others?"

Nathan looked on as Leah continued to lie on her back. It looked like she was saying something to the person lying right next to her. Her pale face somehow looked peaceful, but her clothes were worn and tattered. Blood stained her white shirt, and strands of brown hair lay strewn across her face. Slowly, she reached out for the hand of the other person.

Nathan gasped again, this time almost losing his balance. "Jonas!" he said softly through clenched teeth. "B-but how?" It felt as if his entire body was trembling. "How did they get Jonas, and what do they want with him or with Leah?"

Suddenly, Nathan's thoughts were interrupted by the sounds of laughter and giggles. He thought the voice was familiar; it was definitely a female voice. He looked towards the center of the plaza and that's when he saw her, standing near the tall white obelisk.

Her back was towards him so he couldn't see her face. Her long white dress floated seamlessly as she laughed in the arms of a tall, red-hooded figure. Slowly, her fingertips traced her partner's face, causing her sleeves to hang delicately off her arms.

Nathan noticed that this figure's red cloak and hood seemed different from the others'. The tall man's cloak was intricately ornamented in gold, and the silver rope and gold tassel that hung from his waist were thicker and longer. His skin was luminous, like the long strands of white-blond hair that hung from underneath his hood and down to the crest of his cloak. Abruptly, the woman stopped caressing his chiseled chin, and he released her. Nathan watched as he seemed to vanish right through one of the tall white archways surrounding the plaza.

The woman dressed in white gracefully walked past the bodies lying on the ground.

Nathan's eyes followed her closely. "What is she up to?" he murmured.

The woman seemed to glide across the floor, the long train to her dress flowing behind her. At each archway she passed, she nodded. There were more hooded figures, but they were dressed in black, not in red. There was a black-hooded figure in the shadows of each archway. The dark-hooded figures blended in with the shadows so well that Nathan almost didn't see them.

The woman stopped in front of Jonas and Leah. Nathan's eyes were fixed intently on Leah's face. To his surprise, Leah still seemed calm. He didn't see an ounce of fear. The woman knelt down, her long, curly blond hair falling in front of her, making it impossible for him to see her face. She was very close to Leah now, and her hair seemed to caress Leah's face.

Nathan shifted his shoulders. His hands still trembled and they were very warm. "What is she doing?" he said in a frustrated whisper.

Suddenly, the woman grabbed Leah's arm and Jonas's hand fell to the ground. Leah didn't flinch, but Nathan saw the fear swell in her eyes. A black-hooded figure emerged from the shadows of the nearest archway and stood beside the woman holding Leah's arm. Desperately, Nathan strained to see his face, but couldn't. He looked around the plaza to the faces of the other hooded figures, but couldn't see them either. The woman casually stretched out her hand, and the black-hooded figure gave her a small silver dagger. Quickly, she plunged the tip of the blade into Leah's arm, violently piercing her flesh. Leah screamed as her attacker slowly proceeded to press the blade downward.

Nathan stood up and, without hesitation, darted up the remaining stone steps. His heart pounded against his chest, and his hands pulsated rapidly, as if they were about to burst into flames. "No!" he yelled.

He ran as fast as he could, but everything around him seemed to be in slow motion. He felt the ground give way as the old, weathered steps crumbled beneath him. He fell to the ground, but not before catching a glimpse of the faceless red-hooded figures that were now upon him.

Nathan lay motionless on the ground of the second level. Through the cloud of dust that now filled the air from the crumbling stairs, he could see that one of the red-hooded figures was getting closer to him.

Slowly, he attempted to get up, as whispers and hissing sounds trickled down from the top level. Red- and black-hooded figures were now looking down at him. "What the heck is all that hissing noise?" he mumbled. "Are these guys snakes now?"

"Ah, my head!" he moaned, before immediately falling back down.

The red-hooded figure was closer now, and Nathan could see the gold-and-silver crescent-shaped medallion around his neck.

Nathan placed his hand on his head and moaned. His hands burned a bright red, but felt cool to the touch. "I have to get up," he cried. "I have to save Leah!"

Nathan tried to get up again, but this time fell to his knees. He looked towards the crumbling staircase and saw that the red-hooded figure was almost upon him. The figure stretched his palms out towards Nathan, and the gold-and-silver medallion around his neck radiated a bluish hue.

Nathan's eyes grew wide in astonishment. "Um, this doesn't look good." he stuttered.

Finally, he managed to stumble to his feet, but a blue ball of light was headed straight towards him. He dove out of the way, missing it by inches. The ball of blue light hit one of the mausoleum walls behind him, pulverizing it. He ducked as pieces of the wall went flying everywhere.

Nathan lay on the ground again, and his head throbbed with pain. He took a look at the wall and surveyed the pieces of it that now lay all around him.

"Yup," he uttered. "Like I said, not good at all." He thought about getting up, but his head continued to throb. Another ball of light was hurling towards him, but he couldn't move. He closed his eyes and expected the worst.

There was a brief moment of silence followed by a soft thud. Slowly, he opened his eyes, and in front of him was a pair of pink and gray sneakers. "Lafonda?" he said, confused. "W-what are you doing here?"

"Saving your ass, of course," she responded, helping him to his feet.

Nathan smiled. He looked over her shoulder, where the red-hooded guy with the gold-and-silver medallion around his neck now lay slumped over a pile of rubble from the staircase.

"B-but how?" Nathan stuttered.

Lafonda's smile quickly faded. "I —"

A black-hooded figure suddenly appeared behind her. She gasped, and her brown eyes grew wide. Nathan watched helplessly as a small trickle of blood fell from her mouth. The faceless hooded figure withdrew his double-edged sword from her back, and Lafonda's legs gave way underneath her.

Nathan reached out to grab her, and they both slumped to the ground.

Other black-hooded figures appeared, their silver swords clutched upright against their chests. Nathan held tight to Lafonda's lifeless body while trying to fight back the tears that swelled in his eyes. "No," he cried. "No!"

Suddenly, something began to burn deep within his stomach. It wasn't anger that churned inside of him; this was peaceful. His hands stopped trembling and burning, but his entire body felt like it radiated energy.

More black-hooded figures appeared, and Nathan's

heart pounded relentlessly against his chest. He could see his reflection in the blades of their swords as they prepared to strike and the fiery bright blue flame in the palm of his hand.

CHAPTER TEN

BLUE FLAME

Nathan let out a huge gasp, instantly sitting up in bed. His breathing was labored, and he was covered in sweat. "How did I get back here?" he wondered, frantically.

Slowly, he looked around the room, but his heart continued to beat hard against his chest. *I must've fallen asleep after the bonfire last night,* he thought, while staring at the clock in his room.

He recalled walking back to Lawrence Hall with Lafonda and the rest of the campers, but everything else was a blur after he got back to his dorm room.

Nathan wiped the sweat from his brow. It was almost 7:00 in the morning. *I must've been so tired that I crashed once I hit the bed. But if that was a dream—it felt so real.*

His thoughts were racing as he tried to recall every detail about the dream. "Wait — what's that?" he murmured. "What's that blue light?"

He squinted as his eyes continued to adjust to the dark room. Nathan inched forward to investigate, and without warning he thought he saw a blue spark fly from his hand.

"Aaah!" he yelled, springing out of bed.

Nathan examined his hand hysterically, but piercing through the darkness was a flickering blue light burning at the foot of his bed.

"Fire!" he yelled.

Desperately, Nathan looked around the room for something to use to put out the fire. He grabbed a towel that was hanging on the door knob to the closet and repeatedly beat the towel against the bed until the last flame had been extinguished.

Nathan sat on top of the desk in his room and laughed. "I don't know why I didn't just throw the towel on top of the flames," he chuckled. "I guess I wanted to beat the flames to death."

He looked down at the scorched bed sheets, and his face went blank. "Those flames were blue," he uttered. Nathan looked down at his hands. "In my dream a blue flame came out of my hand. B-but this can't be real."

He continued to examine his hands. "But if it was just a dream, where did the fire come from? And the spark?"

Quickly, he jumped off the desk and searched around the room for any source that could have caused the fire. He examined his hands again. "If I caused this fire," he muttered, "then, what other parts of the dream are real too?"

Images of the dream flooded his mind, and his stomach tightened. First, he recalled running through Grimm Cemetery. Next, he remembered seeing the mysterious red- and black-hooded figures and the strange woman dressed in white. "Jonas and Leah!" he cried. "And Lafonda!"

He sank down on the edge of his bed. Images of Leah being stabbed in her arm by the lady in white tormented him. He remembered her screams, and his stomach continued to tighten. The faceless black-hooded figure came to life again, as did the silver sword that the villain plunged into Lafonda's back. A feeling of dread came over Nathan, and he felt like he was holding her again. He trembled as he remembered her lifeless body.

Nathan's thoughts were suddenly interrupted by the sound of an approaching bouncing ball, followed by a quick knock at his dorm room door. He took a deep breath and sighed with relief. Quickly, he tossed the towel over the scorch marks and opened the door. "Jonas!" he smiled.

Jonas's shaggy, curly black hair looked wet, and the T-shirt he was wearing looked damp.

Nathan shook his head and laughed. "Jonas, did you just get out of the shower?" he asked.

Jonas's eyebrows frowned slightly beneath his wet curls. "Um, not just," he said.

Nathan smiled and playfully took the basketball from him. "You know, they do have a thing called bath towels," he said. "You know, to dry off with?"

Jonas frowned again, appearing slightly confused.

Nathan grinned and pointed to the water dripping from Jonas' hair down on to his shoulders.

"Oh, that," he said, his face lighting up. "I didn't want to be late for breakfast."

Nathan gave Jonas a doubtful but playful look. "Jonas, you're never late for breakfast," he said.

"Oh, okay," Jonas said, reaching for his basketball. "But it's almost 7:30."

Nathan held back the basketball, and Jonas frowned. "Not quite," said Nathan, glancing at the clock in his room.

The elevator bell rang, and they both spun around to watch the doors open.

He handed the basketball back to Jonas and quickly

headed over to the elevator. It was barely 7:00, but he had a good guess who it could be. Lafonda stepped out of the elevator, and Nathan quickly hugged her.

"Whoa! Okay," she said. "Good morning to you, too!"

"You are all right!" he shouted, while holding her in his arms.

Lafonda looked confused. "Of course I am," she smiled, weakly. "Why wouldn't I be?"

Nathan quickly released her from his arms. He was a little embarrassed. "Um, yeah," he said. "Sorry about that."

She tossed back her long black hair over her shoulders and attempted to fix her orange leadership shirt. "What was that all about?" she asked.

He headed back to his room, and Lafonda followed behind him. Jonas was sitting on Nathan's bed. Nathan shook his head at Jonas and grinned. Lafonda raised her eyebrows and stared at Nathan.

He smiled sheepishly back at her. "It was nothing," he said. "I was just surprised to see you."

She looked confused again. "I told you last night that I would give you the yearbook in the morning," she said. "Did you forget?"

He quickly looked to see if the towel was still covering the burn marks on his bed. He then turned to address Lafonda. "N-no," he stuttered. "Of course not. I didn't forget."

She looked skeptically at him, through squinted eyes, and then walked past him into the room. She stopped at the foot of his bed. "Hi, Jonas," she said. "Nice to see that somebody has a shirt on."

Nathan looked down at his bare chest and then quickly put on his IUCF shirt. "Oh," he uttered.

Lafonda smiled sarcastically. "You know," she said. "I

really hope you wash that shirt, based on how often you wear it."

He frowned. "Of course I do," he spouted. "And I do have more than one of these shirts, you know."

She glanced at his bed and then stared at the towel that was covering the burned sheets. "Do you smell that?" she asked.

Nathan followed her gaze and then quickly shrugged his shoulders. "Um — smell what?" he asked.

"I don't smell anything," added Jonas. He had a blank look on his face.

Lafonda raised her eyebrows at him. She then began looking around the room. "It smells like — like something is burning," she said.

Nathan motioned for Jonas to get off his bed.

Lafonda walked over to Nathan's desk and sniffed the air. "I swear something is burning," she said.

Quickly, while she was inspecting his desk, Nathan grabbed the bed sheets and comforter that lay on the floor and made up his bed.

"Nathan," she said, turning around. "You do realize you just made up your bed with that towel still on it, right?"

"Oh," he said. He fluffed his pillows and laid them at the head of the bed. "It'll be fine." He took her by the arm and pulled out the chair from underneath his desk. "Have a seat," he said, with a forced smile. "And let's have a look at that yearbook."

She glared at him and then reluctantly sat down. She placed the IUCF yearbook on the desk and turned around to look at him. "Whatever," she said. "For your sake, I hope that towel isn't wet."

"It's fine," he said, while flipping through the yearbook. "What page is it on?"

She smirked and then slid the yearbook in front of her. "I think the freshman year photos start somewhere near the front of the book," she said.

Jonas dribbled his basketball, and they both turned around to gawk at him.

"Um, Jonas," said Nathan, while scratching his head, "do you mind taking that out into the hallway?"

Jonas stopped and looked up at Nathan with a surprised look on his face. "But you said not to bounce the ball in the hallway," he said.

Nathan paused to look at the clock. "Everyone should be up getting ready for breakfast by now," he said. "Go for it. Have at it."

"Oh, okay," Jonas said with a grin. He happily left the room, and Nathan walked over to close the door behind him.

Nathan took a quick breath and then walked back over to Lafonda. "Okay," he said. "Let's make this quick. I don't want to give the guys the wrong impression. You know, that it's okay to have women on the floor."

Lafonda shook her head and slightly chuckled.

"What?" he asked, with a frown. "You know women aren't allowed on the men's floor."

She laughed. "Nothing, Nathan," she said.

"Um, Lafonda," he protested, while staring blankly at her. "What is it?"

Lafonda laughed heartily. "It's really nothing, Nathan," she said. "It's just that … I can't imagine that anyone would think there would be anything going on between us."

He shrugged and then slowly nodded in agreement. "I guess you have a point," he uttered.

She grinned and then continued looking through the yearbook.

"But wait — hold on!" blurted Nathan in protest. "Why not?"

Lafonda rolled her eyes and then handed the open yearbook to him. "Okay, can I get you to focus?" she said. "There she is, at the bottom of the page."

Nathan took the yearbook in his hands and instantly his stomach twisted in knots. "Okay, here goes," he mumbled, "I am either crazy or not crazy."

"What?" Lafonda muttered, appearing slightly confused.

He quickly scanned the bottom row of yearbook pictures. "Um, nothing."

Nathan was deep in thought. After all this time, he was nervous about seeing Leah's picture in something tangible, something that he knew for sure was real. *What if it isn't her?* he thought to himself. *What if the person I've been dreaming about isn't real?*

Nathan finished looking at each picture in the bottom row and the row above it, but he didn't see her. He looked again, carefully pausing to look at each picture. *But she has to be real, because the blue flame was real and I know that somehow I caused that fire in my room,* he thought.

Then suddenly, there she was. He almost didn't recognize her. She had a smile across her face as if she had been photographed mid-laugh. Her mousy-brown hair was carefully done, and her rosy cheeks were flushed with life. She looked happy. It was as if he was looking at a different person, but it was Leah. It was definitely her.

Lafonda leaned back in the chair and ran her hand through her hair before gently clearing her throat. "So, did you know her?" she asked.

Nathan didn't move. He realized Lafonda had said something but his mind was racing again. "She's real," he repeated to himself. "Leah's a real person."

Nathan closed the yearbook and placed it softly on his desk. Slowly, he walked over to the foot of his bed. Without thinking about it, he plopped down, almost exposing the scorched bed sheets.

Quietly, he stared at the white brick walls to his dorm room. *Does this mean I'm like a psychic, or something?* he thought. He then examined the palms of his hands. *And if I'm not psychic, then I guess it's a safe bet that I have some type of power.*

He had a solemn look on his face. *This is great! I was just dying for a way to be even more different. Yippee! I am so excited to add more weirdness points to my outcast factor.*

Lafonda sat up in her chair and then crossed her arms. "Um, Nathan," she said, "Earth to Nathan."

"What?" he uttered, while blinking his eyes.

"Are your hands bothering you again, or something?"

"No," he said. He turned around to look at her. "My hands are fine."

"Well, you sure are acting weird," she said, relaxing back into her chair.

Nathan let out a slight chuckle. *Weird, huh?* he thought. *You don't even know the half of it.*

He clasped his hands together and then placed them against his mouth. Powers or no powers, the one thing he knew for certain was that Leah was real, and so was the blue flame that had scorched his bed. So that meant the red-hooded *Twilight: New Moon* wannabes were real too, and so were their black-hooded doppelgangers.

With his hands still clasped together against his mouth, Nathan took a deep breath and shook his head. He didn't even want to begin to think about the strange lady dressed in white, let alone her shiny silver dagger. He shook his head again. *Yup, we are definitely in danger,* he thought. *We all are.*

Lafonda sat up on her chair again, this time clapping her hands together before placing them in her lap. "Okay," she said. "So are you going to tell me if you knew Leah or not?"

He continued to stare at the wall. "Why did Jonathan Black have the yearbook?" he asked.

She scowled. "I don't know!" she said. "Something about research. Nathan, are you listening to me or, better yet, can you hear me?"

"W-what?" he slurred, shaking his head and turning to face her. "What are you complaining about?"

She opened the yearbook again. "Ugh!" she growled, while pointing at Leah's picture. "I've only asked you like a million times. Did — you — know — her?"

Nathan could see the frustration building in her face. He wanted to tell her everything about his hands, Leah, and the mysterious black dog he had seen in the forest the day Malick almost drove them off the road. But then he remembered his dreams. A cold shiver ran down his back. He remembered how helpless he'd felt as the black-hooded figure withdrew his sword, and the pain in his stomach as he'd clung to Lafonda's lifeless body.

Nathan stared intently at Leah's picture. Just to make sure, he read the list of names that ran next to the row of pictures: last row, third picture, Leah Davenport.

Tears began to swell in his eyes. "No," he said, while diverting his gaze, "I didn't know her."

Lafonda stood up, leaving the yearbook on the desk. "Jeez," she said, "you acted like I was speaking a different language, or something." She paused to fix her orange leadership shirt and then placed her foot on the wooden chair to tie her shoe. "Well, I guess I'll let you go, then," she said. "I'd better get going before my group realizes I'm gone and decides to act crazy."

"Wait, hold on," Nathan said, staring at her shoes. They weren't the gray-and-pink ones she had been wearing in his dream; they were white.

Lafonda stopped mid-walk and turned around to face him. "What?" she said.

Nathan's forehead wrinkled, and he fidgeted a little before resting his hand on the back of his neck. "Are those your only pair of sneakers?" he asked.

Casually, she looked down and then back at him. "Yes, here at camp," she said. "What? You don't like white sneakers?"

He took a deep breath and smiled. "No, no," he said. "Those are fine."

Lafonda smirked and looked down again. "Yeah, they're kinda plain, huh?"

Nathan almost fell off the edge of the bed. "No, no," he said. "In fact, they are better than fine. Those are great!"

"Well, okay then," she laughed. "Thanks, Nathan. I'll see you downstairs."

The cafeteria to Lawrence Hall was especially bright. Light from the morning sun poured in through the large floor-to-ceiling glass windows that surrounded half the room in the dining area. Nathan could almost see Lawrence Road, despite the many pine trees that lined the back of the building.

Nathan noticed most of the gang was already seated at their usual table. *But where is Jonathan Black?* he wondered. *I guess he wasn't serious about changing his behavior like he promised to Erin the night before.* "Erin is going to kill him," he chuckled.

Carefully, he left the cafeteria counter and tried not to spill his large glass of orange juice that was filled to the brim. He took a seat next to Lafonda. Angela, Alan,

Lafonda and Erin were engrossed in a conversation, and he hoped that no one would notice him. He scanned the cafeteria and caught a glimpse of Jonas joking around with Eva Marie Evans, Samantha Darding and Christina Williams.

A red cardinal landed on the branch of the tree outside the window in front of him, but Nathan hardly noticed it. His thoughts were elsewhere. He couldn't stop his mind from revisiting his recent dream about Grimm Cemetery. "Ugh," he murmured. There was a blank look on his face. *All I know for sure is that it will eventually happen,* he thought. *All of my dreams about Leah happened, so why would this one be any different?*

Nathan's stomach twisted into knots as he remembered overhearing Lafonda and Amanda talking about Leah at Lafonda's birthday party. He blinked his eyes, realizing that was the moment his life had changed forever. Checking the yearbook to confirm Leah was the person in his dreams had been his last chance at denial.

He drew a big breath and then sighed heavily, finally noticing the red cardinal in the tree outside his window as it hopped from branch to branch. The cardinal finally stopped to flutter its wings before choosing to nestle on the side of the tree that received the most sun.

Everything is changing, Nathan thought.

Nathan couldn't remember the last time he had just sat around and done nothing. Sure, this wasn't his first year at camp and he expected to have activities day and night, but this year was different. He couldn't even recall the last time he'd actually had a restful night's sleep without waking up startled by a dream. And when he wasn't asleep, his thoughts were overwhelmed with the strange things that seemed to be constantly happening to him.

He took a sip of orange juice and then stared intently

at his hands. *And now, apparently, I have blue flames that come out of my hands. This is getting way too weird.*

Nathan's vacant expression turned sad as he wished that he knew when it all would happen. A sickening feeling crept into his stomach. *I wish I knew how we all end up in a cemetery.*

The sound of laughter coming from another table interrupted his thoughts. Nathan recognized Jonas's voice and turned around to see a huge smile on the camper's face. Christina Williams had Jonas's basketball and was teasing not to give it back to him.

"Earth to Nathan?" called out a familiar voice.

Nathan turned around to find Lafonda glaring at him. He raised his eyebrows in response to her stare. "What?"

"You didn't hear me talking to you?" she said, her brown eyes scrutinizing his.

Nathan could see that Lafonda wasn't the only one at the table anticipating a response. He opened his mouth to speak and thought about answering sarcastically, but then he saw the look on her face. "Why are you looking at me like that?" he asked.

Lafonda tilted her head and her forehead wrinkled with a look of concern. "You really have been acting strange lately. Are you sure you're okay?"

"Ah, give him some slack," commented Alan. "Let him enjoy his pancakes and orange juice."

"Do you always have pancakes and orange juice for breakfast?" asked Angela.

Nathan was surprised by the question and looked down at his half-eaten plate. He hadn't realized just how often he chose pancakes for breakfast. "Yup," he said. "Pecan pancakes and orange juice — my favorite."

Lafonda pushed her empty tray from in front of her and slapped her hand down on the table. "Whatever," she moaned. "I know something is going on. He even bothered to remember to put on his leadership shirt this morning."

Alan let out a huge laugh. "I guess she has a point there," he said. "What's gotten into you?"

Nathan took a moment to look at the orange leadership shirt he was wearing and shrugged. "I don't know," he said. "It's just a shirt."

Lafonda rolled her eyes before leaning forward. "But you never wear it," she explained. "Well, at least not without coercion."

Angela ran her hand through her carefully groomed locks of blonde hair and smiled. "Well, love is in the air," she said. "Maybe he's in love?"

"Love?" laughed Lafonda. "That's doubtful."

Angela rested her chin on the back of her hand and blinked her long eyelashes playfully. "Why not?" she said. "Summer is the season of love, and I believe the summer love bug has bitten our little Jonas."

Everyone turned around to see Jonas laughing and joking around with Christina Williams. Both of them had huge smiles on their faces.

"And speaking of love," said Angela with a huge smile on her own face, "Lafonda, how's it going with the hunky Jim Darding?"

Nathan sat up in his chair and snickered. He couldn't wait to hear her response on this one.

Lafonda gave him a disapproving glare and tossed her long black hair over her shoulders. "Well," she said. "If you must know, Jim and I have decided to take a break."

"A break?" blurted Alan, instantly scooting back in his chair. "Since when? Does Jim know you two are on a break? When did this happen?"

"At her birthday party, a couple of weeks ago,"

answered Nathan, before Lafonda could respond.

"Nathan!" said Lafonda angrily.

"What?" he shrugged, while raising his eyebrows. "It's the truth."

Alan grinned. "So, that's why Jim left early the night of your birthday party."

"Alan, that's none of your business," spouted Angela. "And how do you know Jim left early? You weren't even at the party."

He smiled and held up his cell phone. "Text, darling, text," he said. "I have friends who were there."

Alan suddenly had an apologetic look on his face. "And my condolences about the dress, Lafonda. I heard it was quite smashing."

"Yeah, me too," winced Angela. "I heard about what happened to your dress."

"Okay, guys," said Erin, after slamming her glass of apple juice on the table. "I'm sure Lafonda would rather not relive that night. Isn't that right, Nathan?"

Nathan looked embarrassed and gave a forced smile.

"It's okay, guys," said Lafonda. She took a deep breath and then smiled. "Really."

Angela quickly pulled herself closer to the table. "Well, while we're on the subject of hunks," she grinned, "I wonder where that Stephen Malick is."

Alan huffed and rolled his eyes.

"Yeah," added Erin. "And I wonder where that Jonathan Black is. He said he would be here early this morning."

Lafonda sighed. "Do we really need to bring him up at breakfast today?" she asked.

Erin looked confused. "Bring up whom?" she asked.

"Isn't it obvious?" said Alan. "Who else does Angela talk about every morning?"

Angela frowned at him and then suddenly had a huge smile across her face. "There he is!" she said. Her rosy cheeks became a deeper hue. "Guys, he's coming this way."

"This conversation is getting old," griped Alan. "I'd better go before my clothes go out of style."

Angela grabbed Alan by the arm and yanked him back into his chair. "Sit down, Alan," she murmured, sounding annoyed. "It's not time to go yet."

She quickly ran her fingers through her hair and smiled. "Hi, Stephen," she said. "How are you this morning?"

Stephen Malick was wearing sunglasses and carrying a tray of breakfast food. Several girls at a nearby table giggled and grinned when he walked past them. "Good morning, ladies," he said. "And gentlemen."

Angela smiled, and her long eyelashes fluttered a few times. "Good morning, Malick," she said.

"Oh, brother," sighed Alan and Lafonda in unison.

He smiled. "Hello, Lafonda," he said. "How are you this morning?"

Lafonda spun fully around in her chair to face him. She had a smirk on her face. "Good," she responded, while crossing her legs and folding her arms. "Still wearing your sunglasses indoors?"

Malick grinned and then quickly removed his glasses. "Thanks for looking out for me," he said, with a wink. "I already ran into LaDonda out in the hallway. Got to make sure we set a good example for the kids."

Lafonda rolled her eyes.

"So, Nathan," said Malick, "LaDonda wanted me to remind you that we are all set to help Argus with the bonfires this Friday. So, north entrance again, a quarter to six?"

Nathan leaned back in his chair and raised his eyebrows. "Sure," he said. "Looking forward to it."

Malick laughed and headed towards the tables that were lined up against the glass windows. "Sure you are," he said.

Quickly, Angela spun around. "Lafonda!" she cried. "No wonder Malick doesn't want to sit with us!" She crossed her arms and pouted her lips. "Why do you have to be so mean to him?"

"Mean?" she huffed. She raised her eyebrows. "To him? Doubt it. He's the one who is mean."

Angela bounced forward in her chair. "What do you mean?" she asked. "He was nothing but nice to you right now."

"Ha!" she responded. "Yeah, right now he is, but he wasn't last night."

Angela's forehead creased. "Last night?" she said. "What happened last night?"

Lafonda placed her hands on her lap and leaned closer to Angela. "You don't remember how rude he was to me last night?" she said. "When I was talking to Jonathan? I was trying to understand the whole Cahokia myth thing, and he made it seem like I was five years old, or something."

"Oh," uttered Angela. "You mean the story about the Fallen Ones."

Lafonda folded her arms and leaned back into her chair. "Yes," she said. "Almost every question I had for Jonathan, Malick followed up with his 'it's just a myth' comment, like I was wasting his time by asking stupid questions."

Alan ran his hand through his blond hair to fix a loose strand and laughed. "I don't know which is more comical," he said, "Angela being all goo-goo eyed over

Malick, like some fourteen-year-old, or Lafonda claiming he's doing something bad to her all the time."

Both Angela and Lafonda turned to gawk at him in protest. "Whatever, Alan," huffed Angela, while rolling her eyes.

He laughed. "Now, Lafonda, before you yell at me," he said, "I don't think you were wasting time by asking stupid questions. I think the whole conversation was stupid to begin with. You were just trying to make sense of Jonathan's ridiculous story."

"Alan!" cried Angela.

"What?" he said. "You know the whole story sounded crazy; all this nonsense about pissed-off angels and parallel dimensions. Now, that was a waste of time. And Angela, don't think I forgot that you wanted to follow Jonathan into some dirty cave." He looked around and then up towards the cafeteria doors. "Where is the lunatic, anyway?"

"Jonathan is not a lunatic, Alan," Angela said firmly. "Jonathan didn't make up the story about the Fallen Ones. He was just interpreting the symbols."

"Whatever," grumbled Alan. "Symbols or no symbols, if he believes that story, he's a lunatic."

"Okay," said Erin. "Even though I have my own bone to pick with our resident archeologist, no pun intended, let's put a rest on the name calling. Jonathan may not be punctual and may be a little eccentric, but he's not a lunatic."

Alan shook his head. "Well, it's time to go anyway," he said. "Looks like Lady D is rallying up the troops."

"Lady D?" asked Angela. "Who is Lady D?"

"LaDonda," responded Alan, confidently.

"My grandmother?" laughed Lafonda.

"Yeah," said Alan. "Lady D."

Angela laughed. "Where did you get that one?" she asked.

"It's short for LaDonda," explained Alan. "Lafonda's name and her grandmother's are too close sounding to each other. It can be a bit confusing."

"Come on, Lafonda," said Angela, standing up and grabbing her tray. "Let's go share with your grandmother the new name Alan has for her."

"Whatever," he sneered. "You just wish you had thought of it."

Nathan watched as the others walked away, but remained seated at the table. He wanted to finish his orange juice before dealing with the guys on his floor.

"Come on, Nathan!" called Lafonda. "My grandmother wants us to assemble everyone and to meet her in the front lobby."

"Okay, I'm coming," he said, quickly finishing the last sip of orange juice while scarfing down another bite of pancakes. He was reluctant to pick up his tray and wished he had another moment to relax and to finish his food before running off to deal with Lafonda and the others. Nathan looked outside the window and saw the red cardinal still resting on the tree branch. He thought about his dream and the blue flame that emerged from his hand. He also thought about the blue flame that mysteriously appeared at the foot of his bed. "Did that blue flame really come from out of my hands?" he pondered. "Just so much to deal with at once."

He turned to look at Lafonda and still felt relief to see her wearing white sneakers. *I just wish I knew when this will all happen,* he thought again.

Nathan sighed. He picked up his tray and paused to look at the cardinal one last time, but it was gone.

CHAPTER ELEVEN

TWO THINGS FOR CERTAIN

It was Friday: the end of the day and the end of the second week at camp. Nathan waited for Malick at the north entrance to Lake Charleston. He was a little early arriving at the entrance this time, but he didn't mind it. He was looking forward to having a break from the guys on his floor. He wasn't, however, looking forward to preparing fire pits for the night's bonfire with Stephen Malick. But he figured that although he had to hang out with Malick and perform manual labor, at least he was outdoors.

A gust of wind passed him, and Nathan let his mind wander aimlessly. He stared at the large and small trees that lined the north entrance and Lawrence Road. Leaning against the forest preserve sign, he tried to block out the sound of the few cars that drove by and tune into the silence of the forest. He tried to welcome the silence but couldn't. The same thoughts that had plagued him all week began to replay in his mind like a broken record.

Nathan had spent most of the week thinking about Lafonda and the others and how he could possibly prevent his recent nightmare starring the mysterious woman in white from coming true. All he could do was to keep a watchful eye on Lafonda's tennis shoes. He would occasionally compliment Lafonda on her shoes of choice, hoping to deter her from buying a new pair. He figured that knowing Lafonda and her love for clothing and everything stylish and modern, it was only a matter of time before she traded up. To prevent the gray-and-pink sneakers from appearing on her feet, he would try everything possible to convince her that white shoes was the way to go.

Although he cringed at the thought of it, Nathan had hoped to revisit Grimm Cemetery again in his dreams. He thought if he had the same dream again, maybe he could learn something he hadn't seen the first time. Maybe there was something he had missed that could help to prevent the dream from happening. Unlike the many dreams he'd had before about Leah, nothing happened. In fact, all week Nathan couldn't remember dreaming about anything. His dreams were just as absent as a solution.

He began to doubt whether or not it was even a dream to begin with, because everything seemed so real. Unlike before, with his dreams about Leah, Nathan had felt like he was actually there. The only thing he knew for certain, the only conclusion he kept coming to over and over, was that the blue flame in his room was real and so was Leah.

Everything happening felt so real, especially for Leah; so real that she was committed to a mental hospital because of it. When he wasn't thinking about his dream at Grimm Cemetery and how to prevent it, he was thinking about Leah. He wondered how she was doing.

Nathan often wished he had at least one trusted person to talk to, one person to whom he could tell everything. He wished he had someone to share the burden of what was happening to him and what he knew, but then he would remember Leah. She had no one to talk to, no one she could trust because no one believed her.

"Hey!" called out a familiar voice.

Quickly, Nathan stood up straight and turned around just in time to see Stephen Malick crossing Lawrence Road.

"Somebody's early," Malick smirked.

Nathan was so deep in thought that he was caught off guard by Malick's remark.

They both stood in silence, and then Malick ran his hand backwards through his hair. "Okay?" he laughed.

"Okay what?" asked Nathan.

Malick shook his head and then proceeded down the path. "Nothing, sir," he laughed again.

"Okay," Nathan sighed, following behind him. "Whatever."

The trail leading to Lake Charleston was still a little moist from the previous night's rainfall. Nathan was glad that he was wearing his hiking boots instead of his tennis shoes. Last time he wore his tennis shoes to the lake, they got so dirty with his filling the wood bin that he'd considered throwing them away. Regardless of the reason for being out there, Nathan enjoyed being outside and in the forest.

Malick continued to walk ahead of him and would occasionally turn around and laugh.

"What?" asked Nathan.

"Nothing," he snickered.

He frowned. *I am not in the mood for this today. Next time, I'll just volunteer to start the fires alone.*

Malick laughed again, this time turning to shake his head at him.

"All right," grumbled Nathan. "What the heck is it?"

Malick stopped walking down the trail and turned around to face him. They had stopped at the fork in the trail that led to the Northern Cahokia Tribal Museum and the cliffs overlooking Lake Charleston. He grinned. "I don't know what you're talking about."

Nathan could feel his ears turning red. "What? Why the heck do you keep laughing and looking at me?"

Malick laughed heartily.

"Okay," said Nathan angrily, as he stormed past Malick.

Malick smiled and grabbed him by the shoulder, stopping him from continuing down the path.

"All right, all right," Malick said. "You really need to lighten up."

Nathan turned around to face him. "Lighten up?" he asked, angrily. "You want me to — lighten up?" His thoughts began to ramble in his head. *This guy has no clue what I am dealing with.*

Malick smiled wide. "Yes," he said. "Have some fun for a change and don't be so serious."

Nathan shook his head angrily. "Yes," he said. "Have fun and be cool like Stephen Malick. No need to worry about anything because I don't have a care in the world."

Malick responded with a laugh, and Nathan's ears and face grew hotter and hotter. He gritted his teeth.

"Okay, okay," Malick said, grabbing him by the arm again. "Calm down for a second. I apologize for poking fun at you."

Nathan took a deep breath. "What do you want?"

Malick smiled. "It's obvious that, aside from your normal brooding self, something is bothering you."

Nathan's jaw fell open. "Brooding?" he protested. "I don't brood. I'm overly sarcastic, maybe, but never brooding."

"Okay, okay. Fair enough," Malick chuckled. "Can we at least agree that something is definitely bothering you?"

Nathan sighed again. "Where are we going with this?" he asked.

Malick's smile faded away. He had a concerned look on his face. "I've noticed over the past two weeks that you've gotten quieter and quieter," he said.

"What do you mean?"

"Not that I am complaining," Malick said, "but there has definitely been a retreat in the remarks and cynicism from your peanut gallery."

Nathan was surprised and tried to hide his smile. "And?" he asked, while trying to keep his poker face.

"And," continued Malick, "you are definitely worrying about something, definitely overanalyzing more than usual."

Nathan looked intently at Malick and blinked his eyes. *He's right,* he thought.

He definitely was worried about something and probably was acting a little different, but who wouldn't be different considering everything that was happening to him? More than anything, he was surprised that Stephen Malick, of all people, had even noticed.

Malick waved his hand and gestured his head in the direction of the trail leading away from Lake Charleston. "Come on," he said.

Nathan was confused. "Come on what?"

"Come on and follow me," he said.

"Follow you? We don't have time for this. Besides, the last time I checked, Argus was expecting us."

"Come on," Malick whined. "We have time."

Nathan checked the time on his cell phone. "Barely," he said.

Malick smiled and nudged him up the trail.

The trail to the Northern Cahokia Tribal Museum was narrow. The museum was located near the base of the cliffs, so the trail led upward. Nathan wasn't as familiar with this part of the trail. He was a lot more familiar with the one that led from Lawrence Road to Lake Charleston. He followed close behind Malick and thought about Leah again and then about Lafonda. He cringed when the black-hooded figure with the silver sword popped up in his head again. Up ahead, the trees surrounding the trail were thinning out and he saw the museum's paved parking lot.

Once out of the forest, Nathan attempted to scrape the mud from the bottom of his shoes. He had been to the museum many times before on school field trips, but he couldn't remember ever using the connecting trail to get there. Most people accessed the museum parking lot from Lawrence Road.

He watched as Malick paced happily towards the museum.

LaDonda had given a large contribution for the construction of the museum years ago, and Nathan thought that explained why the outside resembled a downsized version of the Devaro Mansion. The two-story building, though small, housed many rare Cahokia Indian artifacts and information collected about the Northern Cahokia tribe that had once populated the area.

"What are we doing here again?" he asked.

Malick's eyes were wide and his arms stretched open. "Look at that view!" he shouted. "You can really see how amazing the cliffs are, now that we are closer. I can't wait till we're at the top."

Nathan's mouth fell open. "The top?" he blurted, while staring across the parking lot to the connecting trail. "You said nothing about tracking all the way up to the top." *Come to think of it,* he thought, *he didn't say anything to begin with. Why am I following him, anyway?*

"Come on," smiled Malick.

Nathan checked his cell phone again. "We don't have time!"

Malick glanced over his shoulder and smiled one last time before disappearing into the forest.

The trees rustled and a light breeze of air rushed through, cooling Nathan's face. Being that it was evening, the museum was closed and the parking lot was completely empty. Nathan checked the time on his cell phone again and considered heading back without Malick. "We have stuff to do!" he protested to himself. He stared at the entrance to the cliffs and another breeze rushed over him.

"Those breezes feel more amazing from the top!" shouted Malick from the forest.

Nathan glanced up to the top of the cliffs. "Ugh," he moaned. "I know I will regret this, but ... I'm coming!"

The trail leading from the parking lot up to the cliffs was much wider and wood chipped, so the path was a lot less muddy. Nathan thought this was probably because the museum gave guided tours to the top and to the surrounding Cahokia Caves.

Malick continued briskly along the trail and occasionally turned around to smile. Nathan didn't mind the distance, and after a few minutes could see something yellow blowing in the wind ahead of him. When he got closer, he saw that two trees next to the entrance to the trail that led downward to the caves behind the cliffs had yellow ribbons tied around them. In the ground, blocking the entrance to the trail, were two metal poles, one on either side, with a thick, rusty metal chain running the length between them.

From the middle of the chain hung a red-and-white sign that read:

Closed
Please Do Not Disturb
Archeological Investigation in Progress until August
Trespassers Will Be Prosecuted

Nathan looked down the path between the two yellow-ribboned trees and then glanced upward to see if Malick had noticed he had stopped. "So, this is where Jonathan spends all of his time," he laughed.

Nathan had only visited the caves during school field trips to the museum when he was younger. He didn't remember much about them, just that they were located down the trail and behind the cliffs. Now that he was older, he had no desire to come this far into the forest or to visit the top of the cliffs. He would rather avoid the hike altogether and just hang out by the lake.

Nathan read the sign again and then stood on the tips of his toes to see farther down the trail. "I don't see anything exciting, especially not anything deserving of a Do Not Disturb sign." He returned to standing flat on his feet. "Jonathan did say all the hoopla was about the new cave symbols."

"Hey!" said Malick, approaching from behind. "Are you going to stare at that sign all day?

Nathan jumped. "Dude," he shouted, "you startled me!"

"Sorry; I didn't mean to," chuckled Malick, while pointing at the sign. He gawked at it and laughed. "I'm sure that'll keep out the college students." He gestured with his head and pointed his thumb in the direction of the cliffs. "Are you coming, or what?" he asked. "I'm sure you'll find nothing exciting over there."

Soon, the trail to the top of the cliffs became a straight path upward, and the trees on both sides of the trail began to thin out. Nathan followed Malick out of the forest and stood at the top of the cliffs. A gentle breeze of cool air greeted them as the evening sun set behind them. Nathan looked down at the beach and fire pits below and noticed the beach created a half circle around the lake. In front of him, beyond the beach and the large hill, he could see the roof of the Hiking and Camping Center. Beyond that, all he could see were the tops of the many trees that seemed to stretch out towards the horizon. Eager, he stood on the tips of his toes, trying to catch a glimpse of the Cahokia Falls, which he was sure were nestled somewhere off in that direction. A gentle breeze nudged him again. On his right, beyond the trees, was Lawrence Hall, its skyline revealing only a partial view of the IUCF campus.

"Is that the Cahokia Museum?" asked Malick, standing close to the cliff's edge.

Slowly, Nathan inched towards him. "Yup," he uttered, while hesitantly peering over. "That's it." He raised his eyebrows and then quickly took a few steps back. "And you might not want to be so close to the edge."

Malick turned around only to find Nathan grinning while pointing to the red-and-white sign that had "Danger: Cliff Edge" written on it. Malick shook his head and then pretended to prepare for jumping off the cliff.

"Ha-ha," sighed Nathan. "Funny."

Malick grinned. "Hey," he said, "is that Argus down there?" He ran his hand through his hair as he squinted. "Why does he keep pacing like that?"

Quickly, Nathan stepped beside him. "Argus?" he

asked, while carefully peering over. He pulled out his cell phone from his pocket. "He's probably pacing because he is waiting on us!"

Malick took a deep breath and looked up at the sky before placing a hand on Nathan's shoulder. "Oh, relax," he said. "It will be fine. Just enjoy the view."

Nathan took a quick look at the darkening blue sky and glanced at his cell phone again before placing it back into his pocket. "But we are —"

"Enjoy the view, already!" interrupted Malick with a sigh.

Nathan gave Malick a glaring look and huffed. He took a deep breath and tried hard not to think about Argus, closing his eyes for a moment before slowly looking out into the evening sky again. The trees were calm, disturbed only occasionally by the summer breeze. The lights on campus and from Lawrence Hall were becoming more visible as the sky grew darker. Below, a gold light appeared, and upon close inspection, Nathan could see that it was a street lamp revealing the black asphalt to the Cahokia Museum parking lot. "The view is nice," said Nathan with a shrug. "But we are late and should go."

Malick shook his head and looked down at his feet before turning around to walk away.

Nathan sighed. "Now what?" he said.

A gust of wind swept over the cliffs displacing strands of Malick's hair. Abruptly, Malick stopped and turned around to face him.

Nathan had a surprised look on his face. He thought it must be serious since Malick hadn't bothered to fix his hair.

"Just nice?" asked Malick. A deep crease formed on his forehead. "The view is amazing; not just nice!"

Nathan diverted his eyes away from him and focused on the entrance to the forest behind them. He couldn't believe Malick was making such a big deal about the view. "Okay, okay," he said. "The view is amazing." He took a few steps towards the entrance to the forest. "Can we go now?"

The wrinkle on Malick's forehead deepened. "Sure," he groaned. "I don't know why I bothered to help you anyway."

"Help me?" cried Nathan. He had a confused look on his face. "How are you helping me?"

"You're never in the moment," complained Malick. "You worry too much!"

Nathan's ears burned red. "What?"

Malick paused and drew a deep breath. His eyes connected with Nathan's and the wrinkles on his forehead relaxed. "You don't realize how great the view is because you don't let life happen," he said. "You should be living in the now — not the past, not the future."

Nathan shook his head and huffed. "Look," he said, "you don't know anything about my life and I don't need any help — especially not from you."

Malick raised his eyebrows again, bringing the creases in his forehead back to life. "And what do you mean by that?" he asked.

Nathan sighed. "Look," he said, "I don't expect someone like you to understand anything about being me."

Malick glared. "And ... what exactly do you mean by that?"

Nathan huffed. "No offense, but how could you?" he asked. "You have never been poor in your life. You have no clue what it means to be me. Maybe you can float through life without a care in the world, but I don't have that luxury. I am just the poor brown kid living behind the Devaro Mansion."

"That is where you are wrong!" explained Malick. "That may be your past or current situation, but it doesn't have to be your future." He pointed towards the ground. "You should be living for today," he said. "Living in this moment, because what you do today is your tomorrow."

"I am living in the moment, Dr. Phil!" Nathan retorted. "And in this moment we are late and Argus is waiting on us."

Malick nodded and the creases in his forehead were gone now. "Okay," he said.

Nathan and Malick walked back in silence. The sun had set, so it was dark now, and the trees made the forest even darker. The wind picked up and occasionally howled through the trees, providing them with frequent nudges down the trail. Nathan knew they were about halfway to the Cahokia Museum parking lot after catching a glimpse of the yellow ribbons floating in the wind.

He folded his arms across his chest and looked down, trying to create a little walking distance between himself and Malick. *So, what was the point for coming all the way up here?* he thought. *Did he really think he was helping me to relax and to not worry so much?*

Nathan glanced up at him and then allowed his gaze to wander into the forest. About one thing Malick had been right: his mind was definitely occupied lately.

Nathan knew exactly what he was worried about. He was really concerned about the dream he had had about Grimm Cemetery, particularly the part about the faceless hooded figures and the strange woman in white hurting Leah and his friends. But what was he supposed to say to Malick? More than anything, he wanted to tell someone. But Malick?

He glanced back at Malick. But why not Malick? Despite his failed attempt to cheer Nathan up, he had been the only one besides Lafonda to notice or care enough to say something to him about his change in behavior. But what would Nathan say, anyway, to him or anybody?

Nathan thought about how the conversation would go in his mind. *Yeah, uh, I think I am having dreams about the future and I am pretty sure I dreamed about this girl Leah being attacked the night she was admitted to the hospital. And now I think Lafonda may die. And I have blue flames coming out of my hands.* He chuckled. *Oh, and if I haven't lost you yet — and you don't think I'm crazy — I kinda communicated with this dog the other day. I saw it running in the forest, and I think it saved my life.*

It sounded ridiculous. Nevertheless, he figured he would at least say something to Malick after they entered the trail back to the lake. "So," he said, breaking the silence, "do you think we'll have enough time to set the fires before the others show up?"

Malick looked over his shoulder and grinned. "Oh," he said. "Are you talking to me?"

Nathan smiled. "Ha-ha," he said. "Very funny."

Malick grinned again. "Trust me. We'll make it."

"I don't know if I like the sound of that," replied Nathan.

Nathan and Malick stepped out of the forest and onto the beach of Lake Charleston. The cool breeze that was felt atop the cliffs still accompanied them and continued to provide a welcome relief. Nathan didn't stare as he normally did on first sight of the water.

"Where is Argus?" he said with a touch of panic. "We have to get these fires going."

"Relax," said Malick. "We still have time. I'm sure

Argus just went back up to the Hiking and Camping Center."

"You hope," responded Nathan. "How are we supposed to start the fires without lighter fluid?" He pulled out his cell phone and the light from the LCD screen illuminated his face. "They will be here any minute."

"Okay, okay," said Malick. "I'm sure there has to be some lighter fluid around here somewhere."

"Not likely," said Nathan. "Based on Argus's reaction last time, I wouldn't expect to find anything flammable, let alone lighter fluid, lying around here."

Malick stopped searching around the fire pits and paused to look up at Nathan. "Good point," he said.

Nathan checked his cell phone for the time again and then placed it back into his pocket. "Okay," he said. "So, what are we going to do?"

"Why don't you check up at the Hiking and Camping Center?" Malick pointed to the top of the hill. "See," he said, "a light is on. Argus has to be up there, and I'm sure he has some lighter fluid waiting for us."

Nathan frowned thinking it was just like Malick to volunteer someone else to do the dirty work. He started towards the hill. "Sure, sure," he said.

By the time Nathan had reached the hill the sun had already set, so the path was difficult to see. He hadn't realized how dark it got out there. Although the Devaro Mansion was located in the rural part of town, Nathan had always had at least a flashlight.

After a few tries, he eventually found the path and made his way up the hill. The walk up wasn't that high, but Nathan didn't appreciate the steep climb. "Ouch!" he yelled. He had bumped into something in the darkness. "What the heck," he grumbled, reaching out to feel what was in front of him. "What is that?" he groaned. "Is that a handle?"

He rubbed his knee. "That's going to leave a bruise. Who would do something like this?" He used the light from his cell phone and saw a red, rusty wheelbarrow in the middle of the trail in front of him. "Argus," he moaned. "I promise you, that man is just as bad as Jonas."

Nathan grabbed the handles and proceeded down the trail. In the barrel he noticed there was a bottle of lighter fluid. "The things I have to deal with," he griped to himself. "If it isn't happy-go-lucky Jonas or bad-boy Malick, then it's welcome-to-hippyland Argus."

Nathan didn't make it too far down the hill before he noticed a glow from the lake. "What?" he blurted. He smelled the burning of fresh wood. "Talk about déjà vu," he said. In front of him were twelve bonfires, all flickering heartily with life.

Nathan left the wheelbarrow on the spot and grabbed the bottle of lighter fluid. He jammed the small bottle in the back of his pants and headed towards a grinning Stephen Malick.

"Ta-da!" shouted Malick. "I told you we still had time."

Nathan's eyebrows were raised. "Okay," he said. "And I am just going to pretend that you didn't just send me away, so that you could magically produce twelve fires."

Malick had a blank look on his face. "I don't know what you're talking about," he said. "After you left, I found the lighter fluid bottle Argus must have left for us and presto chango, twelve fires."

Nathan shook his head and frowned. "You mean this bottle?"

"Uh — where did you get that one?" stuttered Malick.

He had a nervous grin on his face.

"From the wheelbarrow that Argus left for us," he said, folding his arms across his chest.

"Hey, Nathan!" called a familiar voice.

He turned around to see Lafonda, Jonas and the other campers from his floor approaching from behind him.

"Good job with the fires again," she said. She paused and glared at Malick. "Oh — and you too."

Malick hesitated. "Thanks," he said with another nervous grin.

"Hi, Nathan!" called another familiar voice.

This time, he turned around to find an overly energetic bunch: Angela and Alan with their group of campers.

"I agree. Nice job," Angela said. She tossed her long, shiny blond hair over her shoulders and winked longingly at Malick. "And you too, handsome."

"Do you have to flirt with him every day?" grumbled Alan. He rolled his eyes in protest. "My goodness."

Angela, Alan, Lafonda and the others continued to walk past Nathan and Malick, towards the fires.

"Shut up, Alan," Angela whispered underneath her breath.

Nathan continued to stare at Malick, and his eyes were wide.

"So, are you going to tell me, or what?" Nathan demanded. "And don't bother saying you don't know what I'm talking about."

The look on Malick's face softened and Nathan caught a glimpse of someone waving from the corner of his eye. It was LaDonda. She was walking with several campers who were carrying a table.

"Yoohoo! Stephen!" she called. "Can you please help us over here?"

"Hey, Malick!" shouted Alan. He was seated with the

others by one of the fires. "I think Lady D is trying to get your attention."

"Don't be mean to him," complained Angela.

Malick waved. "I'll be right there, Mrs. Devaro," he said. He opened his mouth to speak, but hesitated. "Nathan — I can't."

"Why the heck not?" blurted Nathan.

He shrugged. "I'm sorry, bro," he said, while walking away. He had a sympathetic look on his face. "I just can't. It's complicated."

Nathan tossed the lighter fluid bottle into the wheelbarrow and pushed it off to one side. Reluctantly, he headed over to the others. He took a seat next to Lafonda, who was having a conversation with Erin, and stared into the fire. He wondered how Malick could have started those fires — and so fast.

He glanced over at Malick. It looked like LaDonda was giving him instructions on how to set up the table he was carrying. "I know there wasn't any lighter fluid lying around either," Nathan muttered. "Is it possible? Yes, but highly unlikely."

He continued his gaze back into the fire. The voices of the others were becoming secondary to his thoughts. *And where did he find the matches? I would have to check, but I don't even think Argus left matches.*

Nathan heard his name and turned to find Lafonda smiling at him.

"What's up?" she said. "You've been really quiet lately."

Nathan gave a half smile, though he had a somber look on his face. "Nothing," he said. "Everything is fine."

Lafonda's eyes scrutinized his. "Okay, then," she said. "Fine. Don't tell me."

He let out a light chuckle. "It's nothing," he said.

"Really."

"So, there is something," she said.

He sighed. "So, any news on how your friend is doing?"

Lafonda looked confused.

"You know," he said, "your friend in the hospital — Leah."

Lafonda shook her head. "I guess I'm supposed to pretend that you're not changing the subject," she said. She paused for a moment before continuing. "I haven't heard anything, really. I tried her cell, but it goes straight to voicemail." She had a sad look on her face. "If I don't hear back from her soon, I'll try her parents."

"I hope she's okay," said Nathan.

Lafonda frowned. She folded her arms across her chest and crossed her legs. Nathan could see that her right leg bounced impatiently. *Oh, boy*, he thought to himself. *Here it comes.*

"Okay," snapped Lafonda. "Something is definitely up with you."

He stared blankly at her.

"And don't give me that look! You are definitely acting different." She gestured to count on her fingers. "First," she said, "magically, you decided to start wearing your leadership shirt, which I know you hate." Lafonda paused with a surprised look on her face. "And second, you're being nice. When did you become so thoughtful and caring?"

Nathan smiled modestly. He really wasn't trying to be different or nice or caring. The only thing that was different was that he knew their lives were in danger, and because of that, every second counted. He hesitated. "I guess," he said, "I guess it's just that — I appreciate things more now."

Lafonda's mouth fell open; she was speechless.

He sighed. "Okay, you can close your mouth now. I do have a heart and I am human — sometimes."

She happily placed her arm around his shoulder and grinned. "Yes," she said. "Sometimes."

Nathan smiled back.

"Speaking of hearts," whispered Angela, her blue eyes wide and full of life, "I think Sam has a crush on you."

"Who — what?" he stammered. Nathan felt his face turning red. "Samantha?"

He looked up and caught a glimpse of Samantha Darding staring at him from across the fire. She quickly broke her gaze, and Christina and Eva Marie laughed through stifled giggles. Samantha looked embarrassed, but eventually looked back and smiled at him.

"Yup," said Angela. "I peeped it this morning at breakfast." She paused to gaze longingly into the fire. "Isn't it wonderful?" she said. "Young love."

"Oh, brother," huffed Alan. "You sound ridiculous."

Suddenly, she sat up straight and ran her fingers through her hair. "Speaking of love," she said, while rolling her eyes at Alan. "Hi, Malick, I saved a seat for you.

Malick raised his eyebrows and gave a reluctant smile before sitting down. He shot a quick look to Nathan, but Nathan turned his head. Lafonda followed his lead and also looked away.

"We're all happy that you could join us," said Angela. She looked around the fire and noticed the disconcerted faces. "Isn't that right, Nathan?"

"Sure, sure," he responded, barely looking up.

Angela looked like she was going to say something, but after looking at Lafonda's and Alan's faces, decided to sigh in defeat, instead.

"Well, look who decided to show up!" shouted Erin. She had a cross look on her face. Everyone turned to follow Erin's gaze, and there was Jonathan Black heading in their direction.

"I thought you guys had a talk," said Lafonda.

Erin folded her arms across her chest and pouted. "Yeah," she said. "That was about it; all talk." She rolled her eyes. "Obviously, Mr. Indiana here doesn't have a watch or is too smart to understand the concept of time."

"Oh," said Lafonda, diverting her eyes.

"Hello, everyone," said Jonathan. He yawned and rubbed his eyes. "Sorry I'm late," he said, looking straight at Erin. He had an apologetic look on his face. "As usual, I got caught up with my research and lost track of time."

Angela perked up, and her blue eyes sparkled. "Hey," she said, "maybe Erin could call you or send you a text message, so you won't be late."

Erin loudly cleared her throat and gave Angela a cold look. Angela quickly slouched down and mouthed the words *I'm sorry* to her.

Erin uncrossed her arms. "All right," she said. "I know you are dying to tell us: what did you find out?"

Jonathan took a seat next to Erin and then stared suspiciously at Malick. "Yes," he said. "I took Angela's advice and did some research on the Internet."

Angela perked up again. "See," she said, turning to gawk at Alan. She then turned to face Jonathan. "Did you learn anything interesting about those studly male angels?" She suddenly glanced down, and her face had turned red. "I mean, the good ones, of course."

Jonathan paused for a moment, as if he was thinking about something, and then spoke to Angela. "Good or bad," he said, "in the Bible, a union between an angel and a mortal woman was an unforgivable sin and was the catalyst for the great flood."

"Oh," she responded. Angela looked embarrassed again.

Alan laughed heartily. "Don't go causing any floods, Angela," he chuckled, "because I'm not dressed for it!"

"Oh, be quiet, Alan!" she barked in frustration.

"What about the cave wall?" asked Lafonda. "And the secret chamber?"

He turned to look at Malick again. "Nothing yet," he said. "We just started excavating with the new equipment Dr. Helmsley borrowed from a neighboring university. But in the meantime, I am finding some really interesting information on the Internet."

"Well," said Malick, interrupting Jonathan, "I'm sure you won't bother us with anything that isn't conclusive."

"Don't worry," said Jonathan. "When I am done, there will be no codswallop, and everyone will want to hear what I have to say."

"Codswallop?" asked Angela.

"Oh, I'm sorry," responded Jonathan. "In other words, no baloney."

CHAPTER TWELVE

THE SPACE BETWEEN

The elevator to the eighth floor opened, and Nathan quickly got out. He took a huge breath and waved his hand a few times in front of his nose. "Whew!" he said. "You guys definitely need to hit the showers before you go to bed."

Jonas stepped out of the elevator first, followed by Andy and Hugo. Andy tried to take the basketball from Jonas before hopping up on the common room table. The table almost toppled over, but luckily for him, Hugo had climbed up to sit on the opposite side.

Andy smiled wide and laughed. He paused to take a whiff of his underarm. "Dude," he said, "we don't smell that bad."

Nathan turned around to look at him and laughed. Andy's face was covered with sweat, and his red hair was wet and spiky. His nose also was a bright red.

"You look like a clown," Nathan chuckled. "And you are definitely a comedian if you expect me to believe that one."

Hugo leaned in to take a whiff of Andy. "Dude!" he shouted. "You do smell!"

Andy laughed. "Whatever, man," he said. "I could

179

smell you in the elevator, and it wasn't nice."

Hugo playfully swung his long, beefy arm at Andy, almost knocking him off the table.

"Hey!" Hugo groaned. "That wasn't me; that was Jonas." He grinned, revealing big, horselike teeth. "Unlike him, I actually use deodorant."

Jonas glowered and placed his basketball underneath his arm. His shaggy, curly hair was drenched with sweat. Jonas smiled big. "Hey!" he said. "Christina doesn't have a problem with it."

Andy quickly hopped off the table, and Hugo barely prevented himself and the table from falling over.

"Whoa-ho-ho," yelled Andy. "He's got a point there, big guy." Andy paused to lean against the wall to scratch his back. "And unless Jonas royally screws up," he said, "he has a for-sure date to the banquet."

Jonas continued to dribble his basketball, but he had a confused look on his face. "Uh, banquet?" he uttered.

"You know," said Andy, while raising his eyebrows. "The banquet on the last day of camp."

"Oh," he said, before starting to dribble again.

Andy shook his head at Jonas and laughed heartily.

"How are you guys taking dates to the banquet when your parents will be there?" asked Nathan.

Andy raised his eyebrows again, and his eyes were wide. "Duh," he said. "You have to dance with somebody." He playfully elbowed Hugo in the stomach. "And in Hugo's case, that's nobody."

"Grr!" growled Hugo. "Who are you taking, then?"

Andy paused before speaking. He looked proud of himself. "It's a done deal," he said. "I'm taking Samantha Darding."

Nathan grinned and tried to hold back his snicker.

Hugo's face contorted, and Jonas instantly stopped

playing basketball.

"In your dreams!" laughed Hugo. "If Sam is going to dance with anybody, it's going to be me."

Suddenly, the bell to the elevator rang, and to everyone's surprise — except Nathan's — out stepped Lafonda.

"All right, guys," said Nathan. "Enough messing around. And hit the showers."

"Saved by the bell," sneered Hugo. He proceeded down the hallway to his dorm room and shouted, "Girl on the floor!"

"Hi, Lafonda," said Andy, with a huge grin.

Lafonda responded. "Hello, Andy."

"Okay," said Nathan. "Good night, Andy." He gave Andy a slight nudge. "Go get your shower, and you too, Jonas."

Andy smiled again at Lafonda, and Nathan noticed that Andy's cheeks matched the color of his hair as he walked away.

"That guy," she mumbled.

Nathan chuckled. "So, what's up? What brings you up here tonight?"

"Nathan," she smiled, "I stop by practically every night."

He laughed. "Yeah, I noticed."

Lafonda protested halfheartedly and smiled. "Would you rather I came back after you've showered?" she said.

"Are you implying that I smell?" he chuckled.

Lafonda grinned. "Not exactly," she said, "but you did just spend the evening outdoors; not to mention preparing the bonfire."

"Whatever," he said, while taking a whiff of his underarm. He smiled and then gave her an ornery look. "You won't be visiting long tonight, anyway."

Lafonda smiled. "You are correct," she said. "I can't stay away too long from the girls." She took a seat atop one of the common room tables. "Unlike your guys, the girls on my floor can take a shower without my direction."

He smiled wide and sat in the chair that was closest to the table.

She took a deep breath and looked around the room. "You know," she said. "It's always strange for me to see you up here."

Nathan looked confused. "Why? What do you mean?"

Lafonda glanced down and gently twirled her gold locket between her fingers. "It's nothing, really," she said. "I'm just used to seeing Leah and Amanda when I come up here."

"What?" he asked abruptly. "Why would they be up here?"

She looked up and blinked a few times before speaking. "What?" she asked, appearing slightly befuddled. "I know you never came over to visit me, but you know I stayed in Lawrence Hall last year."

Nathan slowly raised his eyebrows. "Yeah," he said. "And ..."

"And," she continued, "Leah, Amanda and I lived on this floor."

His mouth fell open. "You never told me you stayed on this floor, Lafonda."

"Oh," she said, pausing to lean back on the table. "It's not a big deal. I thought you knew."

"Well, it's a big deal to me," he said.

She sat up straight again and shrugged. "I don't understand why it would be such a big deal to you."

I don't know. Maybe it has something to do with the fact that I've only been dreaming and thinking about Leah constantly for almost two months now, he thought.

There was confusion in her face, and he knew the only remedy was to confess everything, but he decided not to. "You are right, Lafonda," he said. "It's not a big deal."

She paused and her eyes looked into his. "You are hiding something again, Mr. Nathan," she said.

He tried to appear innocent. "What do you mean?"

She tossed her long black hair behind her shoulders. "I am going to go along with it this time," she said. "But in all these years, I've never heard you tell me I was right about anything without an argument first."

Nathan smiled wearily and shrugged. "I guess there is a first time for everything," he chuckled.

"Yeah," she added, pointing at him. "Like you deciding to wear your orange leadership shirt."

He laughed nervously. "I guess so …"

"Anyhoo," she said with a laugh, "you are actually staying in Amanda's old room, and Jonas is staying in Leah's room, and Andy is staying in mine."

"Amanda's old room?" he asked.

Lafonda glanced down and twirled her locket again. "Yes," she said solemnly. "Amanda became Leah's roommate after Jamie died."

"Oh." Nathan looked confused. "Who is Jamie?"

She quickly looked up with a surprised look on her face. "You don't know?" she asked. "It was all over campus and in the news."

Nathan raised his eyebrows and shrugged.

"A story about it even appeared in our yearbook," she continued, still sounding surprised. "It was a memorial piece."

"Sorry," he said, with remorseful eyes.

Lafonda shook her head. "You know," she said, "you really have this escape-into-your-own-world thing down pat."

"Can you just continue with the story?"

She rolled her eyes before continuing. "Jamie's body was found outside Grimm Cemetery at the end of our first semester, last year," she said.

Andy stepped out of his room, and Lafonda lowered her voice. Andy had a towel in his hand and looked like he was headed for the shower.

"From what I remember," she said. "Leah and Jamie went to a party, and Leah left the party early without Jamie. Leah said she came back to the dorm room and fell asleep — and didn't realize Jamie was missing until morning."

She leaned towards Nathan and whispered, "I think they asked Leah to identify the body." Her voice grew thin and she looked sad. "Leah said there were deep wounds and scratches on her arms and legs. She was really shaken up about it, and I think she blamed herself — that's probably why she was having nightmares."

"Nightmares?" he asked.

"Practically everyone on the floor knew. We would often hear Leah screaming in the middle of the night." Lafonda clenched her chest. "Some nights her screams would be so bloodcurdling."

"That's awful!" he said.

"Yeah. And unfortunately, sometimes she would get teased by the girls on our floor."

"That's messed up," said Nathan. "Why would you tease someone who's been through something like that?"

Lafonda shook her head. "I don't know, Nathan. I wanted to help Leah as much as I could, but she rarely talked about it."

Bam, bam, bam!

Nathan and Lafonda looked up to see Jonas dribbling

his basketball with only a towel wrapped around his waist.

Nathan shook his head and stood up from his chair. "Jonas," he called, "it's late. Can you give it a rest?"

Jonas looked up, placed his basketball under his arm, and quickly secured his falling towel.

Lafonda diverted her eyes and hopped off the table. "On that note," she said, "I'm leaving."

Nathan laughed.

She stood in front of the elevator and pressed the down button. "Good night, Nathan," she said, cheerfully. "See you in the morning!"

The doors opened and she stepped into the elevator. "Oh, and good night, Jonas," she added. She gave him a quick wink and a thumbs-up. "Good catch grabbing that towel."

Jonas raised his hand to wave good-bye, but quickly had to secure his towel again.

Nathan looked at the puddle of water that was accumulating at the base of Jonas's feet. "You are a mess," he said. He took the basketball from underneath Jonas's arm. "Can you do me a favor?"

"Sure," he said.

Nathan grinned and said slowly, "Go — to — bed."

"Oh, okay," said Jonas.

Nathan sighed heavily and walked into his room.

Later, after his shower, he lay in bed staring at the ceiling. He thought about what Lafonda had said about Leah and her roommate Jamie. *It had to be tough dealing with all of that. And to top things off, she was having nightmares and having to defend herself from those monsters,* he thought.

He turned over to his side and stared at the clock. It was getting late and he couldn't fall asleep. "I still don't know what those creatures were that I saw attacking her. And they were nowhere to be found during my last dream about Grimm Cemetery," he said.

Nathan shivered. Just the thought of Grimm Cemetery and what might come frightened him. There was a knock on the door, and he jumped and glanced at the clock again. *Who in the world could that be?* he wondered.

He then heard someone say his name in a low whisper. Nathan shook his head. "Jonas," he said to himself. He shoved his feet into his shoes and opened the door. "Jonas," he snapped, but in a whisper, "do you know what time it is?"

Jonas cast his eyes away from him and hung his head down low.

Nathan took a deep breath and relaxed his shoulders. "What's wrong? Why are you still up?"

"I can't sleep," said Jonas. "I was going to the bathroom and then I saw that your light was still on, so I figured you couldn't sleep either."

Against his better judgment, Nathan nodded. "Yeah. I'm having a hard time falling asleep too."

Jonas smiled and quickly slid past him, taking a seat on his bed.

"Oh, no you don't," Nathan warned. His eyes were wide. "It's time for you to go to bed, and we're not about to stay up late talking."

Jonas hung his head down low again. He looked disappointed. "But you said you can't sleep either," he protested.

Nathan raised his eyebrows. He had a stern look on his face. "Yeah, but that doesn't mean I am done trying." He pointed towards the door. "Back to bed, Mr. Riley."

"Okay, okay," Jonas said, getting up and heading for the door. But he stopped and stared at the orange-and-black basketball that sat in the back corner of Nathan's desk.

Nathan grinned and shook his head. "Go ahead and take it," he said.

Jonas smiled and bounced the ball.

Nathan cringed. "Don't bounce it," he said. "It's too late for that; you'll wake everyone else up."

"Sorry. I forgot."

Nathan sighed. "Just promise not to do it again."

Jonas had a wide smile on his face. "Oh, okay," he said. "I mean, I promise."

Nathan held the door open and whispered, "Good night, Jonas."

"Night, Nathan," he replied.

* * *

Bam, bam, bam!

Nathan tried to adjust his eyes to the darkness. "What was that?"

Bam, bam, bam!

Nathan sat up in bed. It was the wee hours of the morning, still dark outside. *That sounds like a basketball,* he thought.

He got out of bed and opened the door to his dorm room. There were voices and chattering coming from the hallway, so he gradually put his head out from his door. "What's going on out here?" he asked.

Andy stuck his head out from his dorm room doorway to look at Nathan. "I have no clue," he said with a shrug. "I was in bed sleeping when I heard a loud noise that sounded like a basketball."

"It was Jonas," shouted Hugo, after sticking his head out from his door.

Nathan started to walk towards Hugo when he noticed that the door to Jonas's room was wide open and the lights were off. "Where is he?" he said. "And how do you know?"

Hugo yawned and his eyes looked heavy. "As soon as I heard the dribbling I got up," he said. "That's when I saw Jonas with his basketball." He yawned again, this time covering his mouth. "He was acting weird. I called his name, and it was like he didn't even hear me."

Nathan turned his head to look down both ends of the hallway. "So, where did he go?" he said.

"He went that way," pointed Hugo. "Towards the end of the hallway."

Nathan hurried past Hugo and quickly glanced into the bathroom and shower area.

"He went that way," said another camper on the floor. "He turned the corner at the end of the hall."

Nathan continued past several campers who were now standing outside their rooms. At the end of the hall was Jonas's basketball nestled in a corner. Nathan could hear the sound of shuffling feet approaching from behind him. "You guys go back to your rooms," he said sternly. "I'll look for Jonas."

Andy pouted, but followed Hugo and the others back to their dorm rooms.

Nathan decided to leave Jonas's basketball and turned the corner at the end of the hallway.

"Jonas," he sighed.

Jonas was standing at the door to the staircase a little ways away.

"Jonas!" Nathan called

Abruptly, Jonas outlined the perimeter of the door with his index finger before stopping, palms out, towards the middle of the door.

Nathan squinted and slowly continued towards Jonas. "What is he doing?" he grumbled. Suddenly, his eyes grew wide and his mouth fell open. A blue light crept from Jonas's hand and engulfed the door in blue light.

"Jonas!" he cried out.

Jonas vanished through the door as if it wasn't solid, and Nathan went into hot pursuit behind him. He stopped at the foot of the illuminated door, closed his eyes, and stepped through.

Slowly, he opened his eyes and saw that everything was shrouded in gray. The air was humid, and it felt like he had just stepped into a muted vacuum.

"Jonas, where are you?"

Nathan immediately noticed that his hands felt warm and that they were red again. Scratching and faint shuffling noises came from below. "Déjà vu much?" he asked himself. "Is this a repeat of Grimm Cemetery, but the stairway edition?"

Cautiously, he peered over the banister. "Jonas!" he called out.

Jonas was down below. His shoulders were oddly held back, and he was walking with a strange gait.

Nathan took to the stairs and caught up with him. The sound that he would normally hear while walking on the metal staircase was missing.

"Jonas!" he cried, but Jonas continued to walk forward, not even flinching or blinking.

The scratching and shuffling noises drew closer. It sounded to him like an army of little feet. Suddenly, there was a soft high-pitched wail that came from down below. It sounded like grinding metal.

Nathan's hands started to tremble, and his eyes grew wide. He looked over the banister. "I've heard that sound before," he said. "In my dreams about Leah."

He saw what looked like small black or gray creatures running up the staircase. He could tell they had very sharp teeth because several of them had stopped to gnaw on the railings.

"Jonas!" he yelled, but Jonas continued to walk down the staircase.

Nathan grabbed Jonas by the arm. The high-pitched sound screeched louder as the creatures drew closer and closer.

"Jonas," he yelled, "wake up!"

Jonas didn't try to resist Nathan's pull, but his legs continued forward. Nathan tried standing in front of him and shaking him by the shoulders.

"Jonas," he yelled again, "snap out of it!"

Nathan's hands trembled. The patter of little feet sounded like the creatures were directly behind him.

Jonas's eyes were definitely glazed over. Nathan paused and reluctantly slapped Jonas in the face.

"Wake up!" he cried.

Jonas moved his head and fluttered his eyes a few times before focusing on Nathan's face.

"Nathan," he murmured. He looked confused. "What's going on? And what are we doing in the stairway?"

"No time to explain," said Nathan, glancing over his shoulder. "We gotta move!"

"Why?" slurred Jonas. "I want to sit down for a second." He placed his hand to the side of his head. "I'm dizzy, and I think something's wrong with my eyes."

The stairway suddenly got cold and a metallic screeching sound filled the air. Jonas shivered.

"What was that?" he blurted.

The sound of shuffling and scratching grew and so did Jonas's eyes.

Nathan intently looked him in the face. "Look," he said, "there is nothing wrong with your eyes."

Jonas looked confused again, and Nathan sighed.

"You are supposed to see gray," Nathan said.

Jonas shook his head. "Oh, okay," he said. "But why?"

Nathan pointed over the banister. "That's why."

"What the —" stammered Jonas. "What the heck are those?"

"You see those teeth?" asked Nathan. "Run!"

They stumbled up the staircase with the gray-and-black creatures not too far behind them. Nathan felt like they couldn't move fast enough. The creatures were now on the same level as them. They were trying to surround Nathan and Jonas by climbing up the walls and ceiling.

"They're everywhere," Jonas shouted in panic. "Like roaches!"

"Head for the door!" Nathan shouted.

Jonas hurried for the door and Nathan followed. One of the creatures sprung from the ceiling, landing at the heels of Nathan's feet.

"Aaah!" he yelled.

The creature's small, hairy arms and hands swiped repeatedly at his legs and feet. Furiously, Nathan kicked it, trying to avoid its sharp teeth and long nails. He was finally able to kick the creature in the head, sending it flying over the heads of the others and down the stairs.

"The door won't budge!" said Jonas.

"What?" Nathan cried, pushing him to the side. "This door shouldn't be here. There was a blue door here!"

Jonas tried the door again. "What blue door?" he yelled. "There is no blue door." Relentlessly, he pounded on the door, but every hit was met with silence. "Help!" he yelled. "Somebody help us!"

Creatures from the ceiling were dropping down in front of them and on top of the others, starting to surround them by the door. There was a deep growl from some of them and a high-pitched screeching sound from the others. For the most part, they appeared cloaked in shadow, making it hard to track their movements.

Jonas placed his back against the door and covered his ears. "Why are they making that noise?" he groaned.

Nathan could see them up close now. They were just how he remembered them in his dreams about Leah, especially their sharp teeth and long nails. He remembered how they'd clawed at her flesh, scratching her and biting her. Nathan thought the creatures looked like overstuffed hairy gerbils, the size of small cats, but with flat faces and no tails. He found himself as equally disturbed by their manic red eyes as he was by their claws and teeth.

Nathan felt Jonas cowering behind him, and several of the creatures looked ready to pounce. Nathan's breath labored. His heart pounded against his chest. "Stay behind me!" he cautioned Jonas.

Stealthily, several of the creatures launched into the air, their claws pointed at the boys and saliva falling from their mouths. Nathan crouched down, and his hand shook uncontrollably as he raised it to shield his face.

Without warning, a huge ball of energy emerged from Nathan's hand, knocking several of the creatures unconscious and leaving a trail of blue light. The force from the discharge of energy sent Nathan and Jonas hurling backwards, forcing the door open, and landing them on the floor on the other side.

Nathan shook his head and stood up.

Jonas placed his hand against his head, and Nathan helped him to his feet.

"How did you do that?" asked Jonas.

Nathan looked down at his hands. They were still red and trembling. "I don't know," he said. "But my hands are still shaking, so I don't think we are out of this yet."

"But I don't see them," said Jonas, while cautiously looking around.

Suddenly, a metallic screeching sound reverberated through the air.

"Yeah?" said Nathan. "Then what the heck was that?" He pointed to the wall. "And look — everything around us is still in gray!"

Jonas was shaking in panic. "What are we going to do?"

"Come on," said Nathan, gesturing with his hand. "We need to find another door."

Nathan and Jonas turned the corner to the hallway leading to the dorm rooms and the bath and shower area. Jonas noticed that his basketball was now gray, and it was sitting in the corner.

"It's like frozen!" he said.

Abruptly, Nathan stopped. "What's frozen?" he asked.

Jonas had a vacant expression on his face. "My basketball," he said. He reached down and attempted to pick it up. "See, it's like frozen, and it feels like a wall or some barrier is stopping me from picking it up."

Nathan raised his eyebrows and gave him a stern look. "Jonas, let's go," he said. He hurried over to the nearest door, but it was locked.

"Why are we checking doors again?" asked Jonas.

"Well," said Nathan, while continuing to check each door. "I'm guessing since we came through a door, that you activated by the way, we need to go through another one to get back."

"Me?" Jonas frowned. "That I activated?" He wrapped his arms around himself and shivered. "It's getting cold again," he stuttered.

A high-pitched sound filled the hallway again, followed by scratching and growling noises.

"What are we going to do?" Jonas asked.

Nathan placed his hands on his hips. His hands had started to tremble more. "We have to do something fast."

"Can't you do that hand thing again?" asked Jonas.

Nathan looked down at his trembling red hands. "I don't know," he said. "I don't know if I can."

"Look," shouted Jonas. "This one is open!"

Swiftly, Jonas stepped aside and Nathan opened the door. Nathan tried the light switch, but it was stuck in the off position.

"Is it safe?" asked Jonas, attempting to enter the room. "Can we go?"

Solemnly, Nathan shook his head and closed the door.

"Everything was still in gray," Nathan said. He took Jonas by the arm. "Jonas, I need you to try and activate this door."

Jonas eyebrows were raised beneath his shaggy curly hair. "What?" he exclaimed.

"I need you to try and connect this door back to the other side," said Nathan.

"What side?" said Jonas, with a hint of panic in his voice.

"Back to our floor," said Nathan. "Back to Lawrence Hall. Back to Colorville!"

Jonas swallowed hard. "But what if I can't?" he stammered. "How am I supposed to do that?"

"You can do this, Jonas," encouraged Nathan. "I've seen you do it before."

"But I don't remember," stuttered Jonas. "I don't even know how we got here."

"I need you to try, Jonas," Nathan said.

Jonas's eyes were like a deer's in headlights.

"Look," said Nathan, stretching his arm out towards the door. "First, you traced the outline of the door with your finger and then you faced your palm out towards the door."

A very loud metallic sound rang out from the bathroom, and several gray-and-black creatures sprang out into the hallway.

Jonas gasped in horror. "They're here!" he shouted. "What are we going to do?"

Nathan took Jonas by the shoulders. "Relax," he said. "I need you to concentrate on the door."

"B-but, what about them?" he asked, pointing at the small but frightening creatures pouring out of the bathroom.

"Don't worry about them," said Nathan. "Like you said, I'll take care of them."

"But how?" panicked Jonas. "You said you don't —"

Nathan interrupted him. "I figured out how," he said.

Jonas stared at Nathan with a blank look on his face.

"Just concentrate on the door," said Nathan reassuringly.

Jonas nodded. "Okay."

Nathan turned around to face the creatures. They were so close now that he could easily see the saliva dripping from their mouths. *I'm glad one of us believed me*, he thought to himself. *I haven't got a clue how to do this again.*

A deep growling sound filled the hallway and reverberated off the walls.

"Um, Nathan?" uttered Jonas.

"The door, Jonas," Nathan reiterated firmly.

Nathan could hear scratching noises coming from the other end of the hallway. The creatures were now pouring out from one of the other rooms. Nathan stretched out his hand towards the group of creatures closest to them.

"It's not working," he protested to himself.

Nathan tried again. This time, his hands began to

tremble uncontrollably. He wondered if he and Jonas were going to die there. The muscles in his arm stiffened, and without warning, a streak of blue light fired from his hand, sending several creatures hurling backwards like bowling pins.

Nathan paused to look down at his hands. Jonas had a surprised look on his face.

Nathan barked, "Jonas!"

"I know, I know," said Jonas. "The door."

Several creatures had now climbed the wall and were closing in on Jonas. Nathan raised his hand and another beam of blue light shot out, knocking the creatures unconscious.

A high-pitched screeching sound followed by deep growls sounded all around them. Nathan and Jonas covered their ears as more and more creatures filled both ends of the hallway.

Jonas cowered behind Nathan. "What are we going to do?" he cried. "My hands aren't working!"

They both stood in silence as the creatures surrounded them, but then Nathan noticed his own trembling hands.

"That's it!" he shouted. "That has to be the trigger! Try again," he said to Jonas. "I want you to think about Lawrence Hall. I want you to think about your room. Think about holding your basketball again!"

"I am, I am," said Jonas, throwing his hands up in the air. "But nothing's happening!"

Nathan took Jonas by the arms and looked him in the eyes. "Jonas," he said, sternly, "if you don't do this, we are going to die!"

Jonas's body went rigid and a bead of sweat trickled down the side of his face. Soon, his hands started to tremble and a bright blue light emanated from the palm of his hand.

CHAPTER THIRTEEN

THE TIES THAT BIND

Nathan and Jonas hit the ground with a thud. Nathan's eyes adjusted to the darkness, and he saw a red comforter hanging off the foot of the bed.

"You did it Jonas," he said. He placed an arm across Jonas's shoulders. "You did it!"

Jonas smiled weakly. "Are you sure? Are we back?" He sat up and looked around the room. "Did we make it?"

Nathan pointed to the red comforter and the colored posters made visible by the moonlight that shone on the wall. "Look," he said. "We made it."

Jonas reached up and pulled the bedspread off the bed. "Just wanted to make sure," he said. "You know, to make sure it wasn't frozen."

Nathan laughed.

There was a clicking sound, and light from a desk lamp lit up the room. In front of them stood a groggy-eyed Hugo dressed in his pajamas. "What are you guys doing in my room?" he muttered.

Nathan turned around to examine the door. It was solid again, and the blue light that once engulfed it was gone. He realized that the unlocked door must have been Hugo's room.

Nathan stood up and helped Jonas to his feet.

"Uh …" Nathan uttered, looking at Jonas.

They both had blank expressions on their faces.

"See, Jonas was sick and, and —" Nathan said.

"And Nathan was walking me back to my room," finished Jonas.

Nathan smiled at Jonas. "Right," he said. "And we thought this was his room."

Hugo scrunched his face. He looked confused.

"The hallway lights were off," Nathan explained with a shrug.

"Yeah," added Jonas with a nervous chuckle. "Somebody was probably playing a joke."

Nathan nodded and smiled nervously. "Yeah," he said. "We couldn't see."

Hugo's face was still scrunched and his eyes were red. "Can I go back to bed now?" he asked.

"Y-Yeah," stuttered Nathan. "We should probably get out of here so you can go back to sleep."

Jonas nodded and followed briskly behind him.

Nathan closed the door, and Jonas beelined down the hall to pick up his basketball.

"It was a lot easier to pick up this time," he said. "Wherever we were before, it was like frozen in place." He placed the ball underneath his arm. "Where were we, Nathan?"

Nathan whispered softly, "Shh," and motioned him to follow.

The door to Jonas's room was still open, and Nathan stepped in to check the lights. "Looks like everything is back to normal," he said. He paused. Although the room didn't look much different than his own, it looked so familiar now. This was Leah's room. It felt odd staring at the empty white walls that had been filled with posters in his dream. He wondered if Leah's room was the connection and if that was the reason why they were attacking Jonas.

Jonas placed his basketball on the floor and checked underneath his bed. "Nope, no monsters," he said. He took off his shoes and sat on the bed.

Nathan looked down at his hands and then at Jonas. *But Jonas has a power too,* he thought. *Is that the connection?* He closed the dorm room door and sat on the opposite bed, wondering if that meant that Leah had a power too.

Jonas spoke softly. "Nathan," he whispered, "what was that place? Where were we?"

Nathan continued to stare at him and pursed his lips. *I have no clue. It was like we were here, in Lawrence Hall, but not here.*

His mind continued to race as he gazed aimlessly around the room. *It was like we were here, but we couldn't see the people,* he thought to himself. *When Jonas opened a door back to Lawrence Hall, it was like we really didn't go anywhere; we were just able to see everything again, to move things, to see the people in the space. It was like we were in a space within the space.*

Nathan focused on Jonas again as he lay stretched out on the bed. Jonas's eyes were red and he looked tired.

A space within the space, he thought to himself. He recalled Jonathan saying something about a space in between the space at one of the Friday night bonfires. *Is that stuff real?* he thought. *Is there some truth to what Jonathan was talking about?*

"Nathan," said Jonas. His voice was shaking. "Do you think they will come back — those monsters?"

Nathan noted the worry on Jonas's face. "No," he said, reassuringly. "We're safe and everything is all right."

Jonas sighed. He was starting to look restless. "How were you able to do what you did?" he asked. "How was I able to do what I did?" He sat up in bed. "Do we have some type of power?"

Nathan smiled reassuringly again. He remembered how it felt in the beginning, when all this was happening to him. "I'm still trying to figure out everything myself," he said.

Jonas looked disappointed. "Then I guess you don't have an answer as to why I don't remember us going there."

Nathan shook his head. "Sorry, I don't. But I do know that you did great back there and that you have an amazing ability."

Jonas smiled. "Was tonight the first time you used your power?"

"No, not exactly."

Jonas had a confused look on his face. "What do you mean?"

Nathan thought about his dream at Grimm Cemetery, and about how instead of a blue light or ball of energy, a blue flame had come out of his hand. He took notice of the clock on Jonas's desk and sighed. "It's getting late," he said. "You should rest. We'll talk more in the morning."

Jonas cast his gaze downward and nodded. "Okay," he said, and rested his head on his pillow.

Nathan stood up and turned off the light. "Good night, Jonas."

Jonas sat up again. "Wait," he pleaded. He was hesitant to speak. "Can you stay a little while longer — until I fall asleep?"

"Sure," said Nathan slowly. "Okay." He sat back down on the opposite bed and Jonas lay down again.

"Nathan?" he said.

"Yeah?" replied Nathan, while removing his shoes.

"How did you know it would work?" He fluffed his pillow. "I mean, how did you know how to turn on my ability, my power?"

Nathan lay on the bed and turned on his side to face Jonas. "I realized that my hands would only turn red and start shaking when there was danger or when I was in trouble," he said. "Before tonight, I thought maybe stress or getting upset triggered it."

"Oh, okay," said Jonas. "Is that why you told me we were going to die?"

Nathan's voice grew softer. "Yeah. Sorry," he said. "I figured if that was how it worked for me, it would work for you."

Jonas yawned. "It's okay," he said. "I understand. We might be still there — or worse — if you hadn't figured it out."

* * *

The bright sunlight poured in from the cafeteria windows, and Nathan tried to shield his eyes, but couldn't while carrying his tray. He squinted and kept his head down low, but the light reflected back from his plate of pecan pancakes and tall glass of orange juice.

"Good morning, Nathan!" said Angela energetically.

Nathan raised his eyebrows. "Good morning, Angela," he replied. He took a seat on the other side of the table so that his back faced the cafeteria window.

"Yes," commented Alan. "She is always this perky. Every morning."

Angela rolled her eyes. "That's a different side for you," she said.

Nathan put down his fork and pointed behind him. He tried to talk without showing the food in his mouth. "Sunlight," he mumbled.

She smiled.

Alan stopped looking at his cell phone long enough to

look around the room. "Still no Lafonda," he said. "This is unlike her. She is usually the first one here."

Nathan took a moment from eating to look around the table. He was surprised as well.

Angela reached into her pocket and pulled out her cell phone. It was bright purple and had gold-and-silver stars on the back of it. "I'll send her a text message," she said with a smile. "There, it's done."

"Wow, that's a first!" blurted Alan. His eyes were as wide as saucers. "Erin and Jonathan actually walking in together."

Angela checked her cell phone. "Still no message," she said, sounding slightly gloomy. She gave a quick glance to Erin and Jonathan. "Erin must have taken my advice and started picking him up."

"Quick!" whispered Alan, turning around so that he faced the table. "Before Erin and Jonathan leave the cafeteria counter and make it over here" — he leaned in and lowered his voice further — "did you guys notice the weirdness last night between Jonathan and Malick?"

"Yeah," responded Nathan, while chewing his food.

Angela nodded and leaned in as well. "Yeah," she whispered. "I noticed there was some tension whenever there was talk about the caves." She leaned back from the table and glared at them. "But," she added, "I also noticed that Jonathan isn't the only person having a problem with Malick."

Alan huffed and Angela continued to glower.

"I wonder why Malick would have a problem with the caves," Alan said while grinning. "He probably feels like me and just gets tired of hearing Jonathan go on and on about it."

"Ouch, Angela!" cried Alan. "What did you do that for?" He winced again. "Ouch!" he yelled. "Stop hitting me! I'm not ignoring you!"

Angela folded her arms across her chest. "Yes, you are!" she whined.

"What's your problem, Angela?" he groaned. Alan rolled his eyes. "Malick is just getting what he deserves."

"I feel like nobody in this group is giving Malick a chance to fit in," she said, sounding slightly disappointed.

He frowned. "You know, there are other counselors at this camp, Angela," he retorted.

Nathan looked up and Angela sighed.

"Well, there are," Alan grinned.

"Good morning, guys," said Erin, stepping up to the table.

Erin and Jonathan were carrying trays of food.

"Where is Lafonda?" Erin asked.

"The sun is bright this morning," complained Jonathan through squinted eyes. "Do you mind if I sit on the other side, next to Nathan?"

Erin shrugged. "Fine by me, Mr. Indiana," she said. "I'm just glad you made it down in time for breakfast. A girl can get tired of rallying up the troops by herself, you know."

Jonathan smiled.

"She's almost here!" shrieked Angela, while placing her cell phone back into her pocket.

"Who's almost here?" asked Erin.

"Lafonda," Angela replied happily. "I texted her this morning and I just got a text saying she'll be here, like in five minutes!"

Erin nodded.

"Oh, and here comes Malick," Angela continued with a grin. "And it doesn't look like he has his sunglasses on or with him this morning."

Alan shook his head.

Nathan looked up after finishing his glass of orange juice and caught a glimpse of Malick. He also noticed Jonas talking to Christina Williams.

"Looks like Lafonda is going to miss her chance to see that," added Erin.

"No, she won't," said Alan. "Here she comes."

"Hey," said Malick, pausing to run his hand through his hair. "How's it going?"

Angela adjusted her shirt and fidgeted with her curly blond hair so that it lay neatly on her shoulders. "Hi there," she said with a grin.

"Hey, guys!" said Lafonda, as she approached the table. She sounded almost out of breath. "Sorry I'm late."

"Uh, Lafonda," uttered Angela, with a wink. "Did you notice Malick doesn't have his sunglasses on this morning?"

Lafonda gave Malick a quick look over. "Good for him," she sighed.

Malick grinned and then headed to his regular table by the window.

"Enjoy your breakfast!" shouted Angela cheerfully.

Lafonda proceeded around the table and made room for herself between Jonathan and Nathan.

"Lafonda," said Angela, abruptly. "Aren't you going to have breakfast?

"I'm not hungry," she smiled. "But guess what? I have good news!"

"What is it?" asked Alan enthusiastically. "Is there a sale at Burberry?"

Lafonda laughed. "No, not quite," she chuckled. "Leah's coming home!"

Nathan quickly spun around. "What?" he said, almost spilling food from his mouth.

"I just got off the phone with Leah," she continued

excitedly. "She is being released from the hospital on Monday!"

"Like tomorrow?" Nathan asked.

"Yes," said Lafonda. "Leah is going home tomorrow, and I plan to visit her in about two weeks."

"When?" asked Angela. "Isn't camp like over in two weeks?"

"I know," said Lafonda. "I was thinking about visiting her on the Friday before the closing ceremony on Saturday. Leah mentioned she didn't want to be stuck with her parents all summer, so I thought maybe I would bring her back here in time for the banquet and closing ceremony."

"That's a great idea," said Angela. "Especially since the banquet falls on the Fourth of July holiday!"

"I hoped you would feel that way," said Lafonda. "Do you think you could cover for me for like a day? I would be gone in the evening and return sometime in the afternoon the next day. I've already cleared it with my grandmother. I just need someone to help Nathan with the girls that day."

Angela was going to say something, but then paused to look at Alan. He was busy texting on his cell phone. "That sounds like a great idea," she said finally. "Of course I'll help!"

"Thanks!" Lafonda said happily.

Angela paused to look at Alan again. "What are you doing, Alan?"

"Texting," he said.

"Texting who?" she asked.

"Oh, just a few people," responded Alan. He had a huge grin across his face. "This is big news!"

Quickly, Angela took Alan's cell phone out of his hands. "Give me that!"

"Hey," protested Alan ardently. "Give me back my cell phone!"

Angela and Lafonda laughed.

"Later!" Angela chuckled, while pocketing the cell phone.

"What's the big deal!" he pouted. "It's big news and other people will want to know."

"Yeah?" retorted Angela. "But what kind of people?" She folded her arms across her chest. "Probably not anyone that actually cares about Leah."

"Go ahead and give it back to him," sighed Lafonda, while rolling her eyes.

Angela frowned but gave Alan his cell phone.

"Thank you!" he rejoiced.

"So, is everything okay?" asked Erin. "I mean, I didn't know her, but I ... heard about what happened."

"Yes," said Lafonda softly, while nodding. "Everything is fine. Leah said the doctors want her to relax and gave her a clean bill of mental health. They are calling it stress-induced hallucinations."

"What does Leah think about that?" asked Nathan. "Does she think it was just stress?"

Lafonda paused and then glanced at her cell phone. "She didn't say," she said. "But her mom is talking about keeping her home for a semester."

"That sucks!" commented Erin. "Well, at least she is okay and gets to go home."

"I agree," said Lafonda, with a nod. "I think Leah is just glad to get out of that place. She's ready to put the whole ordeal behind her."

"Ooh," uttered Angela, "and if she comes up for the closing ceremony, she gets to relax and hang out with us. Isn't the ceremony going to be outdoors and in the evening too? She'll get to see the fireworks!"

"I know," said Lafonda. "We talked about doing some shopping at the mall down there to pick out some dresses."

"Shopping too?" exclaimed Angela, with a smile. "Gosh, I wish I was going. I haven't gone shopping since camp started."

Alan abruptly stopped texting and smirked at Angela.

"What? I said I *haven't gone* shopping," she said. "The Internet doesn't count.

Angela rolled her eyes, but suddenly looked concerned once she was facing Lafonda again. "What's wrong?" she asked. "I know I won't be there, but you can still text me pictures of dresses so I can see."

Lafonda responded with a half-smile. "That's not it," she said, appearing slightly gloomy. She forced a small chuckle followed by a quick wink. "Oh, and don't worry, I'll still send you pictures."

"Then … what's wrong?" Angela asked. "You look down all of a sudden."

Lafonda's smile disappeared and she seemed hesitant to speak. "It's about something Leah mentioned on the phone," she said. She lowered her voice and leaned in closer to the table. "She said she hadn't spoken to Amanda since the night she was admitted to the hospital and that Amanda hasn't returned any of her phone calls."

"Oh, that's it!" spouted Alan, gesturing dismissively with cell phone in hand. "Maybe she just hasn't had time to return her phone calls."

"No, there's more," explained Lafonda. "I've tried calling Amanda too and haven't gotten anywhere. The last time I saw her was at my birthday party." She began to whisper. "And this is where it gets weird; Leah said Steve's parents called looking for him. They said he's been missing for over a week now, and they can't reach

Amanda or her parents."

Angela reached over to take Alan's cell phone again, but he moved out of the way.

"Alan!" she groaned. "This is not the time."

"What?" he protested. "This is news. And you never know — someone might know where Steve is or where to find Amanda." He held his phone in the air so that it was out of Angela's reach. "We should let people know, Angela!"

Lafonda tossed her long black hair over her shoulder and sighed. "Go ahead and let him," she said. "Maybe somebody knows something."

Alan's cheeks became a deep red and he smiled widely. A spark of passion beamed from his eyes. "I'm all over it!" he said.

"Whatever Alan," protested Angela. "You're such a gossip king."

"Thanks!" he said, over a flurry of thumb movements. "I'll take that as a compliment."

Nathan looked on and laughed as Alan continued to text feverishly. He also thought about Leah and how great it was that she would be finally going home. *I wonder what it will be like to finally meet her,* he thought to himself. *I wonder if she will even like me.* His palms began to sweat. *It feels weird that the closing ceremony will be the first time I actually meet her. I feel like I know so much about her already.*

Over his thoughts, he could hear Lafonda discussing Amanda's and Steve's disappearances again.

"It's strange that they would go missing," Nathan muttered. "Their disappearances have to be connected to each other."

"Hey, Nathan!" called a voice over the cafeteria chatter. Nathan caught a glimpse of someone waving. He looked up to find Jonas standing behind Angela and Alan.

"Hey, Nathan!" Jonas called again. "Can I talk to you for a second?"

"Sure," Nathan responded, feeling slightly embarrassed. "What's up?"

Jonas fidgeted with his basketball a little before securing it underneath his arm. "It's about last night," he said.

Nathan sprang from the table and grabbed his tray. "Hold that thought," he said. He could feel Lafonda's gaze and everyone else's at the table. To his surprise, even Alan stopped texting a second to look at him. "How come I can go unnoticed on some days, but not when I want to?" he muttered.

Nathan headed over to a corner of the cafeteria that was seldom used, and Jonas followed. Nathan looked over Jonas's shoulder to make sure they were out of earshot. He was certain Alan would still try to read their lips. Nathan cleared his throat.

"About last night," he said. "Have you said anything to anybody?"

"No," Jonas responded, while continuing to fidget with his basketball. "I'm not even really sure what it is that I would say."

"Good," Nathan whispered. "We should definitely keep this to ourselves for now."

Jonas nodded, but then suddenly looked confused. "Why?"

"It's probably safer that way," Nathan said. "Until we figure out what's going on and what the deal with those creatures is, we probably shouldn't tell anyone."

"Oh, okay." Jonas paused to look back at one of the cafeteria tables. Christina Williams smiled back at him. "Have you told anybody?"

"No, I haven't," Nathan said. He smiled at Jonas

reassuringly. "I know this is a lot to handle, and believe me, I totally understand what you're going through." He grinned. "You know, Jonas, now that I am thinking about it, you are the first person that actually knows about my ability."

Jonas smiled and Nathan leaned in. "I'm actually relieved to finally be able to talk about this with somebody," Nathan whispered. "And not just with anybody, but with someone that has an ability too."

Jonas relaxed his shoulders. "Yeah, I can see how that would be a relief. I couldn't imagine going through all this by myself. Those little hairy monsters alone make my head spin."

"Yeah, I know what you mean," said Nathan.

Jonas suddenly had an excited look on his face. "And what kind of ability do I have, anyway? It's definitely not as cool as yours. I can still see you blasting those hairy guys into the air!"

Nathan glanced quickly over Jonas's shoulder to see if anyone had heard him.

"Keep it down," Nathan chuckled.

Jonas cringed slightly. "Right," he said, lowering his voice. "I still think what you can do is amazing."

"Your power isn't too shabby either," said Nathan with a smile.

"I guess not," Jonas responded with a shrug. "I'm still not quite sure what it is that I did." He looked confused. "Where the heck were we, Nathan?"

Nathan stared again at the table where the others were sitting as he mulled over an answer to Jonas's question. Jonathan appeared to be having an in-depth conversation with Erin.

"I'm not exactly sure," Nathan said, "but I think I know where to find out."

Jonas stared at him curiously, but nodded. "Last night, you mentioned something about this not being the first time that you've used your powers. What did you mean by that?"

Nathan looked down and fidgeted with his hands. "I figured I would have to tell you eventually," he said. "I just didn't think it was going to be today."

"Oh, okay. It's all right if you don't want to."

"No, no, it's cool." Nathan swallowed drily. "See, I sort of can see the future or the past through my dreams."

"Whoa, that's cool!" marveled Jonas. He had a huge smile on his face. "Really?"

"I guess it's cool," said Nathan. "It probably depends on what you are dreaming about or what you see. In one of my dreams I sort of used my powers."

"Well, I think that's cool," said Jonas, with a nod.

"Well," continued Nathan, while scanning the room, "it looks like everyone is getting ready to leave the cafeteria."

Jonas turned around. Campers were lining up in their groups.

"Besides," added Nathan, "I'm tired of holding this tray."

Jonas laughed.

"Aren't you guys scheduled to work in the computer lab today?" asked Nathan.

Jonas's forehead wrinkled beneath his long black curls. "I think so," he said. "I think we start work on our final projects today."

"Sounds good," said Nathan.

"Nathan, wait," Jonas called. He started to fidget with his basketball again. "There's one other thing."

Nathan turned back around. He looked confused, but

smiled reassuringly. "Yeah?"

"I didn't say anything at the time," stuttered Jonas, "and this is probably going to sound silly, but last night I had this strange feeling, like my brother was there, or something."

"Your brother?" asked Nathan

"Yeah, my little brother," Jonas said. "At first I thought it was just my nerves, but this morning it didn't go away. Somehow I feel like my little brother was there — in that place."

"Are you sure?" Nathan asked. "I mean, did you see him?"

Jonas shook his head and glanced downward. "No," he said. "I know it sounds crazy. It's just a feeling I keep getting, and I'm starting to worry about him."

"Have you tried calling home? To see if he's all right?"

Jonas shook his head again. "No," he said. "I was afraid of what I would find out."

Nathan smiled reassuringly again. "It's probably nothing," he said. "Just call home and check on your little brother. I'm sure he's all right."

"Okay," said Jonas. "I'll call before we go into the lab."

Nathan winked. "Cool. And I'll cover for you so that Lafonda doesn't yell at you for being late or for ditching out to talk on your cell phone."

Jonas smiled and looked cheery again. "Oh, and Nathan, thanks for staying in my room last night. I felt safer having you there with me, you know, because of the monsters and stuff."

Nathan chuckled. "No problem," he said.

CHAPTER FOURTEEN

RAINED OUT

Nathan was staring out the large window with his cell phone at his ear. It had rained all day and fog circled the base of the floor-to-ceiling glass windows in the lobby of Lawrence Hall. It had rained practically all week, and Nathan and the campers spent most of the time indoors, only braving the rain to attend leadership classes. Many of the campers were excited that the week was almost over and didn't mind spending the extra time indoors to work on their final leadership projects. Nathan couldn't believe that camp was drawing to an end and that there was only one week left before it was all over.

"Hello," said a familiar voice on the phone.

"How's it going, old man?" he said.

"Nathan! How many times do I have to tell you that I may be your grandfather, but I am not old!"

Nathan laughed. "Sorry, Grandpa. I forget how young you are."

"You know I would much rather you called me Roy," he said laughing. "I guess I should be happy that my grandson finally remembered to call me."

Nathan paused. "Yeah ... about that," he said, "I'm sorry that I waited so long to call. I had planned to, but a lot of unexpected things kept popping up."

"Oh, really?" laughed Roy. "Does a girl have anything

to do with this?"

Nathan chuckled and then shook his head. "No, Grandpa," he said. "Where did you get that one?"

There was a brief silence on the phone. "Nowhere. Just trying to figure out what's captured all my grandson's attention."

Nathan paced in front of the large windows. He looked up when Lafonda entered the lobby. "Lafonda," he said underneath his breath.

"What?" asked Roy. "Is Lafonda there?"

"Don't give me that innocent routine," Nathan said with a frown. "You must have heard something from Lafonda."

Lafonda looked Nathan's way and smiled.

"Grr!" Nathan groaned, while quickly diverting his eyes.

Roy chuckled. "That is true," he said. "I do hear from her. In fact, I think she calls to chat at least twice a week."

"Whatever. What did she say this time?"

"Nothing that I recall," answered Roy. "Then again, we do speak often, and with my old age it's hard for me to remember everything."

Nathan rolled his eyes. "Okay, Grandpa."

"So," said Roy, "how is setting up the bonfires going?"

"Uh — what?" stammered Nathan. "What do you mean?"

Roy paused to clear his throat. "LaDonda mentioned that you were setting up the bonfires out at Lake Charleston on Friday nights, and I was curious about how that was going."

"Oh," responded Nathan. "Everything is going okay, I guess." He suddenly stopped pacing. "What? Did LaDonda say something?"

"Relax, son," Roy laughed. "Not everyone is keeping

tabs on you."

Nathan paused. He caught a glimpse of Lafonda, Alan and Angela setting up additional chairs in the lounge area. "Good," he said, "because at times it definitely feels like it."

Roy continued to laugh. "So are you managing getting the fires started by yourself?" he asked.

"By myself?" said Nathan. "No, another counselor from camp is helping me."

"Oh," responded Roy. "And how is that going?"

Nathan grinned. "Good, for the most part," he said. "At times he can be a pain, but he's all right. Underneath it all, I think he's a good guy."

"Good. Sounds like you might be making a new friend at camp."

Nathan laughed. "I wouldn't go as far as to say that. Let's wait until the end of next week. Camp isn't over yet."

Roy laughed. "Speaking of next week," he said, "what are your plans after camp is over? You'll have an entire month off before school starts up again."

"I'm not sure," Nathan stammered. "I haven't really thought about it."

"Once camp is over, do we need to make an appointment to check on your hands? How's that rash coming?"

Nathan felt his face turning red. "Rash!" he groaned. "What rash? My hands are fine."

"So, you've been using the ointment, then?"

Nathan paused. "Uh — yeah," he muttered.

"So, if the ointment is working for you," continued Roy, "why can I see it on your dresser right now?"

Nathan felt embarrassed. "Everything is fine! I just didn't want you to worry. Seriously, Grandpa, my hands are fine."

"Uh-huh," uttered Roy. "Don't forget you'll be home in a week, and I'll get to see for myself."

Nathan watched as Jonas and Christina emerged from the cafeteria and joined Lafonda and the others. Samantha and Eva Marie joined them shortly after. "Okay, Grandpa," he said. "I'll see you in about a week."

"Or sooner," commented Roy.

Nathan continued to watch Lafonda and the others. He was curious as to why they were setting up so many chairs in the lounge area. "I'll talk to you soon," he said.

Roy laughed. "I'm sure I'll see you before you call again."

Nathan laughed. "Have a good evening."

"You too," said Roy. "And be safe."

Nathan closed his phone and placed it in his pocket. *What did he mean by sooner?* he thought.

"Well, about time you got off the phone," whined Alan. He had a labored look on his face. "We need your help setting up for tonight's wonderful activity."

Nathan scanned the room. "What is he talking about?"

Lafonda stopped setting up chairs and laughed. She wiped the sweat from her brow and placed her hair into a ponytail. "Whew!" she said. "My grandmother is showing a video here tonight, and she asked us to help set up more chairs and tables."

"Oh, okay," said Nathan. He paused to look around the lounge again. "But why?"

Lafonda shook her head. "Seriously, Nathan," she said, "you need more friends. You're starting to sound like Jonas."

Alan let out a big laugh.

Lafonda rested her hands on her hips. "Because of the rain, we are going to watch a video my grandmother wants us to see," she said. "She said the video has something to do with inspiring leadership."

Alan laughed. "Didn't you notice that it's still raining outside?" he asked. "I mean, it's been raining practically all week. Did you honestly think we were still going to have a bonfire with all this rain?"

Angela gave Alan a mean look. "Knock it off, Alan," she said. "I wish you would stop putting on your grumpy pants whenever you actually have to do work."

Alan looked down at his pants and dusted them off with his hands. "That's just it," he complained. "I didn't know that LaDonda would volunteer us to set up these grungy chairs today!"

"Why not?" asked Nathan in a playful tone. "It's been raining practically all day. Didn't you know not to wear your nice pants today?"

Alan rolled his eyes, and his upper lip curled. "Ha-ha. Funny."

Angela laughed.

Nathan turned around to look at Lafonda. "I figured because of the rain we weren't going to be outside today," he said. He spoke louder so that Alan could hear him. "I just didn't know what we would be doing instead!"

Alan looked at Nathan briefly, but turned his attention back to his pants. "Ugh! Look, Angela!" he grumbled. "This black smudge mark is not coming off. I am going to the bathroom to try to wipe this off!"

"Wait!" said Angela. "Shouldn't you wait until we are done setting up? What if you get more spots on your pants?"

"If I get one more smudge on my pants," he protested, "I am going upstairs and you can just tell LaDonda I got sick!"

Nathan shook his head as Alan trotted off to the

men's bathroom. "So, where do you want me?" he asked. "What do you want me to do?"

Lafonda stood up again and pointed to where Christina, Eva Marie and Samantha were setting up chairs. "Can you help them?" she asked. She squinted and then scratched her head. "And I don't know what Jonas is doing over there by himself."

Nathan nodded. "Okay, I'll see if I can help the girls." He stopped mid-walk and grinned. "And I'll check on Jonas."

Nathan approached Christina, Eva Marie and Samantha from behind and paused. He figured by the tone of their voices and by the look on their faces, it probably was best not to interrupt their conversation.

"And I don't know what's up with him," mumbled Christina. Nathan could see the worry on her face. "He's been acting strange all week."

"I don't know either," shrugged Eva Marie. "You need to ask him what's going on instead of just talking to us about it."

Christina looked over at Jonas as he attempted to set up a table. "What do you think Sam?" she asked.

"Sorry," she said. "I agree with Christina. You won't know how to react until you know what's going on. As far as you know, you could be overreacting."

"Overreacting!" she howled. "Ugh!" Christina glanced up and looked embarrassed when she noticed Nathan. "Oh — uh — hi Nathan," she uttered.

Nathan grinned. "Hi, Christina." He tried to smile reassuringly. "So, Lafonda said you guys might need my help."

Christina hesitated and her voice quivered. "Uh — sure," she said.

Eva Marie smiled and kindly stepped in front of her.

"Excuse Christina," she said, while giving Christina a quick look. "She's a little sick today."

Christina's mouth fell open.

Eva Marie glared at her, raised her eyebrows, and then continued to talk to Nathan. "Can you grab more chairs from the closet for us?" she asked.

"Sure," said Nathan.

Samantha laughed. "Hi, Nathan," she said.

"Hi, Sam," he smiled.

Eva Marie gestured her head towards Jonas. "See, Jonas over there was helping us in the beginning, but it looks like he is preoccupied at the moment."

Nathan and the others looked up to find Jonas struggling to put up the table.

Eva Marie pointed. "The closet is over there," she said.

"Okay," Nathan nodded. "I'll be back with more chairs."

Before heading to the closet, Nathan decided to chat with Jonas, who was bent over and trying to balance the table with one hand while trying to get one of the legs to open with the other. Nathan reached out with his hand and balanced the table. Jonas looked up and smiled. He then proceeded to lower all the legs of the table.

"Thanks Nathan," he smiled, sounding relieved.

Nathan grinned. "No problem."

Jonas proceeded to set up the chairs that were now on the floor next to the table. Nathan could tell by the look on his face that something was bothering him — he didn't even have his basketball with him.

Nathan grabbed a chair and set it up. "So?" he said. "How's it going?"

Jonas continued working. "Good," he responded.

Nathan had a good idea of what was bothering him.

Oddly enough, he didn't think it had anything to do with Jonas learning about Nathan's ability or that he himself had powers. He didn't think Jonas was too worried about the creatures they encountered in the pseudo stairway, either. He knew this was mostly about his brother.

"So," he said. "What's new with your brother? Were you able to talk to him again today?"

Jonas's eyes lit up, but there was a hint of sadness in his voice. "Yeah," he said. "Mom's been calling me after she picks up Bobby from Aunt Carol's after work."

Nathan nodded. "Right," he said. "You mentioned before that your aunt was watching him while your mom worked."

"Yeah, and he's also in summer school," said Jonas. "He didn't do too well last year and has to attend summer classes to catch up." He had a somber look on his face. "But it's only temporary."

Nathan paused to set up another chair. "You mean the part about him being watched by your Aunt Carol?" he asked.

Jonas smiled. "Yeah," he said. "Because I'll soon be home again."

"Wait, wait, wait!" called out a familiar voice. "Sorry, but the tables and chairs are facing the wrong direction."

Everyone stopped working to find LaDonda Devaro standing in the middle of the lounge area. She wore a dark blue poncho, from which water dripped on the floor.

"Sorry guys!" she said in a cheery voice. "I need all the chairs and tables facing the other way."

Lafonda stood up and wiped the sweat from her face. She paused to look at the rows of chairs. "But why, Grandma?" she protested. "Why can't we leave them the way they are?"

LaDonda held up a red, white, and blue DVD that was

in her hand. "Because you guys will be watching this tonight," she said. "And the screen and the projector are facing that way."

Lafonda's forehead wrinkled. "Oh," she said. She soon had an apologetic look on her face. "Sorry guys, my mistake. We have to turn the tables and chairs the other way."

"Ugh," sighed Christina.

Eva Marie mumbled words of protest underneath her breath, while Samantha helped Angela to turn some of the tables around.

"What are you guys doing?" blurted out Alan.

Lafonda looked up to see Alan standing outside the restrooms.

His mouth was wide open. "We're turning the tables and chairs around?"

Alan's pants leg was wet and he had a distressed look on his face. "Why?" he said. "For what? I thought we were close to being done."

Lafonda pointed to the projector and then the retractable screen. "It's my fault," she said. "I didn't know we were using the projector to watch the movie."

"Who said we were using the projector?" grumped Alan.

Lafonda looked past him. "My grandmother."

Alan turned around to find LaDonda instructing Nathan and Jonas where to move one of the tables.

"Freaking unbelievable!" he said.

Eva Marie stopped turning chairs around and walked over to Lafonda. "Dinner is almost over," she whispered, pointing to the cafeteria doors. "And we probably don't have enough chairs set out yet. Do you want me to go find more people to help set up some more?"

Lafonda scanned the room. "You're probably right,"

she said to Eva Marie. Lafonda then turned to LaDonda. "Grandma, dinner is almost over. Do you want us to get more people to help us set up?"

LaDonda headed to the front of the room and stood next to Alan and Lafonda. "We have enough chairs," she said. "If we run out of seats, people can just sit on the floor."

Alan stared at the floor and frowned. "Unbelievable," he muttered. "I am not sitting on the floor."

"Why not?" asked Angela.

He gawked at her and pointed to the dripping water from LaDonda's poncho. "Because it's wet."

Angela's face turned sour. "Oh."

Alan took in a deep breath. "So what movie are we watching, anyway?" he sighed.

"Grandma," called Lafonda. "Can I see the DVD?"

LaDonda handed her the DVD and she glanced at it before passing it to Alan.

Alan frowned and leaned over to Angela to whisper. "We're watching this," he muttered. "What does watching the last presidential inauguration have to do with inspiring leadership?"

"Oh, no!" said LaDonda in a worried voice.

A loud crack of thunder filled the room, and the lights flickered on and off. "I hope we don't lose power because of this storm," she said. "Then what are we going to do?"

"Not stay down here," Alan snickered.

Angela and Lafonda laughed.

The door from the cafeteria opened and the lobby filled with the sounds of chatter and laughter. Erin, Jonathan and the other counselors and campers slowly trickled into the lobby area.

Lafonda looked around the room. "Good," she said with an exhausted tone of voice. "Guys, I think we're done!"

Eva Marie and Christina looked at each other with relief and sat down.

"Awesome!" cried Alan. "Finally!" He glanced down at his pants and then at his hands. "Ugh," he sighed. "I'm going to wash my hands."

"Me too!" said Angela, running to catch up with him.

Nathan watched from the back of the lounge as everyone came in and took seats. He was surprised that, although there were seats still open, some took to the floor. When he turned around, Jonas was no longer standing next to him. *Where did he run off to?* he wondered.

Nathan searched around the room to see if he could find Jonas. He stood on the tips of his toes and tried to see further back and over the crowd. As he was scanning the different faces for Jonas, he saw a familiar face looking back at him. Malick grinned and headed towards him.

"So look who found a way to get out of work today," chuckled Malick.

Nathan grinned. "Ha-ha," he said. "Tonight's bonfire was only canceled due to the rain, and not because of me."

"I know, I know," said Malick with hands up in the air. "I was just teasing you." He ran his hand through his hair. "So, what happened to you?" he asked. "If the bonfire was canceled tonight, why weren't you at dinner?"

Nathan's eyes quickly darted over Malick's shoulder. He continued to look for Jonas. "Oh," he said. "I ate quick and left early today."

Malick had a confused look on his face.

"I knew that LaDonda would have something else planned for us, so I wanted to call my grandfather before whatever that was got started," he said. "You know, before I forgot about it."

"Got it," Malick said.

Nathan's eyes perked up. He got a glimpse of Jonas heading towards the cafeteria doors. "Excuse me, Malick, but I wanted to talk to Jonas about something."

He tried to quickly maneuver through the crowd of counselors and campers while keeping a watchful eye on Jonas.

"Jonas!" he called out.

Jonas froze as if his hands had been caught in a cookie jar. He slowly turned around, but suddenly looked relieved.

"Oh," he uttered, his breath sounding a little labored. "It's you, Nathan."

Nathan was a little mystified. "Yeah," he replied. "Were you expecting someone else?"

"Oh — no," said Jonas. He smiled wearily. "You just caught me off guard."

Nathan had a skeptical look on his face. "Caught off guard from what?" he asked.

"Oh, it's nothing," responded Jonas. "I was just heading into the cafeteria to grab something I'd forgotten."

"Wait," said Nathan, catching Jonas by the arm. "How are you doing?"

Jonas raised his eyebrows. He looked confused.

Nathan leaned in closer and then spoke softly, "You know," he said, "how are you dealing with everything else? You know, with your ability and —"

"Oh, you mean with the monsters and having no memory of how I got there. I just don't think about it," he shrugged. "I just concentrate on something else."

Like your brother? said Nathan to himself.

Jonas took a deep breath. "Well, it looks like LaDonda

will be starting soon," he said. "I better go grab my stuff."

"Wait," said Nathan.

Jonas turned around, and Nathan noticed that this time he looked nervous.

"I'll go with you," Nathan said.

"No!" responded Jonas abruptly.

Nathan was surprised by Jonas's reaction and he frowned.

"I mean, it's okay," said Jonas immediately. "I got it."

Nathan folded his arms across his chest and his eyes squinted. "Hold on," he said. "Something is not right; you are definitely up to something."

"Everything is cool," Jonas said.

Nathan rolled his eyes. "Uh-huh, right," he said. "Something isn't right. You don't even have your basketball with you."

Jonas glanced down. His cheeks began to turn red. "I'm going to see my brother!" he blurted out.

"What?" Nathan quickly grabbed Jonas by the arm and pulled him to the side. "What are you talking about?"

Jonas winced. "I figured that since the bonfire is canceled tonight I would go home," he said.

Nathan shook his head. "You can't go see your brother," he said. "No one is supposed to leave Lawrence Hall by themselves, let alone campus!"

"But I don't live far from here," Jonas pleaded. "We would be back before anyone even noticed that we were gone."

"We?" blurted Nathan.

"Yeah," explained Jonas. "You said no one could leave campus alone; you could go with me."

"Go where?" asked Malick, suddenly joining the conversation.

Nathan rolled his eyes.

225

"Home," said Jonas. "I mean, to my parent's house, to see my brother."

Malick's eyes lit up. "How far away is it?" he asked.

"Not far at all," said Jonas. "It wouldn't take us that long to walk there."

Malick dangled the keys he had gotten out of his pocket and grinned. "Why walk when you can drive?" he said.

"We're not going anywhere," whispered Nathan in protest. "No one is supposed to leave Lawrence Hall and besides, I have duties." He glowered at Malick. "And you have duties too. We both are supposed to be here at camp."

Jonas had a sad look on his face.

Malick looked at Jonas. He then placed his arm around Nathan's shoulder.

"Look," Malick said. "The kid really needs to see his brother. Who are we to stand in the way of that?" He leaned in close to Jonas and spoke softly. "Why are we going to see your brother again?" he asked.

Jonas hesitated. "Uh, he's in summer school," he said. "And my mom said he's been falling asleep in class. I'm worried about him."

"See," said Malick. "It's important."

Nathan shook his head. "You know no one is supposed to leave campus," he said. "What are we going to say to LaDonda and the others?"

Malick paused shortly, and then a huge smile formed on his face. Nathan's stomach twisted into knots; he hadn't felt that way since Malick had challenged him to a bonfire lighting competition weeks before. *Here we go,* he thought. He recalled how Malick had mysteriously started all twelve fires in record time — he had to have cheated.

"We won't have to say anything," said Malick. "We'll

slip out through the kitchen after the movie starts and LaDonda turns off the lights. We'll be back before anyone even notices."

Nathan caught a glimpse of Lafonda looking his way. "Don't count on it," he said underneath his breath.

"All right, everyone," shouted LaDonda. "Quiet now. I am about to start the movie. Please take your seats!"

Malick walked over to the light switch that was closest to the cafeteria doors. "I got the lights, Mrs. Devaro!" he said.

LaDonda smiled. "Thank you, Stephen!" she replied.

Malick looked at Nathan intently. He was waiting for him to signal.

Nathan caught a glimpse of Lafonda looking at him again before she took her seat. He heard Malick clear his throat.

"Jonas," Nathan said, letting out a huge sigh, "do you still feel like your brother was in the stairway that night?"

Jonas responded eagerly, "Yes."

Nathan then slowly nodded, and Malick turned off the lights.

CHAPTER FIFTEEN

MIDNIGHT TRAIN

The back door to the kitchen of Lawrence Hall swung open. Nathan blinked furiously. He was doing his best to see through the rain but he barely missed bumping into the dumpster. The rain continued to pound against Malick, Nathan and Jonas as they darted towards the silver metallic car. Before Nathan could grab the door handle, the polished-looking vehicle with aluminum wheels purred to life while blinking its red lights. Nathan heard the sound of the door locks pop open.

"Wow," said Jonas, "it's really crazy out here!"

Moving quickly, Nathan folded back the front seat so that Jonas could climb in.

"Yeah," Nathan said to Jonas, "and you were going to walk in this?"

Nathan wiped the rain from his forehead, feeling the cool of the leather seats underneath his damp clothes. The Camaro was relatively clean and still had that new-car smell. He glanced over to find a gleaming Stephen Malick grinning at him from the driver's seat.

"What are you so happy about?" Nathan asked.

"I'm sure you never imagined that one day you would be riding shotgun in this car," Malick laughed.

Nathan frowned as he continued to wipe the rain from

his forehead and his arms. "Not exactly," he said. "Not after the stunt you pulled on the first day of camp."

Malick started the windshield wipers and turned on the heat to defog the windows. "Did I ever apologize about that?" he asked.

"No."

Malick grinned. "Oh. Well, now I just did."

Nathan looked up to the ceiling of the car and shook his head. He was caught off guard when he felt a buzz in his pocket. It was a text from Lafonda. "Where are you?" it said.

Nathan's face immediately turned red. "Lafonda knows I'm gone," he said. He placed his phone back into his pocket. "It's just a matter of time before she realizes that you and Jonas are gone too."

The front windows were clear now, and raindrops splattered on the hood of the vehicle. Malick grinned as he put his car into gear. "It's now or never," he said.

Nathan glanced back at Jonas from the rearview mirror. His hair was wet and, aside from the fact that he had clothes on, he looked like he normally did after stepping out of the shower.

Jonas realized Nathan was looking back at him and smiled.

"Just go," Nathan said to Malick.

Malick hit the gas hard. The tires screeched as the car cut through the water in the parking lot. Malick continued to beam as he quickly turned the corner. "Where to?" he asked with a smile.

"Ooookay," said Nathan, while fastening his seat belt. He heard the clicking sound of another seat belt from the backseat. "It is raining outside. Can you try not to kill us?"

"Uh, yeah, he's got a point," said Jonas.

Malick smiled and then reached to turn on the radio.

"Can you not be so excited about breaking the rules?" Nathan asked.

Malick had a mischievous look on his face. "Can you not look so distraught for breaking them?"

Nathan smiled slightly.

Jonas took off his seat belt and leaned over the driver seat to give Malick directions. Nathan looked out the window as the car whooshed by rows and rows of houses. His leg vibrated again, and he had a good guess at who was texting or calling him.

Jonas pointed towards Nathan's side of the window. "Turn right after the railroad tracks," he said. "Our house is the next-to-last one at the end of the block."

The silver car abruptly came to a stop, throwing Nathan and Jonas forward. Jonas held on as tight as he could to the passenger and driver seats, but still landed in the front of the car.

"Ouch!" he said, rubbing his arm. "You could have warned us."

A loud horn suddenly blared, and Nathan saw a flashing red light.

Malick pointed over the dashboard. "Sorry," he said, "but a train was coming." He had an apologetic look on his face. "I didn't see it until the last minute."

Nathan adjusted his seat belt and glanced at Jonas. "That's why you wear a seat belt," he said. He then pointed at Malick and continued, "Especially if his truly is driving."

Jonas made his way back into the backseat and fastened his seat belt. "I hate that freakin' train!" he grumbled.

Nathan's face squinted as he peered through the front windshield. "Where is the railroad crossing guard?" he asked. It was difficult to see because of the downpour of rain. "All we have is a flashing red light?"

"I don't know," said Jonas. "And the stupid train runs right behind our house."

"That sucks!" commented Malick.

"Yeah," said Jonas. "Try sleeping through the screeching sound of an approaching train at midnight."

Slowly, the silver metallic car pulled into the driveway of the next-to-last house at the end of the block. Malick turned off the engine, shutting off the radio and causing the rapid motion of the windshield wipers to come to a stop. He squinted as he tried to look through the fast-accumulating raindrops. "You are right," he said. "You can see the railroad tracks right behind your fence."

"Yeah," responded Jonas. "And it sucks."

Nathan got out of the car and stood outside. The block that Jonas lived on was heavily lined with trees. That plus the rain gave the street an ominous appearance.

Malick rested a hand against the wet car, and Jonas walked across the grass to the concrete path that led to the front door of the house.

Nathan waved his hand through the air. The heavy rain was now a light mist. "At least the rain has finally let up," he said.

"I know," commented Malick in a drawn-out voice. "I was really getting tired of being trapped indoors."

Nathan watched as Jonas sprinted up the steps to the red door of the gray, one-story bungalow. The modest house with sloping roof and white trim had a cheery appearance, and the red potted flowers that hung from the porch and adorned the gray steps stood out against the overcast day.

Jonas looked excited as he knocked on the door. "Come on, guys!" he shouted. "What are you standing over there for?"

Nathan and Malick carefully cut across the grass. Malick made an effort not to get mud on his shoes.

"I've never seen you be so particular about walking in mud before," said Nathan.

Malick looked up. "It's rude to track mud into somebody's house." he said.

"Oh," said Nathan, as he rubbed the bottom of his shoes against the yellow straw mat in front of the red door. "Jonas," he said. "Don't you think your parents will find it odd that you're showing up like this? I mean, technically you should really be at camp."

"Nah, it's okay," he said. "My mom is expecting me."

Nathan looked confused. "What?" he asked. "Why?"

Jonas smiled. "I was going to sneak out regardless of whether you were coming," he said. "Remember? I told my mom I was coming home yesterday."

Nathan slowly nodded. "Oh — yeah — right," he said. Then he suddenly looked confused again. "And she went along with it?"

The red door to the front of the house quickly swung open.

"Jonas Bartholomew Riley!" shouted the woman at the door. "Give your mother a hug!"

Jonas smiled big and embraced the lady with curly blond hair. She was short in comparison to Jonas, and his arms could probably wrap twice around her tiny waist.

"I love you, Mom," he said, while still wrapped in her embrace.

"Aw," she uttered, "I love you too, honey!" She attempted to comfort Jonas by rubbing his back. "These three weeks away from home must have really gotten to you."

"Jonas!" shouted another voice.

Jonas quickly released his mom. "Bobby!" he yelled with excitement. Jonas playfully ruffled the dark curly hair of the boy in front of him. "Did you miss your big brother?" he asked.

Bobby winced playfully. "Um, a little," he said, and then he grinned. "What's to miss when you've called practically every night this week?"

Jonas playfully put Bobby into a headlock and continued to ruffle his hair. "I am going to take that as a yes!"

Jonas' mom turned around to glance at Nathan and Malick. "Oh, my goodness, how rude of me," she said. "And is it still raining?" She paused briefly to stick her head outside the door. "Come in, come in," she said, with a hand gesture, "before it starts raining again."

She closed the door and faced them, peering over her glasses, which sat oddly crookedly on her nose. "Ah," she said. "Let me guess — you must be Nathan."

Nathan paused. He was a little startled by her accurate prediction. "Yeah," he said. "That's me."

Jonas's mom clapped her hands together and smiled. "Oh!" she said, dragging out the word. "I am just so thrilled to meet you."

Nathan raised his eyebrows and gave a quick look to Malick before rewarding her with an awkward smile.

Linda placed her hands on her hips and laughed so loudly that Malick jumped back.

She smiled and fluttered her eyelashes. "Don't act so surprised," she said. "Jonas talks about you all the time!"

She extended a hand first to Malick and then to Nathan.

"As you probably already guessed," she said, "I am Jonas's mother, Linda Ann Riley."

Nathan still had a surprised but awkward look on his

face. "Nice to meet you, Mrs. Riley," he said, while shaking her hand.

"Aw," she said. "Just call me Linda." She fluttered her eyelashes over her glasses again and grinned at Malick. "And I apologize; what's your name?"

Malick gave a cynical smile. It looked like he was trying not to laugh. "Stephen," he said, "Stephen Malick, but just Malick will do."

Linda stared at Malick. She raised one eyebrow and twitched her lip. "Malick," she said. She hesitated before speaking again. "Oh, okay. Well, then have a seat, Malick. And you too, Nathan."

Nathan sat down next to Malick on a yellow-and-white floral upholstered sofa, and Linda sat in the matching armchair. The living room was neat and sparsely decorated. In the corner, next to a bronze floor lamp, a Siamese cat was sprawled out on the hardwood floor. Nathan thought the cat's bright blue eyes were hypnotizing.

"Jonas!" said Bobby. He had an excited look on his face. "Guess what?" he asked. "I finally completed the last board of *Wizards and Warriors!*" Bobby grabbed Jonas by the hand. "Come on," he said. "Do you wanna see?"

Jonas smiled. "Oh, okay," he said. "But you need to say hello to Nathan and Malick first."

Bobby quickly looked over at Nathan and Malick. It was as if he had noticed them for the first time.

"Oh, hi," he said. He slowly walked over to Nathan and put out his hand. "Nice to meet you," he said. "I'm Bobby. Do you play video games?"

Bobby looked tired, and there were what appeared to be faint scratches on his forearm. Nathan noticed the scratches were red, so he assumed they were probably recent. "I play a little," he said with a smile. "But it's been a while since I've last played a video game."

Bobby turned to Malick. "Do you play?" he asked.

Malick ran his hand through his hair. "I've played my share," he responded cockily.

Jonas turned to look at Nathan. "I'll make it quick," he said.

Nathan nodded and Jonas hurried around the corner with his little brother.

"Jonas is really good with his little brother," said Linda. "He really does look out for him. He's done a great job encouraging Bobby with school and with his studies."

"He mentioned Bobby has been having problems in school," said Nathan.

The Siamese cat that had been spread out on the floor next to the floor lamp was now at the foot of Linda's leg. It purred as Linda rubbed its back.

"This is Lacey," Linda said. "She helps to keep me company."

Linda paused. She suddenly appeared uncomfortable. "He's a young boy," she said. "Considering everything that happened, I think he's doing well." She looked sad, but still tried to smile. "He's still doing the normal things most boys his age do," she said. "Playing video games, roughhousing with his brother — you know, the normal stuff."

Nathan was a little confused. He didn't know what she meant by "considering everything that happened."

"So are things better now?" he asked. "I mean, did something happen at school?"

"Well," she said, "things have gotten a little better. His teacher said he's turning assignments in on time, but falling asleep in class is still an issue. I think he sneaks at night to play his video games, but I don't want to come down too hard on him."

Lacey attempted to sit next to Malick, but he shooed her away. She meowed and Nathan leaned over to pet her.

"This might sound strange," Nathan said, "but I noticed there were some scratches on Bobby's forearm. Did he fall recently?"

"Oh," said Linda, looking slightly surprised, "he probably got a few scuffs and scrapes climbing trees." She smiled. "You know, just being a typical nine-year-old. His father was so good at keeping him in line and watching after him when he played outside. It's just been so difficult for Bobby, and for Jonas too, I'm sure."

"Wait," said Nathan. "I know that Jonas is close to his brother, but why has it been so hard for him?"

Linda looked confused. "Wait. What?" she said. She paused for a second and then suddenly placed her hand to her mouth. "You don't know, do you?" she asked. "I thought Jonas had told you."

Nathan felt clueless. He turned to Malick, who only shrugged.

"Told us what?" Nathan asked.

Linda looked as if she was fighting back tears. "They lost their father not too long ago." she said. Her nose began to run and she started to sniffle.

Malick grabbed a tissue from the nearby end table and handed it to her.

"The police believe he may have been murdered," she said.

"Jonas hasn't said anything," said Nathan in a somber tone. "I'm so sorry. I didn't know."

"It's okay," she said. "That's why I don't want to be so hard on Bobby. I'm sure climbing trees and playing video games is his way of dealing with losing his father." Linda blew her nose into the tissue. "They need time. I want them to be able to grieve in their own way."

Nathan could feel his cell phone vibrate in his pocket again. He quickly placed his hand in his pocket to turn it off. "I apologize for asking this," he said. "Do you mind saying what happened?"

A tear ran down her face and she blew her nose again. "See Bart —" she said.

"Bart?" interrupted Nathan.

"Yes. Bart, my husband, used to work late." She paused and then smiled. "In fact, he liked to work late. See, Bart was a little bit of an insomniac. Bobby reminds me of him; I think he works better at night too." Linda's smile faded away and her face became more somber. "He would often work on projects when he couldn't sleep, sometimes even driving to the office late at night," she said. "I didn't notice it at first, but Bart's nightly disappearances were really starting to affect Jonas."

Nathan looked confused again. "Why did it bother Jonas?"

"Jonas is a light sleeper, unlike me," she said. "And he would often wake up to the sound of Bart's car leaving the driveway. Jonas knew this was typical of his father, but would try to stay up until his father returned, anyway."

Nathan looked concerned. "Did this affect Jonas in school?"

"No," said Linda. "Bart would come home to find Jonas asleep on the sofa. And again, Jonas is a light sleeper, so sometimes after Jonas had woken up, they would end up talking, particularly about basketball." Tears were building in her eyes. "But that was before things got worse," she said. She blew her nose and wiped the tears. "Bart would return back home extremely tired and sometimes bewildered or confused. It got to the point that I begged him to see somebody, to see a doctor, but he wouldn't listen."

"About his insomnia?" asked Nathan.

Linda nodded and her crooked gold-rimmed glasses started to slip down her nose. "He insisted that it was just stress from work, that things would get better. But things didn't get better. See, one night Jonas woke up from what he said sounded like a train; I think he said it was about midnight. Jonas walked the house like he normally does after he wakes up and noticed that his father was gone, but Bart's car was still in the driveway."

A few creases formed on Nathan's forehead. "Where did he go?" he asked.

There was angst in her voice. "We don't know," she said. "We looked everywhere, but we couldn't find him." Linda paused to look down at her hands. "It had snowed that day. Jonas's hands and feet were so blue from searching all day and night. We got a call from the police about a week later; they found Bart's body somewhere out on Route 7."

She sobbed and Malick handed her another tissue.

"I know they miss their father," she sniffled. "The last gift Bart gave Jonas was an autographed basketball from Jonas's favorite player. Jonas still carries it around with him."

"I am so sorry about your husband," said Nathan. "How long ago did this happen?"

"Back in December," Linda sobbed. "Of last year." She removed her glasses and dabbed her eyes. "The police have no leads, but the case is still open."

Laughter suddenly filled the room as Jonas and Bobby filed in.

"I beat you fair and square!" shouted Jonas.

"How about a rematch?" asked Bobby. "I know my warriors will take out your wizards!"

Jonas attempted to grab his brother and tickle him. "I'll give you a rematch," he said.

Nathan watched Jonas roughhouse with his little brother. He was still astonished by what he'd just learned.

Malick stood up and stretched, and Lacey suddenly ran away.

"We probably should be heading back," he said.

Nathan glanced at the yellow-and-silver trimmed clock on the wall. "You're right," he said. "We probably should get going."

Linda's glasses lay crooked on her nose again as she smiled. "Okay," she said. "I am so glad you got a chance to visit, Nathan. It was so nice to finally meet you. And you too, Malick."

Malick grinned. "You too, Mrs. Riley," he said, while nodding his head.

Linda took Nathan by the hand. "Thank you for bringing Jonas home," she said.

"No problem," replied Nathan.

"Okay, bro," said Jonas. "I'll see you in about a week, and then we'll see about that rematch."

Bobby smiled.

Linda opened the front door, and Lacey darted outside. Nathan quickly raised his leg to avoid stepping on her.

"Will you be coming to the closing ceremony on Saturday?" he asked Linda.

"Yes," she smiled. "I'll be there."

"What about Bobby?" asked Jonas.

Bobby awaited a response, intently.

Linda looked down and peered over her glasses. "We'll have to see," she said. "It depends on whether Bobby intends to keep turning in his homework."

"You heard it, bro," said Jonas. "If you want to come, you will have to finish your homework."

"I got it," said Bobby confidently. "Done!"

Jonas glared at him incredulously.

Bobby laughed. "I'm serious," he said.

"Cool," said Jonas, hugging his brother.

Malick fired up the silver Camaro once again, and Jonas waved good-bye to his brother and mother. Nathan reached inside his pocket to turn on his cell phone; it was vibrating furiously.

"Look at all these text messages," he said nervously. "Lafonda's going to kill me!"

CHAPTER SIXTEEN

PNEUMA NOVO

Nathan spent most of the day by himself. It was Saturday and almost the end of June, so although it had rained heavily practically all the previous week, this was summer. And not just any summer, but a blistering hot and humid Illinois one, which meant no trace of water anywhere. The moist and muddy ground beneath Nathan's feet had already started to form dry cracks.

Nathan stepped out of the woods and onto the small pebble-and-rock beach surrounding Lake Charleston. The heavily wooded trail leading to the lake provided a much-welcomed shade from the sun, but he got no relief from the evening sun when he walked over to the edge of the lake.

Nathan glanced into a few fire pits; some were dry, but some were still damp. He didn't know how LaDonda expected them to have a bonfire just a day after it stopped raining. He reached into the pockets of his shorts to pull out his cell phone. "Not a single call or text," he murmured. "Lafonda is definitely upset with me."

Lafonda was upset with him for leaving camp the night before. He wasn't surprised that she had kept it secret from LaDonda. Since they were kids, they'd had an unwritten rule to cover for each other if it meant saving the other person from being in major trouble. She had figured out that he had left with Malick and Jonas, but she wanted to know where they had gone. Nathan knew that he had made matters worse when he repeatedly dodged her questions.

He sighed. Just thinking about having to hide more things from her was starting to get to him, but he was convinced the less she knew the better. He was determined to prevent his dream at Grimm Cemetery from coming true, even if it meant having Lafonda upset with him for keeping her in the dark.

He watched the motion of the water as it made small waves around the lake. Besides the occasional birds and splashing sounds made by fish, it was quiet. Nathan found a dry patch and sat down. He had a little time before Malick would show up to help with the bonfires, and he figured it would be a while before Argus appeared with his wheelbarrow and bad jokes. Nathan looked down at his hands. It had been a week since he followed Jonas into the pseudo stairway and discovered that he too had a power. But he still didn't have answers to why Jonas was in a trance, why he felt his brother was there with them, and who or what those creatures were.

Nathan picked up a rock and skipped it across the lake. *But those same creatures were there in the beginning,* he thought. *They were there in my dreams about Leah.*

"What do they want?" he murmured. "What do they want with Jonas and Leah?"

He stopped searching for rocks and paused to look at his hands.

"How did Leah end up all those times in the pseudo reality?" he asked himself. "Does Leah have a power too?" He felt himself becoming more frustrated. "Where are Malick and Argus, anyway?" He looked down at his hands again; they were a little dirty, but they looked normal. He didn't want to admit it, but he was apprehensive about using his powers again. He glanced over his shoulder and then around the lake and chuckled. "I wonder if I can get this to work without my life being in danger"

Nathan stood over one of the fire pits. "How did I get that blue spark to come out of my hands before? I know I set my bed on fire. I just don't know how I did it."

He looked around again, to see if anyone was coming, and placed his hand over the fire pit. He focused on the charred pieces of wood and stiffened his hand, but nothing happened. "Ugh!" he moaned. "Why didn't this gift come with instructions?"

He took another deep breath and stretched his hand over the fire pit. This time, he thought about his dream at Grimm Cemetery. Images of the woman dressed in white and the silver dagger flooded his mind. Suddenly, the muscles in his hand twitched and he felt the cemetery steps crumbling beneath him again. His head rang with hissing sounds as the red-hooded figure with the crescent-shaped medallion closed in on him. The muscle fibers in his hand twitched again and his fingers and palms turned red. His arm went rigid and the muscles in his hand tightened, forcibly releasing a brilliant ball of blue light from his hand.

Nathan quickly ducked as pieces of wood flew over his head. There was the sound of water splashing as several pieces hit the water. He slowly looked into the bin to examine the remaining blown-up pieces. "Still no blue flame," he grumbled. "But I guess this is a start."

Nathan continued to concentrate and, with his hand stretched over the pit again, released another ball of blue light. This time, he quickly shielded his eyes as pieces of wood sprung from the fire pit. He smiled, but was suddenly distracted by something shimmering in the sunlight: a gray-and-red aluminum can rested on top of one of the smaller wood bins. He raised his hand and a beam of light pierced the air, pulverizing the top of the wood bin and sending the pop can high into the air.

"I didn't mean to do that," he laughed. "But cool."

"What on earth are you doing?" someone yelled.

Nathan jumped; he'd thought he was alone. He dropped his hand and spun around just in time to see Argus charging towards him.

"I can explain," he said nervously. He pointed to the shattered wood bin. "It's not as bad it looks."

Argus placed the wheelbarrow he was pushing to the side. "Are you crazy?" he asked.

"It's okay," said Nathan. "It's probably easy to fix … really." Nathan attempted to demonstrate how it could be fixed, but the wood bin pieces crumbled in his hand.

Argus's eyes burned red with anger. "This is not about some stupid wood bin," he said.

"What?" asked Nathan.

"What are you doing using your powers so openly like that?" Argus demanded. "My brother must have lost his mind! Do you know what will happen if you are exposed? All the lives put in danger, and everything that would be lost?"

"Wait!" said Nathan. "My powers, your brother; you know about my powers? But how?"

Argus waved his arms in the air. "Of course I know about your powers! I've been keeping an eye on both of you."

"Both of us?" asked Nathan.

Argus turned his head, and Nathan saw Malick hastily coming towards them.

"Why do you think I stopped leaving matches and hardly any lighter fluid?" Argus continued. "I wanted to be sure, but to actually catch you out in the open?"

Malick now stood behind Argus.

"And I've been watching you too," Argus said, turning around. "I've had my eye on you since you got here. I know who you are."

Argus picked up the handles to the wheelbarrow and rolled it beside one of the fire pits. He tossed in a bottle of lighter fluid and a box of matches from his back pocket. Then he leaned in and whispered angrily to Malick, "If you try anything, I promise you, you will regret it!"

Argus's right eye trembled and he glared one last time at Nathan and then at Malick before storming up the trail to the Hiking and Camping Center.

"What the heck was that?" asked Nathan. "Why was he threatening you? And what did he mean by he knows who you are?"

Malick grabbed Nathan by the arm, pushing him backwards. "Who are you?" he asked. "Who is your family?" His grip tightened. "Are they a part of the Order?"

Nathan's forehead wrinkled. "The Order? It's just me and my grandfather." He wrestled his arm free from Malick's grip. "What are you talking about? What the heck is going on?"

Malick's eyes bulged and bored into Nathan's for a long time. Finally, he dropped his gaze and turned around. "Did you see the tattoo on Argus's arm?" he asked. "Does it look familiar to you?"

Nathan's forehead wrinkled again. "I've seen it before. But what does this have to do with anything?"

Malick sat down on one of the logs surrounding the

fire pits. "It's used as the symbol for the Order," he said. "It's a part of their crest."

"Wait a minute," said Nathan. "I know where else I've seen that symbol. At the first bonfire. Jonathan said it was one of the Cahokia symbols he had trouble deciphering."

"Look," said Malick, "all you need to know is to stop using your powers in public or anywhere that isn't safe."

"What?" said Nathan. "How did you know? Are you watching me, or something?" The frown lines on Nathan's forehead deepened. "And Argus said he has a brother; is he watching me too?"

Malick's face had a slightly haughty expression on it as he raised his eyebrows. "I don't know if they are watching you," he said. "But chances are they are both a part of the Order." Malick huffed. "And no, I am not watching you, but I did however, see you using Pneuma to destroy that wood bin."

Nathan's eyes were wide but skeptical. "Pneuma?" he asked. He folded his arms across his chest. "And for the record, I wasn't aiming at the wood bin. I was trying to hit the soda can."

Malick gave a quick glance at the destroyed wood bin. "Okay," he chuckled. "Whatever you say."

Nathan rolled his eyes in protest.

"Pneuma is your life force, or your spirit energy," Malick said finally through stifled chuckles.

"Life force? Spirit energy? Are you for real?"

"Um, are your powers real?" asked Malick.

Nathan twisted his lip to the side of his face and nodded. "Good point," he said. "So what does this Pneuma have to do with me? Why am I able to do this stuff?"

"Everyone has Pneuma, Nathan, not just you," Malick said with a grin. "Pneuma is everywhere: in the trees, the air, the water, in animals; even the Earth has Pneuma."

Nathan had a sour look on his face. "Okay, I got it," he said. "But you can answer the question without being condescending?"

Malick lowered his voice. He suddenly had a serious look on his face. "What you just did is called Pneuma Novo," he said. "And having the ability to manipulate your Pneuma is a rare gift and shouldn't be taken lightly."

Nathan took a seat next to him.

"Spirit energy manipulation can take many forms," continued Malick. "And you just performed one of them."

"What do you mean?"

"When you used Pneuma to hit the soda can, you were manipulating spirit energy to form a projectile of energy; sort of like a weapon."

Nathan looked impatient. "So why me? Why am I able to do this stuff?"

"I don't know. It's usually hereditary," he said. "Are you sure no one in your family is a part of the Order?"

Nathan paused. "Not that I know of," he said. "It's just my grandfather and me."

"What about your parents?" he asked. "Your mom or your dad?"

Nathan's face grew soft. "I don't know," he said. "At least I don't think so. My parents died shortly after I was born."

Malick grew quiet as he gazed into the lake.

"So what does all this have to do with you?" Nathan interrupted. "Why was Argus threatening you?"

Malick had a serious look on his face again. "Look," he said, "I am not the person you should be worried about. There are dark and powerful forces out there looking for people like you and me."

Nathan's eyes grew wide and his mouth fell open. "You and me?" he asked. "Dark and powerful forces — what are you talking about?" Nervously, he rubbed the back of his neck. "Are you talking about the Order? What do they want from me?"

Malick had a strained tone. "Like I said before, all you need to know is to stop using your powers. The less you know the better, Nathan." Malick's expression lightened up and became reassuring. "Just stay low and don't use your powers," he said. "If you do that, you won't have anything to worry about."

He stood up and walked over to the wheelbarrow Argus had left behind. Nathan watched as Malick filled the pits.

Dark and powerful forces? Nathan thought. His mind began to flood with images of Grimm Cemetery, the silver sword, Lafonda.

"Wait!" he blurted out, springing to his feet.

Malick jumped, abruptly dropping the wood in his hands back into the wheelbarrow. As he slowly turned around to face Nathan, his eyebrows were raised.

"What do you know about dreams?" Nathan asked, sounding almost out of breath. "Can Pneuma be used to see the future?"

Malick paused, but then continued to fill the fire pits. "Yes," he answered slowly. "I assume you're asking because you're having dreams that are coming true."

"Well, yeah!"

Malick looked surprised. "I'm impressed," he said. "Your list of abilities is starting to rack up, and you are learning about them all on your own."

A look of gloom washed over Nathan's face. "Well, it hasn't been all that great so far," he said with a shrug. "And I wouldn't say being different is necessarily a good thing."

Malick grinned. "Using Pneuma to see the past or future through dreams or premonitions is another form of spirit manipulation, or Pneuma Novo," he said. "It's not as common as some of the other forms of spirit manipulation, but it is one of them. Many Dream Walkers have a difficult time mastering it."

"Dream Walkers?"

"Yeah," he nodded. "Some cultures, including the Cahokia Indians, affectionately referred to those who could see the past or future as Dream Walkers, and I guess it just stuck."

Nathan leaned over to help Malick fill the wheelbarrow with more wood from the smaller bins lined around the beach.

"Why is it so hard to control?" Nathan asked.

"Controlling spirit energy to see the past or future is just hard to do," said Malick with a shrug. "And many Dream Walkers never master it."

Nathan remained still for a moment before twisting his lip and nodding. "So, I guess it's safe to assume you can do Pneuma Novo, too."

Malick grinned. "Yeah," he said. "I guess so." He suddenly looked serious again. "But you have to promise to keep this a secret," he said. "It's not okay to tell people about your ability, like I said."

"I know," interrupted Nathan, while rolling his eyes. "Dark and powerful forces."

Malick nodded ardently. "Yes!" he exclaimed.

Nathan helped Malick pile wood into the fire pits, until he got a splinter in his hand. "So," he said, trying to remove the splinter without placing his dirty fingers into his mouth. "Can everyone who can do Pneuma Novo release energy as a weapon or see visions?"

"No. For the most part, your ability or the forms it can take are innate. It's rare for someone to be able to learn a new ability that wasn't first hereditary."

"So basically how you can perform Pneuma Novo or the different ways in which you can manipulate spirit energy is limited to your parents."

Malick smiled. "Or your parents' parents. Pneuma Novo has been known to skip a generation, and so have powers. Just because you can dream walk doesn't mean that one of your parents could; it could have been a great-great-grandfather or a grandmother."

Nathan's eyebrows were raised. "So, when exactly are you going to tell me what you can do?" He laughed and made quotation marks with his fingers in the air. "And don't give me any of that 'it's complicated' or 'it's dangerous' stuff."

Malick grinned and then laughed. "I'll do better than that: I'll show you. But first …" he reached into his shirt and pulled out a silver chain; a brilliant silver pendant dangled from it. "It's an arrowhead," Malick continued, while carefully examining it with his hand. "It's enchanted with prayers and stuff to keep my powers hidden, but I still have to be careful not to be seen in public; it keeps me hidden from —"

"The dark and powerful forces," interrupted Nathan. He raised one eyebrow in protest. "Which you haven't told me about, by the way."

Malick grinned, but then suddenly looked serious. He raised his hand and cast his gaze over the surface of the lake. A blue light began to glow around his hand. Then, it shot out of his hand like a rocket, smashing into the middle of the lake. A huge amount of water was violently thrown into the air, only to return back slowly to the Earth.

Nathan looked up towards the sky. Sprinkles of water landed on his shoulders and face, cooling him off. "I needed that," he said with a smile.

"I know what you mean," responded Malick eagerly. "I've wanted to do that since the first bonfire. This summer sun is killing me, and it's an easy way to cool off!" He continued to fill the fire pits. "Just stay cool and keep your powers under wraps for now, and I'll see about finding you something to cloak your powers with."

"But wait!" Nathan blurted out. "There's more!"

Malick stood up straight and rubbed his lower back. "Can this wait?" he asked. "It's really getting late, and we haven't even started the fires yet."

Frown lines appeared on Nathan's face again. "It's about Lafonda," he said.

"Don't worry," interrupted Malick. "You'll be able to tell her all about your ability with time."

"No," Nathan said, "that's not it." Nathan's eyes grew weary. "It has to do with my dreams, and I really don't know what to do about it!"

"Remember what I said the other day?" Malick said. "About living in the present and not in the future?"

Nathan reluctantly nodded. "Yeah, but —"

"Well, it even applies here too. You can't live in the future, Nathan."

"No!" demanded Nathan. "This is serious and I need your help!" His hands trembled. "In my dream Lafonda died, and I am not talking about watching it from afar — she died in my arms!"

Malick grew silent. His face was blank but there was a hint of sadness in his eyes. "Look Nathan," he said, placing a hand on his shoulder. "I know this will be difficult to hear, but you can't prevent the future. You have to live for today. Besides, dreams or premonitions of the future are never certain; they are based on peoples' current choices, and people change their minds every day."

"But what about Lafonda?" Nathan protested. "Are you telling me to just let her die?"

Malick lowered his eyes. "The one thing that I have learned, living in our world and with our abilities, is that you have to live in the present, Nathan," he said. "And not in the past or the possible future. You have to write your own destiny, live your own truth — not what people, the past, or the future say it should be."

Nathan still looked frantic. "There has to be something I can do!" he pleaded.

"I'm sorry, Nathan. The best thing you can do is to not let fear of the future dictate your choices. Live in the present and allow for the natural course of life to happen, regardless of what you think you already know."

"But —"

Malick quickly interrupted. "What you do today or what Lafonda chooses to do will decide the future, not some premonition or dream."

Nathan stood idle while watching Malick fiddle with the lighter fluid bottle.

Occasionally, Malick would look up, and Nathan would turn his head away.

The best thing I can do is do nothing? Nathan thought. *How can I do nothing and just let Lafonda die? What's the point of premonitions and prophetic dreams if you can't do anything about it?*

Nathan wiped water from his ear. His hair was still damp from the sprinkles of water. He turned around to look at Malick again, this time focusing on his hands. He watched as Malick continued to have difficulty with the lighter fluid bottle and matches to start the fire.

"You were an expert at that about a week ago," Nathan laughed.

Malick grinned. "Well, that was a week ago," he said, passing the bottle to Nathan.

Nathan smiled nervously. He glanced at Malick's hands again. He remembered how much control he had in casting the energy ball into the lake. Nathan stared at the lighter fluid bottle in his hands.

"What about fire?" Nathan blurted out.

"Yeah," chuckled Malick. "I thought that was the goal here."

"No, not that!" said Nathan with frustration. "Is fire an ability of Pneuma Novo too?"

Malick's eyes carefully studied Nathan's face. "That's an interesting question," he said. "Why are you asking that?"

Nathan hesitated. "In my dream," he said, "after Lafonda died ... something else happened."

Malick looked on curiously, "What?"

"In my dream," said Nathan, "a blue flame came out of my hand, and I am pretty sure it wasn't just a dream because when I awoke, the foot of my bed was on fire."

Malick had a blank look on his face. Slowly, he sat down on one of the logs again. "Are you saying you set the bed on fire with like a book of matches?"

Nathan rolled his eyes. "No!" he protested.

Malick continued to look on skeptically.

"I admit I wasn't sure myself at first, but I know that fire came from out of my hand," Nathan said.

"Maybe you just don't remember setting the fire," Malick said doubtfully.

"The fire was blue!"

Malick lowered his head. "This can't be true," he said, underneath his breath. "I mean what are the odds? This has to be next to impossible!" He looked into Nathan's longing and inquisitive face. "But if what you are saying is true …" He sat in contemplation for a moment. Then he softly bit his lip before abruptly springing to his feet. "This just keeps getting worse!" he grumbled.

"What?" asked Nathan eagerly. "What is it? I mean, why is it impossible?"

Malick shook his head. He appeared slightly gloomy. "You sure are racking it up in the gifts department," he said.

"So fire is a form of Pneuma Novo?" asked Nathan.

"Yes," answered Malick. "Not only is it a form of Pneuma Novo, it's the rarest one there is." Malick began to pace around the fire pit. "There is only one person ever known to manipulate Pneuma into fire, Nathan," he said. "And the story about that person sounds more like something you would tell around a campfire or read in a fairy tale."

"So what does this mean? Am I in danger?"

Malick faked a chuckle. "More than you apparently already are?"

Nathan didn't look amused.

Malick slowly nodded. "Yes," he said, "you are in more danger than I first realized."

Nathan grew silent. His thoughts were racing and he felt overwhelmed. He didn't know where to start or what to do. First Leah was in danger, then his friends, and now he was too.

"Have you used your ability since the dream?" asked Malick.

"No," answered Nathan slowly. He paused. "But then again — well, technically, yes."

Malick looked confused. "You mean today, when you produced an energy ball to hit that wood bin?"

"Right, but not exactly," Nathan said. "The other day I used my ability to produce an energy ball to protect myself and Jonas from these creatures."

Malick pursed his lips. "Little black-and-gray furry ones with razor sharp fangs that will cut into you like fire ants at a picnic?"

Nathan nodded. "Yes."

Malick began to pace again. "This just keeps getting better and better," he responded sarcastically. "You know," he said. "Feel free to just stop talking at any time."

"Sorry!" apologized Nathan. "But what does this all mean?"

Malick paused to wipe the sweat from his forehead. "Wow, this is intense," he said. "And Jonas is involved in this too?" He stared blankly for a moment before slowly running his hands through his hair. "Well, I guess it's a safe bet that they know who you are if they are sending Shadow Creatures after you."

"Shadow Creatures?" asked Nathan.

"Yeah. They are called Shadow Creatures because normally they are cloaked in shadow." Malick had an ornery look on his face. "The cute little black-and-gray furry ones with sharp claws and teeth are called Necrocritters."

"That would explain how they could be here one moment, then gone the next," responded Nathan.

"Yeah," said Malick. "When they are cloaked in shadow they are very difficult to defend against because they are so hard to see."

Nathan nodded. "But you know what?" he said. "I don't think they were after me."

A few wrinkles appeared on Malick's forehead. "What do you mean?" he asked.

"I don't think they were after me at all. I think they were after Jonas."

"Jonas?" asked Malick in disbelief. "Why would they be after Jonas?"

"Last week," said Nathan, "the night of the bonfire, I woke up to find Jonas in a trance, and when I followed him," Nathan took a moment to lean in, "somehow he created a doorway to some type of pseudo dimension. I don't know how else to describe it. It was like a black-and-white version of our world, just absent of people. I know I've been there before, in my dreams about Leah and in my dream about Grimm Cemetery. It's like everything there was frozen."

"Wait," said Malick. "Who is Leah? Is she another person at camp?"

"No," said Nathan. "It's a long story, but I think Leah was being attacked by the same Shadow Creatures."

Malick looked confused again. "So how did she get into the Spirit Realm?" he asked.

"The Spirit Realm?" asked Nathan.

"The Spirit Realm or the Space In Between," said Malick. "If Leah was attacked by the same Shadow Creatures she had to have been in the Spirit Realm."

"Why is that?" asked Nathan.

"Some Shadow Creatures are sensitive to natural light and are afraid to cross over into our realm," said Malick. "Trust me, if Leah was attacked by the Necrocritters she was not here."

Nathan stood in silence as Malick attempted to kindle another pit from the fire Nathan had started.

"It's been a week since you've encountered them, right?" Malick asked.

Nathan nodded.

"And your friend Leah, she's okay, and so are Jonas

and Lafonda, right?" he asked.

Nathan nodded again. "Yeah."

"Then for now it looks like they are safe," said Malick. "And we should concentrate on finding a way to cloak your powers."

"But why?" asked Nathan. "You said that as long as I don't use them, I should be safe."

Malick paused. "Yeah, they won't be able to detect you if you aren't using your powers. However, it doesn't help you any if you are forced to use your abilities to protect yourself," he said. "It also doesn't help if you are unconsciously using them in your dreams." Malick chuckled. "I guess it's just another challenge to being a Dream Walker."

Nathan shook his head. "You're telling me," he said. "It's becoming more like a curse. Having the ability to see the future sounds good, but it hasn't been working out for me." He looked down at his hands again before staring into the fire. "And to top things off, it's probably going to get me killed."

"We'll figure out something," said Malick. "And make sure Jonas doesn't use his ability either."

"That shouldn't be a problem, because I don't think he even knows how to."

Malick let out a slight chuckle. "Good," he said.

"But wait," said Nathan. "If you knew all along about the Space In Between stuff and about the Cahokia symbol, why did you try so hard to convince Jonathan that none of it was real?"

Malick frowned. "Because Jonathan doesn't know what he's getting himself into," he said coldly. "And the less he and everyone else know the better." His tone suddenly softened. "For his sake, he needs to stay in the dark as long as possible. Knowing this stuff changes lives,

Nathan. I've seen it destroy people."

"How?" What do you mean?"

Malick looked sympathetic. "Some people panic and become reclusive after discovering about the world that lies beyond their white picket fences. Others become obsessed," he said. "They become fixated on knowing more to become a part of something new, and when they do, they either disappear, get killed or become a part of the walking dead."

"Well, it doesn't look like I have a choice," said Nathan.

Malick got on his knees and took a deep breath. He slowly blew air into the wood chips and the rising smoke that kindled the last fire. "This is really strange," he said. "Both you and Jonas can Pneuma Novo, but neither of your families are a part of the Order. I wonder what else is going on at this camp."

CHAPTER SEVENTEEN

HEROES

Nathan sat quietly in the small computer lab in the basement of Lawrence Hall. He didn't like being stuck in the square, white room another day while campers worked on their final leadership projects. He wished LaDonda had scheduled them in the much larger computer lab in Fisher Hall next door. Fisher Hall's computer lab was on the first floor and had a nice view of the quad.

Nathan stared blankly at the black computer screen. Over the soft hum of the air conditioner and the sharp clicking sounds of neighboring keyboards, his mind wandered. Occasionally, his thoughts were interrupted by ongoing conversations about the end of camp and the closing ceremony and banquet on Saturday. They had been at camp for three weeks now and most campers were sad to be leaving their newfound friends. But still, for the most part, everyone was excited to finally be able to see their families and loved ones. Nathan was excited too. An entire week had gone by without an attack from the Shadow Creatures, and his dreams were just as absent of any impending danger. In fact, most of his dreams had been about food. In his latest dream, no matter how much he ate, his plate would automatically refill with a tall stack of his favorite food: pecan pancakes.

Nathan was also relieved. He had taken Malick's advice and stopped using his powers, and he knew that soon Leadership Camp would be over. Every day since his first dream about Leah and the dream about Grimm Cemetery, he'd felt very responsible for Leah, Lafonda and Jonas.

He had an overwhelming sense of duty to help Leah and to keep his friends safe, but Leah was back home now, and soon Jonas would be too; and he and Lafonda would be back at the Devaro Mansion. Nathan couldn't wait until this was all over. In fact, he often caught himself daydreaming about sitting outside by the pool behind the Devaro Mansion.

Only a few more days now.

He didn't want to think about anything other than what he would be doing for the rest of the summer, but his stomach continued to twist into knots. He tried not to think about all the unanswered questions that plagued him after he'd been discovered by Malick.

Nathan sat back in his chair and sighed. He had so many unanswered questions. And how long did Malick expect him to stay in the dark?

Nathan tapped his fingers on the armrest of his chair. "Who is Argus's brother?" he asked himself. "And why did Argus threaten Malick?" He tilted his head to the side as the slew of questions continued to spill out. "What did he mean by 'don't try anything'? What had he been afraid that Malick would do?"

A couple of campers were trying to exchange phone numbers, and Nathan tried to tune them out. *Who are these dark and terrible forces?* he pondered.

He remembered how adamant Malick had been about keeping him and everyone else in the dark. *Was it really for our safety?* he thought. And why did Malick know so much about Shadow Creatures and about the Order?

Nathan sat up in his chair. He saw his reflection in the black computer screen. He paused for a moment, stopped tapping his fingers, and then suddenly decided to turn on the computer. "Shadow Creatures," he mumbled.

The black screen came to life and he clicked on the web browser to launch the search engine. Nathan typed in *Shadow Creatures* and pressed enter. "Shadow Creatures," he read to himself, "also known as Shadow Men, Shadow Ghosts or Shadow People." He raised his eyebrows and huffed, surveying the claw marks still visible on his shoes. "I know one thing," he said to himself, "these scratches weren't made by ghosts or people."

He leaned in closer to the screen and clicked on another website. "Paranormal entities," he read, "that are seen mostly in peripheral vision." He chuckled. "Sounds like Necrocritters to me." He turned around to see if anyone was watching him or listening. Hugo and Andy had looked up, but buried their heads back into their computers. Two nearby campers were chatting about sending friend requests over a social networking site and weren't paying attention.

"Let's see," Nathan said. He typed in the word *Necrocritters.* "I guess that's how you spell it," he said, underneath his breath. The search results produced nothing on the word, just alternative spellings that he was pretty sure were completely off.

He typed in the phrases *the Space In Between* and *Pneuma Novo* and the search engine produced several results, but nothing relevant to what Malick was talking about. He then tried *Dream Walker,* and the search engine took him to a website that described a Dream Walker as a person who works through dreams to understand others, to guide and to teach.

"I don't know about that one," he said to himself. "I don't understand half the stuff that has happened to me and the little that I do know is because of Malick. How on earth would I be able to guide or teach?"

He took a moment to stretch his neck and then his back, then typed in the words *the Spirit Realm* and got back 30,000,000 similar results. The first website he clicked on related the Spirit Realm to the realm of the Angels, which was similar to what Jonathan had said about the Fallen Ones at the first bonfire.

"Wait," he blurted out. "Are they real too?" Nathan recalled Malick saying something about the Fallen Ones being just a myth, but considering Malick's "hero complex" of hiding things to keep people safe, he decided to type it in anyway.

The search results for the Fallen Ones didn't return anything about the Cahokia legend, but he did stumble upon a website that talked about Nephilim, the offspring of fallen angels with humans, but nothing specific about the Fallen Ones being fallen angels.

He yawned and tried to see what would happen if he searched the phrase *Dark and Powerful Forces*, but got back a list of websites that were more about *Star Wars* than anything else.

Nathan was frustrated. He had hoped that with the Internet searching he would find answers. For fun he typed in *Black Cloaks*, *Red Cloaks*, and even *Dark Cloaks*, but much to his dismay, only images of various cloaks and several links to where he could buy them popped up.

Nathan took a deep breath and sighed. He decided that his best bet for answers was Malick, but he was sure he wouldn't be getting anything out of him. Maybe Argus could help. But Nathan was almost certain that if Malick wasn't telling him anything, then for sure Argus wouldn't either, especially if he was a part of the Order. "The Order," he blurted out loud.

Nathan looked around to see who in the lab had heard him. Hugo and Andy had looked up from their computers like before, and Eva Marie Evans, who was walking past him at the time, kept walking and sat down at her computer.

Nathan typed in the words *the Order* and pressed enter. The search engine returned over 520,000,000 relevant results. He scanned the first few pages of links and quickly read the descriptions, but none of them really seemed to fit. He almost gave up, but came across a link to an article written by Dr. C.W. Colvers entitled *Brotherhoods, Secret Societies, and Secret Government-Funded Organizations*. In the middle of the article, the Order was mentioned in a list of about 200 secret organizations, right between the Secret Order of the Throne and the Order of the Sphinx.

Nathan laughed. "The Order of the Sphinx," he said. "Isn't that like a Harry Potter book?" He glanced at the long list of organizations again. "Is this guy for real? That's a lot of so-called secret organizations." He sighed. "Well, this is the best I've got. Maybe this guy knows something." He typed in *Dr. C.W. Colvers* and a slew of articles popped up. From what Nathan could tell, most were self-published in Colvers's online newsletter called "Now Is the Time to Know."

"Really?" he mumbled. "That doesn't sound too credible." Nathan twisted his lip in defeat, sat back in his chair again, and tapped his fingers in a rhythmic pattern on the arm of his chair. "I don't want to waste time trying to find this guy just to hear him ramble on about conspiracy theories," he said to himself. "There's got to be another way to check him out that doesn't involve me reading a bunch of articles or me having to call him."

He could now hear the sound of familiar male and female voices behind him. It sounded like there was an argument about whether or not there was enough time to check research. Nathan's face lit up. "Jonathan!" he said. He turned around and saw Erin Rosales and Jonathan Black in the doorway to the computer lab.

"It won't take long," Jonathan said. "I just want to check a few websites and my e-mail."

"Just whatever," she said, waving her hand. "Just meet us in Fisher Hall's computer lab."

"Thanks, Erin!" responded Jonathan happily.

"Do you have to be so happy about it?" she asked mockingly.

Jonathan paused, secured the backpack on his shoulder, and smiled.

Erin raised her eyebrows. "I am so glad this is almost over," she muttered while walking away.

Nathan sprung to his feet. He wanted to catch Jonathan before he walked past him. He quickly bent over his chair and peered at his computer screen to see if the article and online newsletter by Colvers were still open. "Okay," he said. "Now I just need Jonathan to see this without telling him why."

"And where are you going?" asked Lafonda.

Nathan was surprised to find Lafonda standing in front of him. They really hadn't spoken to each other since the day he, Malick and Jonas had snuck out to Jonas's house. He could tell by the look on her face that she was still upset. He could also see he was losing his chance to stop Jonathan.

Out of habit he checked to see if she was still wearing her white tennis shoes. She was.

"Um, hello to you too Lafonda," he smirked.

Lafonda glowered. "Just in case you were planning on leaving," she said, "we aren't scheduled to leave here for a few more hours."

Nathan watched as Jonathan approached them. "I'm not leaving Lafonda," he said. He smiled sarcastically and then sidestepped her. "Hey, Jonathan," he said.

Jonathan stopped abruptly. It was as if he was surprised to see them. His eyes were wide, and they looked irritated, as if he had been rubbing them.

"Hi, Nathan," he said. "And Lafonda."

Lafonda stood there; head cocked to the side and her arms folded. "Hi, Jonathan," she said. "Shouldn't you be in the other computer lab?"

Jonathan hesitated. "Um, yes," he said, "and I am headed there after this."

Lafonda tossed back a long lock of her dark hair over her shoulder. "And why can't you just use the other lab?" she asked.

Jonathan sneezed and then paused to reposition his square-rimmed glasses.

"Bless you," said Nathan, eyeing Jonathan suspiciously. "Do you have a cold or something?"

"No," he responded. "Allergies."

Nathan still eyed him suspiciously. "Oh."

Jonathan pursed his lips. "I need to use this lab because last night I convinced the tech guy on duty to allow me to download a large file from a colleague of mine in London," he said. He held up the slim black drive that was in his hand. "I didn't have a large enough storage device to get it off the computer. Pretty much any computer will do; the tech guy was nice enough to show me how to save it to the Lawrence Hall public server."

Lafonda stepped aside so that Jonathan could pass

them.

"Wait!" blurted out Nathan.

Jonathan jumped. He seemed startled.

Both Lafonda and Jonathan awaited an explanation. "What I meant to say," Nathan said, "is that you can use my computer."

Jonathan looked perplexed. "But I can use any computer. Look, there are plenty of open ones."

"Yeah. What's the big deal?" asked Lafonda. "Are you trying to leave, or something?"

Nathan cut Lafonda a disapproving look. "No," he said. He took Jonathan's backpack off his shoulder and placed it next to his computer.

Jonathan looked confused, but put up little resistance. "Sit down Jonathan," Nathan said.

Jonathan sat down and repositioned the chair closer to the computer. He paused and then leaned in to the computer screen. Nathan could tell that he was reading the article.

"Find anything interesting?" Nathan said. "Is he a real doctor? I mean, does he seem legit?"

"Real doctor?" asked Lafonda suspiciously.

Jonathan stammered, "I-I don't know," he responded. "Is there a reason why you are looking at this?"

Both Jonathan and Lafonda stared at Nathan awaiting a response. He could hear Malick in his head, warning him to keep everyone in the dark.

"Oh, I stumbled upon it," he said. "I thought it was interesting, his research on secret societies and stuff. The newsletter says he has a Ph.D. Do you think he's a professor at a university or something?" He paused. "Oh, and if it helps, I also noticed he has several YouTube videos."

Jonathan hesitated again. "I-I don't know," he said. "I

don't think I can help you."

Both Lafonda and Nathan looked surprised by Jonathan's response.

"Let me see," she said. "Maybe I can help."

"No!" shouted Nathan and Jonathan in unison.

Jonathan closed the browser window and proceeded to place his storage device into the USB drive. "Excuse me," he said, "but I promised Erin I wouldn't be long."

Nathan looked confused and wondered why Jonathan didn't want Lafonda to see it.

Lafonda rolled her eyes and shook her head. "Whatever," she said. "Are you all set for the banquet on Saturday?"

Jonathan continued to copy the file to his drive from the public server.

"Hello. Nathan," said Lafonda, obviously annoyed.

Nathan jumped slightly. He had been so engrossed in what Jonathan was doing that he forgot to answer her.

"Oh — um, sorry about that," he stammered. He paused to scratch his head. "Yes, I am definitely ready."

Lafonda rolled her eyes again. "Most likely you won't see me on Friday because I am leaving early to drive to St. Louis to pick up Leah."

Nathan smiled. He was excited about finally meeting Leah, but he was even more excited about the close of camp. He felt like once camp was over, things would go back to normal again.

"And you don't have to worry about the girls," she said. "Angela will cover for me, and chances are you guys won't even have a bonfire on Friday because it's supposed to rain."

"Woo-hoo!" shouted Nathan. "No more bonfires!"

Lafonda chuckled lightly, but then pursed her lips. "Don't get too excited," she said. "I said that it's supposed to rain; I didn't say that it will."

"But wait," he said. "What about the fireworks on Saturday?"

"There is a chance for rain on Saturday too," she said. "But I guess we would just move the banquet indoors."

Nathan peered over at Jonathan. His file was almost completely downloaded. Nathan stretched his neck to see if he could read the name on the file.

"So how is your buddy these days?" Lafonda asked in a sarcastic tone.

"My buddy? Who? Jonas?"

Hearing Nathan say his name, Jonas looked up and smiled. He was sitting next to Christina Williams.

"He's doing okay," Nathan said.

Lafonda grinned. "I meant your buddy Malick."

Nathan's face turned red after he realized that she was serious. He hardly thought Malick was his buddy. "Ha-ha, funny," he said. "And how is your buddy?"

Lafonda's forehead creased. "My buddy?" she asked.

"You know," he teased. "Leah."

Lafonda fixed her gaze on Nathan and then tossed back her hair. "She's fine," she responded confidently. "In fact, I received a text message from her this morning."

Nathan nodded. "Okay," he said. "That's good, but don't bother asking again about Malick because I don't have an answer for you."

Lafonda grinned. "Leah said she was looking forward to seeing campus again. She also said she was excited to finally have the chance to meet you."

"What? Really?" Nathan blushed. "I mean, why would she be excited to meet me?"

"I told her about you," Lafonda said. "And don't worry, I only told her about the nice Nathan that was sincere and caring; not the rebel-without-a-cause Nathan who abandoned us a week ago."

Nathan glowered. "Ha-ha. Funny, Lafonda. I am not turning into Stephen Malick."

"We'll see," she said.

Nathan frowned.

"Lafonda," called Eva Marie. "Can you please help me?" She had a hint of desperation in her voice. "My computer just froze!" She frantically pressed several buttons on the keyboard. "I hope I hit save."

"I'll be there in a second," Lafonda responded.

Jonas headed over to help Eva Marie. The computer lab technician was coming over to help as well.

"Okay, well, you know the deal for Friday and Saturday," Lafonda said. "And lucky for you, my grandmother made sure everyone was prepared as far as dress attire for the banquet."

"What is that supposed to mean?"

Lafonda grinned. "Now you don't have to fret about what to wear to impress Leah."

Nathan's face turned red again. He remembered the hard time he'd given Roy about packing the slacks and loafers LaDonda recommended on the dreaded gold paper.

"Lafonda!" called Eva Marie again.

"Coming," Lafonda said. She smiled one last time at Nathan and walked away.

Jonathan suddenly pushed back his computer chair and stood up. Nathan took a few steps back to avoid getting hit by the chair.

"All done?" he asked.

Jonathan peered over his shoulder before turning his attention back to the computer screen. "My apologies, Nathan," he said. "I am sort of in a hurry."

"Did you get what you needed?" asked Nathan.

Jonathan quickly deleted the file from the computer, closed the Internet browser, and placed the slim, black storage device into his pocket.

Nathan frowned. "Hey," he said, "I was looking at that."

"Sorry again," Jonathan said. He placed his backpack over his shoulder. "You really should come up to the Cahokia Caves sometime," he continued. "We will be entering inside the secret chamber any day now, and there are a few things that I would like to show you." Jonathan cautiously looked around the room before whispering. "And I think you will find it very interesting."

Nathan raised his eyebrows. He didn't know what Jonathan was talking about or why Jonathan would think he would find the caves interesting. "Okay," he responded slowly.

Jonathan patted him on the shoulder and proceeded to walk away.

"Wait," said Nathan. He paused and Jonathan looked at him inquisitively. "I have a question for you," he said. "It's about your research."

Jonathan adjusted the backpack on his shoulder and repositioned his glasses. "Yes?" he said.

Nathan drew a big breath. "In your research," he said, "have you come across anything about . . . dark and powerful forces?"

Jonathan stood there for a moment and then leaned in. "That's a very good question," he said softly. "There are many dark creatures mentioned in Cahokia mythology. But there is one story that is often repeated and stands out; and that's the legend about the Fallen Ones."

"But that's just a myth, right?" asked Nathan.

There was a vibrating sound and Jonathan pulled out

his cell phone from his pocket. He stood in silence as he read the text. From the look on his face, it appeared serious. "Please forgive me," he said, "but I really have to go."

"What is it?" Nathan asked.

Jonathan stumbled, placing his phone back into his pocket. He fidgeted with his backpack nervously. "Everything's fine. I just have to see Dr. Helmsley immediately."

"But wait!" said Nathan.

"Everything will be okay," said Jonathan reassuringly. "The dark may have its minions, Nathan, but the righteous have their heroes."

CHAPTER EIGHTEEN

A LIGHT IN THE DARK

Nathan sat quietly, looking into the fire. Darkness had set in and a cool breeze gently nudged the flames towards the lake. He thought about the evening and how Malick had repeatedly dodged his questions about the Order. He had hoped that by the time they were done filling the fire pits Malick would have at least answered one of his questions. But he hadn't. The only thing Nathan was able to get out of him was a slight reaction when he mentioned his theory that the Order was a part of some secret organization. Based on Malick's reaction, particularly his repeated attempts to find out how he developed this theory, Nathan concluded he was probably on the right track.

Nevertheless, he was still clueless, and Malick apparently wanted him to stay that way. He'd insisted that Nathan was better off not knowing and told him to stop asking questions. Nathan recalled his exact words were "remain in the dark." By the time the fires were set, Nathan was so frustrated that he was relieved when Malick volunteered to help LaDonda escort a sick camper, Drew Waters, back to Lawrence Hall.

Nathan continued to look into the fire but his gaze

was broken by the sound of laughter followed by a sudden crack of thunder. Lightning struck violently across the sky and a dark gray thunder cloud slowly made its way over Lake Charleston and the bonfire area.

"Wahoo!" shouted Hugo. "We made it to the last bonfire before it rained."

Jonas and Christina Williams sat on the other side of the fire while Andy high-fived Hugo behind them. "Yes!" he yelled. "Camp is officially over."

"Come on," said Alan, who was sitting next to Christina. "Camp wasn't that bad, was it?"

"Technically," chimed in Angela, "camp isn't over. We still have the closing ceremony tomorrow."

"Yeah," said Hugo. "But leadership classes are done and there are no more projects!"

"You know, Andy," said Eva Marie, with a cup of water in her hand, "I never saw your last project." She glared at him skeptically. "Are you sure you even completed yours?"

Andy's face turned red, almost matching his hair color. "Yes, I did," he said, sounding rather annoyed.

Hugo laughed. "Yeah, I guess you can call what you turned in finished," he said.

Andy's face went from red to sour. "Whatever," he muttered. "I got it done."

Eva Marie laughed. "I probably didn't get to see it because you probably turned it in late."

"I'll show you late!" shouted Andy. He grabbed Eva Marie by the waist and threw her over his shoulder.

"Aaah!" she yelled, her feet dangling in the air.

Andy had a wide grin on his face. "How about some water to cool you off?" he asked.

Andy headed towards the lake and Hugo let out a huge laugh. Eva Marie windmilled her hands and feet in an attempt to get down. "Don't you dare Andy! Put me down!" she yelled. Eva Marie's cup of water flew out of her hand and landed in Jonas' lap, wetting his pants and spraying water into Christina's face.

"Hey!" yelled Christina.

Angela quickly rose to her feet. She had her purple hairbrush in her hand and pointed it at him. "Okay, Andy, that's enough," she scolded. "Put her down and knock it off!"

Andy sighed and released Eva Marie.

Eva Marie ran her fingers through her hair and fixed her shorts. "You can be such a jerk sometimes," she said, before storming away.

Angela sat down. "Gosh," she said, "they are never this rowdy."

Alan laughed vigorously.

"Why are you laughing, Alan?" she asked, slightly annoyed.

"At you!" he said, while holding his stomach. "What were you going to do? Hairbrush them to death?"

Erin tried not to giggle and Nathan laughed.

Angela looked down at the purple hairbrush in her hand and placed it in her back pocket. "Shut up, Alan," she said.

Alan said, "You are hurting my stomach from making me laugh so much."

Angela rolled her eyes. "Ugh!" she said. "I'll be glad when Lafonda comes back." She slowly rubbed her neck. "Watching my girls and hers is way too much for one person."

"Tell me about it," protested Erin. "I've been practically by myself for four weeks!"

"Sorry, Erin," said Angela empathetically. "Where is Jonathan, anyway?"

Nathan broke his gaze from the fire to look around for Jonathan.

Erin placed the front of her shoulder-length brown hair behind her ears and sighed. "I don't know," she said. "He's been gone pretty much all week and hasn't told me anything."

"You don't know where he is?" asked Nathan, surprised.

Erin scoffed. "Nope," she said. "I haven't really talked to him since Monday. I guess he figured camp is over, so why bother."

"That really sucks," said Angela. She had a sad look on her face. "You should say something to LaDonda."

"I'm done with Mr. Indiana," Erin added. She stretched her legs out in front of her, causing them to become illuminated by the fire. "I'm just glad camp is over and I don't have to deal with it anymore."

Alan tossed a small stick into the pit but missed the fire. "Oh, well," he joked. "He'll turn up eventually. He's probably lost in a cave somewhere."

Erin laughed.

Alan paused to toss another stick into the pit. "So, when is Lafonda coming back with Leah?"

"She's supposed to be back tomorrow morning," said Angela cheerfully. "I can't wait to meet Leah and to see what clothes they bought." She suddenly grew quiet, but then abruptly checked her silver-and-gold–starred cell phone. "I am, however, surprised that I haven't received one single text message asking for my opinion on dresses."

Alan shrugged. "They probably got caught up in the moment with shopping," he said. "I know I do."

"True," said Angela, tilting her long, curly blond hair to the side. "I guess I'll just have to wait until tomorrow."

Alan leaned in and whispered, "So, I wonder what it will be like to meet Leah?" he said.

Nathan looked surprised because he was wondering the same thing. He often speculated about her personality and wondered how her laugh would be. He already knew what she looked like from his dreams, but thanks to the yearbook that Lafonda borrowed from Jonathan he had an image of her that wasn't a terrifying memory. Nathan's eyes slowly drifted into the red glow of the fire. He remembered how he felt looking in the yearbook and finally seeing her bright smile.

"I wonder if she'll be crazy," said Alan abruptly. He had a weird but serious look on his face.

Nathan couldn't believe what he was hearing.

"Really, Alan?" asked Angela.

"What?" asked Alan. "I know everyone is thinking it — you're just not saying it out loud!"

"Hardly," said Nathan. "After all she's been through, I can't believe you still think she's crazy."

Alan looked like he was trying not to laugh. "I'm not saying she is," he said. "I'm just throwing it out there. I heard she was like a crazy woman when they found her — so crazy they had to call the police!"

"That rumor was started by Steve and Amanda," protested Nathan. "And Amanda is known to be a little dramatic."

"Well, the police part isn't made up," responded Alan.

"It was campus security," said Nathan, through beady eyes.

"Same thing," said Alan confidently. "They had to call law enforcement to get her."

Nathan stood up and kicked a rock into the water. "Whatever," he said, "I've had enough of this conversation."

Angela punched Alan in the arm.

"Ouch!" he yelled. "Why did you do that?"

"Because you made Nathan leave, that's why," she said. "Why did you say all that stuff about Leah?"

The sound of their voices faded as Nathan walked away. The last thing he heard was Angela saying something about Steve and Amanda still being missing. He stood in front of the refreshments table and picked up one of the wind-strewn cups that rolled back and forth across the table. He wanted a drink of water, but the container was empty, and so were the bottles of fruit juice and bags of chips.

Nathan sighed. He wasn't in the mood to rejoin the group, so he decided to clear the table. He found a black trash bag and started to put the utensils that had been used in it.

"Wow, that table looks like a war zone," said a cheery voice behind him.

Nathan sighed again. *Who is this now?* He turned around and was surprised to see Samantha Darding standing in front of him. Nathan cleared his throat.

"Oh — hi, Sam," he said.

She smiled. Her hair was loosely pulled back into a bun, and a long strand of curly brown hair hung freely to the side of her face. "So, there's nothing left?" she said, eyeing the table.

"No," said Nathan. "When it comes to food, these guys are like vultures."

Samantha laughed. "Here," she said, placing her empty cup into the bag, "I'll help you." She looked up into the ominous sky. "I assume we will be leaving soon, anyway."

"Yeah, I suspect that as soon as LaDonda and Malick return, she'll be ushering us out of here." Nathan paused to look up at the sky. He noticed the trees had begun to sway and the air seemed cooler. "I'm surprised she hasn't texted one of the counselors yet, instructing us to head back to Lawrence hall."

"Yup, it definitely looks like a storm is heading our way," she said. "I hope it doesn't affect the banquet or the fireworks tomorrow."

Nathan chuckled. "Don't worry," he said. "LaDonda already has that covered. I was told that if it rains, we'll just have the banquet inside." He paused to start folding the tablecloth. "And in the past, if it rained on the Fourth of July, they would usually just have the fireworks display the following day."

Samantha took the other end of the tablecloth to help him. "I know," she said, with a smile, "I live here too, remember?"

He smiled, placed the folded tablecloth in a maroon bag that had plastic cups in it, and nodded. "Yeah. That's right," he said, feeling slightly embarrassed.

"My parents will be here tomorrow for the banquet and closing ceremony," she continued. "Jim too. I suspect he's only coming because of Lafonda."

Nathan nodded and attempted to collapse the table. A bolt of lightning lit up the sky and a crack of thunder sounded off in the distance.

"I'm sure Lafonda will be excited," he said, with a chuckle.

Samantha smiled and then stood in silence for a moment. "How come I haven't seen you at any of Jim's parties or when Lafonda comes over?" she asked.

Nathan could feel his face turning red. "You mean, at your house?" he stammered.

"Well, technically it's my parents' house," she responded. "But yes."

Nathan's ears burned so he knew his face had to be

bright red. The truth was, he just didn't think he would fit in. He shrugged. "Um, no reason," he said.

"Good," she said enthusiastically. "Because I am having my seventeenth birthday party next month and I want you to come."

His eyes were wide. "Me?" he asked, in surprise. He didn't want her to know he was surprised so he relaxed and spoke with a more confident voice. "I mean, you want me to come?"

Samantha nodded and tried not to giggle. "Yes," she said, "you can just come with Lafonda. It will be fun; and I've invited some people from camp too."

"Am I missing something here?" he asked. "Are those two back together?"

Samantha's eyebrows were raised. "I don't know anything," she said, with a grin. "I'll let them tell you."

He frowned. "I'll take that as a yes."

A bolt of lightning streaked across the sky, illuminating the clouds directly above them. The sound of loud rumbling thunder followed and Samantha jumped. Nathan looked down and saw that Samantha was holding his arm.

"That was loud," he said.

Nervously, Samantha released Nathan's arm and fidgeted with her clothes and hair. "Yes," she said. "It was."

He looked down again. This time it was because his cell phone was vibrating in his pocket. "I bet that's LaDonda calling me," he said.

Nathan spoke on the phone for a while and then ended the call. "Yup," he said. "It was LaDonda. She said she's almost here, but wanted me to clean up and break down the table."

"Check," said Samantha, while eyeing the folded-up

table and closed garbage bag. "You are way ahead of her."

Overhead, another bolt of lightning lit up the sky, followed by a low rumble. LaDonda and Malick were walking swiftly out of the forest, and Nathan was surprised to see Argus close behind them.

"Listen up, everyone!" LaDonda said loudly. "As you can see, there is a storm heading our way, so let's pack up and head back to Lawrence Hall."

Nathan could hear grumbles from some of the campers. He overheard Hugo and Andy being obnoxious about having to leave early.

"Hey," he said assertively, "you guys knock it off or you're likely to get in trouble."

"It hasn't started raining yet," protested Hugo.

Andy moaned. "Ugh, why do we have to leave early?" he asked. He started to sit back down. "What if we don't want to leave?"

"What?" asked Nathan. "Are you guys drunk, or something?" He paused to look in LaDonda's direction. "You keep this up and LaDonda's going to kill you."

Hugo flippantly waved his hand in LaDonda's direction. "Whatever," he said. "She isn't the boss of me."

"Hey, settle down!" LaDonda demanded, arms flapping in the air. "I'm not going to say it again. Now everyone get your donkeys moving, or you will be sorry!"

Andy and Hugo quickly stood up at attention.

Nathan snickered heartily. "See, I told you," he said.

"Hey," said Malick. "LaDonda wants us to quickly put out the fires before the storm hits."

Nathan tried not to frown. After today, being stuck with Malick again was the last thing he wanted. He took a deep breath and tried to relax. "Try to be appreciative," he told himself. "Even though he's acting like Fort Knox or the CIA when it comes to certain information, I would be completely clueless if it weren't for Malick."

"Nathan!" called Jonas, approaching on his left. "Can we chat for a second?"

Nathan had a pretty good idea what Jonas wanted to talk about, but he really didn't know what to tell him. Nathan wanted to keep Jonas safe at any cost, even if that meant keeping him in the dark a little while longer.

"Yeah, sure," he responded with hesitation. "But right now really isn't a good time."

Jonas suddenly looked glum.

"But let's chat later tonight," Nathan continued. "After I get back to Lawrence Hall."

"Come on, guys," said Samantha. "Let's get going so Malick and Nathan can put out these fires before they get rained on."

Nathan smiled.

She held the end of the folded-up table. "Can anybody help a lady carry a table?"

"I'll help you," responded Andy quickly.

Hugo's large forehead formed frown lines. "No, I'll do it," he said. "Look, I can carry it all by myself."

"Good," said Samantha, before Andy could get a word in. "Then Andy can carry the garbage bag, and you can carry this one" she told Jonas as she handed him the maroon bag.

"No problem," responded Andy cheerfully, with saucer eyes.

She smiled. "See you at the banquet tomorrow, Nathan," she said. "Good night, Malick."

Nathan smiled. "Good night, Sam."

Malick nodded.

"Don't forget to pack, guys!" shouted Nathan after

them. "I want to see some packing going on when I get upstairs."

"Yeah, yeah!" yelled back Hugo.

"I'm serious, guys," he said. "Your parents aren't going to like it if you're not packed tomorrow."

"We got it!" shouted Andy, before stepping into the forest.

Malick stared at Nathan and grinned.

"What?" Nathan asked defensively.

Malick smiled. "Nothing."

"She's only sixteen," protested Nathan.

Malick laughed. "Uh-huh," he murmured playfully.

Nathan rolled his eyes. A loud crack filled the air followed by a deep, long rumble. "Whatever," he said. "Let's get going before we're rained on, or worse, electrocuted."

Just a few fires remained. Nathan kneeled down and filled the bucket again. The surface of the lake was completely black now, and he could hardly see his reflection. The pit sizzled as he filled it with water.

"So, how did you and LaDonda end up with Argus?" he asked.

Malick tossed more water into the pit. "I don't know," he said. "They were in the lobby together after I took Drew upstairs. They were having a conversation about something, but stopped after they saw me."

Nathan turned around. A light was on at the Hiking and Camping Center. "Has he said anything to you since …"

"Nope, not a word." Malick had a grin on his face. "Just our usual communication — a bottle of lighter fluid and some matches left inside a wheelbarrow."

Nathan looked down. His phone was vibrating in his pocket. He saw that it was Lafonda and decided to just let it go to voicemail. "What about a pendant?" he asked abruptly. "Have you found a way to cloak my powers yet?"

Malick paused. "Not yet," he said. "But I'm working on it. There's a guy I heard of in London. He specializes in this sort of thing — protective enchantments and stuff."

"London?" Nathan asked. He had a surprised look on his face.

"Yes, London," responded Malick. He suddenly looked serious, and there was panic in his voice. "Have you been using your powers? Did you have another dream? What about Jonas?"

"No," responded Nathan. "I haven't used my powers and I haven't dream-walked either." A raindrop landed on his neck. "And I don't think Jonas has either," he said. "I mean, at least I don't think he has. He would have told me."

Malick had a look of relief on his face. "Thank God! You almost gave me a panic attack." He ran his hand backwards through his hair. "I'm waiting to hear from a good friend of mine to talk to her about what has happened here at camp," he said. "You know, about the Shadow Creatures, your friend Leah, Jonas, Grimm Cemetery, and everything else. She has a better handle on this stuff than I do. I really think there is a connection here. We just haven't seen it yet."

Nathan stood behind Malick as he filled his bucket with more water.

"I think there is a connection too," Nathan said. He reached into his pocket and saw he had missed another call from Lafonda. "Maybe this would be a good time to tell you what else I saw in the dream."

Malick quickly stood up, causing the water to swoosh

around the sides of the bucket. "What do you mean?" he asked. "Were there others?"

Nathan stood there for a moment. A cold chill went up his spine while remembering each detail that led up to Lafonda's death. "Yes," he stuttered, remembering the silver double-edged sword. "There definitely were others." Nathan swallowed hard as Malick looked on intently. "There were these black-robed figures with swords — they were hooded, so I guess they were dressed in cloaks," he continued slowly. "And then, there were their red-hooded counterparts. It looked like they were performing some kind of ritual."

"The guys with the swords are called Shadow Guards," Malick interrupted. Nathan noticed he had that serious look on his face again. "And the red-hooded figures are called Scarlet Priests."

Malick walked over to one of the remaining fires that now flickered in the wind.

"There also was this woman dressed in white," said Nathan.

"A woman?"

"Yeah. And one of those red-cloaked guys — I mean, one of those Scarlet Priests — he had a medallion around his neck."

Malick tossed the water into the pit and froze. "What kind of medallion? I mean, what did it look like?"

"It was a gold-and-silver crescent-shaped medallion."

Malick stood still.

Nathan could have sworn for a second he saw fear in Malick's eyes, but it faded quickly when he smiled. Nathan looked down; the phone in his pocket was vibrating again. "It's Lafonda. It's the third time she's called. I probably should call her back."

Malick blinked a few times and nodded. It was as if he

was slowly coming back to life. "Yeah," he murmured. "Go ahead and call her back."

A gust of wind pushed through the trees, followed by a low rumble. Nathan felt a few drops of rain on his neck. "I can't get through," he said. "I've never had this problem out here before."

"It's probably the storm," said Malick. He had a reassuring look on his face. "Go ahead and head back. And see if you can get a signal. I'll finish up here."

"Are you sure?" asked Nathan.

Malick tossed a bucket of water into the last remaining pit. "Yeah," he said. "We're done here. I just want to walk through and make sure all the fires are completely out. I'll be right behind you."

Nathan paused. A bolt of purple lightning sprawled across the sky, revealing a swirl of dark grey clouds above the lake. "Okay," he said. "But hurry. It's getting bad out here."

Nathan entered the trail back to Lawrence Hall and nearly stumbled. The dark clouds circling above blocked any moonlight from entering the forest. The wind had picked up, causing the leaves and branches of the trees to sway back and forth like currents in a storm-wracked ocean. He stopped to try his cell phone again.

"Still no signal." He squinted, trying to adjust his eyes to the dark forest. "Why didn't I bring a flashlight?"

He continued up the path, hearing the sound of rain drops all around him. A cold trickle of water slowly made its way down his back. "Ugh," he uttered. "I'm going to get wet." The trail in front of him seemed to gradually get wider, so he assumed he was nearing the split in the trail that led eastward to the Cahokia Museum. "Almost halfway there. If I can just make it before the downpour."

Just then, the sound of raindrops increased, making

intermittent sputtering sounds. Nathan tried to make a run for it, but soon he couldn't see anything. His eyes blinked profusely under the pouring rain. "If I can just make it under a tree," he mumbled. Through fluttering eyelashes, he tried to make it to a large oak tree, but slipped on a protruding tree root and went headfirst towards the ground. The rain had stopped, and he wiped the water from his eyes. Nathan sat up to inspect the damage. He had used his right hand to shield himself from the ground and it throbbed.

Slowly, his eyes adjusted to the darkness, and he could hear the intermittent sound again. *Great, it's about to rain again*, he thought. He attempted to stand up, but froze instead; it looked like there was movement along the trail. The intermittent sound drew closer, and he quickly realized it wasn't rain, but something coming towards him.

Nathan crouched down and tried to conceal himself behind the large oak tree. He hoped it wasn't those things — those Shadow Creatures. Malick had said those Necrocritters hate natural light, and there was definitely no light there.

Soon the approaching sound slowed and then stopped altogether. There was the silhouette of someone standing on the trail a few feet in front of him. *Who is that? Who would be out on the trail this late at night and in a thunderstorm?*

Nathan's eyes strained as he attempted to make out the face of the dark figure. A small green light pierced the darkness, revealing a pair of square-rimmed glasses. "Jonathan!" he blurted out. He didn't know why Jonathan wasn't at Lawrence Hall with Erin and the others.

Jonathan appeared to be distracted and didn't hear Nathan say his name. The green glow from his cell phone continued to illuminate his face. Nathan stood up as

Jonathan took the path to the Northern Cahokia Tribal Museum. "Where is he going?" he said softly.

Nathan attempted to wipe the dirt from his pants and quickly went after Jonathan. His eyes squinted as he tried to catch up to the green light. The trail seemed to get darker and darker the farther they went; he could barely make out the shape of Jonathan anymore. *I should have caught up to him by now. Is he running?*

He picked up his pace, following the green light as it bounced sporadically around the trees. The light seemed to grow as Nathan got closer and then it seemed to rest in one spot. *He must have stopped.*

Nathan stopped running; he could make out the shape of Jonathan again. "For a guy that spends all of his time researching, he sure can run fast," he gasped. He was out of breath. "Jonathan!"

Jonathan continued to look into his phone. It appeared that he still didn't hear Nathan. Nathan paced forward. "Jonathan!" he called again, but with a labored voice.

Jonathan frantically closed his phone, almost dropping it, and the green light disappeared. Nathan could still make out his silhouette in the darkness. Jonathan appeared to look quickly around, and then a haze of blue and white lights circled him, illuminating him again. Nathan's eyes grew wide at the display of brilliant light, but the light vanished as quickly as it had appeared, and so did Jonathan. Nathan took a few steps forward, but suddenly froze. He thought his eyes must be deceiving him. He peered into the darkness, trying to make out the new shape that was forming. Where Jonathan once stood was the silhouette of a small animal.

CHAPTER NINETEEN

SOMEONE TO COME

Nathan couldn't believe what he had just seen. Jonathan Black had changed into what looked like a small animal right in front of him. He tried to make out the silhouette of the animal in the darkness. A brilliant bolt of lightning struck above, revealing in a split second the surrounding trees and the shaggy black face with piercing blue eyes staring back at him.

"The disheveled black dog," Nathan mumbled. "The day we left for camp — that dog in the forest — it was you?"

Nathan inched forward and a loud and long rumble of thunder filled the air. A moment later, the forest lit up again and Jonathan took off.

"Wait!" shouted Nathan, taking off after him.

His heart beat rapidly as he tried to keep up. He was breathing hard by the time he exited the trail. He looked up just in time to see Jonathan dash across the well-lit museum parking lot and into the trail leading to the top of the cliffs.

The trees on both sides of the parking lot swayed with the wind and dark gray clouds were gathering above. Nathan paused to wipe the raindrops from his forehead and the beads of sweat from his nose, and then continued after Jonathan, wondering if he was headed to the caves.

Nathan entered the trail, and it was soon dark again. He could barely see in front of him and couldn't tell if Jonathan was far away or near. Lightning from above lit up the forest, revealing two yellow-ribboned trees. *He has to have gone to the Cahokia Caves.*

A thick silver chain ran across the entrance to the trail and Nathan stepped over it. "So much for the Warning: Do Not Enter sign," he murmured.

He carefully continued down the trail that led to the series of caves behind the cliffs. This trail wasn't as well maintained as the others, and mud accumulated at the bottom of Nathan's shoes. The path to the caves opened up to an enclosed meadow surrounded by tall trees on one side and the cliff wall on the other. The meadow stretched downward several feet before leveling out and meeting the cave wall. Nathan carefully maneuvered past squared sections of dig sites that were marked by ropes and yellow flags.

He caught a glimpse of flickering light from within one of the caves and pressed forward thinking it was probably a safe bet that Jonathan was inside that one.

Nathan stood outside of the cave. He could now see a torch attached to the right side of the cave wall. He peered inside, but suddenly flinched back at the sound of scuffling. There was a woman's scream followed by a growl and then a low whimpering sound. "That has to be Jonathan," Nathan said, charging in. "But who else is there?"

He ran towards the sounds echoing from within the cave. Every few feet a torch burned, illuminating the smooth, light-brown limestone walls. Every so often the torches created unusual shadows from the large stalactites that sprung out of the ceiling.

Nathan heard what sounded like huge rocks hitting the ground. A few rock pieces flew towards him, barely missing his head. He dove behind two large boulders. Near the back of the cave were the black dog and a slender woman dressed in all black. Jonathan the dog growled; it looked like he was blocking her entrance into another chamber. On the ground, slumped against a pile of rubble, was an older woman with glasses. *That must be Dr. Helmsley,* thought Nathan.

The woman in black folded her arms across her chest and sneered. "You really need to move out of my way," she said. "I know you're just a simple Spirit Walker, but if you keep getting in my way you'll be going back to the Spirit Realm — permanently."

Jonathan growled, this time showing his sharp teeth.

She sighed and threw several energy balls, missing Jonathan by a second because he had disappeared. Jonathan reappeared behind her and tried to bite her in the leg. Before he could sink his teeth in, she spun around and attempted to kick him in the head, but Jonathan was gone again.

Nathan's mouth fell open. He was surprised by the speed with which Jonathan was here, but not here. *He's moving like a Shadow Creature.*

Jonathan reappeared on top of a boulder and leaped at the woman with claws and teeth aiming at her throat. She quickly ducked, but he was still able to rip a hole into her long, black, leather trench coat. Still bent over, she retaliated by hitting him with a blue energy ball, sending him forcibly into the air and making him crash into the cave wall.

Jonathan let out a slight whimper and tried to get to his feet. She adjusted her coat over her shoulders and walked towards him. She grinned and raised her right eyebrow confidently over her silver-rimmed sunglasses. "I gave you a chance," she said. "Now it's time to meet your fate, like your friend over there."

Nathan took a deep breath. His hands trembled uncontrollably. "It's now or never," he whispered, before springing to his feet.

She stretched her arm out towards Jonathan and his bright blue eyes winced under his black furry face.

"Ciao," she said.

"Not if I can help it," Nathan shouted, sending a bright blue energy ball straight into her back.

The woman fell down so hard that he paused to look down at his hands. "Wow," he said, "that's impressive."

"I'll say," she commented, while slowly getting to her feet. "Who are you? And who invited you to the party?"

Nathan frowned. "Hmm," he said, "I would like to ask you the same questions, but something tells me you're not in the mood to tango."

"Nope," she said.

But before she could move, Nathan quickly sent another energy ball at her.

Instantly, she launched herself into the air performing a forward summersault, missing the energy ball entirely, and kicking Nathan hard in the chest.

Nathan smashed violently against the ground of the other cave room. "No one told me agility was an ability of Pneuma Novo," he groaned, while clutching his chest.

She tossed back her long blond hair and laughed. "That's because it isn't," she said.

He tried to get up, but couldn't. He stumbled backwards until finally resting against the wall of the back chamber. She slowly continued forward, one eyebrow cocked over her sunglasses, and one hand stretched out towards him.

Nathan jumped when Jonathan materialized next to him — now back in his human shape.

"Jonathan. Nice to see you again."

Jonathan held his side and tried to smile. "Hello, Nathan," he said in a whisper. "You have an impressive talent."

Nathan glanced up at the approaching blond woman and struggled to help Jonathan to his feet.

"Sort of," Nathan said. "But that's a nice dog show you have there. Why don't you perform that disappearing trick and get us out of here?"

Jonathan winced. "I would if I could," he said. "But I don't think my ability works that way. Besides, I've only been able to move between realms when I am in animal form, and currently I am all out of juice. I can't change back."

"Why didn't you just leave?" asked Nathan.

Jonathan's forehead was drenched with sweat and his glasses slid down his nose. "I wasn't going to leave you alone to fend for yourself."

"Okay," snarled the woman. "I hate to break up this heart-to-heart session, but this little college town is cramping my style. And frankly, I would like to get back home in time for tea."

Nathan attempted to balance himself while holding Jonathan to free his hand. "Well, I'm sorry to inconvenience you," he retorted.

She smirked. "Ciao, boys!" She raised both hands and fired a stream of energy balls directly at them.

Nathan and Jonathan dove forward with pieces of rock falling behind them. Nathan placed his hands over his head and stayed close to the ground. After a few moments of silence, he slowly opened his eyes. The small chamber swirled in a cloud of dust and pieces of rubble lay in clumps all around him. "Jonathan!" he called out.

"I'm right here," responded Jonathan, through coughs.

Nathan turned around to find Jonathan slowly getting to his feet. He quickly surveyed the room, searching for their mysterious visitor, but he couldn't see her. He then hobbled over to the chamber entrance. "I think she's gone," he said.

"Are you sure?" asked Jonathan, caressing his side. His face suddenly went white. "Dr. Helmsley!"

Dr. Helmsley's body still lay slumped over outside the chamber against a pile of rubble. Jonathan kneeled down beside her and checked her pulse. He gasped. "Thank goodness!" he shouted. "She's alive, and I think she may be all right. I think she's just unconscious."

Nathan stood over Jonathan as he examined Dr. Helmsley. He was looking around the cave when a shiny object caught his eye. He picked up the gold necklace he spotted and headed to the small chamber. The torch to the room was still lit so he held up the necklace. The charm attached to it cast a shadow next to the symbol on the wall.

"It's the symbol for the Firewalker," said Jonathan, while standing beside him. "It's the same symbol used — "

"As the crest for the Order," finished Nathan.

Jonathan nodded. "Yes, you are correct." He stood closer to the wall with the symbol and inspected the damage. There was a sad look on his face as he traced his fingers across the remaining symbols. "What I don't understand," he said, "is why our nefarious visitor was trying to kill us."

Nathan walked over to the wall and wiped the dust from the hieroglyphs. He then stood back. "I don't think she was trying to kill us," he said. "Dr. Helmsley maybe, but not us."

Jonathan raised his eyebrows and then surveyed the rubble and damage in the room. "And how do you surmise that?" he asked.

"Because she had us," he said. "She could have killed us if she wanted to, but she didn't." Nathan placed the gold necklace into his pocket. "I don't even think she was aiming at us," he said. "From the looks of it, I would say she was trying to destroy the wall."

"That is quite plausible," said Jonathan. "Tonight I received a text from Dr. Helmsley saying that she felt like someone was following her, and that's why I came here. About a week ago, she told me that after she contacted Dr. Colvers about her discovery, she felt like someone was after her; that her life was in danger."

"But it's just a symbol," said Nathan. "I mean, what could be so threatening about it that you would want to kill someone over it? What exactly did Dr. Helmsley discover?"

Jonathan pushed his glasses farther up on his nose and pointed to the symbols. "See, it's not just about the one symbol," he said. "I mean, it is a very important one, but it's what all the symbols together say about the Firewalker that makes it so special."

Jonathan ran his index finger across the wall. "See these symbols," he started to say, but paused as more pieces of the wall crumbled beneath his finger. "Well, what's left of them, they tell a story, a new legend to add to Cahokia mythology. Together, these symbols tell us the Legend of the Firewalker."

"All this craziness for just another story?"

"No, not just any story. This one is different; this one is prophetic in nature. It talks about someone to come."

Nathan looked confused.

Jonathan sighed. "Look," he pointed. "Based on what we were able to decipher, the legend says ..." He paused, attempting to read the symbols and to fill in the parts that were now missing. "In the time before the last battle, he will emerge, igniting the spirit from within, bringing down the veil that separates Spirit and Earth, restoring balance back to the spirit of man. And he will wield the power of the three; Earth —"

Jonathan paused.

"What is it?" asked Nathan.

Jonathan pointed again. "That's strange," he said. "Dr. Helmsley didn't record it like this in her notes, but the symbols for Earth and Spirit appear on top of one another, as if it should be read as Earth and Spirit and Fire."

"So what does that mean?"

"I'm not sure," Jonathan said. "Probably nothing." He took a step back from the wall and repositioned his glasses. "There are still parts to the legend that we haven't figured out yet, and that's where Dr. Colvers comes in. We were hoping he could help us decipher the rest."

"It doesn't look like it matters now," said Nathan, pointing to the damaged wall. "There are parts missing and the bottom part is completely gone."

"That's not entirely accurate. While I deeply regret we couldn't preserve such a rare find, all is not lost." Jonathan smiled. "The first time we entered the chamber I took pictures of the entire wall with my cell phone."

Nathan shrugged. "Well, I still don't understand why a person would be willing to murder someone over this," he said. "Regardless of it being a never-heard-of Cahokia prophecy. It's just a story ..."

"That's exactly it, Nathan," Jonathan said. "What if it's

not just a story?" Behind his glasses, Jonathan's eyes were as large as saucers. "What if what Dr. Helmsley was close to discovering was something bigger, something that could profoundly affect all of us?" His voice lowered. "Someone was willing to go to great lengths to keep that something hidden. And whatever that was, was on that wall."

"Yeah," Nathan said. "And now on your phone. Do you think Dr. Colvers is behind this?"

"No. The only reason Dr. Colvers is involved is because of his research. And I suspect because of how vocal he is with his conspiracy theories about the Order, they are probably monitoring him; and that's how they learned what Dr. Helmsley was working on."

"And that's why you wanted me in the dark about Dr. Colvers."

"Precisely," said Jonathan. "I didn't want to risk the Order coming after you too. And thanks to the little gold souvenir left behind by our dangerous femme fatale, I am almost certain they are behind our little visit today. I believe we were close to learning something they didn't want us to know, and they were willing to do whatever is necessary to stop that from happening."

Nathan's face lit up. "What about Argus?"

Jonathan looked confused.

Nathan continued, "He has a tattoo of the Firewalker symbol on his arm. Malick said he's probably a member of the Order."

"Argus?" Jonathan asked. "Well, he would know."

Nathan shrugged. "What do you mean?"

Jonathan looked at him disbelievingly for a second before continuing. "I am not surprised he hasn't told you," he said. "According to my research, Malick's father is a member of the Order."

"What?" asked Nathan, in sheer disbelief.

Jonathan nodded. "Yes, Stephen Malick Sr. is a member of the Order. This is the first time I've learned anything about Argus being involved, but if he's wearing a tattoo of the symbol, it's highly probable he's a member."

"What about Malick?" Nathan asked. "Is he a member?"

Jonathan had started to pace. "I'm not sure yet," he said. "It's difficult finding anything about the Order — even basic things such as who its members are, what their purpose is, and where they're located." He stopped pacing. "But for now, be very cautious. After tonight, it appears the Order is no stranger to people who have abilities, and until we learn about his involvement, don't trust Malick."

There was a loud moan, and the boys turned around to find Dr. Helmsley's eyes fluttering; she was waking up.

"We should get her back to campus," said Jonathan.

Nathan nodded. "So," he said, pausing for a moment, "the black dog in the forest. The first night at camp —"

Jonathan had kneeled down to check Dr. Helmsley's vital signs. "Yes," he interrupted with a smile. "But it's more like a black fox, not a dog."

"Don't you think you're a little too big to be a fox?"

Jonathan frowned, and his blue eyes glared over his glasses.

Nathan thought he had just received the look of death. "All right," Nathan said, raising his hands as if surrendering. "Whatever you say, black fox."

Jonathan pushed his glasses back on his nose and a smile crept back onto his face. "Could you give me a hand?" he asked.

Nathan reached down and together they slowly helped

Dr. Helmsley to her feet.

"I just want to say thank you," said Nathan. "You saved us that day. I don't know how, but I just knew you wanted us to turn down that road."

Jonathan continued to smile, but suddenly looked uncomfortable.

"How did you know where to find us?" Nathan asked. "And why are you a dog — I mean, a fox?"

Jonathan took a deep breath and looked at the wall outside of the secret chamber. "He will be known by those around him," he said.

"What?" Nathan was confused, but followed Jonathan's gaze over to the wall.

"The first night at camp," continued Jonathan, "we discovered the Firewalker symbol on the wall along with other symbols. We had planned to wait until morning to try and decipher them, but I was so excited I just couldn't wait."

Nathan squinted. He could see the Firewalker symbol on the wall outside the chamber along with some other symbols.

"I figured since there were a few more hours before nightfall, I would come back and start deciphering the symbols," Jonathan said. He pointed with his free hand. "When I touched that one, the Cahokia symbol for teacher, that's when I became the black fox."

Nathan looked to see where Jonathan was pointing. Around the Firewalker symbol were several smaller symbols.

"So how did you end up on the road?" Nathan asked.

"I'm not sure. I have a hunch, but it's just a theory at this point." He paused for a moment, as if he was about to say something, but then looked away. "But I do know for certain that I was drawn there. Before I knew it, I was in that place I was talking about the night of the first bonfire."

"Oh," responded Nathan. "You mean the Space In Between or the Spirit Realm."

Jonathan looked surprised. "How did you —"

"You know," said Nathan, with a nervous chuckle, "I've been doing my research."

Jonathan looked at him skeptically for a moment, but then nodded. "Well, since that night," he said, "I've been doing my own research. I've been trying to figure out what happened to me and what it has to do with the Firewalker symbol and the Order. That's when I discovered the other strange occurrences happening in town and that there were others probably like me."

Nathan looked confused. "I'm not sure I'm following you."

Dr. Helmsley moaned; she was out of it, but surprisingly was still standing. Jonathan looked like he was getting weary of allowing her body weight to rest upon his shoulder. "I'm sorry," he said, after repositioning himself. "See, I found this article in the IUCF newspaper about a student who claimed to be attacked by several small creatures."

"Leah," said Nathan.

"Yes, you are correct," said Jonathan, looking surprised. "Based on her account of what happened to her, it sounded like she had been in the Space In Between."

"And that's why you had a copy of the IUCF yearbook," responded Nathan confidently.

"Yes," said Jonathan. "At Lafonda's party, I heard about a girl named Leah who was attacked on campus. After I got her last name from Alan, I looked her up, and that's when I discovered that she lived in Lawrence Hall, in the same room where —"

"Jonas is staying in for the summer," finished Nathan.

"Yes," responded Jonathan, still surprised. "And that's when I learned something even more interesting but equally disturbing. I discovered that Leah's roommate was found dead not too far from where they found the body of Bartholomew Riley."

"Jonas's father," muttered Nathan.

Jonathan nodded. "They found both their bodies out on Route 7," he continued, "which is right outside of —"

"Grimm Cemetery," said Nathan.

"Yes," said Jonathan. "And I believe they are all connected. After reading in the newspaper about what Leah said happened to her, I am certain whatever happened to her occurred in the Space In Between. And if Leah was there, then it's highly plausible that she has a power as well. I suspect that whatever was after Leah, was probably after her roommate and maybe even —"

"Jonas's father," said Nathan.

"Now if it turned out that Jonas had an ability," said Jonathan, "then we would definitely know we were on to something. But for now, I am almost certain that after we decipher the rest of the Legend of the Firewalker, we'll be closer to discovering how everything is connected: our powers, the symbols, the Order and the strange occurrences."

"We have to go," said Nathan, there was a hint of panic in his voice. "Like right now!"

Jonathan was confused by the sudden urgency but nodded, and they slowly started helping Dr. Helmsley out of the cave. "Nathan," he said, "when did you find out you had an ability?"

Nathan chuckled. "It's a long story," he said. "But it wasn't as magical as touching a symbol on the wall."

Jonathan smiled.

"Let's just say I sort of had a premonition about it and then was forced to use it," he said. "It didn't turn out how I expected, but it pretty much was either eat or be eaten."

Jonathan's eyebrows frowned inward beneath his glasses. He looked confused again. "How long ago was this? And how did you know how to use it?" His pupils were dilated and he suddenly looked really inquisitive. "And what brought you to the caves tonight?"

"It really is a long story," said Nathan, feeling slightly uncomfortable. "I just happened to be on the trail tonight when I saw you transform into a fox. After that, I pretty much decided to follow you."

"I usually don't do that so out in the open," said Jonathan, with a chuckle. "I'm usually a little more discreet."

Nathan grinned and then nodded. "I promise to explain more later."

"Well, now you know why I kept asking you to come out here. After the car incident, I just knew you were connected, somehow."

The torches leading to the entrance to the cave had been blown out, but with it being a full moon, Nathan and Jonathan could still find their way out. Dr. Helmsley was semiconscious and silent almost the entire way to the entrance to the cave, so they both were surprised when she actually said something.

"What's going on?" she stuttered, slightly in a panic. "Where is she?"

"She's gone," Jonathan responded, raising his free hand to calm her. "Everything is okay."

Her eyes still looked dazed when she glanced over to Nathan. "Who are you?" she asked.

Jonathan and Nathan turned to look at each other, and Nathan removed the broken glasses that now dangled from Dr. Helmsley's face.

"Just a friend of Jonathan's, Dr. Helmsley," Nathan replied. "I'm here to help you."

She opened her eyes wide, and her head gradually fell from side to side until it stopped square in his face.

"What a nice young man," she said groggily. "You may call me Janet."

She lifted her arms from their shoulders and attempted to walk forward, but quickly passed out.

Jonathan reached out to grab her, but he wasn't fast enough. She hit the ground with a thud. "Ouch," he said, while wincing. "That's going to hurt."

Nathan and Jonathan both bent over to prop Dr. Helmsley against the entrance to the cave. A trickle of blood ran from the crest of her head, and Jonathan attempted to stop the bleeding with the bottom of his shirt.

Nathan stood up and wiped his forearm across his brow. "It will take forever to get back to campus at this rate," he said.

"I agree," said Jonathan. "And it appears Dr. Helmsley needs immediate medical attention. I fear she may be suffering from a slight concussion."

"Crap," said Nathan. "Check your cell phone. My phone keeps dropping the signal."

Jonathan opened his cell phone revealing once again the green light Nathan saw earlier while following him in the forest. "My phone isn't working either," he said.

Nathan noticed the ground was soft beneath his feet. He looked up and a few raindrops landed on his forehead. In the distance, past the meadow, a deep rumbling sound echoed at them somewhere above the trees. He glanced over at Jonathan and saw that the bottom of his shirt was soaked with Dr. Helmsley's blood. He thought about what Jonathan had said about Leah's roommate and Jonas's father and how whatever attacked Leah could be the cause of their deaths. He also thought about what Jonathan didn't know: that Jonas did have an ability and that the same creatures that attacked Leah had attacked Jonas.

"It would be quicker if you stayed here with Dr. Helmsley and I went back for help," he said.

Jonathan stood up and gazed upward at the sky. "Yes," he said. "I agree with your conclusion. It doesn't look like the storm is over, however; you should leave before it starts raining again."

Nathan nodded and started to trot off. "I'll call for help as soon as I can," he said. "I probably will get a signal when I am close to campus."

"Nathan," called Jonathan. "I'm glad you were here tonight."

Nathan smiled and then ran as fast as he could up the meadow. The grass was wet and he almost fell a few times, but soon he entered the forest. He thought about what Jonathan had said about his transformation as he passed the two yellow-ribboned trees. *Malick said our powers were hereditary. Did Jonathan really become a black fox just because he touched some symbol?* he thought.

He stepped out onto the black asphalt just in time to see the last parking lot lamp flicker out.

"Great," he mumbled. "And I still have no signal."

He was relieved he didn't have to worry about bumping into anything because the lot was empty. He could feel mud stuck beneath his shoes and tried to clean them in the grass before continuing down the trail. The path leading out of the forest and on to Lawrence Road was darker than normal because the streetlights were out. Before crossing the road he could see that most of campus still had electricity, including Lawrence Hall.

He could tell from the sidewalk that the lobby to Lawrence Hall was empty. While on the trail, he figured it would be best just to tell everyone there had been an accident and that part of the cave had collapsed, injuring Dr. Helmsley. He had intended to tell this story to the front desk attendants so they could call and ask for emergency medical assistance, but their area was vacant as well. Nathan thought it was odd, but proceeded to the elevators and pulled out his cell phone.

The elevator doors opened and he pushed the button for the eighth floor. He was surprised that he finally had a signal, considering he was riding in an elevator. His cell phone vibrated, reporting he had six missed calls and four unheard messages. "My goodness, Lafonda," he mumbled as he dialed 911.

Nathan felt a little strange dialing that number because he had never had a reason to do so before. He waited as the phone rang on the other end while the elevator bell rang between floors. He watched patiently as each elevator number lit up, but the elevator slowed as it approached the seventh floor.

He was a little surprised because the seventh floor was Lafonda's, and everyone would normally be in their rooms for the night.

Nathan jumped: a high-pitched scream had pierced the elevator. The doors to the elevator opened and in ran Samantha Darding, her nightgown tattered and her hands stained with blood.

"Nathan!" she screamed. "They took her! They took Eva Marie, and I can't find Christina!" Her hands trembled as she clung to Nathan's shirt, her eyes filled with horror. "They were like shadows," she continued frantically. "And Angela! Oh, my God! They took Angela!"

CHAPTER TWENTY

911

"911 dispatch," said the voice over the phone. "Please state your emergency."

A cold shiver shot down Nathan's back, and his mind was suddenly flooded with images of Leah as she tried to defend herself from an unseen attacker. He quickly closed his cell phone and placed it into his pocket. "What happened?" he asked. "Who took them?"

He attempted to exit the elevator, but Samantha pushed him back. "We can't," she said anxiously. "We have to get out of here. They move so quickly! They're everywhere!"

"Who's everywhere?" Nathan asked, peering out of the elevator.

The common area was in disarray; the round tables once set upright were now toppled over. From what he could tell, there were several scratch marks on the walls.

"I don't see anyone," he said.

He turned to look at Samantha. She was clutching her arm and her entire body was shaking. Nathan noticed the rips in her nightgown and her blood-soaked hands. Instantly, he was reminded of Leah again.

"Are you hurt?" he asked.

Samantha leaned against the elevator wall and raised

her sleeve, revealing a deep cut on her shoulder. She placed her hand on the wound and winced in pain. "I don't think it's that bad," she said. "It probably would have been worse if it weren't for Angela."

"Angela?" he asked, while inspecting the wound.

A loose strand of hair dangled in her face. With the back of her hand she attempted to move it out of the way, but ended up smearing blood on her forehead and face.

"They were all around me," she said. "I didn't know where to run." She paused to wipe the tears that swelled in her eyes. "One second they were in front of me, but then they were gone. After they cut me, I fell to the ground; that's when Angela showed up. She saved me, but then they took her."

He took a moment to look at the slashes on the walls again. "Where did the creatures come from?" he asked. "Did they come out of the stairway? The bathrooms?"

"Creatures?" she muttered.

"Yeah," he responded, after peering out of the elevator again. "How many creatures were there?"

Samantha shook her head. She looked confused.

"You know," he said, pointing to her injured shoulder. "The black-and-gray furry things with long claws and sharp teeth."

Her body shook again, but this time her eyes trembled.

"No, no, no!" she shouted. "There were no claws or furry creatures; just black empty faces and shiny silver swords!"

Nathan's heart instantly kicked into overdrive as if it was trying to leap out of his chest. "Shadow Guards," he muttered. "Jonas!"

Defensively, he stepped out of the elevator with his hand poised to fire.

"Stay here," he said.

Samantha nodded.

Slowly, he proceeded down the hall with his hand stretched out in front of him. Up close he could see the marks on the walls weren't scratches, but deep slashes made by either a big knife or a sword.

He turned around and faced the elevator. Sadness began to wash over him. He realized those same marks were on Samantha.

"Sam," he said, sliding his cell phone over to her. "Call the police. Tell them you need immediate medical attention." He then remembered Jonathan and Dr. Helmsley. "Also, tell them there has been an accident at the caves behind the cliffs overlooking Lake Charleston," he said. "It's the cave closest to the archeological dig site."

Samantha stood in between the elevator doors so they wouldn't close and picked up the cell phone. He wasn't sure if she had got it all because her face was still in shock.

He recalled what had happened the previous time with the Necrocritters and carefully peered into the bathroom. It appeared empty, so he slowly crept forward. He quickly froze after he heard crunching noises beneath his feet. He looked down and inspected the shattered pieces of glass. "At least now I know what happened to the lights," he said to himself.

It was night, so the hallway was extremely dark. His heart continued to pound; he expected someone to jump out or ambush him at any second. A faint creaking noise came from somewhere in front of him, followed by low shuffling noises. He was practically tiptoeing now as he eased forward. Muffled voices emanated from one of the dorm rooms on his right. With his palm open and his arm stretched down to his side he was prepared to throw an energy ball. The energy pulsated in his arm as he slowly turned the door knob.

The door opened and he heard a gasp. Standing in front of him with a wooden desk chair over his head that looked rather small compared to his size, was Hugo. Crouched behind him were Christina Williams and several other campers.

"Nathan," he yelled. "Thank God it's you!"

Nathan put down his hand and placed it behind him. "Hugo," he said, his heart still racing. "What are you doing down here and on the girls' floor?"

"Oh, my God, Nathan," he responded. "There were these guys, these hoodlums! I thought it was a prank or a joke at first, but then they grabbed Jonas."

"Jonas," Nathan interrupted. "Where is he? Where did they take him?"

Nathan turned around as other doors opened. Other campers started to appear out of their rooms.

"Christina?" asked a familiar voice.

He turned to find Samantha standing next to him.

Christina hurriedly embraced Samantha. "I thought they had taken you," she said.

Samantha recoiled, quickly placing her hand on her shoulder.

"You're hurt!" Christina shouted. "Sam, you're bleeding!"

"I don't know," said Hugo, his voice sounding huskier than usual. "It was dark and I couldn't see their faces. They moved so fast and they had weapons — swords! We followed them down the stairway, but we just couldn't keep up with them, and that's when we heard the screaming." He paused to eye the scratches on his hands. "In the midst of it all, I lost track of Andy," he continued.

"They were everywhere and they just kept coming!"

"They took him," said Christina while attending to Samantha. "I saw them carry Andy down the stairwell."

"Hugo," Nathan said, "watch after Sam and move everyone that is injured to the lobby downstairs; stay off the stairwell and use the elevator. I'm going to check the stairs." Nathan's eyes softened as he turned his attention to Samantha. "Are you okay?" he asked.

She nodded and tried to muster a smile. "The 911 dispatcher said the police are on their way, and they are sending an ambulance," she said, while handing him his phone. "I tried not to get any blood on it. Oh, and I told them there had been an accident at the caves."

He smiled reassuringly. "Thanks," he said.

Nathan headed down the stairwell fast, but based on what Hugo had told him, he figured he was probably too late. He thought Jonas might have gotten away or could be on the stairs, injured.

The stairwell echoed as each swift footstep caused the metal stairs to rattle and shake. When Nathan approached the next landing, he saw something purple with gold stars on it on the floor. "Angela's cell phone," he said. His stomach, already spiraling, began to twist.

He heard footsteps fast approaching from the landing down below, peered over the railing, and caught a glimpse of Alan coming up the stairs. He immediately picked up Angela's cell phone and placed it into his back pocket.

Alan frowned when he saw Nathan and removed his own cell phone from his ear. "What the heck is going on up there?" he asked. "What's the reason for all the noise? My guys said they heard screaming."

Nathan tried not to look upset.

"What?" asked Alan, speaking into his phone. He attempted to pass Nathan on the stairwell.

911

"And where is Angela?" he asked Nathan.

Nathan caught Alan by the arm. He had a sad look on his face. "She's not up there," he said, almost in a whisper. He cleared his throat. "Just come with me."

"What do you mean?" Alan protested. "I just left from up there like fifteen minutes ago."

Nathan held on to Alan's arm and continued down the stairs.

"Hey," Alan groaned. "What the heck are you doing? And where is Angela?"

He was now speaking into his cell phone. "I don't know what he's doing," he said. "He won't let go of my arm." He reluctantly continued down the stairs. "Again," he said, while speaking into the phone, "I said I don't know."

Nathan just shook his head and kept walking.

"Okay, fine!" Alan snapped, after yanking his arm from Nathan's grip. "Here!"

Nathan raised his eyebrows and frowned. "I don't want your cell phone," he said. "I am dragging you along just in case I may need backup."

"Backup?" he asked. "For what?" Alan rolled his eyes and shoved the phone into Nathan's hand. "You better answer it," he said. "It's Lafonda."

Nathan paused to take a deep breath and sighed. He could only imagine how upset she was that he hadn't returned any of her phone calls. He placed Alan's cell phone to his ear and winced.

"Hello?" he said slowly.

"Nathan Urye!" she responded angrily. "I have called you several times and left several messages. Why haven't you called me back?"

"Um," he uttered, while mentally recalling the events of the day. "I would say I have been very busy."

"Whatever, Nathan. You could have at least texted me. And what's going on there? Alan said the guys heard screaming on my floor. I tried calling Angela, but it just goes to voicemail."

He heard a door open and close on the stairwell and proceeded down the stairs, trying to remain calm. "Lafonda, I couldn't call anybody. There was a storm tonight and I had no signal."

"Hey," protested Alan, while following close behind him. "Where are you going with my cell phone?"

Nathan just ignored him and kept walking. "Plus," he continued, "you can't imagine the night I've had. Jonathan and Dr. Helmsley were —"

"Leah's missing," she said.

He froze and Alan almost ran into him. "What?" he asked. "What do you mean? What happened?"

There was a brief silence on the other end of the phone. "We had just returned back to Leah's parents' house after shoe shopping," she said. "Leah wanted to change clothes before we went out for dinner."

"Shoe shopping?" he asked.

Alan's eyes lit up. "Shoe shopping?"

"Yes," she continued. "I waited for her downstairs with her mom in the kitchen. She wasn't gone that long. Her mom had just taken the peach cobbler out of the oven, and that's when we heard this loud screeching noise."

A cold shiver ran down his back. "Did you say screeching noise?"

"Yes," she said. "It almost sounded like grinding metal."

Nathan remembered the sound the Necrocritters made while on the pseudo staircase with Jonas. He also recalled the scratches on Bobby's arm, and the comment

Jonas had made about the train behind his house. "Like the sound of a train?" he asked, proceeding down the stairs again.

"Yeah," she replied. "How did you know?" Lafonda waited for a response, but after a moment of silence continued. "We followed the sound back to Leah's room, and when she didn't respond, her mom opened the door. The room was a mess, Nathan — feathers everywhere and her bedspread ripped to shreds. It reminded me of her dorm room the night she was taken to the hospital."

There was silence on the phone again.

"What kind of shoes did you buy?" Nathan finally asked.

Alan nodded, eager to hear the response.

"Shoes?" Lafonda asked, sounding a bit confused. "I bought a pair of sneakers."

"Are you wearing them now?" Nathan continued. "What color are they?"

"Yes. They're pink and gray," she replied, annoyed. "And why on Earth are you asking me about my shoes when Leah is missing?"

"Where are you now?" he asked.

Lafonda huffed. "In my car," she said. "Driving back to campus."

"No!" Nathan exclaimed. "I mean — you should stay there!"

"I need a break," she said. "We just spent hours looking for her and talking to the police. I'm tired and just want to go home. I told her mom to call if there were any news."

"That's the reason why you should stay there," he said. "You shouldn't be driving; you're tired. And what if Leah comes home?"

She sighed. "I'm already on the road, Nathan. And

besides, I am almost there. Are you going to tell me what's going on?"

He was nearing the bottom of the stairwell when he caught a glimpse of Erin standing there with a basketball in her hand. "Everything is fine," he said.

"I want to talk to Angela," she demanded.

Nathan rolled his eyes. "Everything is fine," he said. "And we'll see you when you get here."

"Ugh," she groaned.

Nathan looked distressed. "Bye," he said, before hanging up the phone.

"What the heck was that all about?" asked Alan. "Why did you say if Leah comes home? Where is she?"

"What's going on?" asked Erin. "What's up with all the ruckus on the stairs tonight? The girls on my floor were complaining about loud noises. They said it sounded like a fight on the stairwell. I came out here and that's when I saw the weirdest thing." She pointed to the exit at the bottom of the staircase. "I saw two guys dressed in black walk straight through that door, but the entire door was like engulfed in a blue light. And when I reached the bottom to investigate, the blue light was gone and so were the guys. I checked the lobby too. Unless my eyes are deceiving me, I promise you, those guys just disappeared."

Alan held out his hand to Nathan. "Give me back my cell," he demanded. "Are you going to tell me what's going on, or should I just call Lafonda?"

Nathan took a deep breath. It was Jonas's basketball in Erin's hand.

"Angela is missing," Nathan said.

"What?" blurted Alan.

Nathan nodded and his face frowned sympathetically. "Yes," he said. "Jonas, Andy, and Eva Marie are also missing."

Alan's mouth fell open. "You got to be kidding me," he said. "Is this a joke?"

Nathan shook his head and gave Alan back his phone. "I'm not joking," he said. "And Leah's missing too. That's why Lafonda called; she was calling to tell me about Leah."

"That's crazy!" groaned Alan. "We have to call the police."

"The police are on their way, but trust me," responded Nathan, "they can't help us."

Alan looked confused. "What are you talking about?" he asked.

Erin pointed her thumb to the exit again. "Does this have anything to do with those guys dressed in black?" she asked. "And who are they?"

Nathan nodded. "Yes. But I can't explain right now."

She had a doubtful look on her face. "Are they some type of gang?"

"Gang?" spouted Alan.

"No, they're not a gang, but some of the campers might think they are," he responded. "And for now, I think we should keep it that way."

Frustration was building in Alan's eyes. "We need to go after them!"

"That's what I plan to do," responded Nathan sympathetically. "And I think I might know where they're heading next."

"Then I am going with you," vowed Alan.

Nathan reached into his back pocket. "You can't," he said. "I need you to stay here with the others." He gave Alan Angela's cell phone and suddenly sadness gripped his face. "Sam and some of the other campers have been injured and the paramedics are on their way. With

Lafonda gone and now Angela, I need you guys to stick around and make sure everything is all right."

Erin nodded. "Okay," she said.

Alan rolled his eyes in protest, but proceeded up the stairs.

"Erin," said Nathan. He stuttered a little before speaking. "I need a favor— this is very important."

She took a few steps closer and stared at him intently. "What?" she asked.

"When Lafonda gets here," he said. "Under no circumstance can you allow her to leave Lawrence Hall."

She looked confused. "But —"

He grabbed her by the arm. "Please," he said. "It's really important. It's a matter of life or death."

"Okay, okay," she said. "Relax. I'll keep an eye on Lafonda."

Nathan started towards the exit but spun back around. "What time is it?" he asked.

"Almost midnight," she responded.

"I hope I still have time."

"Nathan," she called out.

He turned around again, and for the first time that night he could tell that Erin was worried.

"I sure hope you know what you are doing," Erin said.

"Me too," he mumbled. "Me too."

Nathan stepped out of the stairwell and into the lobby of Lawrence Hall. The rush of cool air greeted him, and so did the glaring red and blue lights from the ambulance sitting out front. *Good, they're here.*

He caught a glimpse of Samantha being examined by a paramedic, while a watchful Hugo towered over them. A trickle of campers and counselors began to fill the lobby.

Soon the police would arrive and so would LaDonda. He figured now was a good time to slip out unnoticed.

He had a gut-wrenching feeling as he stepped outside through the kitchen. The door slammed shut behind him, and he was alone in the parking lot. "I hope Sam will be okay," he said. He remembered seeing the cut on her arm and how relieved she had been to see him. Feeling frustrated, he slammed his fist against the dumpster. "I feel like I am deserting them!"

He looked to see if anyone was around and then headed towards Jonas's house. Nathan sprinted as fast as he could, cutting across unfenced yards and through a couple of alleys. He turned a corner, and a couple of feet in front of him were the railroad tracks that ran behind Jonas's house. He remembered the modest home with a sloping roof and white trim, and headed up the driveway to the back of the house. All the lights were off, except for the one on the front porch. It was a little past midnight and, as he expected, there was no train.

"I hope I am not too late," he mumbled to himself.

The back of the house was completely dark, but there was a faint glow of light from one of the back windows. "I hope he's still there," he said. "I hope they didn't come for him." Nathan stood atop a brick that rested against the house to get a better look inside the window. "If he's gone, how on earth will I get in?"

Inside the window, he could see Bobby playing video games in the dark with the light from the television reflecting on his face. Nathan lightly tapped on the window, and in a flash Bobby turned off the television and hopped into bed.

Nathan chuckled. "Bobby," he whispered while continuing to tap on the window.

Bobby slowly opened his eyes and stared at the window for a moment before getting out of bed. "Jonas?" he asked.

Nathan smiled. "No," he said. "It's me, Nathan."

"What are you doing out there?" asked Bobby, while raising the window. "Is my brother out there too?"

"No," he said. "Have you seen him tonight?"

Bobby shook his head.

Nathan glanced around the room. The box for Bobby's video game *Wizards and Warriors* was on the floor, and there was a *Wizards and Warriors* poster on the wall. "I need to talk to you," he said.

"Am I in trouble?" Bobby asked. "Please don't tell my mom. If I get in trouble again, I won't be able to go to my brother's closing ceremony tomorrow."

Nathan chuckled. "A strange man is looking through a little boy's window in the middle of the night and you think you're in trouble?"

Bobby tilted his head and folded his arms across his chest. "You're not a stranger, Nathan," he said. "We've met, and besides, I'm not a kid. I'm almost ten years old."

"Okay, all right," said Nathan. "I want to show you something, but first you have to promise me you won't be opening windows anymore for anyone after tonight."

"Okay," said Bobby, pausing to take a seat on the windowsill.

Nathan took a quick glance at the poster on the wall again and stepped back. "Um, Bobby," he said.

Bobby looked back at him with eager anticipation.

"Have you seen anything strange or odd lately? Any weird creatures or people, like in *Wizards or Warriors?*"

Bobby's face suddenly looked peculiar as if he was trying to remember something. "There was this black cat in the tree once," he said. "It was really hairy, not like Lacey. It growled a bunch and it had sharp teeth."

"What did the growling sound like?"

The boy twisted his lip and stared off somewhere over

Nathan's shoulder. Suddenly, his eyes lit up and he spoke again. "Like Lacey, but when she's been accidentally stepped on — I think?"

Nathan nodded. "Gotcha," he said. He took a few more paces back, standing closer amongst the trees. "They must have erased his memory, like they did with Jonas," he thought. "And they probably did the same thing to their dad."

Nathan held his arm out with his palm facing upward toward the sky. He could feel the energy building in the muscles in his hand. Out of the corner of his eye, he could see the anticipation building on Bobby's face, and he grinned. Slowly he released the energy, and a stream of white and blue lights began to hover over his hand, coalescing into a swirling ball of energy.

"Whoa!" said Bobby, attempting to hop out of the window.

"Hold on," Nathan chuckled, quickly closing his hand and heading over. "It's way too late, and you need to stay inside."

Bobby's eyes were wide and he beamed. "Are you a wizard?"

Nathan grinned. "No," he said, "I am not a wizard."

"Then you must be a warrior!" said Bobby.

Nathan pursed his lips in a lighthearted way and nodded. "Not quite," he said, "but I appreciate the compliment."

"How did you do that?" Bobby asked.

"One sec," Nathan said. He peered into the window and climbed in. "That's why I am here tonight — I need your help."

Bobby's face frowned in the same way Jonas's did when he didn't understand something.

"Don't worry," said Nathan. "You can do it too."

"Me?" asked Bobby, his eyes wide in amazement.

"Yup," he said. "And Jonas can do it too. And so could your dad."

Bobby's face radiated. "What do you need me to do?" he asked.

"Okay, I need you to close your eyes and focus," Nathan said. "Listen closely and follow my instructions. This is like level 99 of *Wizards and Warriors,* and you only have one board to go."

Bobby's eyes were closed shut, his entire body looked stiff, and his hands were balled into fists.

Nathan smiled. "Are you ready?" he asked. "Do you have your game face on?"

Bobby nodded.

"Okay," said Nathan. "I am going to tell you exactly how Jonas does it. Take two steps back from the window and hold out your hand. Now, I want you to think about Jonas and your dad—think about all the good times you've had together. Imagine that feeling growing, getting stronger!"

A few moments passed and silence fell on the room. Nathan was about to give up, but Bobby's arm slowly started to tremble.

"Now," Nathan said. "Release it through your hand!"

A small bluish-white light slowly crept from Bobby's hand as he instinctively traced the window.

"You did it!" Nathan said.

Bobby opened his eyes to a glowing blue window. "Amazing!" he said. He turned to face Nathan. "Did I do that?"

"Yup," said Nathan, while inspecting the window. "You did it, just like Jonas!"

Bobby beamed. "Like Jonas?"

Nathan nodded then smiled. "Yup," he said. "Exactly

like Jonas!"

"And my dad?"

"And your dad."

With caution, Nathan slowly put his hand out of the window, and then his head. As expected, everything on the other side appeared frozen and shrouded in gray — the trees, the grass and the houses. Everything was as it was in his dreams about Leah and in his dream about Grimm Cemetery.

"Okay," Nathan said, while standing in the room. "It's way past your bedtime, mister."

"I figured you were going to say that," Bobby said, while climbing into bed.

Nathan grinned. "Now remember," he said, taking a seat on the bed, "no more opening windows for anyone whether you think you know them or not, and no more video games!" He headed towards the window. "Oh, and no using your powers — at least until tomorrow," he said with a wink.

"Nathan," Bobby called out, "is my brother in trouble?"

"Everything will be all right now," he said. "Thanks to your help. Now off to bed. We'll see you tomorrow."

The Space In Between was just as Nathan remembered it. The moon and the stars shone exceptionally bright, and to his dismay, Nathan was way across town and nowhere near Grimm Cemetery. By now, he figured the portal that Bobby opened had closed and there was no sense in turning back.

He continued to jog down the lifeless and muted streets, pausing here and there to catch his breath, sometimes stopping in awe at the barren streets and empty houses. "I sure hope Jonas can get us out of here," he said to himself.

He recalled his dream about Grimm Cemetery, the black and red-hooded figures, their swords and the malicious blond woman dressed in white. He huffed. "Yeah, that's if I can figure out a way to save them."

By the time he reached Lawrence Hall to begin the trek down Lawrence Road to connect to Route 7, he felt hopeless. Until now, he had never really realized just how far away Grimm Cemetery was. "At this rate," he grumbled, "I'll never make it in time." When he was a kid, he used to bike there from campus with friends, but being that he was in the Spirit Realm, he was almost certain that any bike he found would be unmovable, practically frozen.

It wasn't until he reached the road leading to the Cahokia Museum parking lot that the pain in his side forced him to take a break. He figured all of the running had finally caught up with him, and since he knew for sure there would be no traffic, he decided to sit in the middle of the road.

Although everything was in black and white, the road that stretched out in front of him was picture-perfect, with motionless trees and twinkling sky. He supposed the scene would make a great photograph with him, the only thing in color, being the focal point and center of attention. Right now, however, the last thing he wanted was attention. He hoped he would continue to go unnoticed up to the very last moment, until he had no other choice but to reveal himself to save his friends.

He stood up, and before he could take a step forward, he felt a warm burst of air on his neck and back. A bright flash of light soon followed and Nathan shielded his eyes. "What was that?" he mumbled. He tried to open his eyes, but there was something big and bright in front of him. He squinted and could see the light gradually diminishing, revealing what looked like an outline of two enormous hands placed side by side together. Soon he could see what looked like a feather, and another feather, and then multitudes of them.

Nathan reached out to touch one and the wall of feathers abruptly sprung open. He instantly stepped back and recoiled, but was ready to defend himself. The light grew smaller and smaller, and then it was gone. He gasped and blinked his eyes furiously. He couldn't believe what was in front of him. "Uh," he stammered. Nathan was speechless. "Are you, uh, wings?" he asked.

The tall man that stood in front of him smiled, and Nathan suddenly realized the bright light that blinded him had emanated from the man.

"Who are you?" Nathan asked hastily.

"A friend," said the tall man, while extending a hand.

Nathan hesitated, staring incredulously at the deep bronze-colored hand in front of him. He could see himself reflected in the gold breastplate as he reached out to shake hands, and in the brief moment that their hands touched, they were gone in a blinding flash.

CHAPTER TWENTY-ONE

MYTHS BECOME REALITY

Nathan blinked a few times, trying to focus his eyes. He thought it was odd that he was on the ground when moments earlier he'd been standing up. The man that had declared himself a friend was standing in front of him. From Nathan's current viewpoint, the tall man completely dwarfed him, leaving Nathan in complete awe of his stature. The gold breastplate the man wore fit him like a glove, and the individual straps with gold buttons that hung from his brown leather belt appeared fit for a king. His bronze skin was a nice contrast to the snow-colored wings now nestled behind him. Although without a sword, he reminded Nathan of a giant replica of a Grecian warrior prepared for battle.

Nathan eyed the empty brass scabbard with red jewels that hung from his belt.

"Where are we?" Nathan asked warily.

"Do you not recognize it?" responded the man in a clear and pleasant voice.

Nathan got to his feet. The blades of grass beneath his hands had felt like little shards of plastic. He looked around and immediately noticed the shadowy trees surrounding the meadow they were in. "Well, we're definitely still in the Space In Between," he said. He continued looking around and eventually caught a glimpse of the old monastery off of Route 7 in the distance. "We're in Lynn Field," he said, sounding surprised.

The tall man beamed at him with welcoming amber eyes and nodded.

"Am I still in time to save my friends?"

The mysterious-looking man started to walk away, and what appeared to be a white door of light appeared in front of him. Nathan quickly followed, and the pit of his stomach became warm and relaxed as he got closer. Light from the door fell upon him, and so did a feeling of peace.

"Wait," he called out, and the man turned around to meet him. "What about my friends? Aren't you going to help me?"

"As in all moments in time, this too shall pass. But the choices and the outcomes of today will shape your future and that of your friends."

Nathan looked up at him in bewilderment. "What are you saying?"

His bronze skin and amber eyes seemed to sparkle in the light. "After all the choices have been made, after all the happy moments, setbacks, doubts and failures," he said, "rest assured that your life, your story will be a guiding light for many people."

"Wait," exclaimed Nathan. "Why are you saying all this?

Nathan continued to follow earnestly behind him, but the man quickly spun around exhibiting a firm hand. "You are neither dead nor an immortal spirit, and cannot enter."

Nathan was caught off guard by his command and he froze. He watched as the bronze man with wings continued forward, disappearing in a mist of white light.

He stood there alone again, pondering what had just happened and staring at the empty space that once was a door of light. "How can this get any crazier?" he mumbled, while throwing his hands up in the air.

He couldn't help feeling angry as he followed the stone path to Grimm Cemetery. He was close enough now to read the familiar Latin words carved at the base of the large oak tree. "Speak no ill of the dead. How ironic, I feel like it's referring to me, now that I've been left here to die. Why help me on the road only to abandon me?"

He shrugged in protest and then sighed again. He felt a little strange when he approached the black iron gate of the cemetery. Everything looked the way it had in his dream, but something was different. In his dream, a sense of urgency had been there; he had heard Leah scream, but now everything was quiet.

He caught a glimpse of a loose stone in the walkway and instantly remembered tripping over it in his dream and falling into the gate. "Well, that matches up," he mumbled, as he proceeded carefully past the gate. "Let's try not to repeat that episode." He was mindful of the various plants entwined around the gate too, recalling that they had startled him.

As soon as Nathan entered the gates, he remembered feeling vulnerable while on the first level. He quickly ran past the rows of small headstone crosses to take refuge on the second level. He didn't bother stopping to hide behind any of the taller monuments because he didn't think they provided much cover.

He felt a sense of déjà vu as he darted up the

dilapidated stone steps and ran to the closest mausoleum. Nathan's breathing labored as he slowly peered around the weathered brick wall. "I'm not repeating that part of the dream," he mumbled, while glancing back at the crumbling stone steps. He peered around the wall again, surveying the graveyard. "There has to be another way up to the plaza."

Nathan carefully made his way to another crypt, stooping low, hoping not to be seen. From this angle, he had a clear view of the surrounding white archways and the tall white obelisk on the third level. He noticed things were much quieter than in his dream; there wasn't any chatter or chanting.

He dared to go a little closer by moving to another mausoleum. This one was familiar, however; it had been in his dream. *This was the crypt that was hit by the energy ball thrown by the priest with the crescent-shaped medallion,* he thought.

Nathan peered from behind the wall, and it was almost painful for him to look at the stone steps leading up to the third level. "I am not going up those stairs," he mumbled, while recalling what happened next. A cold shiver ran down his spine. "There has to be another way!"

Nathan scanned the top level again. He was still astonished by the absence of activity. "Am I too late? Did they take them somewhere else?"

Suddenly, out of the corner of his eye, something moved. He ducked instantly. "Shadow Creatures," he muttered, while taking protection behind the wall. One by one they appeared, darting across the brick and mortar floor. Fear gripped his chest, and his stomach began twisting in knots. "Relax, Nathan," he repeated to himself.

The Necrocritters continued toward one of the

archways and seemed to disappear as they passed through it, leaving Nathan to wonder where they were going. He relaxed his shoulders, but his relief was short lived. Something else had moved. In each dark archway they slowly appeared. "Shadow Guards," he whispered.

Soon after, two Scarlet Priests also appeared, both wearing red-hooded cloaks. Tied around their waists were decorative gold ropes that flowed to the ground. "Looks like I'm not late after all," he said softly.

The two priests stepped aside and another figure emerged from the archway. "Jonas!" he blurted.

Nathan quickly ducked behind the wall to the tomb again, hoping he hadn't been heard. When he emerged, it appeared as if no one had heard him. He could see that Jonas's hands were bound and that his clothes were badly roughed up. Following behind Jonas was a tall, muscular-looking guy that appeared to be escorting him. "Who's that? Where did they get this guy? He looks like he just stepped off the football field."

The hefty guy pushed Jonas forward then stopped him in front of the two priests. He tried to force him to his knees, but Jonas refused. It looked like they were preparing to perform some kind of ritual. Jonas tried to put up a fight, but the hefty guy overpowered him, knocking him to the ground with a violent blow to the head.

Nathan clinched his fists and gritted his teeth. His anger burned, and he could feel something else growing and burning inside of him. "I'm going to kill that guy," he vowed.

Jonas lay in agony on the ground, his hands still bound. The two priests appeared unamused by what just transpired and hissed loudly. The muscular guy quickly reached down and yanked Jonas by the arm, bringing him to his knees.

One of the priests raised his hand from beneath his ruby-red cloak, revealing a long glass vial in his thin, decayed hand. The other priest withdrew a shiny silver dagger similar to the one used to stab Leah in Nathan's dream. In the blink of an eye, his dark, decaying hand was wrapped around Jonas's arm as he prepared to pierce it with the silver dagger. But before he could strike, Jonas yanked back, freeing himself from his grasp. In the same instant, the burly guy slapped Jonas hard across the face, leaving behind a trickle of blood.

Nathan's hands trembled uncontrollably and the burn in the pit of his stomach intensified. "Not yet, Nathan," he repeated to himself. "Not yet." He took several deep breaths, trying to ease the pounding in his chest. He noticed that his hands were bright red, like they had been on the night of Lafonda's birthday party.

Loud hissing sounds echoed from the plaza. The priest with the silver dagger grabbed a fistful of Jonas's dark hair and yanked his head hard to the left, fully exposing the blood coming from his mouth. The other priest carefully placed the long glass vial underneath Jonas's chin and collected his blood. After it was filled, he shook it as if to mix it with something, and the blood-filled vial soon sparkled a bright blue.

The priest released his grip and Jonas's head slumped forward. He was held down by the back of the neck as the two priests stepped into the dark archway. Not too long after they had gone, the Shadow Guards also disappeared.

Everything was quiet now, and except for Jonas and the muscular guy, the plaza appeared empty. Nathan couldn't bear to watch Jonas suffer another second and figured now was his opportunity to save him. But before he could decide on how to attack, Jonas had sprung to his feet, knocking his captor off balance.

Nathan took off running. He only had seconds to reach the top before the guy recovered. He knew Jonas didn't stand a chance while his hands were still tied. Nathan decided to ignore what he knew about the stone steps and ran up them anyway, carefully avoiding parts that were already crumbling. The hefty guy regained his balance and raised his hand to hit Jonas. Nathan also raised his hand, sending a big ball of energy straight into his back. The big guy slumped to the ground, and a huge look of relief washed over Jonas's face.

"Nathan!" he shouted joyfully. "I knew you would come! But how the heck did you cross over?"

Nathan untied the rope around Jonas's wrists and helped him to his feet. "I am surprised that I made it too," he said with a slight chuckle.

Jonas's eyes followed Nathan inquisitively.

"Let's just say I had some help along the way." He examined the bruise forming around Jonas's mouth and then scanned the plaza. "Now quickly," he said. "Where are the others?"

Jonas started to answer, but was interrupted by whooshing sounds coming from each archway. One by one, the Shadow Guards appeared, each one with a long silver sword held upright against their chests.

"Stay close to me," said Nathan. He tried to back up, but couldn't; they were all around them. Nathan opened his hand and formed an energy ball. He was prepared to fight for their lives. A few moments passed and the Shadow Guard in the archway to the right of them stepped aside. Two Scarlet Priests appeared, followed by another one. Nathan gasped.

"It's the priest with the crescent-shaped medallion," he

muttered.

Soon after, another red-hooded figure appeared, but this one was different: he was taller and stockier. Nathan caught a glimpse of his chiseled chin and whitish-blond hair and recognized him from his dream.

The blond figure removed his hood, revealing his ocean-blue eyes and luminous skin. His long hair was just as vibrant. He glared at Nathan and sighed heavily as if agitated by his presence.

"Do you want to die?" he asked with a devilish grin. His mesmerizing eyes scanned the plaza. "Stand down, or I will kill you myself."

Nathan's heart pounded against his chest, and he could feel the sweat accumulating on his forehead. He was about to close his hand, but he remembered how brave Jonas had been.

"No," he said, while gathering his courage. "I will not stand down. Give me back my friends!"

The man with the chiseled chin snarled, revealing his perfect white teeth. "Stupid humans," he said.

In a blink of an eye, a flurry of what looked like red bolts of lightning sprung from the tips of his fingers.

Nathan tried to cast the energy ball in his hand, but dropped to his knees in pain. Jonas tried to get at the man but was knocked to the ground by another red bolt of lightning.

The attack ceased, and Nathan felt like he had just been electrocuted. Smoke rose from the plaza floor and the clothes on his body.

The man laughed. "Humans. They get a little power, and they think they're invincible," he said. "Come, my dear. Please tell me, where did you find this one?"

From out of the shadows of the archway stepped the lady in white, the long train to her dress flowing behind her.

Nathan staggered to his feet and quickly blinked his eyes. He couldn't believe who was standing in front of him.

"Amanda?" he shouted.

She kissed the blond man teasingly on the ear and gently traced the side of his face with her finger. She then focused her attention on Nathan, glaring at him with her sparking green eyes.

"He's no one," she said. "Just a boy I considered toying with while looking for the one we seek."

"Like you toyed with that one?" he said, pointing to the muscular guy, who had recovered from Nathan's energy ball and was just now getting to his feet.

"Who? Steve?" she snickered. "He serves a purpose."

The blond man pointed towards Nathan. "I thought you had brought only five of them this time," he continued. "Where did he come from?"

She suddenly looked flustered. "I don't know," she said, turning around to gawk at the priest with the gold-and-silver medallion. "Why wasn't he with the others?" she yelled. "Are you trying to make me look like a fool?"

The priest quickly lowered his head. "My apologies," he responded with a hiss. "We weren't aware of him. My magic has detected the one you seek, but unless they use their ability, it's hard to tell which one."

"Then we'll have to test them all," she demanded. "Bring them here!"

The priest with the crescent-shaped medallion vanished into the archway.

Steve stumbled over to a pillar that made up one of the archways. He placed his hand to his head, and he looked bewildered. "W-where am I?" he stuttered.

The man with the chiseled chin sighed. "Time is a

precious commodity these days, my dear," he said haughtily to Amanda. He had a petulant look on his face. "And you are wasting it!"

Flippantly, she tossed back her long, curly blond hair as if to show disapproval.

He rolled his eyes at her display of protest and pointed at Steve. "And please tell me, why in all the realms did you decide to keep that pitiful thing?" he asked with disgust. "Do him a favor and kill him already; put him out of his misery."

She headed over to Steve, whose muscular frame was slumped over.

"Get rid of him?" she laughed. "My pet? But he's so useful."

Steve looked up at her, the confusion in his eyes starting to fade.

"Amanda?" he asked. "What happened? What are we doing here?"

She leaned over and gently stroked his face with the back of her hand. "There, there," she said, with a mothering voice.

The confusion on Steve's face suddenly disappeared. He stood up and looked empty-headed again.

"See my darling," she shouted, joyfully. "As good as new and as obedient and loyal as a dog — just like all mortal men are who feel my touch!"

It suddenly dawned on Nathan why he felt compelled to dance with Amanda the night of Lafonda's birthday party. "She touched my arm," he murmured. "I knew something was up. I would never voluntarily subject myself to public humiliation by dancing!"

"You!" she snapped. Her green eyes suddenly filled with rage. "Shut up!" She motioned at Steve. "And you," she commanded hysterically, "what are you waiting for?

CHAPTER TWENTY-ONE

Tie them up!"

There was a whooshing sound, and the priest with the crescent-shaped medallion stepped onto the plaza again, followed by Andy and then the others.

"Ah," she said, while clapping her hands enthusiastically together. "Pius, you have returned."

"Yes," he responded with a hiss. He bowed graciously, causing the metals in his medallion to glimmer in the moonlight. "And I have brought the others."

Nathan watched as two Shadow Guards lined his friends in front of the tall white obelisk. Andy was lined up first, followed by Eva Marie, and then Angela. Their hands were bound and their clothing appeared dirty and in disarray. Leah was the last one to join them. Her face formed a slight grin when her eyes met Nathan's. He was content about finally meeting her, even under the current circumstances. Leah continued to look back at him and Nathan focused on her brown eyes. He wanted to form a memory of her that wasn't from a picture or a dream.

"See, Lucas, my love," Amanda flirted, while twirling her fingers through his long blond hair. "I have everything under control."

"Don't toy with me, Lauren," he exploded, seizing her hand. His voice boomed and the priests and the guards appeared to cower. "I am not one of your human dogs!"

Amanda took back her hand and glowered ferociously. "You know I would never do such a thing!"

His ocean-blue eyes seemed to take on a fiery red and Amanda quickly bowed, conceding graciously. "My love," she murmured, "you know my powers do not work on immortal spirits." Cautiously, she drew near him and attempted to caress his cheek. "Besides, we belong together — and you know how much I love it when you call me Lauren."

"I am done here," he shouted.

Amanda looked confused.

"And you will discover how he got here," he demanded, while gawking at Nathan.

"But my love —" she stammered.

"He knows how to use Pneuma, Lauren!" he shouted. "So he's accountable to someone, and I want to know who!"

"Pius!" he yelled.

"Yes, my Lord," he responded, his voice trembling.

"Do you still believe we are close to finding the one we seek?" he asked.

"Yes, my Lord," he responded again, but pausing to divert his eyes. "I am almost certain."

Lucas placed his red hood back over his head and proceeded towards the dark archway. "He wants results Lauren," he shouted, before stepping in. "And your success or failure will not be determined by me."

"Aaaah!" she screamed. The sound reverberated around the plaza.

The three priests slowly inched away in anticipation of her wrath.

"Pius!" she yelled. "You three get over here!"

She spun around and raised her hand as if about to punch the center of the tall white obelisk. Angela's and Eva Marie's eyes grew wide because she headed directly towards them. Angela and Eva Marie ducked as Lauren's fist hit the wall. There was no sound, but the entire plaza vibrated.

"Aaaah!" she screamed again. "Where is the blood that you tested earlier?" she shouted. "Bring it to me!"

Quickly, the priest standing closest to Pius presented him with the sparking blue vial that contained Jonas's blood. Pius placed the tiny bottle into her hand and bowed. Lauren quickly raised it against the moonlight and then howled.

"Ugh!" she moaned, taking a swing at Pius. "Why even bother giving me this when clearly he's not the one we're looking for!"

"My apologies, Amanda," he said.

"Don't call me that!" she threatened. "Call me, Lauren."

"Yes, Lauren," he responded, bowing low and inching away.

She stared blankly for a moment, but before long, her pursed lips formed a maniacal smile. "Contrary to what my love may think, it's not a total waste of time," she said, while twirling the sparkling vial between her fingers. She placed her hands on her hips and surveyed her prisoners. She looked at each one of them in the face and laughed. "Take out your knife, Pius!" she demanded.

She paused to look at the vial in her hand. She smiled, then turned to look at Jonas. "You might not be the one we're looking for," she said with a grin. "But your blood will allow us to keep opening doorways to your world."

Jonas scowled and Lauren laughed at his frustration.

"Don't worry," she said, her sparkling green eyes gleaming with superiority. "You won't be alone long. Maybe your brother has what we need."

"Stay away from him!" he yelled, attempting to get to his feet.

"Ha-ha-ha," she cackled. "Your father didn't like that idea either, but keep it up and you'll end up just like him!"

Jonas slumped down, the tears swelling in his eyes.

"Ask Leah," she continued, turning to look at her. "She knows what happens to those who get in my way." She continued to twirl the vial in her hand. "See, we thought that Leah was the one. And what better way to find out than to become her roommate?" she chuckled.

Pius took out his small silver dagger, and Andy and the others began to squirm uncomfortably, a look of unease across their faces.

"Poor little Jamie," she said with a sarcastic, whiny voice. She quickly spun around to gawk at Jonas. "And imagine my surprise, after going through all that trouble to kill her roommate, to find out that Leah is just like you: utterly useless!"

Nathan's hands trembled as Lauren stampeded towards Leah.

Lauren leaned over, getting close to Leah's face. "And you didn't make it easy for us either, did you Leah?" she asked in a soft but heartless voice. "Poor Leah can't sleep at night. She's depressed over losing her roommate Jamie. Blah, blah, blah!"

Leah looked calm. She glanced over at Nathan and a tear ran down her face.

Suddenly, Nathan remembered his dream. Images of the bodies on the plaza floor and the woman in white as she strolled past them replayed in his mind. "She's going to stab Leah," he mumbled.

Jonas looked up, trying to make sense of what Nathan had said.

"She's going to stab Leah!" he said again.

Nathan struggled to free his hands, but couldn't.

Lauren held out her hand and Pius gave her the dagger. She violently pulled Leah by the hair and brought her face close to hers.

Leah screamed.

"And then," continued Lauren hysterically, while waving the blade in Leah's face, "because of all your whining you got yourself put in a mental hospital!"

"Let go of her, Amanda!" shouted Nathan angrily. He

looked down and noticed that his hands were a bright red.

Lauren stopped to look at him, but she looked confused.

"Lauren, Amanda — whatever your name is — I said let go of her!"

She dramatically released Leah's hair and then headed towards Nathan. "My name is not Amanda!" she yelled. She gave the vial of blood to Pius and pointed the dagger at Nathan's throat. "I'm not done with you yet," she said. She glanced over at Steve and then gave Nathan a devilish smile. "I am going to have so much fun with you."

She laughed and looked up as if remembering something. "I've been called so many things over the years," she said. "The superfluous humans of Ancient Rome used to worship me as Volupia. I hated that name!" She playfully fluttered her eyes and waved the dagger carelessly in her hand. "Because I've found my love, I prefer Lauren now. Lucas and Lauren. It has a nice ring to it, don't you think?"

She smiled, stepped back and then slapped Nathan in the face. Nathan toppled to the ground and his entire head rang. It felt like a million little stings had landed on his face. He could taste the blood pooling in his mouth.

"Now quiet!" she shouted, her voice echoing around the plaza.

Nathan looked up from the plaza floor. His head continued to throb and his vision was fuzzy. He squinted, trying to make out the shapes in front of him, but then he heard Leah scream. "I can't believe this is happening," he protested to himself. He heard Leah scream again and chills shot down his back. "I have to save her!"

He was angry, but he could feel something else building inside of him. In the pit of his stomach, something burned. Nathan continued to work at the rope around his wrists and gritted his teeth in frustration. He blinked furiously, trying to restore his vision. Slowly, he was able to see again, and for a brief second he thought he saw a small dark shape dart behind a tomb on the second level.

"I should drain you dry of blood before I get rid of you," Lauren shouted, severing Leah's ropes and raising the dagger in the air.

She grabbed Leah by the wrist, and Leah closed her eyes before turning away. Quickly, Lauren plunged the silver blade into her arm. Leah screamed in agony.

"No!" Nathan yelled. Instantly his hands stopped trembling, and the burning sensation in his hands now spread throughout his body. Nathan was enraged, but the energy intensifying inside of him felt peaceful. He gave in to the feeling, to the energy, as it consumed every inch of him. He thought he was going to explode; he felt like he was on fire.

The rope around Nathan's wrists sizzled, and it was consumed in a blue flame. Nathan looked down at the ashes from the rope and stood up. Without hesitating, he opened his palm and cast an energy ball at Lauren, followed by another.

The first energy ball hit Lauren in the back, causing her to falter. She spun around and knocked the second energy ball away with her hand. She grabbed Leah and tossed her to the ground.

One of the Shadow Guards who were now encircling them reached down and took Leah by the neck, bringing her to her feet. The Shadow Guard drew his long double-edged sword and Angela screamed.

Nathan felt the burn again throughout his entire body. He exhaled deeply as he glowered at Lauren, then at the priests, and then at the Shadow Guards.

"How did you do that?" protested Lauren, staring at the bits of rope and ash beneath his feet. "How did you get through your bonds?"

"Like this!" shouted Nathan and he released the energy that was burning inside of him.

Out of his hand emerged a blue flame and he aimed it at the Shadow Guard. The guard screeched in gut-wrenching pain until he dissolved into a fine sprinkle of white ash. His sword hit the ground and so did Leah.

Lauren gasped. "That's impossible!"

Nathan took a hold of the rope around Jonas's wrist and watched as it burned a bright blue, eventually turning into ash.

"Lookout behind you!" Jonas yelled.

Nathan turned around just in time to release an energy ball directly into Steve's chest, hurling him into one of the archway pillars and knocking him unconscious. He turned back around to find Jonas smiling at him.

"Do what you can," Nathan said, patting Jonas on the back. "And try to release the others."

"Nathan!" screamed Angela. He spun around to find two Shadow Guards, swords drawn, closing in on him. Nathan ducked as one of them took a swipe at his head. He kept an eye on Jonas as two of the priests tried to subdue him. Nathan raised his hand to throw an energy ball at them, but suddenly, he was off his feet and dangling in the air.

"You!" screeched Lauren, while holding him up by his shirt. Her menacing face quickly melted into deadly resolve. "I've had enough of you. Your life ends here!"

She tossed him into the air like a rag doll. Nathan hit the ground hard, landing in the graveyard below. His head throbbed again, as he opened his eyes to a clear view of the stone steps that led up to the memorial plaza. Blood trickled down from the crest of his head and he tried to wipe it from his eyes with his hand. The two Shadow Guards that had attacked him stared at him from atop the stairs, and on the staircase and approaching fast was the Scarlet Priest with the crescent-shaped medallion.

Nathan felt a sense of déjà vu and tried to get up, but fell back to the ground. He was dizzy and couldn't gain his balance. He remembered what happened next in his dream and started to panic. Any second he expected Lafonda to appear, followed by the Shadow Guards with their swords. "I have to try and prevent this," he mumbled.

Nathan's mind was racing. He rolled to his side, and in a last-ditch effort, cast an energy ball at the approaching priest. Pius smirked as the energy ball passed him by several inches. The medallion around Pius's neck glowed.

Nathan tried to get to his feet again, and that's when he saw her. She emerged from behind the same tomb where he thought he'd seen a small black shape earlier.

"No!" he yelled, reaching out frantically, trying to wave her away.

Out of the corner of his eye, he saw a series of blue energy balls hurling towards him. Quickly, Lafonda dove to the ground and tried to move him. When she realized it was too late, she shielded him with her body.

Lafonda rolled over, and Nathan had a clear view of the pink-and-gray sneakers on her feet and the shiny gold locket around her neck. He also caught a glimpse of the dissipating purple energy shield that surrounded them. Lafonda attempted to help Nathan to his feet. She looked amazed.

"Did that come from me?" she asked.

Nathan quickly looked around, and just like in his

dream, Pius lay slumped against the staircase, knocked down by a rebounded energy ball. Nathan gasped. He looked up towards the plaza and the two Shadow Guards were gone. "Lafonda!" he yelled, while trying to push her out of the way. "You have to get out of here!"

Lafonda looked confused, but continued to help him. Behind her, a Shadow Guard appeared, revealing his long silver sword. Nathan was able to force her out of the way but then another one appeared. The two guards raised their swords, and in a blue blur they were gone, nothing left but their swords, smoke, and ashes.

"Are you two okay?" asked a familiar voice.

Nathan turned around to see Malick standing there with both his hands stretched out. He could still feel the heat from the ashes. Lafonda and Nathan both nodded, and Malick hurried them behind the closest mausoleum.

Nathan glared at him with intense eyes, and Malick responded by raising his eyebrows.

"What?" Malick asked defensively and out of breath.

"You know this means you are a cheater, right?" asked Nathan, glancing down at Malick's hands.

An energy ball slammed above Malick's head causing him to flinch. "Um, can we talk about this later?" he said.

Lafonda inspected the bruise on the side of Nathan's face and the bloody cut near his hairline.

"Are you okay?" she asked.

"Yeah."

"Are you sure?"

"Yes," he said. "I am fine, Lafonda."

"Good," she responded, whacking him on the back of the head.

"Ow!" he yelled.

Lafonda pursed her lips. "If anyone will be doing any talking, it will be you Nathan Urye!" she protested. "You have a lot of explaining to do."

Malick peered out to the plaza and ducked again to avoid another energy ball. "You guys!" he exclaimed. "Now is not the time."

Nathan glanced from behind the mausoleum wall and saw that Jonas had a sword in his hand and was attempting to hold off the two priests. Leah was making her way towards the stairs, and Lauren was in hot pursuit behind her. The remaining Shadow Guards were positioned along the top of the plaza, while Pius continued to throw energy balls from the staircase.

"The priest with the medallion is the one attacking us," said Nathan. "He's blocking Leah's escape, and Lauren's right behind her."

"He's back up again?" asked Lafonda. "I thought he was knocked out."

"Apparently not," commented Malick, while peering out from behind the wall.

Nathan quickly glanced out from behind the tomb wall again. "We have to do something to help Leah!" he exclaimed.

The three of them suddenly heard barking and looked at each other in bewilderment.

Malick smiled. "I know," he said. "And it sounds like now is our chance."

Malick peered out and then stepped from behind the protection of the wall. Nathan followed behind him apprehensively until he saw the snarling black fox at the base of the stone steps drawing Pius's attention.

"Jonathan," he said with a grin.

Malick didn't hesitate. There were only a few moments before Lauren reached Leah and Pius on the stairs. He formed a blue fireball in the palm of his hand and hurled it straight at Pius. It hit him in the center of his chest and

Pius screeched in agony, leaving behind only his gold-and-silver medallion and a pile of charred dust.

Leah hurried down the steps, but stopped for a moment when she reached Pius's remains.

Quickly, Malick headed halfway up the stone steps. He tried not to step on the pile of dust, and noticed the medallion was gone as he passed Leah. He raised his hand and a blue flame appeared. Rapidly, he motioned his arm in the air, and soon the blue flame over his head coalesced into an enormous ring of fire. Lauren froze as he cast it over her, stopping her in her tracks.

A whooshing sound echoed across the plaza and the graveyard below. Several red energy bolts sprung from one of the plaza archways, destroying parts of the stone steps and barely missing Malick. Out of the darkness stepped Lucas, his eyes glowing red underneath his red hood.

Nathan and Malick quickly joined Leah and Lafonda behind the mausoleum wall while particles of tombs and red energy bolts flew around them.

"What are we going to do?" asked Nathan. "We have to save the others."

Leah held out her arms. There was blood on her hands and shirt. She winced a little from the pain, but nodded reassuringly at Nathan. "He's right," she said. "We can't leave them."

Malick attempted to look out from behind the mausoleum wall. "We have a plan," he said.

"We?" asked Nathan.

Lafonda also looked confused.

Everyone jumped after Jonathan suddenly materialized in a swirl of blue and white lights. He was human again.

"My apologies," he said. "I haven't yet figured out how to make an entrance without scaring anyone."

"Perfect timing," commented Malick. "I was just about to explain our plan."

Nathan looked shocked. "Uh," he mumbled, "you and Jonathan have a plan?" He raised his eyebrows in suspicion and pointed at both of them. "You and Jonathan?"

"When did you guys develop a plan?" asked Lafonda, while crossing her arms in protest. "And when were you going to tell me about it?"

Malick responded by shaking his head at both of them.

"You know what to do," he said, turning to Jonathan. "Nathan and I will distract them and draw fire while you rescue the others."

"Wait, what?" asked Nathan, still surprised. "Draw fire?"

Malick peered over the mausoleum wall again, returning quickly to avoid the continual line of fire. "The guards on the right are still knocked out, so you should enter there," he said.

Jonathan fidgeted nervously with his glasses. "Um, are you sure this is going to work?" he asked. "I've never done this before."

"Trust me," said Malick. "All Spirit Walkers can. Now please, take them back to the monastery."

Nathan remembered the conversation he'd had with Jonathan in the caves earlier while fighting off their mysterious attacker, and he realized what he was planning to do.

"Don't forget Steve," Nathan said.

Jonathan nodded.

"Wait, what? Hold on!" protested Lafonda.

Jonathan squeezed his eyes shut, placed a hand on Leah's and Lafonda's shoulders, and they were gone.

"Spirit Walker?" asked Nathan, turning to face Malick.

"This isn't the time for a Pneuma Novo lesson," he responded. "We have to distract them long enough for Jonathan."

Malick eased his head out from behind the wall and quickly retracted it in time to avoid a shower of stone caused by Lucas's energy bolts.

Nathan followed suit and peered out from the other side. With just a wave of his hand, Lucas removed the ring of fire from around Lauren.

"He's distracted!" Nathan shouted, and he and Malick both cast energy balls at Lucas and Lauren.

Lauren faltered backwards after deflecting Nathan's energy balls with her hand. Lucas did the same, but quickly returned fire, and Nathan and Malick dove for cover again.

"If we keep this up," commented Nathan, while glancing at the rubble around them, "there won't be any wall left."

"We just have to do this long enough to help Jonathan," said Malick.

Nathan nodded and then abruptly returned fire. "I saw Jonathan," he said, trying to catch his breath. "He has Angela and Eva Marie. Jonas and Andy are holding off the two priests."

"Let's try to make it over to one of the other tombs!"

"What?" asked Nathan and before they could move, a blanket of red energy bolts rained down on them, causing them both to retreat.

Nathan caught a glimpse of Lucas standing on top of one of the mausoleums in the graveyard. He scurried behind Malick and returned fire.

"How did he get up there?" he shouted.

They had almost reached cover, but suddenly there was a paralyzing sting in Nathan's back, launching him forward. He hit the ground hard and could barely keep his eyes open. He felt himself being pulled, and that's when he saw Malick.

"Hold on," said Malick. "I got you."

"W-What about the others?" Nathan stuttered.

Malick propped him against the wall and stared at the blood that oozed from Nathan's hand. "Jonathan has them," he said. "He should be here any second."

Nathan tried to focus on Malick's face, but his vision was blurred. A sharp pain rippled through his arm, followed by a prolonged burning in his hand. "Who are they?" he mumbled.

Red bolts of energy flew over them, and Malick shielded him from falling debris.

"Remember when I told you about the dark and powerful forces?" Malick said.

Nathan nodded and fought to keep his eyes open.

"Well, that's them," he said. "And he's one of the Fallen Ones."

Nathan attempted to frown, but the wound near his hairline pulsated. "You told Jonathan that was just a myth," he mustered the energy to say.

"Well, I guess myth just became reality," Malick said.

Malick turned as if he was talking to someone, but Nathan couldn't make out what he was saying nor keep his eyes open. He attempted to speak, but his speech slurred.

"Hold on, Nathan," said a familiar voice.

Nathan's eyes closed, slipping into darkness.

CHAPTER TWENTY-TWO

LOOSE ENDS

Nathan slowly opened his eyes and blinked a few times, allowing his eyes to adjust. He could tell that he was lying down. He waited for a second for his mind to reconnect with his body. His thoughts started to come back to him as well. Soon his heart started racing and he abruptly sat up in bed.

"Look who decided to join the land of the living," said Lafonda.

He blinked a few times while looking at her and then quickly scanned the room. "What are we doing back at Lawrence Hall?" he stammered. "And where are the others? Is everyone safe?"

He threw back the bedspread that was covering him and attempted to get out of bed.

"It's okay," said Lafonda, pausing to place a hand on his arm. "We're okay; everyone is safe."

He stared at her for a moment and then slowly sank back into bed. The back of his head slightly throbbed. He raised his hand to massage it, but noticed the white bandages around his hand.

"Jonathan and I cleaned and dressed it," she said with a smile. She pointed at his head. "And the cut on your forehead."

He lifted his bandaged hand to touch it. "Thanks," he said. He sat back to relax, but winced a little when his back touched the pillow.

"Your back and the side of your face are still bruised," she said. "But from the looks of it at least some of the swelling has gone down."

Nathan looked down and noticed he didn't have a shirt on and that his midsection and back were wrapped in a white bandage. With his eyebrows raised, he gave her a puzzled look.

Lafonda grinned. "It was Jonathan's idea," she said. "He said we needed to check for injuries."

Nathan's cheeks started to redden.

"Don't worry," she said, standing up and heading over to the wooden desk and bringing back a glass of water. "I didn't stay for that part; I left the room."

He took a gulp of water and she handed him two pills. "For the swelling," she said.

"How come Jonathan's a doctor all of a sudden?" he asked, pausing to take a drink of water to swallow the capsules.

She sat near him on the edge of the bed again. "I asked him the same thing," she smiled. "He said being out in the field so much with his dad, they both became certified in CPR and First Aid. Of course, Jonathan went the extra mile to become an EMT."

There was a gentle knock at the door, and Malick walked in. "Hey, you're up," he said. "How are you feeling?"

"Okay," said Nathan, still sounding groggy. "Aside from being slapped in the face, tossed around and electrocuted, I'm good."

"Well, it sounds like you're back on track to your old self," announced Malick with a grin.

Nathan took another drink and nodded. "So how did I end up back in my room?" He gently massaged the back of his head. "How did we get back here?"

Lafonda glanced over at Malick.

"Bobby," Malick said.

"Bobby?" asked Nathan, almost spilling his drink. "Jonas's little brother?"

Malick laughed. "Yup," he responded.

"But how?" he asked. "How did you know about Bobby — I mean, his ability? And how did you know where to find me?"

Lafonda uncrossed her legs and leaned over to take the glass out of his hand. "Well," she said, turning to glare at Nathan. "When I got back to Lawrence Hall, after finally talking to you on the phone, I was surprised to find the police and the paramedics here, especially since someone had refused to tell me what was going on." She paused to lean over to place his glass on the floor. "I knew something was terribly wrong after Alan told me Angela, Jonas, Eva Marie and Andy were missing and that you had gone after them. What I couldn't figure out was why you just didn't go to the police. It wasn't until Erin tried to stop me from going after you that I knew you were in trouble."

"Well, she obviously did a good job holding you back," Nathan said sarcastically.

Lafonda rolled her eyes and dramatically laid her hand on the bed. "We were all worried for you and the others, Nathan" she said. "All she knew was that some gang or possibly some fraternity boys had taken them."

He was silent for a moment and then slowly nodded. "What story ended up sticking with the police and LaDonda anyway?" he asked. "And what about me and my injuries? She's bound to notice."

"Don't worry," Lafonda responded confidently. "I modified your gang story a little and said that it was a fraternity prank on Angela, which is more believable because she's in a sorority. So, as soon as we reported that to the police, they seemed less interested. Plus, I'm sure it helped that Erin's dad is chief of police."

Lafonda paused to cross her legs again. "And as far as your injuries," she said, "I figured we would tell my grandmother you were with Jonathan and Dr. Helmsley during the cave accident."

"So, LaDonda doesn't know yet?" he said, surprised.

"No, not yet," she replied, sounding a little more concerned. "We'll have to see how well that goes over. Both of you were supposed to be at Lawrence Hall and not at the caves last night."

"And what about Angela, Andy, Eva Marie and Jonas?" he asked. "How are they handling it? Are they okay with that story?"

She looked away for a second, but looked at Nathan again. "I guess everyone is dealing with it in their own way," she said. "See, after Jonathan got us back to the monastery — well the monastery in the Space In Between — Bobby was the one that brought us back to the monastery on our side."

"Bobby?" he interrupted.

"Yes, Bobby," she said. "Jonathan went to our side to tell Bobby to make another door so we could pass through."

Nathan's forehead wrinkled and he winced a little from the pain from his cut. "Wait," he said. "Where was Bobby?"

"At the monastery on our side waiting for us," she said. "That's how we crossed over."

"You took Bobby to an abandoned monastery and left

him there in the middle of nowhere!" he exclaimed.

"No," she said. "Well, yes, but he was fine. Alan was there with him."

Nathan relaxed his forehead a little and then shook his head. "I told Bobby after I left not to open the window for strangers," he protested.

"He didn't," interrupted Malick with a chuckle. "He told us he couldn't open the window for strangers, so he opened the front door instead."

Nathan shook his head again and grinned.

"Well, like I was saying," she continued, slightly annoyed, "after we got back to the monastery on our side, we all decided on the car ride home — after Jonathan declared you were okay, of course — that that would be our story."

Nathan nodded slowly. "But you still haven't told me how you guys knew where to find me. Or about Bobby."

Lafonda grinned. "I was just getting to that," she said. "After Erin and Alan told me what was going on, Jonathan confirmed my suspicions that something was wrong."

"Jonathan?" he asked, sounding surprised. "I thought he was at the caves with Dr. Helmsley?"

"I guess after they picked up Dr. Helmsley, the paramedics dropped him off here," she said with a shrug. "He came up to me shortly after I got here and said that you were going to need all of our help."

"How did he know?"

"And after that," commented Malick, "that's where I come in." He stood closer to the foot of the bed. "I learned what had happened to Angela and the others and had gone to the lobby to find you. I didn't learn that you had gone to rescue them until after I heard them talking."

Lafonda laid her arms across her chest. "Yeah," she

said with a frown. "More like eavesdropping."

Malick grimaced and huffed in protest. "Then I heard Lafonda say something about her friend Leah being missing too," he continued. "After I heard what Jonathan had to say about it and his theory about Leah, and Jonas and his dad, I remembered your dreams about Leah and what you had told me about Jonas and his abilities. It all just clicked."

Malick sat down on the edge of the bed. "After I clued Jonathan in on Jonas, it clicked for him too," he said. "We both figured that, like Jonas, Bobby must have an ability too, and that's where you must've gone."

Lafonda looked confused. "What dream?" she asked. "You never mentioned dreaming about Leah. How is that even possible? You didn't even know her."

Malick raised his hands as if surrendering. "I'll let you explain that one," he said.

Lafonda gawked at Malick, then at Nathan. "Okay," she said sarcastically. "Don't all speak at once."

"It's complicated," Nathan said finally.

She rolled her eyes.

"But," he said, before she could respond, "to make a long story short, I didn't want to tell anybody about my powers or my dreams until I had a better handle on what was happening to me. Plus, I didn't want to endanger anyone."

She thought for a second. "So how did you know it was Leah when you had never met her?" she asked. Lafonda's eyes lit up. "Wait!" she blurted out. "The yearbook!"

Nathan smiled and Lafonda smacked him on the arm.

"Ow!" he yelled, while trying to rub his arm with his bandaged hand.

"That's why you were acting so strange!" she

exclaimed. "You could have told me, Nathan. You didn't have to go through all of this by yourself."

Nathan inspected the small red bruise forming on his arm. "I wasn't totally alone," he said, while grinning at Malick. "I had a little help along the way."

Malick smiled back, and Lafonda glowered while pursing her lips.

"I also suspected that it was Leah in my dreams after hearing you and Amanda — I mean, Lauren — talk about what had happened to Leah the night of your birthday party."

Lafonda nodded. "Speaking of Amanda, aka Lauren, and her band of creepy friends," she said, "who are they?"

Nathan turned to look at Malick and Lafonda responded by rolling her eyes.

Malick took a deep breath and exhaled slowly before speaking. "They're the Fallen Ones," he said finally. "Well, at least one of them. I don't know who Lauren is. I had never heard of her."

"Wait a minute," Lafonda responded eagerly. "Like the Legend of the Fallen Ones? Like what Jonathan was talking about?"

Malick nodded. "Yup," he said. "The very ones."

"You've got to be kidding me!" she said, turning to seek confirmation from Nathan.

Nathan shook his head. "No," he said. "He's not joking."

"Then, what do they want?" she asked.

Nathan looked at Malick.

"I'm not sure," Malick said with a shrug. "But I did hear them say they were looking for someone, and they thought that person could be Jonas or Leah, but why the others, I do not know. Does this mean they have powers too?"

"I've asked them," Lafonda said. "And none of them knows."

Malick stood up. "Regardless of whether they have powers or not," he spouted, "everyone should stay low and refrain from using their powers. And that includes you, Lafonda."

"Me?" she said, sounding puzzled.

Malick nodded and leaned against the desk. "Yes, you too," he sighed. "I've seen people use Pneuma as a shield to reflect energy balls, for example, but as an entire body shield? That is unheard of."

"So what does that mean?" she asked, looking concerned. "I didn't even know I could do that."

Malick stood up straight. "Well, somebody did," he said. "The ability to perform Pneuma Novo is hereditary, and I find it hard to believe that it's just a coincidence that so many people in one location would possess the ability to use Pneuma and not know about it." He paused to take a deep breath again and sighed. "I know my grandmother was a member of the Order, and since our grandmothers are good friends, I would start there."

Lafonda spun around and the frown lines in her forehead deepened. "Are you implying that someone in my family, specifically my grandmother, is hiding something from me?" she asked defensively.

"I don't know," said Malick with a shrug. "But somebody in your family or Nathan's has to know something."

Lafonda stood up and headed towards the door.

Nathan had a befuddled look on his face. "Lafonda," he said, "are you okay?"

She stopped to cut a look at Malick before opening the dorm room door. "Yeah, I'm fine," she said. "I've just reached my limit on this conversation." She glanced in the room again before shutting the door. "I guess I'll see you tonight then," she said.

"Tonight?"

"Yes," she said, "at the closing ceremony."

Nathan nodded. He still looked surprised by her sudden exit.

"Yeah," he said, raising his bandaged hand. "But I can't promise how good I'll look."

She forced a smile and then shut the door.

"What just happened?" asked Nathan. "She does that all the time. She says she's okay, but is she really?"

Malick laughed. "She seems like her normal self to me," he said. He grinned, but suddenly got quiet. "But she was pretty shaken up last night when Jonathan and I brought you to the monastery," he said. "I'm sure it was just because she'd never seen you like that."

Nathan sighed while lowering his head and twisting his lip.

"Anyhow," said Malick, trying to lighten the mood, "I'm glad you're doing okay, but I'd better get going. Steve's resting in my room. He's a little dehydrated and still slightly confused, but he'll be all right. We still haven't decided what to tell his parents yet."

"We need to talk," said Nathan. Malick's forehead frowned and he had a puzzled look on his face.

Nathan inched closer and whispered. "About your ability?" he said. "You know, about this rare gift of fire that we both seem to have?"

Malick grew silent.

"And your grandmother," he continued, while recalling what Jonathan said about his father. "Is she the only member of the Order?"

Malick's face went blank for a moment, but then he

sighed heavily. "I said she was a part of the Order," he responded, finally breaking the silence. He paused to take a deep breath again. "Let's talk about this later, okay?"

Malick headed towards the door while a puzzled Nathan watched him.

"By the way, I think there's a certain lady that's looking forward to seeing you tonight," Malick said.

Nathan appeared flustered by the sudden shift in the conversation and just nodded.

A few hours later, Nathan stood at the glass door to the ground-level walkway that connected Lawrence and Fisher halls. He watched as counselors, parents and campers mingled in the pristine courtyard that stretched out to the campus quad. It was dusk and the setting sun created a gradual shade of pink to deep purple across the sky.

Nathan stepped outside and onto the freshly mowed grass. He was surprised to see how well-dressed and well-behaved the guys were on his floor. Most of them were excited to be going home and wanted to impress their parents or that special someone during the dance.

Nathan felt a little embarrassed and a little out of place with the white bandage around his hand and the flesh-colored Band-Aid on his forehead. He scrutinized the brown khakis and brown leather shoes recommended by LaDonda. He refused to wear the shirt, tie and jacket she had also recommended and decided on a navy blue polo instead.

Nathan saw Jonathan Black sitting alone at one of the many white-clothed round tables and headed towards him. Carefully, he maneuvered through the crowd, smiling sporadically as his eyes connected with a few people. He had almost reached Jonathan when someone grabbed his arm.

"Ha!" shouted a female voice.

He turned around to find a small woman dressed in a loosely fitted blouse staring back at him over her gold-rimmed glasses. Her blond tight curls appeared slightly wild, and her blouse was patterned in pink and red roses.

"It's not a coincidence finding you here now, is it?" she exclaimed.

"Hello, Mrs. Riley," he said with a smile, while trying to fight the awkwardness. "No, it isn't."

She abruptly clapped her hands together causing Nathan and a few other people to jump. "Aw, just call me Linda," she said with a big smile. She pointed to his bandaged hand. "I heard you guys had a rough night."

"Yeah," he said, trying to hide his discomfort. "I guess so."

"You know," she continued lightheartedly, "dealing with fraternities is just another part of being at a university."

Nathan smiled weakly and nodded.

She peered over her glasses and happily waved at someone.

Soon after, Jonas and Bobby joined them.

"Look who I found," she said, while placing an arm around Nathan. She then gently tilted Jonas's chin to examine his face. "And it looks like you two have matching bruises."

"Uh," stuttered Nathan.

"It's just a coincidence," said Jonas with a fake laugh.

"Uh, yeah," said Nathan. "I probably got mine while out at the caves. "Uh, there was a little accident. And Jonas, you got yours …"

"Playing basketball," he interjected nervously, but with a smile. "Yup, just playing basketball."

Bobby nodded reassuringly.

Linda fluttered her eyelashes behind her glasses and looked at the three of them suspiciously.

"Um, look Mom," said Jonas, breaking the silence. "There's LaDonda. Didn't you say you wanted to talk to her?"

LaDonda was standing by the stairs to the small stage that was set up for the closing ceremony.

Linda stood in silence for a moment and then finally acknowledged Jonas by turning to look at LaDonda. "Yes," she said slowly. "I was going through some of your father's old things and there was a picture that I wanted to ask her about."

"A picture?" asked Nathan.

She nodded. "Yes," she said. "The photo was taken when Bart was younger, probably around the age Jonas is now." She glanced back at LaDonda. "I didn't even know she knew him."

"Well, now is your chance to catch her," said Jonas. "Before she gets busy or goes on stage."

"Right," she said. "Yoo-hoo, LaDonda!" she called, quickly heading over to her.

Jonas had a big smile on his face. "You look good," he said to Nathan. "Minus the bandages, of course."

Nathan laughed. "You don't have to be nice to me," he said with a chuckle. "Camp is officially over."

Jonas smiled, but looked a little sad. "Um, Bobby," he said, "how about you grab some more punch and meet me over there by Christina?"

Bobby stood on the tip of his toes and smiled when he spotted Christina.

"Oh, okay," he responded enthusiastically.

He gave Nathan a hug around his waist, and Nathan ruffled his hair.

"When are you coming to visit again?" asked Bobby.

"Soon," he said, and Bobby smiled again before taking off.

Jonas was silent as Nathan watched Bobby weave through the crowd of people.

"Nathan," he said finally. He paused again and looked as if the words were difficult to say. "Thanks for coming to save us."

"No problem," said Nathan with a smile. He gave Jonas a quick side pat on his shoulder. "You would have done the same for me."

Jonas nodded. "So, I guess it's true then," he said before taking a pause. He hesitated and swallowed hard before he spoke again. "What the woman in white said about my father?"

There was a brief moment of silence, and then slowly Nathan nodded. "Yes," he said softly, placing a hand on his shoulder. "I'm sorry."

Nathan tried not to notice, but there were tears swelling in his friend's eyes. Jonas tried to force a smile.

"So, was that a promise you'll come visit?" he asked.

"You got it," said Nathan. "And don't forget, you can always visit me."

Jonas smiled. "Well, I'd better get over there to Bobby and Christina," he said. "Before he drives her crazy."

"Okay," said Nathan, giving him a pat on the back as he walked away.

Nathan looked around the courtyard and caught a glimpse of Jonathan again. He was still sitting alone at one of the tables near the stage.

"Hey, you clean up well," he said.

Jonathan responded by turning around. Jonathan looked happy to see him.

"Not dressed in wolf's clothing today?"

Jonathan's face turned red. "It's a fox," he said. He

looked around. "And keep your voice down. What if someone hears you?"

Nathan pulled out one of the foldable wooden chairs and sat down. "Relax, Jonathan," he said. "Even if someone did hear us, they wouldn't have a clue what we were talking about."

Jonathan shifted his glasses and moved his chair closer to Nathan. "You look well," he said. "How's your hand?"

Nathan raised his hand to examine it. "It's okay," he said. "And thanks for everything you did last night. You know, with saving our asses and patching me up."

Jonathan smiled.

"By the way," said Nathan, "how is Dr. Helmsley?"

"She's still in the hospital," responded Jonathan, sounding slightly sad. "They're keeping her another night for observation."

"Oh, will she be all right?"

Jonathan paused to reposition his glasses. "I think so," he said. "I believe it's more of a precaution than anything."

A few minutes passed while Nathan fidgeted with the bandages around his hand. "Jonathan," he said, breaking the silence. "How did you know where to find me yesterday? How did you know I was in trouble?"

Jonathan cleared his throat. "I wanted to talk to you about that. I just wasn't sure the best way to bring up the conversation."

Nathan looked confused. "What do you mean?"

"Hey, what's up!" shouted Alan. He looked like a walking Ralph Lauren ad with his pastel colors and corresponding blazer.

"You know what, Alan? You are definitely making me sweat with that jacket on," responded Nathan with a frown. "It is way too hot to be wearing a blazer."

Alan chuckled. "Not at the expense of fashion," he said. "You know you have to work it and keep it together!"

Nathan shook his head. "Go have a glass of water," he said. "You're sweating all over the place."

"Angela's bringing me water," he said with a smile. "Everyone's heading over here."

"What?" he asked suddenly. "Why?"

Alan pointed towards the stage. "That's why," he said. "LaDonda will be starting the closing ceremony soon."

Nathan looked up to see LaDonda inching towards the microphone. "Oh," he said.

"Um, Nathan," said Jonathan, standing up, "can I talk to you in private for a moment?"

"Sure," he said, jumping to his feet.

"Excuse us, Alan," said Jonathan.

Alan rolled his eyes. "Whatever," he said, brushing them off and burying his head into his cell phone.

Jonathan slowly made his way through the crowd, and Nathan followed. He looked up just in time to see Angela.

"Hi, Nathan!" she said. The sleeveless silk dress she wore made her blue eyes even more captivating underneath the courtyard lights. She smiled. "Glad you're feeling well enough to join us!"

Nathan stopped for a moment while keeping a watchful eye on Jonathan. "Thanks," he said. His eyes diverted to the two cups of water she held in her hands. "And how are you holding up?"

"Good as can be," she said, trying to smile. "Lafonda's clued me in on some of the details, but I'm just glad that it's over." She tried to blow a loose strand of curly hair out of her face and then focused on Nathan again. "Thanks for coming after us," she said in a whisper.

He couldn't help but feel sorry for her. He could only imagine the stress she was experiencing dealing with all that had happened. "No problem," he said, trying to sound reassuring.

"Are you coming to join us?" asked Leah, joining them from the rear.

Her curly, mousy-brown hair had been straightened and lay close to her bare shoulders. Nathan didn't understand why, but her infectious smile made things feel almost normal again.

"I hear LaDonda will be giving her closing speech soon," she said.

"Um, sure, in a second," he said, remembering Jonathan. "I'll meet you guys over there."

They both smiled and he continued in the direction he had last seen Jonathan.

LaDonda started her speech.

Jonathan was standing near the back of Lawrence Hall, fidgeting with his long-sleeve white shirt. He appeared to be having difficulty rolling up his sleeves.

"Hey," shouted Nathan. "Sorry about that. I ran into Leah and Angela."

Jonathan stopped what he was doing and nodded. "I saw that," he said. "How are they doing? Is Leah's arm well?"

Nathan's eyes grew wide. He had noticed the white bandage around Leah's forearm but forgot to ask about it. "I believe they're okay," he said, feeling slightly embarrassed.

"Nathan," said Jonathan, after clearing his throat, "do you remember the inscription on the wall outside of the secret chamber? The one that says 'That he will be known by those around him'?"

Nathan's forehead wrinkled. "I think so."

"Do you remember what happened after I touched the symbol for teacher?" he asked.

"Yeah," Nathan said. "You became a black fox and were drawn to the road we were driving on."

Jonathan nodded. "Well, the same thing happened last night."

Nathan shook his head. His eyebrows were scrunched and he looked confused. "What do you mean?" he asked.

"Last night, after the paramedics brought me back to Lawrence Hall, I had that feeling again." he said. "But this time I wasn't drawn to the road, but to Grimm Cemetery. That's when I saw you and the others."

"Wait, when I was on the ground of the memorial plaza," said Nathan. "For a second I thought I saw something moving in the graveyard below. A small dark shape. Was that you?"

Jonathan nodded.

"But I don't understand," responded Nathan. A few moments passed and he grew silent. He looked at Jonathan and then slowly his eyes grew wide. "Wait, are you saying you are drawn to me? Why on earth would you be drawn to me?"

Jonathan cleared his throat again. "Uh, I don't know how else to say this, but I think ... you're the one."

"The one what?" asked Nathan, looking confused.

"The one your ancestors were looking for," he said. "The one to come, according to the legend." Jonathan drew closer and with enthusiasm whispered, "You're the Firewalker!"

"What?" exclaimed Nathan. "Are you insane? Did you hit your head?"

Jonathan beamed. "It makes sense," he said. "The inscription on the wall outside the secret chamber said 'He will be known by those around him.'"

"Yeah, yeah, I got that part," interrupted Nathan. "Get to the part about me being the Firewalker."

"Right," continued Jonathan excitedly. "On the same wall, around the Firewalker symbol, are five smaller symbols. The Cahokia symbol for teacher or Spirit Walker is one of them, as well as the symbol for protector, healer, traveler and guide."

Jonathan's piercing blue eyes behind his dark-rimmed glasses were bright, and Nathan was surprised because he hadn't seen him look this rested in weeks.

"And considering what happened to me after I touched the symbol, I must be the teacher," Jonathan continued. "And if I am the teacher, then after last night, Lafonda's clearly the protector."

Nathan cocked one eyebrow and stared at Jonathan in disbelief. Nathan almost had a grin on his face. "So, I'm the Firewalker. And Jonathan Black is my teacher. And Lafonda Devaro is my protector."

"Precisely!" exclaimed Jonathan.

"You might look rested," responded Nathan, "but I think you might need more sleep."

"No, no, I'm serious," continued Jonathan. "It fits; even the part of the legend that says he will wield the power of the three: Earth and Spirit and Fire." He leaned in close again. "It's you, Nathan," he whispered excitedly. "You have the gift of fire!"

Nathan continued to shake his head and huffed. "Yeah, but so does Malick," he said. "And besides, you said there would be five around him and you've only mentioned you and Lafonda. Who and where are the others?"

Jonathan looked away and fidgeted with his sleeves a little. "I haven't quite figured that part out yet," he said. He paused. "But I have a theory."

Nathan looked towards the stage and watched as LaDonda continued speaking. "Uh-huh," he said. "And there are also parts to the legend you haven't decoded yet."

They both grew silent.

The microphone from the stage echoed loudly, startling everyone, including LaDonda.

"Sorry about that," said LaDonda with a smile. "Now as I was saying, the Outstanding Counselor Award goes to the counselor who has demonstrated teamwork, integrity, responsibility and leadership. The recipient of this award was nominated by his peers."

LaDonda paused to take a look at the paper in her hand. "We had a tie this year, and I'm not surprised because both of them were so helpful to me this summer," she said. "This year's award goes to Nathan Urye and Stephen Malick."

Nathan was surprised and felt embarrassed by the sounds of applause.

Jonathan nudged him forward. "Go, Nathan," he said, while clapping. "Go up there."

Nathan reluctantly headed towards the stage, smiling weakly at the smiling faces in the crowd.

Andy high-fived him right before he met Malick at the stairs.

"Are you just as surprised as I am?" Nathan whispered.

LaDonda smiled and gave them both a diamond-shaped glass plaque that had their names engraved in them.

"And that concludes this year's ceremony," she said. "Please enjoy the food, music and tonight's fireworks display." She waved a hand to the crowd. "Happy Fourth of July, everyone!" she shouted. "And I hope to see some of you next summer."

Nathan and Malick headed down the stage stairs.

Malick playfully held his plaque in the air, trying to reflect the light. "I saw you and Jonathan huddled up in the corner over there," he said. "What was that all about?"

Nathan looked up because he heard music playing. He caught a glimpse of the DJ on stage and noticed that people started to dance.

"Oh, nothing," he said, glancing back at Malick. "Just Jonathan being Jonathan."

Malick raised an eyebrow and stared at him suspiciously. "Well, that guy I told you about checks out," he said. "And we should be able to get a charm or something to cloak you guys with in London. He has a store there. We should go check it out."

A few frown lines suddenly appeared on Nathan's forehead. "Check it out?" he said. "In London?"

"Yeah," continued Malick. "And the friend I told you about, the one that knows more about this stuff, she lives there too."

Nathan grew quiet for a moment. He thought about asking him when they were going to talk about the Order and their powers, but decided to just nod instead.

"There is one other thing," said Malick. "I keep thinking about it and I haven't been able to figure it out. If you were having dreams about Leah before you came to camp, back when you were at home, why didn't they detect you there?"

"Congratulations, Mr. Urye!" said a familiar voice.

Nathan looked up to find Lafonda standing in front of him. Although she looked different with her hair in curls, he recognized her immediately.

"Thanks," he said with a smile. "And by the way, you

look nice."

She smiled and then ran her hand across the hem of her dress. Her dress was a bright berry color and designed from a lightweight fabric. The same fabric was looped as a belt around her waist, and the gold locket that lay bare against her skin shone in the courtyard lights.

"Do you really think so?" she asked, surprised. "I got it in St. Louis, when Leah and I went shoe shopping."

"Yes," said Malick, chiming in. "Nathan is right. You do look nice."

She glanced at Malick suspiciously, but finally smiled. "Thank you," she said. "And congratulations to you too on your award."

Malick nodded with a grin.

"I'm just glad that it didn't rain today," she continued. "Otherwise we would be forced to have the banquet indoors."

"Yeah, and our Fourth of July would have been a wash," said Angela, joining them.

Leah was at her side.

Nathan noticed the music had changed and several people around them were starting to slow dance.

"Um, Leah," he said, sounding slightly nervous. "Would you like to dance … with me?"

Leah smiled and Angela beamed.

"Sure," she said. "I would love too."

She headed over to him, but suddenly he started looking around and scanning the ground. Nathan held up the plaque in his hand and chuckled.

"Maybe I should place this somewhere or put it in my room first," he said.

"Gibberish," said Angela, her blond curly hair bouncing on her shoulders. "I'll hold it for you. You guys go ahead and dance before you miss the song."

Malick fidgeted with the sunglasses attached to the neck of his shirt before finally running his fingers through his already perfectly coifed hair.

"Lafonda," he said, "would you —"

"I know you're not asking me to dance," she said.

"Uh — treated!" shouted Alan from the table. He had a grin on his face and continued to text feverishly on his cell phone.

Malick grinned. "Why not?" he asked with a chuckle. "Will you?"

Lafonda appeared highly agitated. "I'll pass," she responded.

"Lafonda!" exclaimed Angela. She leaned in close to her and whispered, "Is that any way to treat the guy who saved your life?"

Lafonda folded her arms across her chest. "I would like to think of it as we're now even," she said. "Considering how his reckless driving could have killed us before we even got to camp!"

Malick smiled coyly. "Just one dance," he said.

Lafonda glowered.

Angela swiftly took the plaque from his hands and shoved Lafonda into Malick's arms.

"Go ahead," Angela said. "One dance never killed anybody."

Nathan shook his head and gave his plaque to Angela.

"Shall we?" he asked extending his arm to Leah.

"Yes, we shall," responded Leah, taking a hold of his arm.

Nathan guided Leah to the middle of the courtyard. He laid his hand gently on her waist and they started to dance.

"Do you think Lafonda will kill Angela for making her slow dance with Malick?" he asked.

Leah tilted her head over Nathan's shoulder to get a better view of Malick and Lafonda. "Most likely," she said with a chuckle. "But so far, so good because they're still dancing, and there may even be some talking going on."

Nathan continued to dance. When he was facing them again, he said, "Yup, it looks like they're having a conversation. They're definitely talking about something." Nathan laughed. "But based on Lafonda's expression, I don't know if it's good."

Nathan looked down while laughing and noticed the white bandage around Leah's arm. "So, how is it?" he asked in a more somber tone.

"Oh," she responded after following his gaze. "It's okay." She returned his gaze by examining his bandaged hand. "And you?" she asked. "Are you okay?"

"I'm all right," he said. "Things could be better, but believe me, I'm not complaining."

There was a brief silence and Leah's head tilted a little as she gazed into his eyes. "Thank you," she said, "for coming after us. That was very brave of you."

Nathan blushed and tried to conceal his embarrassment. "No problem," he said.

He quickly looked away and was surprised to see Roy standing over by Argus and LaDonda. It looked like they were having an intense discussion, but Roy quickly smiled after he saw that Nathan was looking at him. He held up a bottle of Wool's Ointment and waved.

"Oh boy," commented Nathan, swiftly looking away. "Talk about embarrassment."

Leah laughed. "What?" she asked. "What is it?"

"Oh, nothing," responded Nathan quickly. He dropped his eyes and tried not to look at his grandfather again. "So," he said, trying to think of something to change the subject. "How are you holding up? I mean, is this all new to you? Did you always know about your powers?"

"No," she said. "In fact, it wasn't until Amanda — wait, Lauren, or whatever her name is — kidnapped me that I knew what was going on." She paused. "I knew I wasn't crazy, though. I mean, after the attack at school, I knew the stuff happening to me was real, regardless of what anyone else thought was going on."

Nathan smiled reassuringly.

"Apparently, in the beginning," she continued, "Lauren tried to kidnap me by getting me into the Space In Between through my dreams. When that didn't work, she decided to just send the Shadow Creatures after me."

"Did she ever say what she wanted?" Nathan asked.

Leah shook her head. "No," she said. "Only that she was looking for someone special — someone with a particular power."

He thought about what Leah had just said about not being crazy, and the thought of her being alone in the hospital made him sad again. He looked over her shoulder, near the refreshments table, and caught a glimpse of Samantha Darding standing next to her brother Jim, Eva Marie Evans and Hugo. Nathan sighed. He was pleased to see Samantha well again.

Leah pulled back a little so that she could see Nathan's face. She smiled and said, "It's okay. I'm not in the hospital anymore. And at least now there are people in my life that believe me and know that I'm not crazy."

Nathan smiled.

"So," she said cheerfully with a grin. "Lafonda tells me you were having dreams about me."

Nathan's face was flushed. He was embarrassed again. "Yeah, sort of," he said. "And I apologize if that sounds weird or freaky." He tried to swallow, but his mouth was dry. "It's just another one of my abilities," he said. "Through my dreams I can see the past or the future."

"It's okay," she said with a laugh. "It probably would explain why I never felt alone in all this. Even when I was in the hospital, I always felt like someone was with me."

Suddenly, there was a series of loud bangs followed by little popping sounds. Nathan and Leah both ducked as the courtyard lights dimmed and a bright display of red, white, and blue dazzling sparkles filled the sky.

They both stood up straight again and laughed. Leah ran her hands through her hair and straightened her dress. "It's just fireworks," she said through stifled giggles. She looked up to watch the sky and then turned to look at Nathan. "What?" she asked, with a smile. "Why are you smiling at me?"

He beamed and the light from the fireworks revealed the happiness in his eyes. "Because your laugh is how I always imagined it would be."

Want to know when Book 2 will be released?

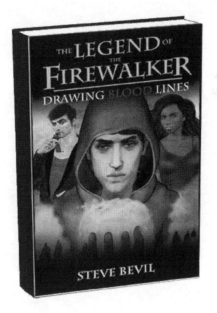

Sign-up today at *www.legendofthefirewalker.com*

By submitting your email, you will be notified of book release dates, giveaways, book signings, receive sample chapters and more!

Also, if you enjoyed the story, please leave a review on Amazon.com. I would love to hear from you!